IRRATIONAL FEARS

WILLIAM BROWNING SPENCER

irrational fears	*william browning spencer*
cover art	*larry perlman*
interior illustrations	*kathleen ryan*
jacket and book design	*john snowden*
art direction	*richard thomas*

Published by
White Wolf Inc.
735 Park North Blvd. Suite 128
Clarkston, Georgia 30021
www.white-wolf.com

First printing August 1998
10 9 8 7 6 5 4 3 2 1

Acknowledgments

This book and others before it have all profited immensely from the world-class copy editing of my friends Hendle Rumbaut and Michael Ambrose. Friends have rallied round when the darkness of the writing life has made self-destruction seem my best option. These people are: Neal Barrett, Brad Denton, Marty Cohen, Susan Wade, Mary Willis, David Pexton, Kelley Perko, Jill Hartman, Carol Dodgen, Wilson Brown, Joyce DiBona, Tracy Nunn, Gordon Van Gelder, Marci Davis, Ellis Smith, Larry Perlman, Bill Putney, Rev. Liz Decker (my religious advisor and sweetheart), and Paul Walters (who, back in 1990, when I was adrift, suggested I might like Austin and why not come on down?).

This book is for my
good friends and writing colleagues,
Jeff Hartman and **Carolyn Banks**.
So here you are in the front of this book, guys.
Plenty of room for the both of you.
No need to do anything
that will get us all thrown out of here.
There. Isn't this nice?

Part 1
Hurley Detox

Somewhere in the echoing innards of the old Seventh Street Hurley Memorial detox, a drunk was shouting. He was shouting *Wu whas wu whas wu whason* over and over, a mantra that might, to many, have meant nothing.

Jack Lowry understood. *I guess you learned your lesson*, that's what the drunk was screaming. He was reprimanding himself, in the voice of a parent, spouse, child...who knows?

The drunk ran down, words turning to slush, silence.

Jack was sitting on his bed in his underwear. He reached forward, snagged his pants from the back of a chair, and tugged them on. He stood up, and the residue of the gin he had drunk washed over some loose brain cells, tumbling them in a cold pine-scented surf.

He walked out into the hall. The light was harsh, the brown floor tiles uneven. His feet were bare.

He had been here before. Twice. This time he'd stayed sober for five months. He had thought he was getting a handle on it.

To his right, a barred window faced out on the night. At the other end of the corridor, a nurse's station guarded double swinging doors.

Halfway down the hall a gurney was parked against the wall. Jack approached the gurney and its recumbent passenger.

IRRATIONAL FEARS

She lay sleeping with her head propped up by pillows, her right arm in a huge, L-shaped cast surrounded by rumpled green sheets and plaster dust. She was a young woman with curly black hair. Her mouth was slightly open, showing a gleam of white tooth. Her left cheek was smeared with plaster. She looked like an angel haplessly caught in some construction site explosion.

As Jack watched, she turned her head and closed her mouth. A small sigh escaped her, the corner of her mouth quivered, and a dazzling smile suddenly flared, as brief and bright as a struck match on a moonless night. Then her features were set, silent, the bones of her face noncommittal. She slept on. He looked at the blue band on her wrist and read the typed-in name: KERRY BECKETT.

"Hey, what are you doing?"

The night nurse was a big-boned woman named Blanche.

"Hey Blanche," Jack said.

She slowed some, seeing who it was. "Oh, it's you. I saw you were back."

"Sorry."

"It's all the same to me. There's probably people you could be apologizing to, so don't waste it on me. I get paid the same no matter what you do."

"That's a good attitude."

Blanche snorted, frowned. "I don't need you telling me good attitudes. You wouldn't know a good attitude if it bit your ass. What are you doing sneaking up on this young thing? Probably trying to peek down her skimpy gown, see some teenage titties."

"What happened to her? Is she going to be okay?"

Blanche shrugged. "Who knows? She's another willful one. Everybody calls it alcoholism these days, that's all the rage, but I call it willful. Steal a car and drive it flat into a tree. Ain't your car, ain't your tree…but that's no matter, just do it."

"She stole a car?"

Blanche frowned and said nothing. She leaned forward. "You stick to your own troubles. That should be plenty to occupy you."

Big Ernie, the nightshift orderly, came up, looking, as always, morose, perhaps dangerously so. "Hey," he said. "We got an *incident* here? We got something going to have to be damn *wrote up?*"

Blanche assured him that this was not the case, and Jack Lowry went back to his room. There were two beds, but, for the moment, Jack had the room to himself.

The room was small and dismal. There were paintings on the wall (so generic that the eye couldn't rest on them), an end table, a lamp, a dresser. Jack tried to imagine that he lived in some impoverished, overpopulated country where such a room would be coveted, would be a sign of great status. A family would live here, many children, several relatives, chickens, a dog, perhaps a goat. They would be happy, grateful for this place.

They would be so happy that others would come and kill them, prompted by envy and malice.

Jack sighed. Positive thinking wasn't for everyone. He thought about Sara. Every now and then, during the six months of their acquaintance, they had gone to a cafeteria where a sign on the wall stated, in hand-printed caps: *ANY FISH CAN HAVE BONES.* Clearly the employees had grown tired of geriatric patrons hobbling back up to the counter with their fillets of flounder and their miffed expressions. Finally some overwrought and underpaid food server had grabbed a magic marker and produced this sign. Jack and Sara had laughed on first seeing it. *Any fish can have bones* became a shorthand for those flawed people, places and events that were the stuff of life. *Any fish can have bones.* Any room in a hospital detox can be less than aesthetically satisfying. Jack closed his eyes, convinced that he would not sleep. But he did.

In the morning, seven people appeared for breakfast.

Jack sat next to an older man, a banker perhaps, wearing a white shirt and tie.

"Tilman," the man said, nodding to Jack. "Ed Tilman."

Jack introduced himself and went off to get coffee.

When he returned, the man named Tilman said, "What are you in for?"

"In for?"

Tilman nodded, smiled. He had a small, round face, round eyes. His white mustache had a faintly parasitic look.

Tilman seemed to be waiting for an answer, so Jack shrugged, sat down with his coffee, and said, "I guess I'm in for alcoholism. Guess that's what we are all doing here."

The man continued to smile. He reached out and clutched Jack's shoulder. "That's what they'd like us to think," he said. He squeezed Jack's shoulder, winked broadly, and released his grip. He stood up, bowed to everyone at the table, turned and left the room.

"Dude's crazy," said a skinny teenager wearing a brown jumpsuit. "Talks a lot of loopy conspiracy shit. 'I ain't interested,' I told him, but he wouldn't stop. How did you break that arm?"

IRRATIONAL FEARS

This last remark was directed at Kerry Beckett, who sat opposite the boy.

She looked up, revealing the bluest eyes Jack had ever seen, eyes that would have made Shakespeare nervous because there was the stuff of bad poetry lurking in those eyes, exaggeration, metaphors to make an academic bark with abrupt, disdainful laughter. *That* blue.

"Car crash."

And there was a voice that would have made angels trip over each other, crowding up loutishly, hollering *back off!*, slamming an elbow into a neighbor's stomach, pinching, anything mean to get closer to the source.

The kid said his name was Al. Jack realized that this boy might be Kerry's age, part of her peer group. Jack studied Al with new interest. Al's head was shaved, one of his eyebrows was pierced with a silver ring, and he might have been wearing mascara. His skin was pale, possessed of a damp luminosity, a blind cave salamander glow.

Jack had encountered enough young people to know that there existed females drawn to this sort of male, for reasons too mysterious to ever yield to rational analysis.

Would young Kerry find her heart beating faster?

Al was now launched on a monologue regarding car crashes he had endured and their legal ramifications. Surely she would not be drawn to Al's mind?

Jack studied Kerry. She sat straight at the table. She wore a flannel shirt—a man's shirt? what man?—and the clumsy white cast (bent at a right angle at the elbow) rested in its sling just beneath the swell of her breasts with something of the aspect of a cradled infant. All this created that powerful vision of nurturing madonna and teenage trailer-park nymph that is so irresistible to the detoxing male.

I'm in love, Jack thought. He thought it the way one might think, after an accident with a chainsaw, "I've just lopped off my thumb," the thought as yet unaccompanied by pain.

After breakfast, they watched a Father Martin video about alcoholism. Father Martin was a cheerful recovering alcoholic and a priest.

There was good news and bad news about alcoholism. The good news was that alcoholics could learn to abstain from drinking (primarily through the auspices of Alcoholics Anonymous). The bad news was that once you were an alcoholic you remained one. Your future didn't hold any convivial, social drinking days.

None of this was news to Jack.

WILLIAM BROWNING SPENCER

After the video, they filed into a small room where chairs were arranged in a circle. As far as Jack was concerned, this was the low point of any day at Hurley detox: group therapy.

Jack hated sharing his feelings or, for that matter, being the recipient of shared feelings. It didn't help that the counselor was Wesley Parks, an intense young man with a goatee, who had been here on Jack's last visit. Unlike most alcoholism counselors, Parks was not a recovering alcoholic and seemed, in fact, to dislike alcoholics.

Jack sat in a chair and Parks said, "Back again, Professor?" Parks insisted on calling Jack *Professor*. This was all part, Jack assumed, of an attempt to impress upon Jack Lowry, Ph.D., just what a liability the intellect was in the battle with alcoholism.

"Do you think you could tell us why you drank again?" Parks asked.

"No," Jack said.

"Come on, Professor, you're an intelligent man. You're very articulate. Give it a try."

"You're not an alcoholic. I don't think you are capable of understanding the compulsion."

Jack knew that this was a sore subject, that Parks was defensive about this.

Parks looked like he might get into it, haul out the old argument about a doctor not needing to have a disease in order to treat it. The discussion would have suited Jack, something to kill the time while dodging the dreary emotional outpourings of group.

But Parks leaned back, took a breath, smiled. "We can discuss my qualifications some other time. Right now, I'd like to go around the room and see how everyone is doing today."

Nobody was faring really well, which is what you might expect from folks who, prompted by DTs, hallucinations, suicide attempts and altercations with the police, had arrived in Hurley Memorial's shabby detox unit.

An unhappy fat woman next to Jack said it was her children's fault she was in the hospital. They had packed her suitcase and brought her. "Throwed out," she growled. "Like a dog that's gone blind or a burned-up pot roast. All I got left is the sweet love of Jesus."

A truck driver named Hinkle told a long story about driving a load of chickens to Texas. He told about all the people he met on the trip. He described them in detail and was able to recall whole conversations.

Parks finally interrupted. "What does this have to do with your alcoholism?"

Hinkle frowned and shrugged his shoulders.

Kerry said she wasn't an alcoholic.

"Sure I drink," she said. "Who doesn't? But that's not my main problem."

Parks asked her what that might be, this main problem?

"I'm a loser. That's all. My daddy was a loser, and my momma is a loser and I got a sister living in Des Moines who is a loser. And my baby brother died in his crib when he was two months old—just expired for no good reason unless maybe he saw his future clear and lost heart."

"That's quite a negative attitude for a young person," Parks said, and Jack had to agree.

"It's negative, all right," Kerry said, nodding her head as though congratulating her counselor on getting the point so quickly. "There's nothing positive about being a loser."

When Ed Tilman was asked how he was, he smiled cagily. "I'm fine," he said. "You can write it down. 'Patient has no complaints.'"

"Are you aware that you have a drinking problem, Ed?"

Tilman's smile expanded.

Parks continued, "Your wife says you have been drinking approximately a case of beer a day since 1982."

"She might say that," Tilman said. "Someone could have gotten to her, *made* her say that. Or someone who sounded like her might answer her phone and say that."

This stopped Parks for a minute, and Tilman nodded as though he'd scored a point.

The teenager, Al, had to be awakened in order to participate. He wanted to know if they'd be graded on sharing in AA meetings and if he could get a paper, some kind of signed document, to hand on to his attorney.

The last man to share was a short bald black man named Gates. "I got four generations of alkyholic in me," he said. "I been to A and A meetings in fifteen states. This place don't show me nothin. Where's your Mister Bill Wilson? Where's your Mister Doctor Bob? This ain't shit for treatment."

Group ended on that note.

In the evening, they were all put in a van and taken to an AA meeting. The driver of the van was an ancient man named Earl Simms, a volunteer who had been a patient at the hospital and hadn't had a drink in seven years. His hands still shook, and he called everyone Joe or Sally, and he drove the van at a consistent thirty miles an hour, which got him some death threats from his passengers. When trucks doing seventy-five would hiss by them on the Beltway, rocking the van as though it were a dinghy on open seas, Jack would feel some anxiety.

"We gonna be dead alkyholics," grumbled Gates.

The meeting was held in a church basement in Alexandria, Virginia.

It was early October, a chilly night. Jack climbed out of the van into the parking lot and walked, with his sullen companions, toward a side door where a clump of people were standing around, talking loudly, smoking cigarettes, laughing. Clouds of smoke rose into a sky full of glittering stars.

Jack had never been to this meeting before. AA's Intergroup listed the meeting as a young people's group, and the detox staff had decided that Al and Kerry needed to see kids their own age "in recovery." It couldn't hurt the older detox patients to see this either. It would be inspirational. Gates, small black cauldron of discontent, was not convinced. "Young peoples got no bidness in A and A. They sposed to be gettin down. A and A's for us old, whupped muthers."

Jack had been to AA meetings before, on his previous stays in Hurley, and he'd even attended some AA meetings between detoxifications, having been told that consistent AA attendance was the long-term treatment for alcoholism. He'd never managed to go to more than a few meetings before drifting away.

The meeting Jack found himself in was, indeed, filled with young people. They sat around a long, low table, balanced precariously on tiny chairs (during the day, the room accommodated small children). Most of the people in attendance appeared to be in their late teens or early twenties. There were a couple of kids who looked to be thirteen, and one disheveled old man named Walt who had been sober for many years, and who saw that the coffee got made. Old Walt enjoyed being of service to young people, prompted by either a genuine affection and concern for their welfare—or some deviant, pedophilic impulse disguised as altruism.

Jack realized that this mean-spirited thought was generated by his own dismal and pathetic desires. He was forty-two years old, and yearning for a girl less than half his age. He realized that this infatuation was the product of boredom, despair, and loneliness. On his two previous visits to Hurley detox, he'd seen unlikely romances arise (a swarthy cab driver and a retired exotic dancer had had to be expelled for carnal high jinks). There was something about withdrawing from alcohol; sexual liaisons arose to fill the vacuum. Jack even remembered, vaguely, nurse Blanche delivering a lecture on the danger. She said it was strongly suggested that new sexual/romantic relations be avoided during the first year of sobriety. Jack remembered, then, studying his companions (an unshaven Charles Manson lookalike, a balding fat man in a rumpled suit, a skinny, near-catatonic girl wearing an "Andrea Dworkin Rules" T-shirt, and a woman in her late seventies who had to continually fight the notion that she was on a Caribbean cruise). Jack felt, at the time, that Blanche's warning was unnecessary, that these people were safe from romantic entanglements, but the Charles Manson lookalike and the fat man actually did develop a relationship that went deeper than simple mutual esteem…and wound up living together, which ended in acrimony and drunkenness, and which served to give weight to the truth of Blanche's lecture.

Jack awoke from this reverie to find that the meeting was in progress. Someone had already read "How it Works" (the beginning of Chapter 5 in the book *Alcoholics Anonymous*, a sort of capsule summary of the program), and now a guy with a ponytail was speaking. "I lie all the time," he said. "It's just a habit I got from my using days. Ask me something, I'll probably lie."

Heads were nodding around the room. It was a paradox that Jack had yet to grasp. People in meetings came to trust each other by sharing candidly about their lives. Obviously, the group liked and trusted the person presently speaking. They admired his honesty in describing an unflattering character defect. But—and this seemed to elude them—he was saying that he was an habitual liar, *not, in fact, someone to be trusted.*

The next person to speak, the boy who appeared to be thirteen and whose hair was purple, spoke interminably about injustices done him by his parents and about how his outpatient treatment counselor had accused him of drug use because of a "dirty urine" when he hadn't been doing any drugs at all and there must have been some mix-up at the lab.

Jack found himself studying the walls. The usual AA signs had been hung, and he was surprised to find himself taking comfort in them: *EASY DOES IT—ONE DAY AT A TIME—LIVE AND LET LIVE.*

Certainly there was something funky and welcoming about AA, this strange grassroots community founded by a failed stockbroker and a despairing proctologist. AA had, literally, saved millions of lives. The fact of its existence had also spawned dozens of peripheral programs using the same twelve-step program, created a mountain of self-help books, and unleashed a horde of opportunistic pop psychologists.

And AA's popularity had generated its share of critics who were unhappy with, among other things, its pragmatism, its God-as-we-understand-him spirituality, and its quaint sense of personal responsibility, community and service.

The response to such attacks was simple enough: Yes, AA was flawed, but one didn't complain about the paint job on the lifeboat when the ship was sinking. Reservations were for less desperate folk.

When it came to treating alcoholism, there were no real contenders. Most recovering alcoholics were in AA.

Jack was thinking these and other thoughts, admonishing himself for his lackadaisical AA attendance in the past, resolving to do better in the future, when he heard applause. A pretty girl got up, accepted a small round medallion, and said, "I'm Sam, and I'm an alcoholic. I'm not much for speeches, but I love you guys and thanks." She waved the medallion over her head (more applause) and returned to her chair. The meeting's leader said, "Anyone else got six months?" No one did, nor did anyone come up to claim a three-month, two-month, or one-month chip. "Anyone need a desire chip?" the leader asked, explaining that such a chip indicated a desire to stop drinking, one day at a time, and was something a new AA member might like to claim.

Kerry went up and got a desire chip. "I'm Kerry," she said, accepting the silver medallion. "I don't know if I'm an alcoholic or not. I guess being an alcoholic is what people would call bad luck, so maybe I am. If it's bad luck, I've got it. I figured I should stand up and get this chip because it's *all* I'll get. I mean, not to be negative, good stuff doesn't exactly come to me, just the *wanting* of good stuff, just the *desire* for it. I'd have to be a moron if I still thought I'd ever really *get* anything worth having." She blinked at everyone as though she might cry, then shook her head and hurried back to her seat.

Everyone applauded enthusiastically, as though she had said something inspirational. AA was that way. You could say, "I hate you all and hope you die," and AA folks would applaud. There were two interpretations for this group behavior. One was that AA members were an easygoing, nonjudgmental lot. The other, more cynical interpretation, was that AA members were not possessed of particularly good listening skills.

Jack realized that he and some of his companions were also eligible for desire chips, but no one else claimed one.

The basket was passed—Jack put in a dollar—and someone announced that a dance was being held at a local AA club. "Okay," the leader said, "let's close." Everyone stood up, joined hands, and said the Lord's Prayer.

IRRATIONAL FEARS

Outside, in the parking lot, a fight was in progress. A stocky, bearded youth was exchanging blows with a taller kid who wore a white dress shirt and a tie. The tall kid's companions—easily identified because they wore the same uniform of dress shirt, tie, and black pants—regarded the contest with a single expression of distaste. Behind them was a shiny black van with tinted windows. This had to be the vehicle that had conveyed the group to the meeting.

There were five of these young men, their hair cut short, their faces smooth and clean-shaven. Their stillness was remarkable; they were linked, holding each other's hands in an absentminded, listless fashion that appeared to be an habitual clinging rather than some show of solidarity.

The meeting attendees, who had now spilled out of the church into the parking lot, shouted at the circling combatants. The bearded youth crouched low, presenting broad shoulders to the long-arcing swings of his foe, an untutored boxer whose feet, in their shiny Sunday shoes, skidded awkwardly in the gravel. A small red-haired girl next to Jack screamed with sudden bloodthirsty volume, "Kill him, Bobby!"

At that moment, the bearded youth darted forward, fired a fist into his opponent's stomach, moved in close for a series of short, pummeling blows, then stepped back and connected with a left to the boy's jaw. The boy wobbled on reedy legs and dropped, eliciting a satisfied shriek from Bobby's cheerleader.

Bobby shouted at his fallen foe. "Don't be coming round here anymore! Don't be fucking with us! You understand?"

Old Walt was pushing through the crowd. "That's about enough!" he was shouting. "What's going on here?"

The girl grabbed Walt's arm. "It's not Bobby's fault," she said. "They were passing out those crazy flyers again, stopping people, trying to keep them from going into the meeting."

The white shirts were moving, helping their fallen companion up, turning and walking him toward the van. They moved quietly, with no display of emotion. One of them pulled back the van's sliding door and they lifted their injured comrade in. The last of them climbed in, and the door closed.

Jack regarded the van with its hidden cargo of mute young men. The vehicle was squat, polished, somehow menacing. Jack couldn't see a driver; the black windshield reflected a row of parked cars.

Jack felt something flutter against his leg, bent down and retrieved a yellow sheet of paper. He saw that similar sheets, animated by a chill, harrying wind, danced over the gravel lot. He blinked at the one in his hand and read the banner line: *YOU ARE IN HELL.*

WILLIAM BROWNING SPENCER

The van's engine came alive, and Jack looked up; headlights flared.

A voice crackled into metallic life. "Children!" The voice boomed from twin trumpetlike speakers on the van's roof. "I do not blame you for resisting the pain of enlightenment. It is your nature to do so. Know that The Clear loves you. The Clear is your salvation. The Unraveling is at hand, but you needn't be afraid. We will save you in *spite* of yourselves."

The engine roared, and the van, tires sending gravel into the air, accelerated. All watched as the vehicle turned sharply and raced down the church's long drive, its brake lights igniting for one red instant as it slowed to negotiate a hard left onto the road.

"Jeez," someone said.

Jack recognized the voice and turned to find Kerry at his side.

"Weird fuckers," she said.

"Troublemakers." This was Walt, who bent down, snatched up a flyer, and crumpled it into a ball. "They call themselves The Clear, some crackbrained cult that believes addiction is demonic possession, or something. Their leader's a nutcase named Greenway. They come around here recruiting. I don't know…" Walt wiped sweat from his brow. Jack studied the old man, saw him for the first time, really, a man with a wash of gray on his unshaven jowls, thick, unruly eyebrows, and that watery-eyed squint that comes to some older folks when the world has taken to taunting them.

"Trouble." He turned away, shuffling toward the church. He paused, looked back, and shouted at Jack, "They always say *Love*, you notice that? All those assholes with an angle, all those self-appointed gurus and flimflam artists and scheming sharks, they all got love on their side, like they got the franchise on love, got it straight from God. I don't blame Bobby. People go on about love, it makes me want to kick their butts." He sighed, shook his head, and turned again, back to the church basement, the coffee pot, the waiting cleanup chores.

Others obviously agreed with Walt. Bobby was the center of a congratulatory crowd. He had not survived the battle unscathed. There was a trickle of blood issuing from one nostril. But he grinned a victor's grin and hugged his red-haired admirer, lifting her into the air. Her legs, encased in black nylon stockings, scissored ecstatically.

In the van, Jack found himself sitting next to Kerry. He'd been staring out the window when she plopped herself down beside him. He knew it was her before turning. He recognized her perfume now, something like cinnamon (enlivened by a second odor, antiseptic, pungent, that emanated from the cast enclosing her arm).

IRRATIONAL FEARS

"So why does Wesley call you Professor?" she asked, not one for preamble.

"Why do you call our Mr. Parks Wesley?"

"Cause he asked me to," she said.

"Well," Jack said, "I didn't ask him to call me Professor. He just took to doing it when he learned that I taught at George Washington University."

"He doesn't like you much."

Jack shook his head. "No, we'll never be close."

"What do you teach?"

"Nothing. I don't teach anymore."

"Okay. What did you teach?"

"American Literature."

That answer silenced her for a while. Jack turned and stared at the traffic. They were on the Beltway again. Ten o'clock at night and the world was alive with automobiles. Jack felt a headache coming on, felt an accompanying panic brought on by a conviction that all this *busyness* was sentient and malevolent. It didn't help that cars rushed by with their horns blaring (*woooooooohank*), infuriated by Earl's overcautious driving.

Kerry's voice was balm.

"I been in a couple detoxes, a mental hospital," she said. "I got this notebook full of poems and stuff I wrote in those places. Maybe you could take a look at it, see what you think."

"I'd love to," he said.

e lay in bed with her notebook. As soon as they had disembarked from the van, she'd run off to fetch it.

It was a notebook that had traveled some. Several different pens had doodled on the brown cardboard cover. Officially, this notebook was a Hammond Spiral (the words commercially printed in blue, block letters) but Kerry had amended this with an inverted V between the words "Hammond" and "Spiral," indicating that the word "Eggs" should be added.

There was a drawing, much scribbled and shaded, of a horse's head, an image encoded in the DNA of teenage girls. It was executed with about average skill. There was a scribbled homework assignment, page numbers, a cryptic note ("Jen. Never never never again."), and two sentences in red block letters: *THIS NOTEBOOK'S CONTENTS ARE COPYRIGHTED BY KERRY ELSA BECKETT. USE OF THESE POEMS WITHOUT HER CONSENT IS AGAINST THE LAW!*

The exclamation point made Jack smile. *You hear that? Against the law!* Cautiously, he lifted the cover. The blue-lined page was inhabited by a single small poem with the title "DEATH."

DEATH hovered over many poems, and it was Jack's experience that it was better not to read such poems—copyrighted or otherwise—unless they had survived centuries of critical scrutiny.

Still, he read it:

DEATH

If I die while I'm asleep
not expecting it
I won't be surprised or disappointed
just a lump under the covers
somebody else's problem.
I won't be sad
like my mom
or scary
like a goblin.
I'll just be dead
no tears, no sobbin.

Jack read the poem a second time. Hey. He liked it. *Did he?* Yes, he really did. He wouldn't have to lie.

He turned the page. The next poem, much longer, was entitled "The Garden," and began, "The beautiful garden in the sun is laced with many-hued flowers and a myriad of colored butterflies that hover daintily in the dawn. My heart is filled with wonder as my feet travel the winding path…"

So you can't win every one. Shakespeare wrote *Titus Andronicus*, didn't he?

Jack read on. He did not, again, discover anything as charming as the first poem. The poems divided into two groups: romantically effusive ones in which words were loved not wisely but too well, and humorous poems that were more successful but—a failing of youth—not overly subtle.

Some of the poems, written in obvious misery, reminded Jack that literature was cruelly indifferent to heartfelt emotion. You could write a really bad line while authentic sadness blinded you with tears. You could sit there on the edge of your bed, sick from stealing and drinking your parents' Jack Daniels, shaky with guilt over that test you cheated on and still failed, frightened that you could be pregnant by your best friend's ex-boyfriend who was, just like she said, a creep. You could be miserable with longing for…well, every teenage yearnable thing…you could sit there, crying shamelessly, writing as fast as you could, and literature, that prig, would respond with: "Clichéd. Mawkish. Childish. Self-indulgent." Literature

WILLIAM BROWNING SPENCER

scorned the genuine article, real, wallowing anguish. It cared—shallow creature—only for appearance.

"These are terrific," he told her.

They were sitting in the day room. She looked radiant, a purple sweater draped over her shoulders, her black, wanton curls teasing the blue in her eyes.

"You really like them?"

The sunlight had come into the room, expressly to lick her throat (*a cat's tongue over cream*).

"Yes."

That night they went to an AA meeting in Falls Church. The young people's group that Hurley's detox patients had attended the night before did not have a meeting on Wednesdays, and, in any event, the hospital staff felt that the patients should be exposed to a variety of AA groups.

This group's members were, for the most part, older, with a substantial senior-citizen population. Jack had actually been to this meeting before, and he thought of it as a fundamental, blue-collar meeting. Nobody here was apt to talk about therapy or inner children or self-actualization. The answers were in the book *Alcoholics Anonymous* (generally referred to as the Big Book). Many of this group's older members were unimpressed by a later book (written by cofounder Bill Wilson) that explained the twelve steps and twelve traditions of AA in detail. These old-timers thought of the Twelve and Twelve (published in 1952, thirteen years after the publication of the Big Book) as a new and heretical text, an elaboration that sullied the pragmatism and simplicity of the earlier work.

It was a speaker's meeting, and an elderly man was standing at the podium telling his story.

It was not a riveting story, the room was overheated, and Jack found himself nodding off.

Jack got up and left the room. He found the rest room, splashed water in his face, and felt better, although he didn't feel well enough to listen to the rest of the old man's talk. The man was in need of an editor, someone to tell him, gently but firmly, "Ease off on the ancestors; cut to the chase. Were you ever stabbed by a hooker? Rob a liquor store? Set fire to your high school? *Anything?*"

Jack left the rest room and walked down the hall. He went out into the night air and sat on the steps. It was colder than it had been the previous night. He could see his breath in the air, feel the cold stars prick at his skin.

A voice behind him said, "He ain't even been born yet. He's still going on about his father's drinking. I reckon they'll have to buzz him or gong him or whatever afore he gets to his own drinking."

It was Hinkle, the truck driver, and he sat on the steps and lit a cigarette, his ruddy, open expression turning, for a moment, falsely pensive as he inhaled deeply. Jack studied the truck driver's profile, trying to guess the man's age. He was probably somewhere in his thirties, but he could have been younger, his face reddened by alcohol and the elements. He had long, woolly sideburns that tapered into an unshaven jaw shadow, like a paved road turning to dirt before petering out. He wore a leather jacket, jeans, and brown boots, all three articles rubbed raw in spots.

"I don't seem to be getting a lot out of any of this," he said, leaning back and spouting smoke at the night sky. "If I had a beer in front of me, I guarantee you I'd have it inside me afore you could say *alcoholism* three times. I reckon I'll just have to take my chances. I get in some scrapes on account of alcohol, but I get in some scrapes on account of women too, and I ain't *ever* thought of giving up pussy."

He grinned at Jack. "Can you keep a secret?"

Before Jack (who dreaded confidences) could answer, Hinkle said, "Don't matter whether you can or not. It's a done deal. My ride's arrived." He looked at his watch. "Right on time." He stood up and dropped the cigarette on the concrete, crushing it with his heel.

The black van had pulled to the curb. Hinkle was running down the steps. Jack stood up. "Wait!" he shouted.

The van's side door slid open and Hinkle hiked himself up, a hand clutching the door frame, foot on the running board. He turned and shouted to Jack, "Tell old Wesley Parks he can kiss my ass. It's like you said, he ain't been down the road we been down. He don't know shit about wanting a drink." Hinkle swung around, ducked, and entered the darkness. The door closed, and the van pulled away.

Jack imagined Hinkle in the van, turning to his unlikely companions, the young, serious men in their white shirts, shirts that flickered in and out of the shadows as they caught the light of passing street lamps.

After the meeting ended and they couldn't find Hinkle, they drove slowly back to the hospital, Earl Simms muttering all the way. "I ain't a baby-sitter. Somebody wants to run off, I can't stop him. Sides, I'm a volunteer. You can't fire a man ain't hired." He loudly proclaimed this to his passengers, convinced, apparently, that he was going to be reprimanded. But all Blanche said, on hearing the news, was, "Nobody's committed here.

WILLIAM BROWNING SPENCER

You want to leave, you can leave. You just sign a piece of paper that says you relieve the hospital of responsibility, and you leave, watching so the door don't bang your butt on the way out. Don't worry about it, Earl. You think I'm worried about it? Look in my eyes. You see even the tiniest bit of anxiety? No. If Mr. Hinkle wants to do more research, more power to him. Let him see if it's any better out there."

It might have been Jack's imagination, his paranoia, but he thought Blanche shot him a meaningful look.

That night, Jack read The Clear's flyer. He'd forgotten to read it the previous evening, distracted by Kerry's notebook, but now, when he emptied his pockets, he found the folded yellow paper, picked it up, unfolded it, and smoothed it on his knee. Having just watched Hinkle board The Clear's van—a fact he had not passed on to Blanche or anyone else (because, he reasoned, it was none of his business)—he felt a more personal interest in the document.

YOU ARE IN HELL it shouted, in bold black type spanning the top of the page. Hell's denizens, in the form of pen-and-ink sketches of winged serpents and fire-breathing gargoyles, decorated the edges of the paper. The drawings had a Victorian flavor, were, perhaps, clip art from some Victorian grotesque collection.

Underneath this stark pronouncement were three columns of text that accounted for two thirds of the flyer's space, the last third being occupied by an order form and a square photo of a man's face. The man was wearing sunglasses and grinning. A caption identified him as Dorian Greenway. The photo was fuzzy, the halftone screen rough; it could have been anyone.

Jack read:

> If you are an alcoholic, you know what it means to live in Hell. Perhaps you've gone to Alcoholics Anonymous for help. They have explained to you that you have a disease, a physical, emotional and spiritual disease. The disease cannot be cured, although it can be arrested. By not taking the first drink, you can be free of all the dire consequences of your drinking; you can lead a productive life. However, if you drink alcohol after years of abstinence, your compulsion will reassert itself, you will again be swept up by your addiction.
>
> Alcoholics Anonymous is a deluded organization of self-righteous fools. Their misguided and arrogant teachings have destroyed many.

IRRATIONAL FEARS

Their basic tenet is flawed. It is not a disease that you have; it is a *damnation*.

You are the progeny of an ancient Tribe, known by many names, but called, most commonly, K'n-Yan. The K'n-Yan were an underground race who worshipped Tsathoggua until that monstrous god's true nature was revealed, at which time the Great Rift occurred. The K'n-Yan were hurled into an asynchronous reality, perversely focused by alcohol and drugs. Hungers were created in this vortex. The hunger for love, for prestige, for money—and the hunger most manifest, the hunger for alcohol and drugs, which granted the accursed a spurious, fleeting clarity.

Have you ever snapped out of sleep in a cold sweat, pitched into the DTs, seen some hideous thing, a nightmare serpent or some unearthly creature?

This is no mental derangement. This is no hallucination, no product of out-of-balance electrolytes. What if I were to tell you, *There is such a place, and the monsters live there.*

Science denies this, of course. But I tell you, you must see these monsters *in the clearest light* if you are to conquer them.

I cannot tell you how the curse is passed down through the generations. It is not simply of the blood. The K'n-Yan, a telepathic race, transmitted it psychically, I'm convinced, so that it transcended all racial boundaries. Almost all Native Americans (living in close proximity to the largest K'n-Yan population) seem to have suffered its effects.

It is truly a war that is being waged. You must prepare yourself for a battle, soldiers of Shub-Niggurath, Yig, Ghatanothoa. The Unraveling is at hand. You will battle ancient and terrible forces as a soldier in the army of The Clear. And you will free yourself forever from the bondage of drug and alcohol addiction.

In my book, *Alcoholism and the Pnakotic Pentagon*, I clarify what cannot be addressed on this single page. That book can be obtained from many local bookstores or purchased by mail using the printed order form below.

You already know, intuitively, what you are. Many of you have united in the fellowship of AA, and this coming together is instinctive—and futile.

We of The Clear number less than a hundred. But we are growing, our best advertisement being the truth. Come with us.

Bill Wilson, the founder of AA, was riven by a wind that showed him the way. He was a pawn to dark forces, although the wind and the torment and the circle of denial are all real.

We are still *inside* the cave, my children. The Clear is the pathway to the true light, to the surface, to freedom.

For more infor...

WILLIAM BROWNING SPENCER

Jack didn't feel the need for additional enlightenment. He saw, however, why AA members might not take kindly to Dorian Greenway's proselytizing. *Hell.*

Someone was always hawking some version of Hell, Jack thought. Sometimes Jack had a clear picture of Hell's origin. Some poor caveman prods his dead companion with a stick, thinks, "Hum. Thrug no move. Smell bad. Fod." And then the lightning cracks and thunder rolls and the caveman thinks, "Me be dead sometime too. Double fod."

And so, coaxing hope out of mystery, the caveman turns to a living companion and says, "I think maybe our spirit go somewhere else, some happy place and live forever when we be dead." And this second caveman says, "Maybe so—and if you not live right here, do something make the gods angry, then you go to horrible place forever, hurt every day, cry and holler and wish you could wake up but—ha, ha—you not asleep. You miserable forever."

Any good idea, any piece of small comfort, is quickly spoiled by the next sour human in line. That's the nature of things. *Any fish,* as Sara was wont to say, *can have bones.*

The next morning, after breakfast, the scheduled alcoholism video (*The Morning After*) was canceled. Parks herded everyone into the dayroom for a special meeting.

Jack figured they were in for a lecture prompted by Hinkle's dereliction, but Parks wasn't thinking of the truck driver.

"I have good news," he said. "Good news for me, and, I think, good news for you. I will no longer be working at Hurley Memorial." He grinned, rocked on the balls of his feet, stood on tiptoe and stretched a bit as though drawn toward the ceiling by a new lightness of spirit. He sank back down, faked a rueful expression, and said, "I know, you are thinking, 'How can it be good news that our beloved counselor, the one person we rely on for guidance, is leaving us?'" He scratched his goatee, frowned with mock thoughtfulness (in the fashion of a skilled mime or apprentice dinner-theater actor). "Hmmmmm. Good question." He rubbed his hands together and smiled.

"And here's the good news: You're all coming with me!"

Wesley Parks had been hired to work at a treatment center called New Way, which was six years old and in need of a counselor to replace one who had quit abruptly. The rehab was county run, and while some of its patients were paying customers, the majority were broke and uninsured.

IRRATIONAL FEARS

For years, a few patients would go directly from Hurley to New Way, which was located on twenty acres of land in the small town of Harken (ten miles west of Leesburg, Virginia).

Most patients, however, refused the offer of free treatment at Harken. Being urban folks (from Washington, D.C. and its teeming environs), they were not eager to travel to primitive outlands for the cure. To these people, the word *country* conjured visions of snakes, centipedes, spiders, outhouses, and grueling, unsavory chores (hog butchering, cow milking, fence mending). The country was that place where the weather was always bad, shelter was primitive, and even the airwaves suffered, radios being devoid of anything but evangelists, farm reports, and banjo music.

Gates was the first to object. "Ah ain't going to no farm!" Gates said, pronouncing it *fahm* (as though it were a foreign word, something loathsome and untranslatable). "Fahms ain't never done right by my people. Next thing you know, I be settin in some tar-paper shack, my fingers all tore up on cotton."

The other members were equally unenthusiastic. Only Eunice (the fat woman whose children had dumped her in Hurley) and Ed Tilman immediately agreed to go. Eunice acquiesced in the spirit of martyrdom (abandoned by her children, she would go into the wilderness and suffer), and Tilman thought it would be a good place to "lie low."

Parks shook his head sadly, disappointed by his recalcitrant clients. "This is a great opportunity to get your feet planted firmly on recovery's path," Parks said. "Free. Fairfax County is footing the bill. There are people who will be paying $20,000 for the sort of treatment program that New Way is offering you."

"I'd just as soon have the money," Gates said, which caused young Al to double over with laughter, shoulders shaking as he leaned forward on the sofa, sneakered feet slapping the linoleum floor.

Parks smiled. "I hope you retain your sense of humor in prison, Al. Laughter is a great comfort in hard times."

Al stopped laughing and went still. He looked up at the counselor. "Hey now. You saying it's this place or jail? That's not right. This is America; I got freedoms guaranteed me."

Parks smiled and nodded. "Of course you do. And New Way is not affiliated with the courts. No one can make you go there. But you might want to talk to your lawyer about all this. A judge could look at your driving record and doubt your resolve to turn over a new leaf. He could see all those DWIs and think, 'This fellow has threatened the lives of law-abiding motorists once too often.' Now if such a judge discovered that you had turned down an opportunity for free alcoholism treatment…" Parks shrugged. "Ask your lawyer how things might go if the judge feels you aren't interested in cleaning up your act."

Al sat with his mouth half open, dazed, as though his chewing gum had turned to stone.

Parks continued: "You all have three days to think about what you want to do. I'd like everyone to come. But I can't make you. The decision is yours. Kerry, I'd like to see you in my office after lunch."

"I'm going to New Way," Kerry told Jack that evening. "Can you believe it?"

Jack looked up from the magazine article he had been reading. The article was entitled "Mapping Your Emotions," and someone had already filled out the questionnaire that accompanied the text, using a red pen and pausing occasionally to draw little stick figures and lightning bolts. The test-taker had scored twenty-two. The recipient of such a dismal score was urged to seek immediate professional help.

"Well," Jack said.

Kerry giggled. "Yeah. Wesley got Jason to agree he won't press charges if I go to New Way."

"Jason?"

"I didn't really steal his car. I just drove it out of the parking lot and into a tree. That was my entire intention. I don't like his car, don't want it. It's one of those racy old Camaro things with the back hiked way up. You know how a cat in heat will wave her butt in the air? That's what comes to mind, and I told Jason that, but he just loved that car, and I probably shouldn't have—"

"Who's Jason?"

"Jason is this guy who thinks he is God's gift to women. Which he definitely is not. Can you believe it, he thought oral sex meant talking dirty."

The AA meeting that night was held in the hospital. It was an older crowd that came. The leader of the meeting was a self-satisfied ancient wearing a plaid sports jacket. He said, "Most of you folks will drink again. You will walk out these doors thinking you got it licked, and you won't attend any AA meetings, and the next thing you know liquor will knock you on your ass."

Gates jumped up in the back row. "What's wrong with you man?" he shouted. "Mr. Bill Wilson be ashamed of a message like that. I wouldn't carry a message like that across the street! Goddam. We a bunch of sick muthers laid up in a hospital, all low and poorly, shakin, seeing things, and you come bustin in saying we got worse ahead. Mr. Doctor Bob would carve your lights out, he hear such low-down talk calling itself a message. Shit." Gates plopped back down, arms folded in front of him, a fierce scowl stamped on his features.

Somebody applauded. The leader, flustered, quickly called on one of his cronies who said that Arnie was just sharing his experience and that it was a sad truth that many people left detox and returned to drinking.

The whole meeting was, Jack felt, contentious, the forces of hope and optimism allied against those who felt the reality of alcoholism required a no-nonsense cautionary delivery.

After the meeting, a large, hearty man in a suit came up to Jack, hugged him, and said, "Hang in there. I love you." Jack smiled wanly and said nothing, embarrassed. He had never met the man and this declaration of love felt presumptuous. *Unconditional-love harassment*, Jack thought. As pernicious in its way as sexual harassment—more so, perhaps, since no one sympathized with the victim, no legal recourse was at hand.

Depressed, Jack went back to his room and lay on his bed. He desperately wanted a drink. A beer would do. Holding a cold beer can in his hand would almost be enough, the silky metal against his palm, the heft of a promise that would be kept. It would quiet him instantly. Of course, drinking would set him to thinking of Sara, and he could travel so far into that black cave that there would be no getting back.

Too jittery to think, he drifted back into the hall.

At the nurse's station, Blanche was speaking on the phone.

Jack heard the tail end of the conversation. When Blanche hung up and turned toward him, he said, "Is Hinkle back?"

Blanche narrowed her eyes. He could see her first impulse was to say, *None of your business*, but then she changed her mind.

She nodded. "He's down in the ER. You'll be seeing him soon enough."

"Did he drink again?"

Blanche faked broad amazement, eyes wide. "Now why would you think a thing like that?"

WILLIAM BROWNING SPENCER

he day came. The sky was overcast, moody weather. For late October it was unseasonably cold, and there were small, damp pockets of even colder air, unhappy autumn ghosts. One such ghost had stepped in front of Jack as he was walking toward the van, and the encounter had left Jack clumsy with a kind of unfocused grief, grief for some future tragedy, remorse as yet unborn.

Jack found a seat on the van and Gates immediately sat down next to him. "Ah can't believe I'm going to some fahm," Gates said. "Ah can't believe it."

Gates was going because he had argued with his son-in-law, Marvin. The exact nature of the argument was unclear, but Gates had pushed tall, lanky Marvin backwards, toppled him over a sofa in the dayroom, and the young man had leapt to his feet and called his father-in-law a "sorry-assed smoke head" and Gates's lovely daughter, Leeda, had come between them, preventing the argument from escalating to blows.

Leeda and her husband had come with the intention of taking her father back to their apartment in D.C., but the altercation killed that plan. Gates refused to budge. "You'll see me percolatin in Hell first," he grumbled.

Now, hunched in his seat, he kept saying, "Ah can't believe it. On my way to a goddam fahm."

Jack was fighting his own battle with credulity. Yesterday morning, he would have laughed at—and *did*—any suggestion that he should sacrifice six weeks of his life to intensive group therapy and alcoholism education.

Then, last night, he'd had a change of heart. In the morning, he'd sought Parks out.

Parks had looked up from the notepad he'd been writing on. He looked very young, skinny and harried, his tie undone, his hair sticking out in two flared wings above his ears, his goatee bristling. His smile was manic, fierce. "Well, Professor. How's the old head? I guess you've learned not to get between an alcoholic and his booze." Parks chuckled. "Guess we'll both be glad to get out of here. Sorry you don't want to come, but—"

Jack interrupted, explained that, in fact, he had changed his mind and would like to come.

Parks narrowed his eyes, said nothing. Then he nodded his head. "Last night changed your mind? Hinkle got you to thinking, did he?"

Jack nodded. "I guess."

Parks grinned, nodding his head violently now. "Sometimes you've got to hit an alcoholic over the head to get his attention."

Jack grinned back. He didn't trust himself to speak. But he knew that this alcoholism counselor was right on one count: Last night had been an attention getter.

"Ah ain't milkin no cow, feedin no chickens," Gates was saying.

Jack thought of Wesley Parks and the notebook Parks had been writing on. The white page had been covered with little red stick figures and lightning bolts, the same distinctive doodles that had adorned the article entitled "Mapping Your Emotions."

According to that test, Jack's alcoholism counselor had the emotional resources of a mollusk.

"And ah ain't cuttin no hogs," Gates was saying.

Jack wondered if he was doing the right thing. But last night had unnerved him, had left him with a strong desire for remote therapeutic havens.

The AA meeting that night had been another in-hospital meeting, and Kerry had leaned over and whispered in Jack's ear, "Look."

He'd already seen them, seated in the back of the room near the water fountain, three young men in white shirts, a clump of silent otherness.

A man named Mort (who wore a black jumpsuit and a black woolen cap suggestive of risky, covert activities) spoke. Mort talked about humility, pontificating at length. He was remarkably boring (a quality that, Jack noted, often accompanied outrageous, declamatory fashion statements), explaining that there were three sorts of humility. He said that he would explain each in detail.

Jack thought the lecture was drawing to a close when the first two types of humility had finally been delineated, but then the final variety came under examination. "This kind of humility can be divided into four parts," the man said, and Jack lost all hope, setting his mind free to roam elsewhere. He thought of a time when he was eleven years old and a neighborhood dog named Pudgy would bite him every morning. He remembered how everyone gave him advice on how to avoid this (just as people will suggest various hiccup cures). *Befriend him*. Pudgy would bite. *Run at him*. Pudgy would bite. *Ignore him*. Pudgy would bite. Most of the kids agreed that Pudgy's biting was probably the result of some flaw in Jack's character.

"Pudgy hates me!" Jack would wail, full of helpless rage.

Jack's friends would smile sadly, perhaps look away, disdainful of such a cheap dodge. *Sure, blame it on a dog.*

When the meeting ended, Jack was prepared to hurry back to his room where he was reading a medical thriller entitled *Spleen*, but Kerry clutched his arm.

"They went into Hinkle's room," Kerry said.

"Who?" Jack asked. But he knew who would go into Hinkle's room.

Hinkle had been brought up to the floor that morning, lodged in room E4, and nurses, orderlies, and Hurley's resident, Dr. Barrett, had all visited him.

Jack had peered into the darkened room, but Blanche had sent them away. "He's not up to visitors yet," she had said.

Now a contingent of The Clear was in room E4, preparing, no doubt, to shine their special light into the truck driver's alcoholic darkness.

"Come on," Kerry said. She moved quickly down the hall, an imperious young woman powered by conviction. The big cast on her arm didn't slow her.

Jack followed, reluctantly. He never cared for the thick of other people's problems. In this case, Hinkle had sought these folks out. Kerry didn't know that...needed to know that, and if he could just overtake her...

IRRATIONAL FEARS

Kerry turned slightly, pushing the door open with her shoulder, and Jack followed her into the room.

It was darker here than in the hall, the only light coming from a floor lamp near the nightstand. One of the young men was crouched on the floor. His two companions stood at the head of the bed. The figure in the bed lay flat, a sheet drawn up to his chin.

"Hey," Kerry said. "What the fuck do you think you are doing?"

Jack blinked at the man squatting by the side of the bed. He was creating a straight white line on the carpet by tapping a small canister in his hand. The powder formed an inch-wide line that seemed luminous in the gloom.

One of the young men left the side of the bed and came over to Kerry and Jack. "Please leave immediately," he said. "Your presence cannot be a benign influence. We must complete the pentagram. Your friend left us before he could experience the necessary purging, and he is consequently unprotected and in grave danger. We have come to complete the process and bring him to a place of knowledge and safety. If you will leave the room, we will execute the rituals."

"I'm not going anywhere," Kerry said. "I'm not leaving Hinkle with you wackos, not for one second."

The man at the head of the bed began to chant. Jack recognized the rolling, liturgical tones of Latin, mixed with some other language, guttural and primitive.

"Hey," the youth on the floor said. "Not yet. I'm not finished here."

The chanting stopped. "Nothing will stir until the second invocation," the chanter said. "So work while I prepare the gate, numbering the portals. There is much to do and little time." With that, he began again.

While chanting, the young man swayed slowly from side to side. He raised his arms. In one hand he held an empty shot glass, in the other— *Jesus!*—a pint of bourbon.

"Hey!" Kerry shouted. She too had seen the bottle. She ducked past the man in front of her and charged toward this inappropriate high priest.

Just then, Hinkle came alive on the bed. He lurched into a sitting position, arms flaying the air, eyes wide, galvanized by some nightmare. He yelled, "Nooooooooooo!"

"What's going on in here?" It was Blanche at the door now, behind her the bulk of Big Ernie, the nightshift orderly.

Blanche moved past everyone and leaned down to enfold Hinkle in her arms. "It's okay," she said, patting his back. "Nothing but bad dreams.

WILLIAM BROWNING SPENCER

I'll get you something that will send those nightmares back under the bed. Hush now. Hush."

Hinkle rocked in the nurse's arms. Blanche looked over his shoulder; took in the room with a slow turn. "Everyone out," she said. "Visiting hours are over."

Blanche, formidable in her authority, sent them all tumbling into the hall.

The young men of The Clear fled, down the hall and out the door with the last of the meeting's stragglers.

Neither Kerry nor Jack made any effort to stop them, but Kerry shouted after them (turning all heads except for those attached to the miscreants themselves): "Assholes! You sonofabitch assholes!"

Then Kerry slumped back against the wall and let gravity slowly slide her into a sitting position.

"Hinkle will be okay," Jack said.

Kerry looked up at him, the look in her eyes one he would have paid to avoid. "You don't know that," she said.

"No. Actually, no."

"What were those creeps doing here, anyway?"

"Well," Jack said, "I believe Hinkle knew them. When he left that AA meeting…" Jack hesitated. "I saw him leave in their van. I don't think he actually embraced the tenets of their faith; he just saw them as a convenient means of escape."

Kerry's mouth was open and she was staring up at him with shocked disbelief. "And you didn't tell anyone about this? You didn't think it was worth mentioning?"

"I believe in free will," Jack said. "I think that a person has a right…" He stopped speaking. He almost said, "I didn't want to rat the guy out," but that sounded so hopelessly immature, so stupid. "I don't know," he said.

Kerry rolled her eyes. "Great. I thought we were supposed to be looking out for each other. Just great." She stood up, turned away, and moved down the hall toward her room. She reached her door, clutched the handle, and then she looked back. Jack wanted to comfort her, to explain that he wasn't worth any big emotional outlay, hadn't been for years, had retreated into passivity and intellectual solitude and, of course, alcohol.

He might have mumbled some apology, but she spoke before he could. Her voice was calm, defeated. "My mistake," she said, and she opened the door and went into her room.

* * *

IRRATIONAL FEARS

Jack was sleeping when the new weight at the end of his bed caused him to roll. He awoke instantly.

Hinkle was sitting there. He was wearing a leather jacket, a baseball cap and white boxer shorts. He put a finger to his lips, urging silence.

Hinkle leaned forward and whispered, "They think they got us skinned and salted, but they don't."

He stood up then, reeled a little as he lifted the bottle to his lips and took a swig that seemed to knock him back, making him stumble. He giggled and turned, lumbering out the door.

Jack scrambled into his jeans and went after the man.

The hall was empty.

Hinkle was easy to find. He was back in his own room, sitting on the bed. Barefoot moments before, he now wore a single boot, part of a dim and poorly executed plan to achieve fully-clothed status. The rest of his attire remained the same: cap, jacket, boxer shorts.

Hinkle reached over to the nightstand and lifted the bottle. He bumped the floor lamp, which wobbled; shadows reeled drunkenly on the wall. Hinkle held the bottle out to Jack. Jack shook his head, *no*.

"Giving it up, huh?" Hinkle said. "I been that route. I can't recall all the details, but it was unpleasant. You ever been to Hell?" Hinkle held up a hand. "You don't have to answer that. You might think you've been down some hard roads, but you haven't, not really. Cause if you've really been to Hell, you know it right off, no question, you've been where worse is just more of the same. I been there."

Hinkle tilted the bottle to his lips again. He grinned. "Those Sunday boys sent me right to Hell. Don't know how they done it, the details aren't clear, but they done it. Then they hauled me back and asked, 'How you feeling, Hinkle?' and I said I was feeling like varnished shit, and they said, that's cause you ain't had enough; we got to send you to Hell again." Hinkle grinned. His eyes were shiny, the left one drifting toward the ceiling. "They underestimated me. I busted loose. Cleared out on The Clear. Hah ha."

"Hinkle," Jack said, "I'm glad you're okay. But it wouldn't be good if anyone caught you drinking in here. It—"

Hinkle stood up, suddenly truculent; the hand that wasn't holding the bottle formed a fist. "You wouldn't rat me out, would you, Professor?"

"No," Jack said, taking a step backwards. "Of course not."

Hinkle smiled, leered. "I come to and I'm in old Hurley detox again and old Blanche is hugging me and cooing in my ear. What do you think of

WILLIAM BROWNING SPENCER

that? She got her a good pair, under all that starch, and she ain't so bad to look at in the right light. Better yet, when she leaves I lean back on my pillow, feel something uncommonly hard, slide my hand under and find a pint of Old Midnight Arkansas Bourbon. I think, 'I been in Hell and now I'm in Heaven.' You sure you don't want any of this?"

"This is Hurley detox," Jack said. "People come here to stop drinking. That's the plan."

"And a fine plan it is," Hinkle said. He hiccuped, giggled. "Next year you might plan on growing wings or porking Madonna or being less of an asshole or—" Hinkle hiccuped again. His face went rigid, his mouth opened wide, he gagged. The bottle fell from his hand, bounced off the toe of his boot and spun on the carpet. The reek of strong booze filled the air.

Hinkle stumbled into the bathroom and began to vomit violently.

Jack stood by the door to the bathroom. "You okay?" he asked. It was, he thought, his day for ineffectual gestures, lame offers of aid.

The retching stopped. Silence.

The bathroom, identical to the one in Jack's room, was an exercise in minimalism: a sink, a shower, a toilet, a towel rack. Hinkle was on his knees in front of the toilet.

The room was dark, and Jack reached in, found the light switch, and flipped it. An overhead fluorescent light came alive with an angry buzz, casting a fitful glare over brown tiles. Hinkle's broad, leather-jacketed back gleamed like the sleek carapace of some prehistoric beast.

Hinkle's face, slick with sweat, was in profile. A single drop of blue water hung on the end of his nose, then fell.

He clutched the edge of the toilet bowl with shaking hands, leaned forward, stared in horror into the porcelain depths. "Go away!" he screamed. He reached up, fumbled for the silver handle.

"WHO ARE YOU TO COMMAND?"

The voice was too big for the small room, and it filled Jack's head. It was a voice inflected with evil, implacable, inhuman, and Jack believed, instantly, without a tremor of incredulity, without so much as a discreet pause to shake off the skepticism of a rational life, that a demon had spoken.

"Aaaaaa," Hinkle screamed, and his pale, clumsy hand slapped at the handle.

The toilet flushed, an explosive crack that roared into echoing torrents, the noise rising to a scream, tormented by the smallness of the room. Hinkle howled too, fell backwards. His baseball cap flipped off and dove, bat-like, into the bowl.

IRRATIONAL FEARS

A gray towel unfurled from its rack, undulated in the air like a live thing and dove into the blue turbulence of the toilet bowl. It disappeared with a shriek. A red toothbrush leapt from its holder. Toiletries swarmed in the air: a bar of soap, a tube of toothpaste, a safety razor, a glass bottle of shampoo which, suddenly shattering, became a writhing green blob with an honor guard of glittering shards. All plunged into the toilet bowl, swallowed (*pock pock pock*) by something that raged as it came.

Came. Was coming. Of that, Jack was certain. Something was approaching, furious, frenzied.

A roll of toilet paper unraveled, leaving a spinning cardboard tube. The shower curtain flapped, twisted, stretched to find the toilet bowl. Two of the plastic rings popped; the others held.

The toilet bowl was straining to swallow the curtain, which was stretched on a diagonal, shaken as though harried by an invisible terrier.

The shower rod buckled and fell. The intact rings swarmed free; the curtain snapped brightly and disappeared into the groaning bowl, a clatter of rings, a last straining, gagging, keening sound and then the steady, satisfied boom of water stirred by hurricane winds.

Something was happening to the light in the room. The corners of the room were in shadow. Hinkle, shoved back against the wall, was also in shadow. The light was dimming, no, narrowing. It was being drawn into the toilet bowl, marshaled by a hideous power that fashioned it into a single cold beam traveling from light fixture to porcelain bowl.

The door to the bathroom slammed in Jack's face, bringing stark, impossible silence. Jack hurled himself against the door. "Hinkle!" he screamed.

Jack's voice was loud, crazy with terror in the stillness. He slammed his shoulder against the door, and it gave some, releasing the hurricane roar and Hinkle's screams. The noise was a physical assault, battering Jack's skull.

Jack peered through the grudging inches where door and frame were parted by the pressure of his shoulder. In the gloom, he could see that something black and wounded was crawling across the tiled floor. A dog, perhaps, beaten, abject.

Where's Hinkle?

Jack's eyes found the trucker, crouched in a dark corner of the shower stall. Hinkle's white belly caught the ambient light, glowed like the moon underwater.

Of course. It was the leather jacket that crawled toward the omnivorous porcelain mouth.

WILLIAM BROWNING SPENCER

The jacket ascended the white, bulging belly of the toilet, seemed to pause at the gleaming rim, hesitated, and was swallowed, three gulps, the sound: *whup, whup, whup*. Then Hinkle's single boot jauntily bounced the distance and disappeared.

Jack strained at the door, but his efforts failed to widen the three-inch gap.

Hinkle suddenly screamed and lurched forward. He was leaning over the toilet, his right arm plunged into thrashing blue water, his face squashed up against the upraised toilet lid. Grimacing under the column of light, the trucker looked like one of those late-night wrestlers, illegally pinned against the ropes, writhing in anger and agony while the crowd roared and the referee looked the other way.

"Hinkle!" Jack shouted.

The door was jammed; perhaps if he backed up and ran against it. Jack turned to look at the room behind him. As he watched, the tall floor lamp in the corner shed its lamp shade; the light bulb blazed. The lamp leaned forward as though trying to peer past Jack, fascinated by what it sensed.

The floor lamp lifted in the air and tumbled toward Jack. It spun end over end, an illuminated baton.

The door to the bathroom slammed shut. Jack reeled in the jarring silence.

Pop. Instant darkness. The sound, Jack later realized, was that of an electrical plug wrenching free of its outlet as the lamp flew beyond the reach of its cord.

In the blackness, Jack heard the flailing lamp cord snap against the wall behind him. And that was it. A burst of light, the false illumination of pain, bathed the inside of his skull.

"We way in the boondocks," Gates said, frowning at pine trees as the van bumped over a dirt road. "That trucker maybe had the right idea. He shouldn't have hit you with that lamp, that was uncalled for, but gettin out of Hurley before this sorry country bullshit…that might have been a good idea. How you suppose he escaped?"

Jack rubbed his forehead, winced when his hand came into contact with the bandage—seven stitches—and shrugged.

He just slid right down the toilet, Jack could have said. *I know he was kind of a big man, and so it might be hard to credit, but there was something in that toilet—I guess you'd call it a monster—that squeezed Hinkle good, squeezed that big truck driver as easy as you or I would squeeze a tube of toothpaste. No, I*

IRRATIONAL FEARS

didn't actually see it happen. I was knocked unconscious by a flying lamp. And, to tell you the truth, I would be happy if I were mistaken on this one. I'd be pleased to be wrong.

Gates leaned forward in his seat and shouted at the driver of the van. "How much longer before we get to this place? We been driving for hours!"

Wesley Parks (rehab counselor and temporary van driver) turned in his seat and beamed. "Patience, Mr. Gates. We are almost there."

WILLIAM BROWNING SPENCER

Part 2
New Way Rehab

rickety wooden gate, latched but not locked, blocked the dirt road. A hand-painted sign read *NEW WAY Alcoholism Treatment Facility*. The sign's lettering was crude but elaborate, executed, Jack assumed, by one of New Way's patients, someone who didn't do much but did it to excess. There might, Jack thought, be some sort of graduate thesis paper in the relationship between ornate lettering and mental illness.

This is not going to be fun, Jack thought.

Wesley got Al to get out of the van and open the gate. The teenager was wearing ballooning red pants, sneakers, and a leather flight jacket. Jack wondered if this outfit was ironic in intent. Al's expression (gloomy, put-upon) didn't suggest that he was consciously engaged in sending up fashion.

After Al got the gate open, they drove past a low, rambling building of brown brick, past a small, muddy pond full of autumnal yellows and reds, past a swaybacked barn. They drove on to the top of a low hill where the sight of a wooden, three-story farmhouse in need of a paint job caused Gates to sigh audibly.

"Ta ta," Wesley said, stopping the van. "Welcome to New Way." He turned the engine off and climbed out of the van. "Come on."

IRRATIONAL FEARS

Eunice, wearing a pink robe over a blouse and black slacks, followed, descending to the muddy earth with a weary sigh. Al was next, then Kerry, then Ed Tilman.

Two dogs banged open the farmhouse's screen door and came barking and bobbing across the porch and down the steps.

Jack watched from the van window. The dogs were big, scruffy, burlap-brown dogs full of rural hatred for outsiders.

I'm not getting out of this van, Jack thought.

Hurley detox's relocated patients were milling around in the weedy yard. Gates was just exiting the van, but ducked back inside. "Sheeeeeeyit. I knowed it," Gates said, turning to look at Jack. "Dog bit to damn death! You call that curin alcoholism?"

Jack didn't. He couldn't take his eyes off the approaching dogs. They were in a fever, a frenzy, of motion. There was something wrong with these dogs. The bigger, darker of the two kept twisting as it ran, was—yes—biting its own shoulder, yipping from self-induced pain. There was something very wrong with these dogs. They were wet, their fur matted. Their eyes were illuminated by angry red fires.

Eunice was running, her pink robe flapping, an impossibly overweight butterfly, never to be airborne, her stubby arms stretched toward the heavens, her fingers wiggling as though seeking an angel's protective grasp.

The dogs saw her. She was irresistible; they turned and pursued her as she lurched and stumbled down the hill toward the pond. Her companions, with the exception of Kerry, clambered back into the van.

"Cowards!" Kerry shouted. "You've got to help her!"

Parks dragged Kerry back into the van and slammed the door. "We'll go get help," he said. "We will—"

"It will be too late!" Kerry shouted.

Eunice's screams turned every head. The smaller dog had the hem of Eunice's robe in its mouth. The woman was leaning away from the dog, yanking at the fabric of her robe with both hands. The bigger dog was circling, head low.

Someone shouted from the tree line. A figure in a long, gray overcoat had come out of the trees and was now running up the hill, moving with long strides. His hat blew off to reveal shoulder-length gray hair, a gray mustache, the face of some Civil War general, crazy with years of deprivation and the denial of defeat.

A shotgun was clutched in his right hand.

WILLIAM BROWNING SPENCER

He was shouting something, at first unintelligible, but then coming through the opened window with surrealistic clarity: "Dr. Bob! Bill! Stop!"

Both dogs were shaking the robe now and Eunice, released from its pink confines, was running again.

The dogs dropped the robe and pursued her.

The man reached her before the dogs. He whirled in front of her and threw the shotgun to his shoulder. "Whoa!" he shouted.

The smaller dog (small being a relative term; a big dog in almost any other company) leapt, sank its teeth into the man's forearm. The man stumbled backwards and fell. The big dog had reached him now and lunged for his throat, its hindquarters trembling, its whole body jittering as though animated by convulsive electric currents.

The shotgun roared and the man was instantly on his feet, standing over the broken corpse and swinging the shotgun in an arc, following the smaller fleeing dog. The man slowed, perhaps calculating the distance, perhaps hesitating. When the shotgun erupted, the dog yelped, tumbled, but raced on, howling, and made the safety of the trees and was gone.

The man studied the trees for a few seconds before turning to regard the van with an expression of unblemished disgust. Then he turned and headed toward Eunice, who had fallen again and now lay on her stomach near the lake with her hands over her head, a posture more defeatist than defensive.

They looked at each other, the van dwellers. Jack did not look in Kerry's direction, for fear she would be looking back at him.

"We need to process this in group," Parks said, and Jack looked then, cheaply pleased to see Kerry's disgusted glare leveled at the alcoholism counselor.

"I say we process ourselves right back to Hurley while the processin's good," Gates said.

Jack agreed but said nothing.

"Bill Wilson was a good dog. Never killed no chickens, never got up on the furniture, never hurt a soul. There were some said, 'You shouldn't go naming a dog after the founder of AA. That's sacrilegious.' I always said, 'This dog honors that name, makes it shine.' He was loyal and he was good-hearted, and anyone who knew him will tell you the same.

"Bill Wilson went crazy today, tormented by a curse, hexed, and the blame don't lie with him. I know where the blame lies, and I'll tend to that.

Right now, I'm sending you off, old Bill. I'm wishing you a Heaven of fat rabbits and bitches always in heat. God love you."

He threw the milkbone into the hole. It made a dull, sad *thunk* on the top of the long cardboard box that had once held frozen poultry parts and now housed the mortal remains of a part ridgeback, part anyone's guess dog.

The man, whose name was Martin Pendleton, picked up the shovel and began heaving dirt back into the hole. He looked up, as though surprised to see the people gathered around him. He pushed the long gray hair from his forehead. "I won't be needing any help here," he said. "You can all go on down to the Residence. I expect you are hungry. Aaron here will see that you get something to eat. I'll be along shortly."

As they walked down the road to the brown brick building, the air filled with swirling white flies, one of which stung Jack on the cheek and melted: Snow.

"Damn snow," Gates said, squinting up at the gray sky. "Damn fahm, damn old dogs, damn snow."

The cook, Aaron, apologized for dinner, which consisted of baloney sandwiches and applesauce. "I'm mortified," he said. "You'll think the worst, won't you? This is grocery day, but I was unable to get into town, so…" He sighed, closed his eyes, and pressed his fingers to his temples. Aaron was a tall, thin man (his tallness exaggerated by a foot of bright red hair that rose toward the ceiling as though drawn by an electrical charge). He was wearing an orange silk shirt. His skin was pale, pinkish, and his lips, painted with glossy red lipstick, suggested a fresh wound.

"You hate me, don't you?" he said.

No one responded; the question seemed rhetorical. Aaron glared at them, turned and stalked off.

They were seated at long tables in a low-ceilinged room. It was already dark outside, and Jack could see fat snowflakes tumbling against the windowpanes.

"He'll get over it," a woman sitting next to Jack said. She was a small Joyce Carol Oates sort of woman with a round face and short straight black hair. Large black-framed glasses magnified her eyes, creating a hopeful, inquisitive expression. "He's always getting his feelings hurt, sulking, accusing the staff of eating his precious peach cobbler pie—as though he paid for it out of his own pocket."

Jack smiled wanly.

WILLIAM BROWNING SPENCER

"I'm Gretchen Payne," she said. "I'm the secretary here. I guess you are wondering where the other residents are."

"Well…"

"I'm not at liberty to discuss it," she said. "I'm just the secretary. I do my job, but I'm not supposed to have any opinions."

"Ah."

"What do you think of our little rehab?" She smiled, folded her hands and leaned forward. She nodded her head. "Well, it's free. That's what Martin—he's the director here—says when anyone complains. He says, 'You don't like it, you can have a refund.'"

"Those dogs—" Jack began.

Martin Pendleton burst into the room, bringing the weather with him. The shotgun was slung over his back. He had reclaimed his hat. His shoulders and the brim of his hat were glazed with snow. Drops of melting snow gleamed from the thicket of his mustache. His eyes were black and angry under bramblelike eyebrows.

Wesley Parks got out of his chair where he was sitting next to Kerry, and hurried toward New Way's director.

"Martin," Parks said, "we've got to—"

The big man nodded grimly, as though he knew the end of the sentence. He brushed past Wesley and walked to the far corner of the room where a white lectern emblazoned with the AA triangle-within-a-circle symbol stood in shadow. He enfolded the lectern in a massive bear hug, lifted it, and carried it to the other side of the room near the door to the kitchen.

He stood behind it, took off his hat, and blinked at his audience.

He didn't say anything for several minutes. In the silence, Jack found himself struck again by Martin Pendleton's resemblance to a mad Confederate general (preparing to urge his troops into some final doomed offensive).

"Ladies and gentlemen," Martin began, "I apologize for this inauspicious beginning." He narrowed his eyes. "Where's that fat woman?"

"Eunice is lying down in her room," Kerry said.

Martin nodded. "I'll apologize personally to her later." He looked around the room. He didn't seem happy with what he saw.

"You haven't arrived in happy times," he said. "If you thought you were bound for a picnic, you are gonna be disappointed. Old brother alcohol and his sister, demon drugs, are a match for all of us, and getting sober is a climb up a steep cliff in a thunderstorm. It ain't never easy." He paused, sighed. "Still, it is usually a sight easier than it is right now. Imagine if Bill Wilson, our founder, had been trying to start AA and someone was always dogging him, harrying him at every turn, pouring whiskey into his coffee when he wasn't looking, filling meetings with dissension and rumor, flat-out lies like *Dr. Bob is popping pills* or *Bill Wilson is screwing the new man's wife while the poor son of a bitch is laid up in detox.* Alcohol is hard enough to shake without people actively set on seeing that you fail."

He paused again, looked sharply around the room as though expecting dissent, some act of insurrection. Jack was beginning to have a bad feeling about this. He closed his eyes and saw Hinkle's face, a rictus of terror as he wrestled with a malevolent toilet.

"We had seven residents last week," Martin Pendleton said. "They stole the van and headed off to California. Jake, my right-hand man here at New Way, he was their ringleader. He left a note saying stress had got to him, and he needed a break. His plan…you want to hear his plan for getting mellow?"

No one said anything, which Martin took as a go-ahead. "He wrote it in his farewell note, said he's gonna take the whole damned rehab to a Grateful Dead concert, gonna get mellow. The man's so out of touch; he don't even know Jerry's dead. I don't like to think how he's gonna handle that.

"I know what scared Jake and the others. That damn cult. We got a crazy, white-shirt-wearing cult here in town; they call themselves The Clear. They been hanging around AA meetings for two years or so now, but they weren't much more than a nuisance at first. Now they are more aggressive."

The Clear. Jack felt his stomach twist.

"We had an incident about six months ago," Martin was saying. "A teenager, a girl named Molly Bluett, was trying to get her act together. Her father, Max Bluett, had been sober for fourteen years—owned Bluett Quick Stop Grocery—and he was seeing that she made an AA meeting a night. Getting sober doesn't always work when the goad is a parent cracking the whip, but Molly was showing up, and we were glad to see her. She had a sunny disposition; she was a sweet thing."

Martin Pendleton's eyes rolled up toward the ceiling, accessing some memory. He sighed.

"My brother died drunk in a bar fight," he said, his eyes shifting back to his audience, "and my parents burned up in bed, snuffed by cigarettes and alcohol. Alcohol tried to kill me too, but I got seventeen years free of it, and I won't go back without a fight. It is a fight. Make no mistake." He paused, collected himself. "So Molly Bluett ran off with The Clear; I imagine they promised her a lot of nonsense, and she was probably restless and bored

WILLIAM BROWNING SPENCER

crazy by the meetings where she was getting lectured by a lot of old men whose dicks hadn't twitched since Nixon resigned. She ran off, and when she came back she was wild in ways that scared people, and her father sent her to me, but this isn't a lock-up here, and she ran off again, and her father and some others went and fetched her—kidnapped her, I guess—from The Clear's commune. Her father took her on home, and locked her in her room, thinking, I guess, that she was just being willful, and she hanged herself with an electrical cord.

"Old Max Bluett started drinking again. One night, roaring drunk, he drove to the Late Niters AA Club and shot down two cult members who were standing in the parking lot handing out fliers. I was there that night. We all came running out of the meeting when we heard the shots, saw old Max reeling under the yellow lights, the hunting rifle hugged against his chest like a holy cross, saw those two dead kids, their white shirts black with blood, busted up. Abe Finners drove Max home, and I remember Annie Bascomb, sober twenty-eight years, shouting out that this was nobody's business and that the rest of the world didn't need to know about it. So everyone kept quiet, and those bodies just disappeared, and never a murmur on the news. A couple days later, Max used that rifle on himself. I expect he saw the truth: The blood of a couple of cult followers wasn't gonna wash the pain out of his heart."

Martin was convinced that the cult was responsible for the strange behavior of his dogs. The dogs had disappeared for a day—and they weren't dogs to miss a meal. A farmboy named Robbie Waller said he'd seen them getting into a black van. "A cult that will meddle with a man's dogs will do anything!" Martin said. "The dogs came back, the very next day, shivering and strange. I knew something was wrong when Dr. Bob growled at me like he didn't know me."

A pause. Then: "I'm hoping you folks didn't come here for a rest cure. Because I'm gonna need the best each of you has to offer. You are in the front lines now. Yeah, Wesley?"

Jack turned in his chair, saw Wesley Parks pushing his chair back, rising from the long table. "It sounds as though we have a situation here that can't be addressed by a therapeutic community. If I'm hearing you correctly, murder has been done, condoned by an AA club—"

"I didn't say that. I didn't say 'condoned.' No one's happy—"

"Still, the point is"—Wesley put a hand to his forehead—"we have criminal activity, a crisis situation. It's out of the question to attempt any sort of therapy in these circumstances. I'm taking my clients back to Hurley tonight."

"Your clients are New Way's clients now, and they are going to an AA meeting. They aren't running off at the first sign of trouble. That's no way to get sober. If they want to learn how to stay sober, they will have to get in the habit of going to an AA meeting no matter what the circumstances of their lives."

"I cannot be a party to this," Wesley said. He drew himself up, shoulders back. "I'm not staying."

"You sure ain't taking the van you came in," Martin said. "I'll be needing that to take these folks to an AA meeting. They got a drinking problem, and it needs to be addressed. Way I understand it, you don't have a drinking problem. You are more one of those *authorities* on the problem. While we are all floundering, bobbing up and down in a rough ocean, goddam *drowning*, you are off somewhere on a rock with a megaphone broadcasting all manner of help, explaining the backstroke and the dog paddle and I don't know what all. Likely you know what you are talking about, but I'm losing interest, going down for the third time. There goes my life flashing in front of my eyes—a sorry-assed show—and I can't make out a word you're saying, and I could surely, surely use someone who fucking *knew how to swim* and who was fucking *in the water!*"

Parks had turned and was walking toward the door.

"Hey!" Martin shouted.

Parks increased his pace.

The shotgun blast shattered the plaque above the door frame, sent fragments spinning, tumbling across the linoleum in a Tinkertoy clatter.

Parks stopped dead, his shoulders hiked up, his arms angled at the elbows like some still shot from a comic dance number.

"We got a war on here, counselor!" Martin shouted. "I'll drop you in your tracks, you try to desert."

It was a subdued crowd that filed out of the kitchen. Jack, eyes downcast, noted the truncated piece of inspiration (Old English lettering, blue on a white background) that had come to rest against the door frame. *GOD GRANT ME THE SER*, it read.

now came out of the black sky in a wild, dizzy rush. The snow seemed to sense that it was ahead of schedule, tried to fake it with enthusiasm, like an uninvited guest backslapping his way to the punch bowl.

"You think they'll hold a meeting? Won't they close up?" Al asked.

The question was directed at Kerry, who was sitting next to Al in the van. It was Ed Tilman who answered, however, leaning forward in his seat behind Al and shouting into the teenager's ear. "The meeting will be crowded," he said. "I've made a study of the alcoholic personality. Your basic alcoholic is stubborn, contrary. You push, he pushes back. Snow falls, slicking up the roads. That's Mother Nature saying, 'Don't be going outside.' So your alcoholic says, 'I'm on my way. You can't stop me!' That's the way he's made."

"I guess I'm not an alcoholic," Al said. "I think we should have stayed inside."

Just then, Martin Pendleton yanked the van's steering wheel to the left, too quickly, and the van skidded, leaning sideways, and every one of its passengers (Ed, Al, Kerry, Jack, Gates, Wesley, and Eunice) made the same high-pitched sound ("Eeeeeeeeeeeeeee"), demonstrating a solidarity of panic, and then the van smacked the curb, jumped forward, and slid through a red light.

"You gonna get us killed!" Gates shouted. He had been curled in the fetal position on the backseat, but Martin Pendleton's driving had knocked him from a sideways sulk to an upright rage. "We gonna be dead in a drift!"

Pendleton ignored Gates, inured, Jack assumed, to the complaints of his charges.

"All right," Pendleton said as they pulled into the parking lot. "I want you to keep an eye on each other. Don't anybody go wandering off alone."

The meeting was in a two-story red brick building on the corner diagonally across from the parking lot. It was an old building, with small, square windows through which unhappy souls could glare at an establishment across the street, a nightspot called Bob's Beer Palace. Crossing the street, Jack could hear country music leaking from the bar, the unmistakable sad, besotted voice of George Jones. Jack felt a strong and sudden yearning to be inside Bob's Beer Palace sitting at the bar, listening to old men and women stuck fast in the past, their voices filled with slowness and regret, the sadness of their stories dulled by the tarnish of endless telling. The sound of their voices would be punctuated by the occasional clink of glass against glass, the frothy hiss of liquid filling a chilled mug.

The bar's sign was clearly homemade, crude cutout caps braced upright on the shack's flat roof. Floodlights illuminated the letters, displaying a glinting, scaled and multicolored surface, which, Jack suddenly realized, had been accomplished by gluing or nailing hundreds of beer cans to the cutouts—a labor of love and surely performed by Bob himself, in a fit of folk-art inspiration purer, in its way, than Michelangelo's commissioned work.

There were five cars in front of the bar, all of them filmed with snow.

Jack and his comrades entered the bar's competition, The Happy Roads AA Club, and were greeted by a blast of cigarette smoke and hot air and hearty laughter.

The actual meeting was held upstairs, the downstairs being reserved for socializing (the drinking of coffee, the smoking of innumerable cigarettes, and the stoic contemplation of bridge hands).

In single file, they ascended the narrow stairs. The blue carpet beneath Jack's feet was faded and worn. Old black-and-white photos of Bill and Lois Wilson, Bob Smith, and Dr. Silkworth (an early AA advocate and author of "The Doctor's Opinion" in the Big Book) adorned the walls. There was a photo of the house in Akron, Ohio where it had all begun.

If AA was a cult, as some disgruntled ex-members maintained, it was a cult with stodgy and decidedly uncharismatic founders. They all looked like Calvinists just out of church.

Jack found himself thinking of quirkier cults and their eccentric leaders. L. Ron Hubbard, the founder of Scientology, came to mind. Hubbard had started out as a writer of pulp science fiction, and he had written a lot of schlocky space operas before Dianetics made his fortune. His devoted followers were legion.

Strange to have as your leader a man whose shrine honored his world-shaking vision and also hawked his weird pulp-fiction tales.

Jack found himself wondering how Christianity would look had Jesus felt compelled to dash off gothic romances in his spare time.

Jack was examining this thought from several angles when he reached the top of the stairs. Martin Pendleton, immediately in front of Jack, pushed open a door and they entered a smoky room that was, as Tilman had predicted, packed.

A tall man in a gray suit came up to them, patted Martin on the back, and ushered them all past rows of seated men and women to where other members unfolded metal chairs to create a new back row.

A cloud of blue cigarette smoke hung near the ceiling, eliciting crackles and pops from an overworked smoke eater. A furnace rumbled, exhaling oily heat. Jack sat in the offered chair and smiled at Wesley Parks who was grimly, grudgingly lowering himself into the adjacent chair. Parks didn't return Jack's smile. The alcoholism counselor looked frightened. Having a shotgun fired over his head had affected him negatively. He kept darting furtive, unhappy looks at Martin Pendleton, who sat on Jack's right and who stared straight ahead, stonelike in his impassivity.

Easy does it, Wesley, Jack wanted to say, but he knew that such input would be unwelcome. At the best of times, Wesley Parks was not happy with AA's anarchy. Being forced to sit in a meeting where his opinions and direction were not required (or even desired) had to be a harrowing experience for the man. Fear still had the upper hand (if Jack read Wesley's expression correctly), but indignation was trying to scramble to the top of the emotional heap. Jack turned his attention to the meeting, already in progress.

An extremely fat man in a gray sweatshirt was speaking. "...And I turned my life over to the Elder Gods, as I understand them, and Yog-Sothoth prevailed and the gate swung wide and a great calm washed over me. *N'ggah-kthn-y'hhu! Cthua t'lh gup r'lhob-g'th'gg lgh thok!*"

Having uttered these curious syllables, the fat man was silent. He smiled beatifically, unfolded his hands and plucked his burning cigarette from the ashtray balanced on his knee. He took a long drag and beamed like a lottery winner.

IRRATIONAL FEARS

A weary-looking woman with a lion's mane of blond hair spoke next. She was wearing a pale green waitress uniform. She talked about how she wanted to drink every time she thought about her ex. She described her ex's pencil-thin mustache and his Clint Eastwood act, always squinting up his eyes and whispering. She talked about how he had chased women and gambled away their life savings. She had everyone hating the guy by the time she finished talking, ending by saying, "Thank Azathoth I'm not drinking! *N'gig them'ln mk'barsoom!*"

A wizened little man spoke next, beginning, "I'm Steve and I'm an alcoholic"—*Hi Steve!* the group shouted—"I'm delighted to be here, delighted to be anywhere, sober. *Ia! Ia! G'noth-ykagga-ha!*"

The crowd laughed. Jack found himself blinking at the opposite wall where the usual slogans were framed. The Old English lettering was familiar from other AA meetings, those tried-and-true slogans... His mind stumbled. *One Day at a Zigmuth,* he read. *Easy N'gamf It,* declared another plaque. And over the doorway, Jack read, *But for the Grace of Azathoth.*

Something's wrong here, Jack thought.

A prim woman with straight hair that was parted in the middle (as precisely as a geometry proof) was speaking: "I've been doing a lot of inner-child work. When I was a kid, I was smothered by over-affectionate parents. It wasn't, technically, abuse, and my parents were doing the best they could, I know, but my sense of self was distorted. My parents, by being too loving, created an abusive situation, you see. When I hear people talk about how mean and thoughtless their parents were, I envy those people, because they were being prepared for an indifferent world. My parents, by unnatural nurturing, made the rest of the world seem monstrous. I've written a poem about it. It's not very long, and if no one objects, I'd like to read it."

No one shouted "Don't read it!" although Jack thought he heard someone moan softly.

The poem was probably not long in comparison, to say, *Evangeline,* but it did march to a measured drum. Many people, skilled in avoiding poems and meandering anecdotes, slipped off to refill coffee cups or avail themselves of bathrooms.

Jack decided he could use a cup of coffee himself, and he stood up as the woman droned on (*"empowered as the stars and the planets that spin around them and the nurturing nurturing gravity and the boundaries that are nurturing and..."*). Turning, he saw that Wesley Parks's chair was empty. How long? Five minutes? Ten minutes?

Jack ran down the stairs. What was the urgency here? he asked himself. If Parks wanted to leave, good riddance. *Right?* Well, *right?*

WILLIAM BROWNING SPENCER

Right.

Jack slowed, entered the noise and smoke of the downstairs coffee bar. People were hunched over tables playing cards. In a corner of the room a television was on. Several old men were watching some sort of sports event in which men in wet suits played shuffleboard on ice. Someone scored, and two of the men watching jumped up and hugged each other excitedly.

Jack turned away and saw Wesley Parks moving toward him through the crowd with speed and purpose, his goatee thrust resolutely forward, his arms swinging briskly.

It was clear he did not see Jack, and Jack was forced to clutch at an arm.

"Aaaah!" Wesley said. He wobbled and then regained his balance. Recognition changed the counselor's expression from terror to distaste.

"Let go of me, Professor."

"I—" Jack realized he had no words for this sense of dread, no way to express the *not-rightness* that was palpable. It was more than the strangeness of the meeting overhead, more than the sum of recent ominous events. It was a certainty that the horizon held disaster. A premonition. He'd felt this way before, failed to act. (*Although he'd had no premonition, that time. He had been deaf while the world screamed. In truth, he'd felt nothing when Sara had said, "I'll do it." Why hadn't an alarm gone off then if he was so damned intuitive?*)

Wesley backed up, wary, as though Jack might grab him again. "This is *not* a therapeutic situation, and I don't condone it. I'm leaving."

"Look, I agree with you. We should all leave. I don't know how—"

"Excuse me," Wesley said. He was peering past Jack, studying the crowd, looking for someone. "A young man was kind enough to offer me a ride to Leesburg. I can take a cab from there. He...ah, there he is. Later, Professor."

Wesley turned and was off, heading toward the door. A tall youth stood next to the door, hands clasped behind his back: A clean-cut young man, respectful, serious, the boy to date your daughter (if you were of the old school that believed good deportment and grooming were the best indicators of good character). The youth wore an overcoat, open to reveal a white shirt and black tie.

"Wait—" Jack said, and he ran after Wesley and clapped a hand on his shoulder.

That was a mistake. Had Jack looked closer into Wesley's eyes he would have seen the panic there, as mindless as a roach just sprayed with Black Flag and scrambling across the linoleum, tiny brain filled with insect *whatthefuck* terror. If Jack had been paying attention, he would have been prepared for the wild swing, the fist that found his jaw.

IRRATIONAL FEARS

Jack slammed backwards, knees water, and knocked over a chair. "Watch it!" someone snapped. He fell, the ceiling's fluorescent panels tumbling like golden dominoes, a shadow enfolding him for one quick, angel-wing beat.

He scrambled to his feet—instantly, he thought, but he was wrong there. Someone had robbed him of a tiny piece of time. There were people around him, concerned, some suspicious (the thought, *Is this guy drunk?* held in their eyes).

"You okay, buddy?" someone asked.

"Fine," Jack said, staggering forward and resting a hand on a card table that trembled. Parks was gone.

Jack hurried to the door and out, skidding, almost falling on the snow-slicked steps. Snow fuzzed the world, wide-screen video static.

The time-thief hadn't made off with much, loose change, a couple of minutes. There was Wesley, getting into a black van.

"Wait!" Jack shouted, but Wesley pulled the door closed and the van pulled away from the curb. Snow devoured the vehicle before it reached the corner.

Again, Jack thought, shoulders hunched against the storm.

Again.

Jack went back up to the second floor and squeezed past folks leaning against the wall and sat down next to Martin Pendleton. The over-nurtured woman was no longer talking, but she had inspired a thin bald man to reflect on his own troubled childhood. "You talk about dysfunctional. You folks don't know dysfunctional. I'll tell you something. The only time my dad ever hugged me was when he was robbing a 7-Eleven and using me for a shield. You don't..."

Jack leaned over and whispered into Martin Pendleton's ear. "Wesley Parks just left."

"Fine," Martin muttered. "Let the sucker go."

The bald man had finished speaking and now the chairman was wrapping the meeting up.

"I think," Jack said, hesitating, realizing then that there was no secrecy required, no confidence to violate, "I think he left with members of The Clear. In fact, I'm sure he did."

"Goddam it!" Pendleton roared, and leapt to his feet. The rest of the room was rising too, preparing to hold hands and end the meeting with a prayer.

WILLIAM BROWNING SPENCER

"Come on," Pendleton said, and he rounded his charges up and had them hurrying down the stairs.

Gates, speaking for all of them, said, "Where's the damned fire?"

They hurried down the stairs. Above them, behind the closed door, the prayer began. Jack couldn't make out words, but the eerie cadence and dark power of the muffled incantation seemed to pursue him, a pressure on his back and shoulders that engendered a queasy echo of guilt, need and yearning.

Definitely not your standard Our Father Who art in heaven closing.

Jack thought he heard a rising shout from behind the closed door, something like *The Poodle, The Poodle, The Poodle*, and then Hurley's transplanted crew, now players on the New Way team, were plunging into the storm. Eunice, her freshly-laundered robe whipping around her, blinked at Jack with blank-eyed puzzlement. She shouldn't have been brought along, Jack thought. Her encounter with mad dogs had sent her into brooding silence, as though she had to think carefully about it all, reflect on just what that unpleasantness had meant, and consequently had no time for the world beyond her skull.

Her dark, close-set eyes fixed on Jack with grim intensity. "Jesus was a social drinker," she said.

"Huh?"

"He could take it or leave it. He could have a little, let the rest sit, go off about His Father's business without looking back."

"I'm not following you, Eunice," Jack said.

Up ahead, Pendleton was preparing to cross the street. He shouted for them to hurry.

Eunice nodded grimly, as though she had expected no better from Jack. "They aren't looking to Jesus for help," she said, and she turned and lumbered after the others.

Jack followed reluctantly.

"it up here with me," Pendleton said. He shook his head disgustedly. "Damn fool thought The Clear would give him a ride to Leesburg, did he?"

Jack climbed into the front passenger seat. Martin Pendleton gave him a hard look and said, "You look like you might have some sense. Ain't much of a lot to choose from. Here." Pendleton leaned over and popped the glove compartment. He reached in, found what he was looking for, and handed the gun to Jack.

"No thanks, Mr. Pendleton," Jack said, surprised into accepting the black revolver even as he shook his head, *no*. "Really. I've never fired a gun." The revolver smelled of oil and gleamed as though sweating death. Jack held it with both hands, pointing the barrel at the van's floor.

"Call me Martin," Pendleton said, turning the key in the ignition. The van shuddered to life. "If you have to pull that trigger, it will probably be too late to matter. You might not know how to shoot a gun, but these fellows we are going to see, they won't know that. Don't tell them. Since you are with me, they will assume you are some sort of ex-felon, someone who knows his way around a Smith & Wesson."

"Still—" Jack said.

Martin roared, banging a fist on the dash. "Fuck that, my man! I don't want to hear your reservations or how you're goddam following Gandhi's path. I lost my right-hand man last week—not to mention seven residents. I could use some support. Maybe Jake had some rough edges, never could quite shed the dope-smokin hippie and get all the way upright, but he could tuck it in when it was required."

"I'm just not sure—"

"Course you're not," Martin said. "Why would you be sure about anything, one day out of detox, looking for your ass every time you stand up?"

"I'm just—"

"You got to be *willing to go to any lengths,*" Martin said. He wasn't shouting now. "If you want to be sober, you got to be willing to go the distance."

"I'm—"

"Give me that pistol," Martin said. He sounded defeated, weary. "Hand it over before you hurt yourself."

Jack handed it to Martin who shoved it into his overcoat pocket. "You are letting me down, and I don't even know you. I just feel there's better stuff in you, down deep."

Jack said nothing; he didn't feel like defending himself.

The snow was wet, heavy, and it made the windshield wipers squeak and shudder ominously.

Once past the abandoned movie theater—the marquee still displayed the last, death-knell feature: *Speed 2*—there was nothing but farmland, the whiteness of low hills, telephone poles and the rare lighted patch that marked a four-way stop or a railroad crossing. They passed a bar called Skeeter's, a little to the right of nowhere, its name a looping scrawl of red neon, and Jack noted that the parking lot next to the bar was jammed with cars. Bad weather wasn't deterring these alcoholics either. It was that stubborn streak, that contrariness.

Gates shouted from the back of the van, "How come we drivin through this froze-up Hellwater? We supposed to be doing something in particular, or are we all just flat-out jump-up crazy?"

Martin chose to respond this time. "I have reason to believe that Wesley Parks, your alcoholism counselor, has been kidnapped. I believe I know where he has been taken, and I mean to retrieve him."

"We could take a vote on that," Ed Tilman said. "I wouldn't be surprised if a majority were in favor of some more prudent action. We could report his abduction to the proper authorities in the morning."

"Tomorrow will be too late," Martin said. "I've seen the way it goes down out there. We got to fetch him before they mess up his mind."

"You mean they'll brainwash him?" Tilman asked, sounding interested.

"He'll be a changed man," Martin said.

"Could be he'll be improved," Gates said. "There was room, plenty of elbow room for improving. Could be he wanted to go with them fellows. He was sick of his tired-ass self and wanting a change and said, 'Sign me up' and they said 'Okay.'"

"No," Jack heard himself saying. "It wasn't like that."

"That's right," Martin said. "Jack says that fool, Wesley Parks, thinks he's getting a lift back to Leesburg, and we'll see about that. I'm guessing he's out there being indoctrinated, slick as a frog being gigged—and there's no free will in it at all, and I'm stopping it before it starts. Those sonsofbitches fucked with my dogs, and now they plan to take liberties with my alcoholism counselor. Not this time."

"Will they just let us go in and get him?" It was Kerry's voice, the first she had been heard from in some time, and Jack peered into the darkness of the van. He couldn't make out her features, saw only the cloudy tangle of her hair. She sounded scared.

"Only the Lord knows what they'll do," Martin said.

Eunice spoke up then, perhaps in response to what was said, perhaps not. "Jesus don't want no part of this," she said.

The storm began to ease off. The flakes that fell grew tentative, lost bravado as their ranks thinned. You could see the road under the whiteness. It wasn't freezing; this stuff wouldn't stay long.

That was fine for tomorrow, but Jack wasn't happy with the moment. The van slid down the road like a refrigerator down a ski slope. Martin Pendleton didn't seem to notice that the vehicle he was operating was more or less out of control.

Amid stomach-lurching swoops, Jack saw them tumbling off the road, dead a dozen times as they rolled end over end down the embankment and then belly-flopped into some icy farm pond for another helping of cold-water death.

For a man with an anxious and brooding temperament, an imagination is never an asset.

Jack tried to distract himself.

"That meeting we were just in," Jack said. "Did you find anything unusual about it?"

Martin turned and looked at Jack. "How so?"

"Well, I know every meeting, every AA group, has a slightly different feel."

Martin was nodding. "Yeah?"

"Well. How did that one strike you?"

Martin pursed his lips. "I guess I'm a little set in my ways. I don't hold with change, and you're right, that meeting has changed since I first went there."

"Ah."

"A meeting will change so slowly that you hardly notice it. Touchy-feely therapy stuff can come in and infect a group before you know it. Hard truths will get lost. Old-timers will stop telling newcomers that they are idiots—in some sort of misguided attempt to be gentle. And I don't hold with that inner-child stuff, and reading poems. I reckon they call it pop psychology because it's a balloon of hot air that you could pop with a pin prick."

"I wasn't thinking so much on those lines..."

"Any meeting that you are not used to seems a little strange. Likely you will have to adjust to country ways."

"Well," Jack said, "I was thinking specifically of the curious foreign language that several people spoke. And the mention of deities that don't seem to be Christian-based, and the wall slogans which weren't your traditional—"

"Huh. Didn't notice that. Here we are."

Pendleton had stopped the van with the engine still running. He leaned back and spoke to his passengers. "I thought of having you folks wait here while Jack and I went up to the house, but I had time to think about that on the way out here, and I think it's a show of solidarity that we're wanting. Think of this as your first twelfth-step call, going out and helping a suffering alcoholic."

"Wesley Parks ain't no damn alkyholic!" Gates said.

"The man can't help that," Martin said. "He may not have a clinical excuse for being an asshole, but he's a human being nonetheless, and I would appreciate it if all of you would close your eyes, take a deep breath, and imagine that you are caring individuals."

It had stopped snowing, but the world beyond the warmth of the van didn't seem inviting. No one shouted, *All right, let's go. What are we waiting for? Our beloved alcoholism counselor needs us.* Ed Tilman may, in fact, have been voicing the sentiments of others when he broke the silence, saying, "They wouldn't be pulling shit like this at Betty Ford's. We wouldn't be playing SWAT team in a stinking snowstorm, getting ready to kick down a door and yank some counselor's bacon out of the fire. We'd be sitting on sofas, maybe sharing our feelings, maybe watching an old *Star Trek* episode on TV, laughing and punching each other on the shoulder, bonding. What I mean to say is, we'd be doing things covered by insurance."

Al had thoughts on all this. "I think if we get Wesley Parks out of this, it should count for something with the law," he said. "Like, we should get rehab diplomas immediately, and something in writing saying all charges are dropped—if, you know, you got charges pending—and maybe—"

"Humpf," Martin said. He climbed out, turned and pulled the shotgun from under the seat. Jack sighed and prepared to get out himself. He saw the keys still dangling from the van's ignition switch, and he leaned across the seat, snatched the keys, and stuffed them into his pocket as he backed out.

"Where we supposed to be going?" Gates said. Everyone was standing outside the van, the lot of them looking like ragged extras in a budget disaster movie. Kerry, a blue windbreaker flung over her shoulders, was hunched forward, as though the weight of the cast was finally a force to be reckoned with. Her eyes were colorless; her features painted with fatigue.

Jack went to her. "Are you all right?" he asked.

She looked up. She opened her mouth, and Jack saw her let the impulse to say something cruel die on her tongue. "Sure," she said. "I'm a little shaky, that's all. And I've got a bad feeling about this."

"Me too," Jack said. He moved closer. "Our leader may be crazy, you know. He's wielding a shotgun and preparing to kick down a cult leader's door. He may have never heard of Waco. I think we would be within our rights to mutiny."

Kerry blinked, not comprehending.

Jack took his hand out of his pocket and showed her the keys. "I've got the keys to the van," he said. "I snagged them when I got out. We could let everyone set off on this crusade and we could fall back, get out of here, get to a telephone and get some genuine help…"

"Just leave them here?" Kerry said. She raised an eyebrow.

Well, Jack thought, *I've animated her features. I've brought life back into her eyes.*

It was angry life. She glared at him—and deftly snatched the keys from his hand. "I think Martin's right," she said. "I think we have to get to Wesley right now. We don't have time to run away and call up the cavalry. Martin's right about that. I think he's wrong about you, though."

"Ah?" Jack said.

"I don't think there's a better Jack Lowry underneath. No, I think what you see is what you get."

She turned her back on Jack and walked quickly to where Martin was standing.

Her shoulders were straight again, braced with censure.

Jack caught up with them as they walked up the gravel driveway. He hoped that Kerry would notice he had joined them, but she didn't look back.

The drive was flanked by oaks still retaining most of their leaves. Jack looked up, saw that every ancient tree trunk was yearning toward the lopsided moon. The silvery moon was full of that cold, arbitrary quality that was life's main ingredient and it frightened Jack.

Main ingredient. The main ingredient of life…how had Sara said it? They had been talking about Sara's first love, astronomy, about the vast, empty distances that separated stars, the ample space between electrons, the blooming vacuum in everything. *Building block*. That's how Sara had put it. "The building block of the universe is *nothing*," she had said.

Who could argue with that?

The drive curved slowly to the left and then, impressively, a mansion presented itself. Gothic? Was that the adjective? Jack was no student of architecture. Had Nathaniel Hawthorne encountered this house, there would have been no stopping him. Eves, gables, spires, towers…ten thousand words to take the wind out of a schoolboy's sails and send him fleeing from literature and into the arms of math and computer science and other less boring—and more lucrative—disciplines.

Gothic?

It certainly inspired lurid description as it crouched on the hill, a black, bristling, spiky edifice of wood and stone and concrete. Some dark gray stone was the main ingredient, and mental illness seemed to be the theme.

The mansion was melodramatically grotesque. And… *I've seen this house before*, Jack thought. That was crazy. Where could he have seen it. *Yes, and there was a full moon behind it, and a girl got a bat caught in her hair and her boyfriend said, "Hey, it's only a bat."*

"No," Gates was saying. "I don't think so. I'll wait here. You all take your time, don't hurry on my account."

IRRATIONAL FEARS

And the audience laughed, Jack thought.

"It was built—altered, actually—for a movie," Martin said. "A comedy, one of those horror comedies that thirteen-year-old boys think are funny, people's heads blowing up, zombies catching fire, eyeballs melting, real first-rate laugh fodder for morons. I can't recall the name. Later a millionaire named Ezra Coldwell bought the place. Harken folks have plenty of stories about Ezra; he was a notorious drunk, and always boiling with resentments. He hated everyone by the time he went mad—maybe bile destroyed his brain—and they shipped him down to the nut ward in Staunton. Next thing everyone knew, a lot more buildings were going up on the property and now Harken's the headquarters for The Clear."

"I saw that movie," Jack said. No one paid any attention to this remark.

"I ain't going any closer," Gates said. "My entire curiosity is satisfied right here."

"Suit yourself," Martin said. "Rumor has it there are some pretty mean-tempered guard dogs roaming the grounds, so you'll want to look sharp, standing out here by your lonesome. The rest of us, we are going to go on in and introduce ourselves."

"Hey," Gates said, grudgingly accompanying the others, unhappy with his options. "I know this here shotgun-toting fellow is crazy, but what about the rest of you? We ain't been invited here, you know. Might be they will shoot first and ask questions later."

But they moved on.

Martin held the shotgun at his side, barrel pointing at the welcome mat, and rang the doorbell. Jack could hear the bell echoing within, a dolorous tolling that suggested vast, empty rooms and long, cold hallways.

The mat at Jack's feet was inscribed, red letters on the gray, stubbled surface:

WELCOME
All pilgrims to R'yleh's Portal
Wza-y'ei! Wza-y'ei!

Martin rang the bell again.

"No one home," Gates said. "Guess we'll have to come back some other time."

Martin turned the doorknob (an elaborate brass fixture, two lizards—dragons?—locked in combat). The door swung open.

WILLIAM BROWNING SPENCER

The room was large and dark, illuminated by several ornate wall lamps that created pale islands in the gloom. To their left, a wide, carpeted stairway rose majestically into grainy darkness.

Jack looked at the carpet beneath his feet and staggered, his mind jostled into vertiginous panic by the conviction that the dark patches in the pattern were empty space, the blackness of a pit. The pattern itself had seemed, for a moment, a nest of thick-bodied serpents, green, brown, yellow, that formed an evil, undulating grid.

This was not so, of course. His feet were firmly planted on a carpet whose intricate design was nonrepresentational, no snakes at all.

Jack lifted his eyes from the carpet. To his right, a large sofa, Victorian in aspect and upholstered in some floral pattern, squatted in front of a wall of books, shelf after shelf of leather-bound volumes, their bindings scuffed and discolored by age.

"Hello!" Martin shouted. "Hello!" His voice drifted away, an absentminded ghost.

"Come on," Martin said, moving into the room. Jack followed, reluctantly. The others came too, fear creating a skittish platoon.

"Visitors!" The voice came from overhead. "I thought I heard the bell, but sometimes I hear it when it isn't ringing, and I really didn't think anyone would be dropping by in such inclement weather."

Jack turned and watched the man descending the stairs, one hand lightly on the banister, dramatic, slightly effeminate, an ingenue's entrance. A *young man*, Jack thought, but then revised upward. Middle-aged but boyish, this man was very pale and wore the obligatory white shirt, tie, dress slacks and polished shoes. Apparently, there was no casual dress for members of The Clear.

"I'm Dorian Greenway," he said, smiling. His teeth were white and even. "And you…" He held up a hand, pale palm outward. "No, don't tell me. I much prefer to guess. The shotgun and the lateness of the hour would suggest that you are the village mob come to slay Frankenstein's monster. But, if that's the case, where are your torches? I really must insist that you bring torches if you wish to present yourselves as a proper mob."

"We didn't have time for the torches," Martin said. "One of our members got himself kidnapped, and we came directly."

Dorian Greenway opened his mouth, widened his eyes, and sat down on a carpeted step in a parody of shock. "Well. I do know you. You are Martin Pendleton, the man at the helm of an alcoholism treatment center called New Way—although, let's be honest here, there's nothing particularly new about your methods out at New Way. Distressingly archaic, I'm afraid."

"We've come for Wesley Parks."

Dorian nodded. "Yes, he's here." Dorian turned to regard Jack. "If people want to come here, we welcome them. We had a friend of yours recently, I think. You were sitting on the steps together." Jack was sweating under the man's scrutiny. "What was that young man's name? Pickle? Winkle? A very excitable person, I remember that. Very impressionable. He had some conversations with my uncle about demons and such—not actual conversations, of course; poor Ezra hasn't spoken a word in years. Anyway, I think your friend took my uncle too literally. That happens. Then we have incidents." Dorian sighed. "And who do you think gets blamed? We are scapegoats, every time. Take your friend, Wesley Parks. Frankly, I can't see why you've bothered coming out here in this frightful weather for Mr. Parks. He's not one of us, you know." Dorian Greenway leaned forward, hands rubbing his knees, and whispered, "He's not an alcoholic."

"Yes. I know."

Dorian shrugged, standing up. "I don't think civilians should be involved." He reached into his pocket, casually pulled out a black shiny object and raised it to his lips. It was, Jack saw, an inhaler, like the epinephrine inhalers used by asthma sufferers.

Dorian squeezed the black inhaler, filling his lungs. His dark eyes widened. He put the inhaler back in his pocket. He ran his hands through his short-cropped, dark hair.

"Only those who have been damned in the great Rift, only those with the K'n Yan-imprint, acquired genetically or by astral accident, will have the self-interest required to be soldiers in the Unraveling. So…" He smiled. "I've taken the liberty of enlightening Wesley Parks. If he is going to play the game, he should understand the consequences."

Martin Pendleton raised his shotgun. "I'm not following you. And, like they say, that's okay. Guess I was never much of a follower. If you could fetch Parks, we'll be on our way."

Dorian Greenway's manner changed. He stood up, a hand to his brow. He was visibly shaking, and when he spoke, his voice trembled. "I hope you are not threatening me," he said. "Because this is not about me or you. It is much, much bigger than that. We are at the center of it, here in Harken. We are a tiny anomaly, just a loose thread in the fabric. But that's changing; pluck at this thread and soon, soon it will unravel. An ancient conflict will be resolved, for good or ill."

Jack saw movement in the corner of his eye and turning, saw that men—and women, the first he had seen of The Clear's female contingent—had entered and stood against the walls in silence. The women wore black dresses that came to their ankles. The men were dressed like their leader. Their arms were at their sides, hands linked, men and women creating a placid, bovine chain.

The effect was unsettling and Jack was fervently wishing he were elsewhere, wishing he hadn't let Kerry snatch the van's keys, hadn't let her shame him into accompanying Martin and the others.

"We come into the world not evil, but hollow," Dorian said. "This hollowness is what calls us to the other side. It is the thing we call love that binds us, the curse and the blessing of attraction."

"This is fascinating," Martin said, "but the hour's late. You'll have to fill me in on Armageddon later. I know you fellows always have some end-of-the-world story, and I'd love to hear it before you drink your poisoned Kool-Aid. But right now—"

"The Elders wept!" Dorian said, suddenly standing up, walking directly toward Martin.

"Easy," Martin said, but Dorian walked past him and stood in front of Kerry.

Dorian dropped to his knees with a gasp, reached up and caught her hand. He stared at her face, enthralled. "It's you," he said. "Here I have been thinking to myself lately, *Dorian, you say your prayers and nothing comes of it*. Such a meager portion of faith have I had." He shook his head. "You are…you are the *image* of her. This means…it means we can alter this tired cycle, we can…" He leaned forward—and licked the palm of her hand.

"Hey," Kerry said, pulling her hand away, frowning.

Dorian stood. "Ah," he said. Jack saw that the man was sweating visibly, his forehead beaded with glistening droplets, an amphetamine madness hissing in his eyes. Whatever that inhaler contained, it was doing its work. "How could you stand in this room and I not know it? We will forge a new cycle."

"Back off," Martin said, nudging Dorian with the shotgun.

Oh Jesus, Jack thought. *Don't poke this madman with a shotgun. Please don't do that.*

But Dorian blinked, turned, and smiled at Martin. "Certainly," he said. "I'm out of line. I can't expect this glorious girl to understand her destiny. What has been instantly revealed to me, must come to her in the fullness of time." Dorian turned to Kerry. "What is your name, my little miracle?"

"Forget it," Kerry said. "You're not my type."

"Tell me your name and I won't have your friends hurt. I'll let them, and you, and your esteemed counselor, Wesley Parks, leave."

He spoke quietly, no menace in his tone.

Martin Pendleton pointed the shotgun at Dorian Greenway's head. "She doesn't care to talk to you," Martin said.

The tribe of The Clear opened their mouths and emitted a rattling hiss.

"Kerry Beckett. My name's Kerry Beckett."

Dorian nodded. His followers fell silent again. "And a beautiful name it is." Dorian tilted his head back and shouted. "Bring Wesley Parks down, will you, Mark?"

Parks sat next to Jack in the van.

"Are you okay?" Jack asked.

Wesley Parks smiled, a rictus, a grimace that was not reassuring. He nodded his head violently. "Fine. Never been better. Ready to listen. Receptive. Might have been narrow-minded, once, but that's the past, ancient history. Ha ha." Wesley Parks shouted then. "I'm listening!"

"What did they do to you?"

Wesley was shaking badly now, his eyes wide. "Oh, nothing. I swear, nothing." Wesley clutched Jack's arm. "I'm a little nervous, okay. That's all. Because I know, you see. I know that any of us can just lean back, just blink, and slip away. This reality sheath is flimsy. You can fall right through. And then you're there. Too bad, but there you are. That's what they showed me. And that's enough, you know, to make anyone a little nervous. They gave me something though, gave me something for my nerves. I'm going to be right as American rain, you watch."

"That's good," Jack said. Jack was thinking of Hinkle again. *Those Sunday boys sent me right to Hell,* he'd said—one of the last things he'd said before being devoured by a toilet.

"For my nerves," Wesley said, opening up his fist, fingers coming unstuck with a rusted, jerky motion.

Jack blinked at something gleaming yellow in the man's palm.

"What's that?" Jack asked, leaning closer.

Wesley snapped his fingers closed. "Mine!"

"Okay. Sure. What is it?"

Wesley Parks was grinning maniacally now. "Heh heh." He opened his hand again, slowly, reverently. "Gummy bear," he said, the way a mother, leaning over her newborn infant, might whisper an endearment.

"Ah," Jack said. The little piece of rubbery candy, accepted on faith by children throughout America to be shaped like a bear, lay on Wesley's palm, a misshapen jewel. "That's a gummy bear, all right," Jack said.

Wesley snapped his hand closed again. "That's enough. Don't be trying to swallow it with your eyes."

Wesley turned away, peering out the van window at the night.

Jack sighed. The day had been unduly long.

Jack looked behind him and saw Kerry in the back of the van, bent low. He thought, at first, that she was crying, sobbing profoundly. That would explain the animation of her shoulders and head. Peering into the darkness, he saw that this was not the case. She had produced a tissue and was furiously rubbing the palm of her hand, frowning fiercely.

Jack felt a sharp pain, a multicolored hurt darkened by the sure knowledge that he was not the one to comfort her.

The van careened toward New Way and the prospect of weeks of alcoholism treatment. Martin Pendleton's driving had not improved since earlier in the evening, and there was still the chance that they would all die in some catastrophic vehicular event.

Jack realized that his mood had degenerated; such a death now seemed hopeful and optimistic.

ope returns, *like a dog to its vomit,* Jack thought. He'd been in New Way a week when the darkness seemed to lift a little.

He'd spoken of Sara in group, not intending to, and then guilt had possessed him like some malign and brutal demon and he'd found himself sobbing, helpless, stupid with grief, and he had fled the room and Kerry had followed him.

"I'm sorry," she said, shouting through the door, and he let her in and told her about Sara and heard himself apologizing, stupidly, saying, "We weren't lovers, we were just friends, just starting to be friends, really…" as though his hurt, the destruction of his world, was unwarranted. As though he had no claim to such grief, that was for Sara's grieving parents, her sullen, inconsolable sister.

It was hard to say what finally brought the outburst on. Eunice had talked interminably about the wrongs her children had done her and about conversations she had had with Jesus in her dreams. It was bad enough, Jack felt, to have to listen to a lengthy, unedited narration of Eunice's conscious day; it was far worse, a much greater imposition, to have to endure long monologues describing what went on when she was asleep. Eunice not only described her plotless dreams, she analyzed them in depth.

Neither Ed Tilman nor Gates had had much to say, although Tilman expressed concerns with security at New Way. "They could come in through the woods. The back door wasn't even locked last night. They could cut our throats while we were sleeping."

"Who this 'they?'" Gates asked—a good question, Jack thought, not sure whether Tilman was referring to The Clear or some covert government group. Tilman just shook his head sadly, and rolled his eyes toward the ceiling.

Al talked about what an old fart his father was, always down on anyone with ideals, like traveling around the country on a motorcycle or getting a tattoo that promotes world peace.

Al was in love with a rock singer named Lisa Perks who sang in Georgetown clubs with a band called *Potamus*. He loved her and went to all her gigs and drank beer and sniffed glue mainly because he was heartbroken and trying to forget her. He had written her a love letter once, slipped it to her by way of a waiter one night, and she had gone up on stage and said, "This next song is for the creep at the back table who can't spell," and she'd sung a love-dissing song called "Get a Grip." After that, humiliated, he'd had to go to her performances in disguise, a false beard that—in combination with sunglasses—gave him a ZZ Top look, which was pretty cool and he thought maybe she'd fall in love with his new style and much later, after they were lovers, he'd have to reveal that he was the guy she'd made fun of once. That sort of thing happened.

He'd had his disguise on the last time he'd been stopped for drunk driving, and he remembered the cop peeling the false beard off him and studying it with distaste, as though it were a dead rat or a rotting flounder.

Kerry had received a letter from her mother. She read part of it to the group. Her mother was dating a man named Reno who was always in trouble with the law. "'Don't get involved with someone who always ducks down in the car when a police cruiser goes by or who has a half dozen names depending on who he's with or who goes for a gun when the doorbell rings,'" Kerry read.

"That's typical loser advice," Kerry said. "People like my mom and her friends got lots of advice for bad situations, like what to do for a black eye or where to cash a rubber check so it will take the longest time getting back to the bank."

Kerry would sit in group rubbing the palm of her hand, her pale forearm resting on her blue-jeaned thigh, as fragile-seeming as blown glass. Martin had driven her into town to have the cast removed. At night, and sometimes during the day, she wore a lightweight plastic splint, but in group her arm was bare, vulnerable. The constant scratching and massaging of the hand that Dorian Greenway's tongue had accosted was habitual now. It worried Jack and was certainly something that Wesley should have addressed.

But to say that their alcoholism counselor wasn't entirely attuned to his clients' needs was an understatement.

Sometimes Martin Pendleton would sit in group too, but he obviously had little patience with therapy and would rarely last more than five or ten minutes. Therapy was Wesley Parks's job, and Martin wasn't much interested. As far as New Way's director was concerned, AA was the treatment for alcoholism, and therapy was just a sop to the mental health professionals.

Martin wasn't in group enough to notice that Wesley wasn't entirely lucid. Jack had plenty of time to observe Wesley Parks, and it was Jack's conclusion that the man was losing his mind.

A new, obsequious note had entered Wesley's voice and demeanor. He would nod his head rapidly when a member was speaking. "Yes, yes," he would say. "Absolutely, right you are." He would lean forward, a shameless earnestness in his shoulders, a sycophant prepared to laugh at the boss's joke.

He had been a confrontational counselor, but that was gone now. Now he was filled with phony heartiness. "It's not that bad," he would say. "We are going to be just fine." It was this "we" that troubled Jack. Wesley Parks had always been remote and, well, disdainful. Now he was frightened and invoking the protection of community. "I'm just one of the guys," he seemed to be saying, with the nervous laugh an aristocrat might muster when the revolutionaries broke down his door.

He would sometimes stand up abruptly, as though a noise had startled him, and leave the room. On returning, he would apologize, saying, "Got a bladder that won't take no for an answer." He would utter a feeble laugh, wiping the beads of perspiration from his forehead with a tissue.

His comments did not always seem to the point. Why, for instance, did he interrupt Eunice's extended oration on her oldest daughter's sloth to say, "Even a blind pig will find an acorn sometimes"?

Skewed platitudes punctuated Wesley's speech now, as though the door to some brain closet of dusty, mutated slogans had sprung open, spilling its contents onto the man's tongue. "Even a dog can look at an exotic dancer," he would say, or, "If you can't stand the heat, get out of the jacuzzi." If he was aware that these were not the original, pristine aphorisms, nothing in his delivery showed it. It was not, in fact, clear to what extent Wesley was participating in group. His eyes often looked as though they were focused on the Dali-esque webs of invisible spiders.

Jack had become accustomed to Wesley's new, Zen-like group leadership, and he found it less irritating, for the most part, than the man's earlier, confrontational mode.

WILLIAM BROWNING SPENCER

Now Wesley would let people talk, which is what they needed to do.

Kerry had been talking about her baby brother, who had died in infancy. She described the thrill of holding him. She had been nine years old, and she remembered holding him in the dappled sunlight, sitting in the porch swing, his warmth and perfect heft a proof that God existed and was good. She had loved God then, before she learned that the God of losers was cruel and arbitrary.

"I miss him," she said, falling silent.

"I miss Sara," Jack had said, and then, appalled, embarrassed by this echo of shared loss, he had added, awkwardly, "A friend. She was murdered…" And his voice had fallen away, shocked by this absolute, this unspeakable thing, given voice.

He surprised himself with tears and fled. Kerry followed.

He'd met her in the backyard of Dean Hirshorn's house on a cool September night, some obligatory faculty gathering. It was the beginning of his third year at George Washington, and he was drinking his first gin and tonic of the day, and the alcohol had just struck a match in his stomach when she came into view, a small woman in a blue dress, her feet bare, her eyes large, brown, and alert in the manner of nocturnal creatures enlivened by the dark.

She smiled when she saw him, a wide, generous smile, and he said, pointing at the sky, "There's Mars."

"Actually, that's Aldebaran," she said. "It's an orange giant, the main star in the constellation Taurus."

"Ah," he said.

"Well, 'There is no sin but ignorance,' as Shakespeare says."

"Actually, that's Marlowe," he said.

She giggled. "We need to find some common ground, something we both know nothing about."

Later, when he knew Sara Janson better, he would discover that she was informed about most things, and that finding a good-sized vacant lot in the land of her learning would have taken some doing. She was a grad student, returning to school in her mid-thirties. Her major was astronomy, but she seemed to be studying just about everything else too.

She had known, for instance, that Shakespeare was not the author of Marlowe's line—and she had confessed as much three months later.

"Correcting a woman picks a man up," she had said. "You looked like you needed a lift. The male ego is a hothouse flower, you know."

Sara Janson was an expert on the male ego and had married one of its more florid examples, Dr. Winslow Janson, chairman of the mathematics department.

IRRATIONAL FEARS

Jack was already acquainted with Dr. Janson from various faculty functions and meetings. Winslow Janson was a big man, the physique of a ex-high school football player now settled in a less active life and beginning to go to seed, bit of a paunch, a ruddy beer-fed face. He looked more like the owner of a successful car dealership than a mathematician. But, by all accounts, he was brilliant.

It was also generally conceded (by colleagues and students alike) that he was an asshole: arrogant, loud, vain, combative, petty, self-satisfied, rude.

When Jack had known Sara long enough to ask, he asked her why she had married the man. "I fell in love with his mind," she said.

Back then, intellect had seemed everything, the power and the glory, the sun at noon in the Sahara. Those annoying personal traits, the container for intelligence, were to be endured with good humor.

Jack had been reading student papers in his office two months after his first meeting with Sara, when he looked up and saw Winslow Janson standing in his doorway.

The math professor beamed. "May I come in?" he asked.

"Of course."

Dr. Janson pulled up a chair and sat down, leaning forward, elbows on the desk. He was wearing a blue sports coat and a white shirt, open at the collar, no tie.

"What is the state of American literature, Dr. Lowry? Is it relevant? Is it just whacking off? I have never cared for fiction, its vagueness, its symbols that cannot settle. It is grown-ups lying when they know better."

"What can I do for you, Dr. Janson?"

"To the point," he said, nodding, smiling. "Fine. All right." He paused, picked a pen from the desk and tapped it against the desktop. "I wish to know if you are sleeping with my wife."

"No."

Janson nodded, grinning. "That is also what my wife tells me. Fine." He sat there, tapping the pen on the desk, blinking. Slowly, he put the pen down and stood up. "I believe you, Dr. Lowry. I believe that you are not taking my wife's clothes off and fucking her in some motel, fucking her the doggie style, the missionary, perhaps the funky chicken. But you *want* to do this. You are hoping, with time, it will come to pass."

"I don't—"

Janson shouted, slamming a fist on the desk and making the coffee cup jump in its saucer, coffee splashing onto a student's Faulkner essay.

WILLIAM BROWNING SPENCER

"You don't find my wife attractive? You are going to tell me you don't find my wife attractive?"

"Your wife and I—"

"No. I don't wish to hear your explanations for your daily lunches with my wife, your laughing and leaning close to each other, brazenly, in the cafeteria. You will tell me that you do not wish to see her dress rising over her head, her brassiere (black lace) unhooked (in front), her breasts shimmering like fruit."

Jack stared at the madman who had stopped talking, his mouth still working, his tongue red and swollen. Janson stood back from the desk, took a deep breath and recovered himself, let his arms fall to his sides. "No more lunches," he said, his voice flat, dust. He waved his hand without lifting it, a gesture of dismissal aimed at some invisible dog. Then he turned and left.

When Jack told all this to Kerry, her role was that of high priest to his confession, and so he sought absolution, speaking the arguments that, over the years, he often repeated in his mind.

"Sara said she would not be deprived of my company because of her husband's jealousy. She was not, no matter how much he might wish it otherwise, chattel."

Kerry nodded. "Sure."

"But I knew…" Jack said, switching to self-condemnation, "I should have known he was crazy, dangerous."

"Hey, knowing a dude is bad don't mean you should bend over and let him kick your ass," Kerry said. "Sara was right."

Sara and Jack had made a concession to her husband's jealousy. They had stopped eating lunch together in the cafeteria. Instead, they had begun meeting in off-campus restaurants. Her husband believed that eating anything other than a piece of fruit in the middle of the day was a custom responsible for many health problems, and so he was always in his office at noon, either alone or in the company of a student he was reprimanding for feeblemindedness.

Jack had, of course, fallen in love with Sara. He did imagine her dress rising over her head; he did envision her falling into him as the world was transformed by desire. He said nothing of this. He suspected that Sara might love him too, but they both understood that the clandestine nature of their meetings required a balancing decorum. They could meet secretly because they were not adulterers. A convoluted thought, perhaps, but one they both understood perfectly.

And then, in the sixth month of their relationship, Jack had said, "You should leave him."

Sara had shaken her head. "No, Jack. I can't."

"Why not?"

"I don't want to talk about it, okay."

"Okay." But it hadn't been okay, nothing like okay.

The red numbers of the clock read 2:14 when Jack answered the phone that morning. At first, he could not understand the voice on the other end, thought perhaps some drunk had dialed a wrong number and was now sobbing incoherently into the phone.

The sobs took form, shaped words: "No more lunches. I told you. *So!* Never now. No doggie lunches, no missionary, no funky—" The phone clattered; a dial tone returned.

Jack recognized the voice. He dialed her number, sick with dread. *Dear God...*

"Hello."

"Sara, my God, are you—"

"You have reached the Janson residence. We are unable to come to the phone right now but..."

Jack dressed and hurried to his car.

There were three police cars, two at the curb, one in the driveway. A news van had already arrived.

And this was the news: Renowned mathematician, Dr. Winslow Janson, had, for reasons unknown, killed his wife and then taken his own life, the instrument of death in both cases being a handgun (later determined to have been purchased three months earlier by Dr. Janson). No note was found at the scene, no explanation, et cetera. The usual media frustration was aired—as though life marched to certainties, was even faintly interested in the logic of appearances.

Sara could have told them. *The building block of the universe is nothing.*

Kerry said she was sorry and that she hadn't known. She had hugged him, kissed him on the cheek, and stood up. "It's not your fault," she had said. "You didn't do anything but love her, and even that's not your fault. I think love is God's meanest joke." And she'd turned and run out of the room, leaving Jack sitting on the bed.

WILLIAM BROWNING SPENCER

After the unseasonable snowstorm, the weather had staged a retreat, hustling back to balmier days. The sun lit up the air.

Martin Pendleton drove with the windows down, his hair flying.

"This is the thing," he said. "If you want to get sober and stay sober, you got to accept that you'll have the occasional bad day. You got to hunker down and let it roll over you. Alcoholics can't stand a bad patch, and they are always looking to fix it immediately, but that don't work."

They were heading into Harken on a grocery run. Jack sat in the passenger seat. New Way's director had, for reasons mysterious to Jack, taken an interest in Jack's recovery, and so Jack was enlisted for store trips during which Martin would impart the acquired wisdom and experience of seventeen years without a drink. "New people are always saying AA don't show them anything. They say it's boring. Hell. Sure it's boring. Where they been? There's a ton of dross in your average day, and if there's one trick you want to learn for survival, it's how to weather the flat times. AA is where you learn that. This whole group therapy thing, this getting at your feelings, I'm not saying it's pointless, I'm just saying that all the drama and insight isn't gonna cut it for the long haul. Learning to hunker down, that's the ticket."

IRRATIONAL FEARS

"Speaking of therapy," Jack said. "I'm worried about Wesley Parks. I don't know if you've noticed, but he seems confused, maybe on the edge of a breakdown."

Aaron, the red-haired cook, shouted assent from the back of the van where he was sitting with Gretchen. Jack was the only patient in the van, and he felt oddly privileged.

"Yes," Aaron shouted. "You are on to something there, Jacky L. That man is like a cat that's been tossed into a dryer and spun round for the full wash-and-wear. He's been saying some nonlinear stuff. Like yesterday morning, he was sitting there studying his omelet for ten minutes, and finally I nudged him, asked if he was all right, and he said, 'Intact. All engines primed and ready for reentry,' and then he got this very intense look and asked me what my tribe was. I didn't think I heard him right, so I got him to repeat it. *Tribe* was the word. 'Got me,' I finally said, and he smiled real sneaky and put a finger to his lips and winked like we had an understanding which—I assure you—we don't."

"Well, I didn't want to say anything," Gretchen said. "Who am I to say anything? I'm a secretary, not a therapist. I don't know from Adam about mental health. But I have to say that I've been having quite a time typing up Mr. Parks's client reports. I mean, he fills the page with drawings—little lightning bolts, stick figures, cartoony things—and the words are all bunched up or moving around the page like ants on a kitchen counter. I said to him, 'Mr. Parks, I can't make sense of this,' and he said, 'That's because it's just the surface,' and I asked him what that meant, and he said, 'Surface. That's just the surface, there,' and I said 'What?' and he kept bobbing his head like a jack-in-the-box that's just popped, and he said, kind of condescending, 'Surface, Miss Payne. Like water. A water's surface is where it stops being water, or starts becoming water—depending on how you look at it, of course.' Then he finished off saying, 'A stitch in time is another man's ceiling.' It wasn't any of it helpful, and I've still got to type up a rat's nest of crazy writing and cartoons. And I'm working forty hours a week and being called part-time with no benefits."

Gretchen's voice rose on this last outrage. Her eyes sparkled behind her glasses, and Aaron reached over and patted her shoulder. "I know, I know. It's a sin. The County is nothing but scoundrels. But one has to look on the bright side. You are doing good work, helping sick people."

"Sick people depress me," Gretchen muttered.

Aaron sighed. "That's true. They do have a way of slouching around that makes me want to prod them with a fork. A lot of them go after suffering like there's an Academy Award in it. You take that Eunice woman—who,

WILLIAM BROWNING SPENCER

by the way, has no business wearing pink—that woman has got gloom down to an art. If she is really having all those conversations with Jesus, all I can say is Our Lord is probably about fed up. *I'm gonna slap this broad* is, I expect, the thought foremost in His mind. There's only so much anyone can take."

"Soda stop," Martin said, pulling the van off the road and into the Glad Whiz convenience store. Martin drank a Diet Coke every fifteen or twenty minutes. At the Glad Whiz he was able to obtain this beverage in a plastic container that required two hands to hold.

The skinny clerk behind the counter was drunk. He was in that condition of inebriation where standing up is a major undertaking, requiring frequent, spastic acts of adjustment. He was smoking a cigarette, and had achieved an impressive length of ash on the butt that dangled from his mouth. He was wearing what Jack at first took to be a bandanna, but which was, on closer observation, revealed to be the Glad Whiz clerk's regulation paper hat, a jaunty red-striped boat that the clerk, dissatisfied, perhaps, with the regimentation of his attire, had torn open and poked his head through.

"No change," the clerk said when Martin handed him the five.

"Huh?" Martin said.

"Fucking little pennies, dimes, nickel shit," the clerk said, glaring at the cash register and reeling. "Fuck em." He shook the cash register, his thin shoulders twisting as though they might snap. "Fucking change!" He turned and handed the five back to Martin with a haughty air. "Get your fucking change at the laundromat," he said.

"Look—" Martin said.

The clerk held up a hand. "That's it. Finished. End of argument." He lifted a beer from behind the counter, raised it to his lips, and drank deeply, his adam's apple dancing.

Martin shook his head and said, "Come on."

At the gas station, the service station attendant was taking a leak against the side of the building when they pulled up. Other than that, he was well-behaved, filling the tank without incident. He did stink of bourbon, and he did proposition Gretchen, but in a shy, gawky manner that wasn't offensive.

"I'm a secretary at a treatment facility," Gretchen said, rather primly. "I'm not allowed to date alcoholics."

The grocery store was filled with inebriated people. Two teenagers were smoking dope and giggling in one of the aisles. A fat man had knocked over a bin of cantaloupes and was wringing his hands and shouting, "Lopes!" (a warning to others?) as the softball-sized fruits rolled at his feet.

IRRATIONAL FEARS

Martin was unmoved by any of this, pushing the cart briskly down aisles and consulting with Aaron on purchases.

The checkout clerk, an elderly woman with gray hair and tiny, silver-framed glasses, worked with a cigarette lodged in the corner of her mouth, pausing occasionally to sip from a wine glass. She rang them up, gave them change, and methodically bagged their groceries. All the while, her lips moved. Leaning forward, Jack was able to hear a whispered litany of obscenities (*mutherfucking shitcrappers limp-dicked asshole cocksuckers*).

Jack and everyone else helped tote the groceries out to the van. In the parking lot, two old men were fighting, a staggering brawl. They were throwing wild punches, falling down, cursing each other ineffectually. A small scruffy dog was barking at them from the sidelines where an old woman guzzled a bottle of wine.

On the drive back to New Way they passed a billboard advertising deodorant (a fat man in his underwear surrounded by babes in lingerie) and a police siren sliced the country calm.

Martin immediately hit the accelerator. "Shit," he blurted.

"Shouldn't we slow down?"

Martin shot Jack a look. "You're right. It's a reflex, still. Some habits are hard to shake." Martin craned his neck, studied the rearview mirror.

Jack leaned out the window and looked back. The cop car had gone off the road, taking out a section of fence. One of the cops had vacated the car and was reeling around in the open field. As Jack watched, the man fell to his knees, yanked the gun from his holster, and fired twice at a cluster of cows, startling them into fleeing over a brown hillside.

"Well," Martin said, speeding up again. "It just goes to show that sometimes the old reflexes are the best. A lot of times, a reflexive action is the wisdom of the years asserting itself."

He said nothing more, studying the road, pleased, no doubt, with the wisdom of this summation.

Jack was silent too, nonplused. Finally, he said, "You'll notice that we didn't encounter a single person in Harken who wasn't drunk. Don't you find that remarkable?"

Martin pursed his lips. "Well, this is a powerful disease."

"Powerful? What? Look. Every time we go into town, everyone we meet is drunk—except at the AA meetings, of course. Don't you find that unusual?"

"Well, it just goes to show. You can't underestimate the importance of regular AA attendance."

WILLIAM BROWNING SPENCER

Jack turned to Gretchen and Aaron in the back. "Doesn't anyone find this crazy?" he asked.

"I think it's crazy," Aaron said.

"Me too," Gretchen said.

"Thank you," Jack said, turning to face forward again. But he wasn't satisfied. He couldn't help feeling he was being humored, like a feminist at a stock car rally or a science-fiction writer attending a literary salon.

At lunch that day, Jack watched, fascinated, while Wesley Parks talked to his jello.

A low, savvy chuckle had caused Jack to glance in Wesley's direction. The alcoholism counselor was sitting by himself at the head of a long table, grinning savagely at his plate.

A squat translucent cylinder of green jello sat alone on Wesley's plate. Wesley held the plate in trembling hands that caused the jello to shiver.

While Jack watched, Wesley leaned forward and said, "No way. No waaaaaaaaaay."

Jack had the distinct impression that Wesley was unaware that it was his own hands that were animating the jello, in the same way Ouija board players are unaware that their subconscious, and not some interested astral party, draws a plastic pointer across a lettered board.

"You think you are soooooo smart," Wesley told the jello.

As far as Jack could see, the dessert had given no indication that it was unduly proud of its intellect, but Jack suspected there was more to the relationship than met the eye.

With one deft flick of his wrists, Wesley sent the plate into the air. It hit the floor, shattering. All heads turned as the green jello landed intact but splayed, flattened on the linoleum floor.

Wesley looked up furtively and met Jack's eyes. Wesley smiled. "Whoops," he said.

After lunch, they all went to the rec room where Martin Pendleton passed out the mail. Jack's mail consisted of a postcard from his mother. Ellen—she had always insisted that he call her by her given name and not Mother, which made her feel old and sadly pigeonholed—never wrote letters. A high-powered businesswoman, she traveled extensively and preferred communicating with her son in succinct paragraphs written imperiously on the backs of cards that featured a photo of some luxury hotel's lobby.

She had written from Seattle: *Dear Jack—A wasted trip. The contract is ludicrous, nothing to negotiate. What were they thinking? I'm off to Chicago, writing from the airport. So pleased you are addressing your alcoholism. Your father—may he rest in peace—left you that legacy, all those Irish drunkards. Sorry you got the gene, but I know you'll do what has to be done and be back in top form in no time. Love, Ellen*

As usual, his mother's no-nonsense encouragement felt like an anvil on his chest.

"Kerry Beckett!" Martin called out, waving a large manila envelope in the air.

Kerry retrieved the envelope and walked into the hall studying it, a puzzled expression on her face.

Group was scheduled for two in the afternoon. Jack went back to his room and lay on his bed. He had time for a nap, but he decided to work on his Fourth Step, part of the Alcoholics Anonymous program designed to get one back in sync with the world. The Fourth Step was a personal inventory in which one reflected, in writing, on people and institutions one resented. Invariably a resentment grew from some perceived threat, real or imagined. The book *Alcoholics Anonymous* urged its readers to consider their own part in the resentment, to rigorously examine where they were at fault.

The Fourth Step was executed by creating four columns consisting of: 1. Who one resented, 2. The cause of that resentment, 3. What was threatened, and 4. One's own culpability in the matter.

Jack drew the columns. For his first resentment, he wrote, *God*. Why resent God? Because God was a crazy hotheaded bully so puffed up with pride that he was ready, if not taken seriously, to fly off the handle and smite all the firstborn. Yes. God who put Job through hell for…well…on a bet. Yes. And when Job asked what was going on, God, unwilling to admit that He had been goaded into torturing Job, took refuge in the cheapest sort of evasiveness. "How can you understand me?" God asked. "I created the giraffe and the behemoth." Covered with boils, Job must have found this a lame excuse.

It was easy to fill out the first three columns but what, Jack wondered, was his own part in all of this?

Believing! That was it. Perhaps not believing in God, but believing in civilization, in the possibility that goodness and decency might prevail. Yes. Jack had forgotten about the universe's prime ingredient.

WILLIAM BROWNING SPENCER

Jack had been told that the Fourth Step, in conjunction with the Fifth Step, would be a freeing experience. So far, it was not producing that effect.

He tore the piece of paper from the legal pad, wadded it up, and tossed it in the wastebasket.

Tomorrow is another day, he thought. Tomorrow and tomorrow and tomorrow…

In group, he shared his Fourth Step difficulties.

"Faith can move mountains," Eunice said.

"I don't know," Jack said. "I read that Billy Graham just took a leap of faith, swallowed it all without question, and I know he is considered one very devout guy, but that looks a hell of a lot like this denial thing we keep talking about. I mean, if you are drinking yourself to death and you believe you are in great shape, that's called denial. It's not called faith, right? A person can believe any number of things that are contrary to logic. If you believe that little green men in the radio control your bowel movements, that's not faith, that's insanity."

"Get thee behind me, Satan," Eunice hissed.

"Hey, hey," Wesley said. "Group's not in session yet. We are missing one of our members."

Kerry had yet to show up. Jack looked at his watch. It was ten after two.

"All right, troops, let's go get her," Wesley said, slapping his thighs and standing up.

Whenever someone was late, the rest of group would fetch that person, the intention being to demonstrate group solidarity—or, perhaps, to lay a guilt trip on the tardy one (*we've all of us had to hike down here thanks to your inconsiderate ass-dragging ways*).

Kerry did not open her door when Wesley knocked. "Hello," Wesley said, pushing the door open. "Someone's forgotten all about her reeeeeeesponsibilities."

Kerry sat at the small writing desk, her back to the door. To her left was a small curtained window, an African violet on the sill. A framed needlepoint of the Serenity Prayer was on the wall, and a wall shelf contained a dozen books, including the ubiquitous Big Book, the Twelve and Twelve, and the popular *Alcoholism for Dummies*.

She did not turn when Wesley called, and Jack, peering past the counselor, felt an immediate sense of foreboding.

"Kerry," Jack said, pushing past Wesley.

IRRATIONAL FEARS

She sat back in her chair, arms thrust forward, her hands flat on the table. The manila folder was torn open, its contents, an eight-by-ten glossy black-and-white photo, revealed.

Kerry was staring at the photo, and seemed, in her stiff-armed, thrust-back attitude, to be attempting to shove it away.

Her left hand was slapped flat on the glossy surface, palm down, and Jack could see the eyes of the portrait staring between her fingers, eyes that, even in a photograph, seemed to glow with sharp, fanatic light.

Kerry was staring at Dorian Greenway's portrait with terrible intent, her mouth partially open, a small, pinched vee of skin between her perfect eyebrows. Her eyes were eerily empty, someone awakened suddenly from a bad dream, her mind still in thrall to nightmare images.

Jack bent over her, smelled the pungent odor of urine, blinked at her feet and the wet yellow pool.

Jack touched her shoulder. He reached for her hand.

"Nothing sudden," someone said, and he turned and saw Ed Tilman beside him.

"Talk to her first, get some response. Don't jolt her."

"Kerry," Jack said. "It's me."

"Move into her line of vision," Tilman said. "Look in her eyes."

Jack did as he was told, no time to marvel at Ed Tilman's new authority.

"Kerry," he said, moving closer, ducking his head under her arms, coming between Kerry and the mesmerizing photo.

Bubbles of spit flecked her lips. Her left cheek was wet.

He moved to touch her cheek and something leapt in her eyes, lightning on a clear day, and she uttered a sharp hissing noise, started to stand up, stumbled.

Ed Tilman caught her. "Got you, girl," he said.

She collapsed in his arms with a convulsive shiver; he staggered back. "Give me some help here," he said.

They got her to the bed. Already she was coming around, moaning.

She sat up and glared at them. "Where is he?" she said.

"Kerry, are you all right?" Jack said.

"Where is he?" she shouted. Her eyes flew past the room's occupants, disinterested, impatient—none of these was the one she sought.

She flopped back on the bed, flung a hand across her eyes, an attitude of defeat. "Of course. Not here."

Then, without warning, she rolled off the bed, hit the floor running, and dashed through the door, already racing down the hall, moving fast, her Nikes earning their keep. Martin Pendleton was just coming through the swinging doors at the end of the hall, and he grabbed for her, got an arm around her waist, hollered, "Whoa."

She threw herself into the air, feet kicking. Her foot found the wall and she shoved, sending Martin back against the opposite wall, knocking the wind out of him. He fell, his thrashing bundle rolling away from him.

She was free, moving like something thrown, a wind through the lobby and through the front door.

Jack was in pursuit, leaping over Martin's legs.

"Don't worry," Martin shouted, "there's nowhere for her to go."

Even as Martin said it, Jack heard the sound of the engine wheeze into life.

In his mind, he again saw Kerry, eyes flashing with righteous anger, snatch the van keys from his hand on the night of the snowstorm.

And Jack knew that she had never returned the keys to Martin, knew without asking that Martin had more than one set of keys and had simply taken another set from his pocket when they left The Clear's headquarters that night.

Jack flung open the door and watched the van bounce down the long driveway.

He returned, defeated. In her room, he found Ed Tilman gingerly studying the photo.

"Don't touch it," Tilman said. "I got a friend I'm gonna send it too. I'm thinking these geeks are more sophisticated than your average cult geeks."

Jack blinked at the photo, baffled, stunned. It was a close shot of Dorian Greenway's head. There was the pale, clean-featured face, short black hair, that supercilious gleam in the eyes. He was staring into the camera—like one of those eyeballing contests kids indulge in—leaning forward. The extreme closeness of the portrait distorted it, creating a ballooning, fish-eye study. Adding to this almost three-dimensional effect was the tongue (specifically, the color of the tongue). Dorian Greenway's mouth was open wide and his tongue was sticking out like a Rolling Stones logo (*yaaaaaaah!*). Although the photo was a black-and-white print, the cult leader's tongue was bright green.

The green was smeared somewhat now (the palm of Kerry's hand had done that).

Ed Tilman nodded at the photo and rocked back on his heels. He was dressed jauntily, a red bow tie giving him a barbershop quartet look but his manner was grim.

"Should have recognized the signs," he said. "Sat there in group with the girl, she fidgeting and rubbing that hand, and I didn't get it. Just shows, I've lost my edge, been retired too long."

Jack clutched the old man's arm. "What's going on?"

Tilman put a hand on Jack's shoulder and squeezed. "We are talking chemical monkeyshines here. First you got something which is skin-permeable. You can transfer it with a touch. Nothing new there. We saw it happen. We stood there and watched him lick that lovely girl's hand, didn't we? Right after he'd taken a blast from that inhaler. What were we thinking?" Ed Tilman shook his head sadly.

"So Kerry's got this chemical buzzing round her system, making her hand itch, but it's not doing anything, just waiting like a government mole waits for a coded message from his control. This is the message." Ed tapped the edge of the photo with his forefinger. "This green stuff here, also skin-permeable, is a catalyst, or maybe the rest of the equation, I'm no biochemist. This stuff activates whatever preexisting condition has been created by the first, entrenched agent. Likely she got a phone call too, something to set her up, something that gave this photo significance."

"What are you saying?" Jack said.

"I'm saying that Greenway fellow has reached out and snatched her. That's where she's heading. Count on it."

aron let them borrow his car (an old Impala, baby blue). "That Kerry's a sweet thing," he said, handing over the keys. "Bring her back."

The rescue team consisted of Martin, Jack, and a strangely revitalized Ed Tilman.

Wesley Parks had volunteered to stay with the residents and help them "process" the loss of one of their members. It didn't take someone skilled in reading people to look at Wesley Parks and see that the idea of returning to The Clear's commune scared him silly.

"What's this 'processin'?" Gates said. "You actin like she's dead or something. You givin me a headache, counselor. I been watching you day in and day out, and I have come to the conclusion you couldn't counsel a dog to bark."

Wesley had shrugged, smiling rather than taking umbrage, the cheesy smile of someone who has been found out and knows he doesn't have a leg to stand on.

Martin drove. "Here," he said. This time Jack took the offered revolver. The car's engine made a coughing, rattling noise, like a robot with a bad cold.

Ed Tilman, sitting in the backseat, checked the clip in a small black automatic pistol.

"You are not supposed to have that," Martin said, looking up at the rearview mirror to send a scowl backward. "Residents are not supposed to have weapons at New Way. You signed a contract when you were admitted."

Tilman looked up, blinked. A grin bloomed under his ragged mustache. "I'd be shark food in the Sargasso if it weren't for this little baby." He snapped the clip home with the heel of his hand.

"Does anyone have a plan?" Martin asked.

"No, but I got a suggestion," Ed said. "I suggest we don't just walk up the drive and knock on the front door this time."

Martin pulled over to the side of the road, and they all studied the map. "This is an old farm road," Martin said. "We could park here and go north through this woods, coming out here. I got a compass to hold us on course."

It took less than an hour to hike through the woods, but Jack was winded by the time they came to the white outbuildings. He hadn't exercised in at least a decade, and he had never been an outdoors person. The main reason for having an outdoors, Jack always maintained, was so that one could have an indoors.

"It'll be dark soon," Martin said. "Might as well wait."

"What about the dogs?" Tilman said.

"What dogs?"

"Heard you telling Gates there were vicious dogs patrolling the grounds."

Martin chuckled. "Just wanted Gates to come along without a fuss. It worked too. Aren't really any dogs, least I never saw any or heard tell of any."

"Hope you are right on that," Tilman said. "Garroting a dog is work for a younger man."

Martin unslung the shotgun and sat down. He laid the shotgun on the ground and stretched out his legs. He tilted his hat back and leaned his head against a tree trunk. Dead leaves crackled when he shifted his weight. He was looking at Tilman with a contemplative air. "You ever garrote a dog?" he asked.

"Once in a great while."

"What sort of work features dog garroting?"

Ed Tilman shrugged and sat down on a big gray slab of glacier-borne granite. "Any job has its unpleasant aspects. I could never tolerate the eight to five routine. I liked to travel."

"You ever encounter anything like these Clear fellows?"

Ed shook his head. "No. I once lived with a tribe of Catholic cannibals. They were good fellows for the most part, very welcoming (*our rain forest is your rain forest*), but they took the whole communion thing too literally. I guess there's no end to the mischief human beings can get up to when they contemplate the infinite."

Jack couldn't get comfortable against a tree. He tried lying flat on his back, but that didn't work either. Leaves and acorns stabbed him. A bug ran across his neck. A fist-sized cloud of gnats rose up and tried to infiltrate his nose, his eyes. He swatted them away, tried to focus on Kerry.

Hang on, he thought. *We're coming.*

Twilight had no time to preen. Its moment was short, time for a half-dozen crows to flap across the sky, silhouettes against the weak-watercolor wash of the sun.

Then it was dark.

"Let's go," Martin said.

They moved quickly past the white wooden buildings. These, Jack assumed, were dorms. Lights glowed from tidy square windows. Jack felt a sense of peace and fellowship, spurious, but that was the lure of the commune, the illusion of unity, of a shared vision and purpose. Too bad that, more often than not, the man at the helm was insane, whipping his poor crew into frenzied pursuit of some deadly white whale.

Still, Jack thought it would be nice to sleep with the herd, to know that like minds, as familiar as old and oft-read books, surrounded him.

You're forgetting one thing, Jack thought. *The Clear are creepy.*

"Here," Martin whispered. He had reached the back of the mansion and already sprung the latch on double doors that lay flat against the ground. Jack and Ed joined him. Martin swung the doors wide and pointed the cloaked flashlight down into the darkness. The oval of light moved like a rippling eel over the concrete steps.

"Over there," Tilman said, and Martin and Jack looked up and followed his pointing finger to where the van was parked out in the drive. "Do you have keys?"

Martin nodded. "Yes."

"Good," Tilman said, "I expect we'll have to leave in a hurry. I didn't fancy a scramble back through the woods in the dark."

They descended into the cellar, into darkness. Martin, in the lead, reached above him and caught a dangling chain. "Close those doors and I'll give this a try," he whispered.

IRRATIONAL FEARS

For a moment, as Jack drew the doors shut behind them, leaving the wide night for a darker, enclosed one, panic came, like a moth in his throat. He swallowed the fear, chased it with anger (*These sons of bitches have Kerry*).

The bare lightbulb flared, at first illuminating nothing but itself, a circle of white surrounding a translucent egg of pale yellow. Jack squinted, ducked under the glare and moved on down the concrete steps, gritty with dirt, following Martin and Ed.

He descended into a chill atmosphere of mold and decay.

With the blazing lightbulb behind him, his eyes could now rally and profit from the light falling over his shoulder. The limits of this light made the room seem vast, bounded by nothing but shadows.

He saw Martin and Ed before him, moving with a shuffling motion (novice skaters, new to the ice). The floor was concrete and bare except for several wooden crates, a squat wooden barrel, a dozen cinder blocks scattered randomly, like dice thrown by a giant.

As they moved into the room, they moved away from the single lightbulb and so back into darkness. Martin's flashlight beam moved in front of them, revealing a wooden table with power tools, jars of nails and bolts, cans of paint, a bale of wire on its side, a withered basketball, and a stack of old *National Geographic* magazines (*de rigueur*, Jack thought, *in all the best basements*).

They had come to the limits of the light when Martin found the wooden stairs. Jack looked behind him, saw the lightbulb burning like a cold sun. Foolish, this look back; turning forward again, he saw nothing but the afterimage of the glowing orb. He bumped into Ed, who whispered, "Easy," and put a steadying hand on Jack's shoulder.

The door above creaked open when Martin laid his shoulder against it. The sound stretched Jack's frayed nerves. Pale light washed over them.

They came out in a wide hallway, the floor carpeted with the same curious pattern that, before, had seemed disturbingly three-dimensional. It seemed flat enough now, but Jack didn't let his eyes linger there.

Martin Pendleton turned off the flashlight and thrust it into an overcoat pocket. He unslung the shotgun from his shoulder.

They moved cautiously down the hall. Fake Victorian gas lamps protruded from the walls, their low-wattage bulbs offering a diluted yellow light, just enough illumination to stretch Jack's shadow into a long, grotesque apparition.

Jack held the revolver at his side. He had grown accustomed to its weight in his hand. It seemed more of a talisman than a weapon, and as Ed Tilman

WILLIAM BROWNING SPENCER

eased a white door open (the first in a row on the right side of the hall), pushing with the heel of his gun hand, a practiced maneuver that suggested he'd done this before, Jack realized that this wasn't his game at all, that he could not imagine pointing a gun at anyone and then pulling the trigger. *Someone could get hurt,* he thought. Martin Pendleton, standing behind Ed with a raised shotgun, was obviously indifferent to such thoughts. Jack saw a narrowing of focus, a fearful purpose in the way Martin Pendleton lifted the shotgun and in the way his eye glared balefully down the barrel. This was a man who was not going back, who was not rethinking anything now.

Ed ducked down as the door swung open revealing an empty bedroom, everything swathed in white sheets, the air of disuse palpable.

So it was with the other doors; behind them everything was shrouded and abandoned. They had surfaced in a wing shut down for months, perhaps years.

At the end of the hall, they came to a wide staircase.

"Up or down?" Martin asked.

The noise seemed to come on cue, a loud *clunk!* like a recalcitrant furnace activated on the first chill day, and then a hum that grew in pitch and made the house vibrate.

The noise came from below.

They ran down the stairs, less cautious now, the roaring of engines creating an unexamined need for haste.

The stairs brought them to a short hallway that ended abruptly at a gray metal door, spotted with rust, a door that looked like a steel collage, some artist's abstract of Auschwitz, great welts of welded metal, bolts the size of a wrestler's fist, a thick black wheel growing from an X of steel beams.

Martin laid the shotgun down and tugged at the door. The noise was coming from behind it, making the door and walls hum.

"Turn the wheel," Ed urged.

Martin grabbed the wheel, shoulders braced for resistance, but it spun easily.

The door swung back violently, banging open like a screen door snatched from one's hand by a gale-force wind. This door weighed, perhaps, half a ton, and if Martin hadn't leapt back and beyond its arc, his backbone would have been shattered between wall and wheel. Instead, the wheel burst through the wall, spraying plaster, lodging there, the door stuck open, shivering, animated by a howl bigger than reason.

Jack felt himself sliding away, fading. The air was full of wetness, the scent of brackish tide pools, rotting fish. The hall's pale blue walls grew speckled with black spots, turning to blotches, blooming quickly to a single blackness; Jack looked at his hands, saw blood, thought some airborne object had cut him, then realized that blood was in the air, a fine spume of bright red droplets.

Jack would have welcomed darkness, but he spied Martin through the bloodstorm. The man crawled slowly toward the shotgun, retrieved it, and then, still crawling on hands and knees, hiked himself through the door into the ravenous mouth of the hurricane. Ed Tilman, also on all fours, followed.

Jack cursed this marvelous stubbornness. And followed, staggering forward at first but quickly dropping to his knees, crawling.

He came out on a narrow, railed-in catwalk overlooking a huge room dominated by a swimming pool filled with churning, black-green water.

Jack recognized the room from the movie. He distinctly remembered that the cheerleader virgin had been dragged here by the high school football coach. The coach (a character actor in a career slump) had been in thrall to malevolent gods intent on world domination.

The gymnasium-sized room was pretty much the way Jack remembered it. At the end of the room was the dark stone deity, looking like two giant squids grafted to a thirty-foot praying mantis.

As sometimes happens in moments of duress, Jack was even, magically, visited by the film's title: *Revenge of the Cheerleader Space Zombies*.

Not a bad movie, actually, a funny little campy horror flick with better-than-average B-movie production values and…this was not, perhaps, the time for a film critique.

A lot was going on down there. The black-green water in the pool was in motion, and something moved beneath its surface, brown and silver and massive. The air itself was filled with black flies, which were, Jack realized, more droplets of blood. The tribe of The Clear, men and women, stood naked, hands linked, encircling the pool. They were swaying slightly in rhythmic sympathy to the undulating roar of monstrous generators. The room's light ebbed and flowed, as though reacting to shifting power demands.

The blood cloud seemed to have as its source the dark water. Something thrashed beneath its surface, something as big as the pool itself or—Jack could not explain this thought that came with terrible conviction—bigger, some small part of a star-sized sentience caught and vexed by being summoned, shaking off this temporal splinter in its alien finger.

The turbulence churned Jack's mind. The Clear themselves were undergoing strange fluctuations. It was difficult to see them as distinct,

WILLIAM BROWNING SPENCER

human entities. They were linked male/female, male/female, but the yin and the yang of it seemed to shift. Picking a single individual, Jack could not with any certainty settle on that individual's sex. Male/female seemed to stutter like a winking neon sign, a this-that image that refused resolution.

Drugs? Jack wondered, remembering Dorian Greenway's chemical skills. Something in the air, skin-permeable, that altered his perception?

Jack hoped it was so—and was fairly certain it wasn't.

As Jack watched, one of The Clear detached himself/herself from the others (who instantly relinked) and dove, headfirst, into the raging waters. Jack felt his heart stutter. The cult member did not surface and—again, was it altered perception?—the rising blood cloud seemed to thicken like the smoke from a campfire when a new log is thrown on the flames.

Jack saw something move to his left and turning, saw that Martin had slung the shotgun back over his shoulder and was climbing down a metal ladder. His hat was long gone, snatched by the storm, and his long overcoat flapped wildly.

A sudden shriek of organ chords, blasting from speakers high in the walls, added to the machine din. Wide double doors just to the right of the horror-film stone god flew open. Dorian Greenway and his entourage made their grand entrance. The cult leader was wearing a tuxedo. He was flanked by male members of The Clear dressed in their traditional shirt, tie, slacks and gleaming shoes. They moved sedately, in time to the howl of the wedding march which, despite its speaker-rattling volume, was muffled and blown into near incoherence by the machine-raging roar and buffeting winds.

Dorian moved to the side of the doors and waited with his honor guard. A second group entered, women in black. There were eight of them, four on either side of a gurney upon which some shimmering, rectangular object lay. In stately accord with the howling march, they guided the gurney into the room.

They joined Dorian and his group and all stood frozen, poised and waiting for the next cue.

Elsewhere, frenzy prevailed. The ranks of The Clear were rapidly thinning as, in twos and threes, they hurled themselves into the water. The water in the pool seemed to levitate. The whole room was growing dark. In the thick of the black foam, savage bolts of lightning skittered. Rubbery black tentacles, adorned with silver, rune-etched rings, rose and fell. One appendage swept the edge of the pool, tumbling a dozen pale bodies into the maelstrom.

"Let's see if we can shut this circus down!" Ed Tilman shouted. Jack jumped. He'd forgotten the old man. Ed had come up behind Jack and hollered in his ear, and Jack had nearly pitched over the railing.

Recovering himself, he shouted back, "What about Martin?" Jack pointed below to where Martin Pendleton was striding purposely around the pool toward Dorian Greenway.

"That John Wayne style ain't gonna get it," Tilman said. "The straight-on macho shit doesn't address the situation. We got a goddam hurricane in a gym, air swimming with blood and hallucinogens, we got a monster in a swimming pool, we got naked cult people feeding themselves to said monster, we got that lunatic in a tuxedo primed for some ceremony that is not gonna be pleasant, we got that sweet girl, buck naked and frozen in a block of ice, we got—"

Jack turned, clutching the rail. Dorian's male contingent had removed the object from the gurney and placed it upright while Jack's attention was focused elsewhere.

Kerry Beckett, in a dazzle of flesh, stood encased in a glittering block of ice. Her hands were at her sides, her eyes open. She was not standing perfectly straight, but tilted to the left. She must have been frozen while lying down. Perhaps two inches of ice separated her toes from the floor.

The ice was translucent, milky-white in places, and the effect was artful—more *Playboy* than *Hustler*.

"God!" Jack moaned.

"She's a looker, all right," Ed said. "Come on."

Jack followed Ed as he ran along the catwalk. "Where are we going?" Jack shouted.

Ed didn't respond. He ran with a crouched, arthritic gait, an old geezer waving a gun, running in baggy brown polyester pants and natty two-tone shoes and a goofy bow tie—surely not the man to trust in a crisis—and Jack followed, scared, confused, and hoping that appearances were deceiving.

Ed had come to a door in the wall, found it locked, and now waited for Jack to catch up. *AUTHORIZED PERSONNEL ONLY* the sign read.

"We want to find the heart and stop it!" Tilman shouted. "Give me your revolver."

"Huh?"

"Give me your revolver." He snatched it from Jack's hand, gave Jack the automatic. "The safety's off, so don't be shooting your dick off." Ed directed Jack to get behind him, and Ed extended the revolver, aiming point-blank at the lock. He turned his head away. "Authorized Personnel only," he said. "Well, here's your authorization." He fired twice and the door popped open. He grinned at Jack, pleased with himself. "Ed Tilman ain't lost his touch," he said.

WILLIAM BROWNING SPENCER

They entered a cold stairwell. The thundering roar of engines pummeled Jack as he followed his manic leader.

"Okay, okay," Tilman chanted as they raced down flights of stairs. "Okay, okay, okay."

The noise could grow no louder, Jack thought. And then Tilman kicked open the door at the bottom of the stairs and they were in a room of black machinery. Jack had half a second to note winking red lights, pumping pistons, a reek of burning oil, a mind-defying roar as though Zeus and Yahweh, the both of them composed of steel and steam, were trading punches at ground zero. A young man, wearing muffled earphones as protection against the din, stood up, the magazine falling from his knees, grabbed for something—and Ed Tilman shot him, the bullet opening his throat, banging him in a heap against the door, bright blood flooding his shirt. The dead man slipped slowly to the right and sprawled across the machine gun.

Tilman, wasting no time, was already past the slumped guard and through the door of the room he'd been guarding.

The room was small, dimly lit, filled with antiseptic hospital smells. A bank of video monitors lined one wall.

A hospital bed dominated the room, facing the wall of flickering monitors. A red-faced dwarf was propped up in the bed, his eyes small, white, and sightless, his lips purple and swollen. His skin was netted with wrinkles; even his scalp, visible though a fuzz of thin white hair, was crisscrossed with tiny lines.

Two IVs dripped fluids into the paralyzed body. To the bed's right a shelf of monitors beeped and blinked, monitoring vital signs. Moving closer, Jack saw that a small silver box, the size of a cigarette lighter, appeared to be stuck to the dwarf's right temple. Wires radiated from this box, stapled into his flesh, one traveling like a scar down the right side of his face to disappear behind his ear, several traveling down his chest. Other wires led off the bed, presumably to power sources or monitoring equipment.

Jack saw something move, jumped, saw that it was his own reflection in the standing mirror next to the bed, a mirror framed with small lightbulbs like yellow ping-pong balls.

Jack turned his attention back to the man on the bed. The man looked dead, not just dead but long dead, dead-with-the-pyramids dead. Maybe he had been taller ten thousand years ago, but now, standing, he'd be about three and a half feet, judging from where his feet punched up the blanket. Dead. The short and the dead. *Like the Bible says.*

Jack felt he was losing it, driven mad by an accumulation of surreal moments.

Ed Tilman was circling the room. He turned and shouted to Jack. "Control central. This is it. So who's running the store? Sure isn't—"

She must have been crouched down behind the bed and the nightstand, although there hardly seemed enough room. In any event, the sound of the bedside lamp crashing to the floor, the sound of a metal pan cartwheeling and coming to rest with a dying, tinny wobble, the sound of the nightstand slamming on its side...these sounds trailed the *oof!* Ed Tilman uttered as she tackled him, head-butting his stomach, knocking him into the wall.

Jack watched, stunned, as Ed struggled with a short, wide woman in a nurse's uniform, white stockings, white canvas shoes, the whiteness a blur to eyes wide-focused for the murky light. There was enough light to see that she was a substantial woman, easily two hundred pounds. Jack could not see her face. Her hair was cropped short, her head and neck a seamless bullet shape tucked efficiently between broad shoulders.

Ed Tilman and his assailant spun, locked together, her hand clenched around the wrist that held the revolver. The revolver smashed through a monitor's face. Both hands, bloody, her hand still glued to his wrist, resurfaced, dripping shattered glass onto the floor. One shard of glass glinted from the base of her thumb. The revolver was gone from Tilman's hand.

Jack saw her other arm swing, high and wide, a southpaw's fastball delivery, bringing the syringe down. Tilman raised his arm to fend off the blow, and the needle stuck into his forearm then snapped, and he stepped forward and slammed his elbow into her nose, and she staggered back, shaking her head, and stumbled against the broken monitor. Her small eyes were pale blue, innocent of all expression, dumbfounded, dazed, her mouth slightly open, a mustache of blood forming over her thin upper lip.

Later, Jack was to understand what a consummate professional she was, how skillful this semblance of confusion.

Thrown against the broken monitor, her right hand had been bounced back, lost again in the jagged maw of the broken picture tube. This was a calculated maneuver. She came up with the revolver in her hand. She pointed the gun at Tilman's head and smiled.

Jack shot her twice. That is, two bullets entered her body. The first bullet entered her chest, an inch below her name tag (BENDERS), the second destroyed her left eye. A stream of bullets found other targets, taking out two more monitors and shattering various pieces of electronic equipment. This was an extremely automatic automatic.

Ed Tilman took the gun from him after Jack thought to relax his trigger finger.

WILLIAM BROWNING SPENCER

"You want a lighter touch," Ed said. "Although I am not complaining."

Jack didn't say anything. He leaned back against the wall, found he was sitting on the floor.

"You just rest there," he heard Ed saying. "I'm going to see about turning stuff off." Ed retrieved the revolver, stuffed it in his belt, and then went to sit in front of the computer banks.

The noise died slowly around Jack, machines spiraling into silence, some refusing to go gracefully, hissing and shrieking, others uttering a last, desperate rat-scramble scrape and sigh.

"Ah," Tilman's voice said. "Well, well, well. Well, *fuck me*."

Jack closed his eyes and concentrated on not throwing up. Time passed, in queasy, single-file seconds.

Ed Tilman clutched his arm. "No rest for the wicked," he said. "We got to gather the troops and get. I seem to have started a countdown. It's not entirely clear what is being counted down, but I got a feeling about these guys, and my guess is we don't want to be around when that last zero winks. Looks like we got fifteen minutes."

Jack stood up. He was shaky, but no longer sick. He blinked at the dwarf on the bed, blinked at the blind eyes, the monitors that no longer beeped and blinked.

"We shut down his life support," Jack said.

Ed turned and joined Jack in regarding the open-mouthed, impossibly ancient husk. "You are saying we killed the Mummy?" Ed shrugged. "Okay. I can live with that. You got to break a few eggs to make an omelet. Besides, this guy should have hung with a nicer crowd. You play with snakes, you are apt to get snakebit. Rest in peace, old-timer."

Ed steered Jack out of the room.

Ed stooped and snatched up the machine gun. "Here we go," he said, and they headed back up the stairs.

They came out on the catwalk again and blinked down at the altered scene.

The room was empty, the pool devoid of water. A red-black rectangle lay at the bottom of the empty pool, like a coffin in some nightmare mausoleum.

They climbed down the metal ladder and ran across the gymnasium floor, the soles of their shoes making pocking noises on the sticky, resinous surface.

Don't think about the blood, Jack thought. Bad advice. His stomach churned.

"Kerry!" he shouted. The hollow room took the name and shook it and gave back nothing.

Jack found the ladder down to the bottom of the swimming pool and began to descend.

"We don't have a lot of time," Tilman shouted after him.

Jack reached the concrete floor, turned, and slipped. He managed to break his fall with his left hand, palm skidding across the slick surface. His left knee banged the floor, pain filling it like air rushing into a vacuum. Trembling, Jack stood and limped onward, leaning into the fear as though it were a strong wind.

The block of ice was imperfectly coated with red-black blood, and he knelt, reached out his hand, wiped away the blood, and saw her face, the blue eyes as empty as a cloudless sky, her flesh pale, frosted and strangely translucent.

"Kerry!"

He seemed to be shouting across a canyon, across death itself, that bridgeless expanse.

A roaring, ravenous sound broke overhead, and he looked up and saw flames boiling from the ceiling, saw dark girders appear magically. The air was suddenly heated, fogged with smoke.

Ed Tilman's face, full of upside-down concern, peered over the pool's edge. "We got to be going," he said.

Not without Kerry.

He turned back to her. The block of ice was melting, so rapidly that Jack could see it dwindle. It appeared, in fact, to be sinking into the floor. Kerry would be released; he would carry her to safety. Perhaps she was not...

Kerry remained encased in the ice, was, herself—no, *yes*—melting. The strange translucence of her features had increased; she was a ghost, fading, the floor beneath her visible. She was an indentation, a shimmer-shape painted on a crystal mold.

The wetness of her retreat soaked Jack's clothing. Two inches of ice, now shed of its blood-veneer, revealed her whole body, perfect and ephemeral, sinking, disappearing.

And she was gone. Jack's hands slapped at the pool of water that remained, the heat around him a swollen, evil halitosis of despair. He sought her, crazy, clawing the already tepid water, breaking his fingernails on the chalky concrete. His palm slapped something round and thin; he closed it in his fist.

A hand clutched his shoulder; he turned and saw Tilman leaning over him. "Come on," Tilman said. "There's nothing you can do here."

The Hollywood god was on fire, the flames revealing the steel-wire frame and the true nature of the simulated stone (paper and glue). Skeletal tentacles writhed as though in agony, animated by blazing paper skin.

It was toppling toward them as they fled through the double doors. In the hall, they almost fell over the recumbent form of Martin Pendleton.

He lay on his back, his coat spread out like a stain beneath him. Crumpled against the opposite wall was a member of The Clear, arm nearly detached at the shoulder where the shotgun blast had caught him.

"Give me a hand," Ed said, slipping an arm behind Martin's back. "He's alive."

As though to confirm this, the director of New Way groaned, then coughed and sat up convulsively.

"Easy," Tilman said. "Can you stand?" Blood was flowing from Martin's forehead and from another cut on his cheek. He stood up, stumbled, and Tilman caught him. Jack came up, took Martin's left arm and steadied him.

They lurched down the hallway, which was filling with smoke. In front of them, a wall of flames rose. Heat bruised Jack's face. He gasped and stepped back, bumping a door that swung open on salvation.

The cellar.

"Here!" Tilman had already seen. With Martin between them, they retreated down the stairs.

They needed no flashlight this time. The cellar was illuminated by burning rafters.

The pain in Jack's knee hummed, keening like a dentist's drill. They walked through the scattered cinder blocks and found the concrete stairs and moved up them like geriatrics in some sack race against death. The doors swung open and the night bloomed over Jack's head.

Jack stared out the van's window and coughed. He watched flames sprout from the mansion's roof. A window was suddenly illuminated. Glass shattered. A gable collapsed, a red lattice tumbling earthward.

A muffled *whump* made the van shudder and the mansion's front door ripped from its hinges and spun, flames billowing in its wake.

"We're out of here," Tilman said, turning the key in the ignition.

IRRATIONAL FEARS

Jack turned and saw Martin, who was sitting up, staring at the burning mansion. New Way's director said, "Sonsofbitches," and wiped the blood from his forehead with his coat sleeve.

Jack felt his knee bite him, winced. The object in his hand vibrated as his fist tightened around it. He opened his fist and blinked at the silver coin. Words circled a silver sunburst: *ONE DAY AT A TIME*.

He was holding the medallion that Kerry had picked up at that first AA meeting they had attended together. A desire chip, the chairman had called it.

Desire.

 week later, back at New Way, engaged in the mechanical process of continuing, of participating in the numbing, pointless process of group therapy, Jack held the desire chip in his hand, felt it vibrate, and thought of Kerry.

Young girls did not melt into nothingness; he knew that. He had, he supposed, hallucinated her image in the ice. Something, some chemical, had been floating in the air, something that briefly altered his perception.

So why didn't he believe that? Why was he convinced that Kerry had, indeed, melted away before his eyes?

Group went on. They sat in a circle, Eunice on the sofa with Wesley Parks, the others perched on flimsy folding chairs (designed, perhaps, to stress the uncertainty of life, the necessity of coming clean before the whole shaky business collapsed).

Gates had been talking about his thirst for whiskey. "It just swoops me up," he said. "Makes me all dizzy and distracted."

He'd got them started, all of them eloquent on this subject. Eunice had talked about how Jesus Himself couldn't wrestle that vanilla extract from her (drunk, she would smell like a cake), and Al said he even drank the sweet, licorice-tasting stuff that his parents kept in the cupboard, knowing it would make him sick but hungering after the buzz.

IRRATIONAL FEARS

Martin Pendleton, who had taken to attending group every day, nodded sadly and said, "Drinking's like hugging your own pain, nothing but hurting and wanting, hurting and wanting, wanting…" He drifted into a mutter. His beating at the hands of The Clear had left no permanent physical damage, but it had wrought some deep psychic change; he was gloomy and fierce. "They meant to kill me," he told Jack and Ed. "I thought I was on my way to Saint Peter, but here I am. Reckon the Good Lord don't want me yet. Reckon I'm still responsible, gotta keep hauling the sorry-assed, suffering alcoholic to meetings, gotta keep shouting the message even if it falls on a deaf ear."

"How do you live with nothing but yearning?" Jack asked, and blank stares were all the answer he got. Still, he felt that the question was critical to his survival. If he could find an answer to that question, perhaps he could live with his alcoholism. This reaching out and being rebuffed (losing love, losing hope) was the oldest joke, and if it was God's joke, then God was evil, no way around it. But "God is evil" was not the answer either, merely semantics.

Kerry knew all about it, her teenage cynicism dead on. You might as well get that desire chip, it was all you could ever claim: Desire. The medallion in his fist tingled, a phenomenon he did not care to examine (subconscious machinations, no doubt) but which was, this trembling life, both a painful echo of loss and a desperate last-ditch connection that he could not relinquish.

"Well, Professor, let's not get too philosophical," Parks said. "Let's just stick with the program, one day at a time, easy does it, et cetera." Parks was a jittery group leader these days, various facial tics working overtime, his head bobbing like a sycophant among VIPs.

Jack had expected Parks to be relieved by the disappearance of The Clear—and they were gone, vanished. The mansion had burned to the ground, the white buildings still stood, and The Clear were definitely gone.

On hearing the news, Wesley Parks had fainted. Revived, he was greatly agitated, a condition which could have indicated genuine concern (the bell tolls for us all), except that Jack was certain Wesley Parks was not moved by compassion or empathy. Something else was operating here.

Gates said, "Whiskey can take up all your thoughts, don't leave no room for nothin," and everyone nodded. They were a dark-hearted, rueful lot in the absence of Kerry. Al now maintained that he had loved her. He would sob himself red-eyed in group, hyperventilate, clutch whomever was handy and moan dismally. Jack wanted to throttle the lugubrious teen, despising these histrionics. The authenticity of Al's grief over Kerry's disappearance was, Jack felt, compromised by Al's inclination to get her name wrong, often referring to her as Lisa.

Jack realized that he was not particularly fond of any of these people. Nor was he much drawn to the people he met in Harken's AA meetings. A large part of AA's strength was this bond of shared suffering, but Jack felt himself drifting away from his fellows, alienated by despair.

Martin had taken them to more AA meetings, two a day, convinced that total immersion was the ticket, but even in AA meetings, seeds of discontent could be sewn. Last night they had gone to a meeting where Bitter Bob (not to be confused with Wanker Bob, an Englishman who, when drunk, was inclined to expose himself) had shared at length. "Every year gets a little worse," Bitter Bob said. He was originally from New York (where he got sober), a fat man with small black eyes that were grim prisoners in his flesh. He had many chins, which shook when he was overwrought (his normal condition). He had been sober for twelve years. He talked for fifteen unhappy minutes, concluding with, "I lost my job. I got high blood pressure. My ex-wives took every dime I ever made. I think this program's a sham. I'd kill myself if I had the energy."

People who heard Bitter Bob for the first time would go to him, offering consolation. He would look surprised, even offended by their solicitude. "Huh? I'm fine," he would say. "This is the way we do it in New York. We just let it all out and then go on with our lives."

The meeting Bitter Bob spoke at was a low-bottom club called Round the Clock in a bad part of town near the bus station. "Low bottom" was an AA description applied to alcoholics who had lost everything or experienced particularly unpleasant and degrading circumstances in the process of hitting bottom. Homelessness, hallucinations, prison, mental wards, hospitals...these were all part of the low-bottom résumé. In AA, the more dreadful your drinking past, the more venerated you were in recovery.

Sometimes this got out of hand, became (an apt metaphor) a pissing contest. "I was way worse than you!" someone might holler. "I'd have been throwed out of Hell for being rowdy!"

It saddened Jack, this jostling for position, but the high-bottom meetings were worse, with men in suits agonizing over stock options while their women fretted over vacation plans and incompetent interior decorators. In one such meeting, Jack had found himself feeling the pain of a woman who had, that day, been betrayed and scorned. She was sobbing, heartbroken. Jack's own heart ached in empathy. Then she revealed the source of her grief, a canceled appointment at her hair salon. After that, Jack was wary about letting his sympathy loose in the presence of vague emotional strife. *Let's have some details*, he would think. *Are we talking chemotherapy or travel plans gone awry?*

But, in truth, Jack knew there was nothing wrong with the AA meetings. His irritation with others was simply a manifestation of his own relentless self-loathing.

He was not only sick of himself, he was sick of being sick of himself, sick, in other words, of the whole echoing mirrorhall of his morbid reflection. He knew all his tricks; and despised them all.

He was certain he was going to drink again. So far, he had resisted the temptation to leave New Way. But he could get away any time he wanted to; no one would stop him. He could hike down the road. At the first gas station, he could call a cab. He could find a bar, hunker down at the end of it. Better yet, he could buy a bottle, find a motel somewhere, sort it all out.

Now people were standing up, milling around. Group was over.

Jack found himself staring at the one member who remained seated. Ed Tilman sat in his folding chair, head lowered so that the pink bald spot on the top of his head gleamed under the fluorescent lights.

Ed was wearing a long-sleeve, blue workshirt. He was rubbing his right forearm vigorously and frowning. He looked up, saw Jack, and stopped. He got up abruptly and left the room.

Ed didn't want to let Jack in when Jack knocked on his door.

"Something's wrong," Jack said. "I can tell."

"I'm fine," Tilman said, peering from behind his door.

"Something's wrong with your arm."

Tilman opened the door wider then, letting Jack in. He closed the door behind Jack. "Yeah, something's wrong. I was thinking maybe if I didn't talk about it, it would go away. Like a little old lady, I was thinking that." He sat on the bed, shaking his head. Then he looked up, staring straight at Jack, letting Jack have a good look at his eyes and the naked fear there. "I'm scared, is all, flat scared."

"What is it??"

"Two days ago, I was washing the dishes. I don't mind taking my turn washing dishes, but I had to tell Aaron I was sick, had to get out of there, because the minute I stuck my arms in that water, well, I felt water in my lungs, in my throat, felt like I'd gone under myself, drowning in a big, gray vat of soapsuds. I could see huge silver objects and two white gleaming disks. As soon as I snatched my arms out of that dishwater, I could see the kitchen again. I told Aaron I was feeling poorly, and I staggered off to bed and lay there, tasting hot soap on my tongue, replaying every detail of my drowning fit. It came to me then. I knew what the silver objects were, knew what those big white disks were too. I'd been bug-sized, under water in the sink, blinking at submerged pots and pans and porcelain dishes that seemed as big as houses.

"I thought about all this some more, and I decided it had something to do with the itching in my forearm. I guess I knew where that came from and just hadn't wanted to think about it either. That big old nurse that attacked me…I thought the needle she stuck me with had broken off before I got a dose…I guess I was spared most of it. But I got *some* of whatever she was promoting. I got a lick of the devil." He sighed, began rolling up his sleeve. "Might as well show you."

Jack blinked at a shimmering silver patch the size of a fifty-cent piece. It lay, like spilled mercury, on top of the old man's forearm, about midway between wrist and elbow.

Peering closer, Jack saw, with that queasy empathy that makes one dizzy at the sight of another's blood, that this silver, roughly circular shape seemed to writhe, its boundaries trembling, shifting.

"Want to see a trick?" Tilman said. Jack didn't think, actually, that he did, but the question was rhetorical. Tilman picked a pencil up from the nightstand and pushed it into the silver, winking radiance. The pencil, shoved point first, disappeared into what was revealed to be a glittering hole. Tilman continued to push the pencil down until he was holding it by the eraser. "Doesn't hurt," he said, shooting his eyes toward Jack. "And you'll notice it hasn't popped out the other side of my arm either." Tilman, still holding the pencil by its eraser, turned his arm slowly in a time-honored magician's gesture (nothing up *this* sleeve). "Now how do you explain that?"

Jack stared, silent, the recipient of another rhetorical question.

Tilman pulled the pencil back. It seemed to shimmer briefly in a blue-white nimbus before turning dull, returned to the mundane world.

"It wasn't there that night I was washing dishes and had my fit. It wasn't there so I could see it anyway. It was staring at me the next morning though. And one thing you don't want to do," Tilman said. "If you acquire one of these silver holes in your flesh, don't be sticking your finger in it. You'll feel sort of inside-out if you do. I can't describe it, but it's not a sensation you would seek out, trust me."

"Shouldn't you see a doctor?"

Tilman smiled wanly. "I sent that photo of Greenway, the one that set Kerry off, to a friend of mine. We go back a long way. He called yesterday.

IRRATIONAL FEARS

He's still puzzling over it. Says that the green dust on that photo is some kind of amphetamine mixed with aspirin. Yeah, aspirin. And that's it. His initial conclusion was that the powder just served as some sort of post-hypnotic cue, didn't, all by itself, get our girl's mind in a brand-new place. That was going to be the extent of his report, but then he decided to look a little closer. I couldn't follow all of what he had to say. He's not an excitable fellow, but this had him in a turmoil. The photographic paper itself is altered, he says, on a molecular level in a way that is making a lie out of some cherished subatomic truths." Tilman shrugged. "That news don't do anything for me, either, but what it makes me think, about consulting doctors, is that that might be a waste of time. I want to consult with Dorian Greenway himself. I want to consult with my hands around his throat."

"How are we going to find him?"

"That's the big question, isn't it? That question is ninety-nine percent of your grade." Tilman was squinting at the brightness on his arm, a tiny sun-flared lake or one of those boiling brain lights that float into your vision prior to a massive migraine.

Tilman sighed. "I think this son of a bitch is growing."

That night, in the dining room, Wesley Parks got in another argument with his dessert. It was a banana pudding that he took umbrage with this time. "Fuck you!" he screamed.

He had triumphed over the jello, and was, perhaps, overly confident. He lifted the bowl, prepared to hurl it against a wall, slipped and fell backwards, banging his head against the coffee cart. A glass pot fell, smashed, and splashed hot coffee on him, spraying his neck and face. He howled, jumped up, and fled the room.

The pudding had, miraculously, landed upright and unscathed except for a small portion of itself that had abandoned the bowl for the floor.

Aaron came out from the kitchen, hurried over to the pudding, and lifted it in both hands as though it were an injured puppy. The cook shook his head, glared at the door through which Parks had made his exit. Then he sighed audibly, stood up and went back into the kitchen, the pudding cradled close to his stomach, shoulders hunched protectively against some new assault.

"Our counselor is crazy," Jack said.

"Hell, you know what *kind* of crazy, too," Gates said. "Crazy drunk!"

Jack turned to Gates. "Drunk?"

"Sure. What you think? Guess I'm the only one with eyes in my head. I been watchin and watchin that muther. I ain't talkin whiskey drunk. I would have smelled that. I'm talkin pill drunk."

WILLIAM BROWNING SPENCER

"What—"

Gates was nodding his head grimly. "I been follerin him, doggin his slippery old self. I seen some stuff. You know why he was all tore up when he heard that those Clear muthers was burned down and run out?"

"Well…"

Gates was still nodding his head. "You know why he ain't still tore up?"

Jack stared at Gates.

Gates smiled broadly. "The muther thought he lost his connection, then he found out he didn't. They still coming round. They still slippin him the stuff; he still getting fried. I been watchin."

"Are you saying that members of The Clear have been—are still—supplying Wesley Parks with drugs? Why didn't you say something earlier?" (Jack experienced a wince of awareness here; Kerry had asked him the same question.)

Gates frowned. "Where you been, Mr. Professor? You think somebody's gonna give this black man a prize for damn investigative reportin? Damn. I'm just watchin out for my own self. I'm telling you cause it might be you could profit from the information."

Back in his room after dinner, Jack thought about what Gates had said, about profiting from the information. Life was lived in a sea of uncertainty, of misapprehension, of impulse. When did you ever have enough information—even to take that first faltering step on life's journey?

Jack didn't know what he should do. If Gates was right, if Wesley Parks was on drugs—scored from The Clear—Martin Pendleton needed to know about it. Jack had assumed that Wesley was simply crazy. If you started firing alcoholism counselors just because they were crazy, a fearsome winnowing would occur throughout the field. No, you had to tolerate some nonlinear behavior or you wouldn't have any troops at all. But an alcoholism counselor who was doing drugs…that wouldn't work.

Jack sighed. He'd never been good at decisions; he still wasn't. He decided to think about it tomorrow.

In the meantime, he settled down to work on his Fourth Step. Martin had said, "No meeting tonight; I want you all to work on your Fourth Steps. Recovery isn't just meetings; we got a program too."

Jack's attempt to write about God had been less than successful. He decided he would tackle the problem of yearning. Group had been no help. Perhaps a written analysis would clarify his question.

YEARNING he wrote at the top of his legal pad. This was still, he supposed, a God-resentment, since it was God who had buried desire and aspiration so deep in the human heart.

Jack wrote quickly once he got going, losing himself in his thoughts.

He seemed to have lived his life out in the cold, full of hunger, with his face pressed up against the glass. He wanted everything. If he were to kill himself tomorrow, he would, no doubt, be reincarnated as one of those angry blue flies, caught mysteriously between screen and windowpane, capable only of buzzing with heated frustration, the rattling of a lost and hopeless soul driven mad by unrequited desires.

Acceptance was the key, of course, but if acceptance was learning to live in the cold and hunger, then suicide seemed the ultimate acceptance, the acknowledgment that life would never grow less implacable.

Bitter Bob's words came to Jack: "I think this program's a sham." *Life* seemed fraudulent, sometimes.

Jack wondered if he didn't ask too much of life. Was he disillusioned because he had constructed willful illusions? The dream of being a college professor (a dream which had driven him to work very hard, to study and strive passionately) had not matched the reality of indifferent students, mindless administrative details, pompous faculty members, and fashionable, thought-free curriculums. The dream of Sara's love had remained a dream, and so it continued to burn without flickering. But was that because it remained unresolved, an immaculate, impossible ghost? And Kerry? Was she a detox infatuation (a clinically predictable phenomenon) that he could now enshrine?

It was not fair that life held so many things that could assail your heart and senses in an instant.

Jack made a list:

1. Sunlight on water and plunging in, shattering summer, the smell of chlorine
2. Sara's eyebrows, her jasmine perfume, her sly interrogations
3. Snow filling a windowpane, a fire in the fireplace and the radio's pretense of crisis when none in fact exists, when all is warm and safe
4. Van Gogh's brush strokes
5. Entering the promise of the dark bar where the waitress knows you and fetches the amber-brown bottle and opens it and a pale serpent of mist lolls out and the beer waterfalls, foaming into the frosted mug (frost you can scratch with a fingernail) and—

WILLIAM BROWNING SPENCER

Jack tore the page from the pad and crumpled it. The intent of this exercise was not, he was fairly certain, self-torture. Once again, he'd taken a turn into hostile territory.

But the question remained: Why was there so much to want and why was so much of the stuff of desire waiting in ambush? You couldn't avoid it. Should it be avoided? What the hell was it doing lying on the path if picking it up meant burning your hand?

"Kerry," Jack said, speaking to the ceiling.

Someone knocked at the door, and Jack jumped, surprised by the sudden lurch of his heart, a fear that must have been crouching there.

It was Gates.

"Come on with me," Gates said.

Jack followed without argument or question, something in the black man's manner so peremptory that action was the only response.

Gates led the way, out past the kitchen and out the back door into the cold. Jack could see his own breath in the night air and was thankful for the sweatshirt that he'd donned earlier in the day.

Gates was moving rapidly, a small, stern man in denim overalls and a green woolen shirt. For all Gates's dislike of farms, for all his urban ways, he would not have looked out of place sitting on the porch of some tumbled-down shack, chickens in the yard, a scruffy hound at his feet. Maybe his fears had been justified and he was becoming possessed by primal, rural spirits.

Gates moved with purpose, not looking back to see if Jack were following. The grass grew taller as they moved beyond the range of the minimal lawn grooming administered by a county work-release crew.

Jack found himself marching through a meadow, moving downhill toward the wall of trees. Stars shone overhead, frosting the autumn-seared weeds.

They entered the woods, leaves crackling under their feet, no way to avoid the rustle and pop of snapping branches.

Suddenly Gates crouched in front of a clump of bushes, turned, motioned with his hand for Jack to join him. "Okay," Gates said. "He'll be along shortly. I heard him on the phone."

Jack had assumed—for no good reason, really—that they'd been hurrying after someone. He knelt down beside Gates.

"Who are we waiting for?" Jack asked.

"Who you think?"

"Parks?"

Gates nodded. "He'll be coming along the path down there. He can't see us from there, and anyway, his mind will be all on gettin that dope."

IRRATIONAL FEARS

"What if he—"

"We got to be quiet now. I expect he'll be along directly."

But he wasn't. In the stillness, the cold leaked into Jack. It came in through the soles of his tennis shoes, his buttocks, thighs, his bad knee. He could feel the intricate pattern of twigs and roots and dead leaves engraving a blue tattoo on his butt. His lungs ached.

He blinked at the faint widening in the path and realized that he had been here once, right after breakfast on a warmer day, when Martin Pendleton, full of morning vigor, had marched them around the grounds while urging them to breathe deeply. "Get that dirty city funk out of your lungs, folks. Inhale some clean living."

Remembering, Jack looked for the plaque on the tree and found it, a small white rectangle. He couldn't read it from this distance, but he remembered what it said, which was: *HI I'M A RED MAPLE (SOMETHINGUS LATINUS)* and a breezy description like: *I'm a highly adaptable species, growing up to 90 feet tall and living more than a hundred years. You can't miss the brilliant red of my leaves, a brilliance that increases with the acidity of the soil. Always opposite, my leaves...* Jack had imagined an entire forest, each tree wearing its name tag, a social mixer for pines, cedars, maples, oaks, hollies, dogwoods, hackberries....

Beyond the tree, Jack remembered that there was a steep drop to a narrow stream. He had watched its brown water hurrying over yellow pebbles, the water animating wet, black leaves that were lodged among the rocks (and Jack had found himself thinking how it had been a month since he had last flossed).

Now there was someone standing next to the tree, perhaps he had even slipped from behind the tree. Jack was sure this person had not come down the path. He was simply, suddenly, there.

He was wearing a dark, hooded jacket, and he was hunched forward, hands in his pockets. He was tall, thin, and unsteady on his feet, wobbling. He removed a hand from his pocket and braced himself against the eponymous tree.

This was not Parks, too tall, too thin. So this was the man Parks was meeting. A member of The Clear? If so, good grooming had been abandoned. His pants were muddy and one of the knees was torn out, revealing pale flesh. His shoes were scuffed. Something was wrapped around one of the man's arms, and, as Jack's eyes sifted the gloom, he realized that it was a necktie, wound and knotted around the man's upper arm.

WILLIAM BROWNING SPENCER

"Sssssh," Gates said, clutching Jack's shoulder with a grip that hurt. Jack hadn't been intending to say anything, but he saw that a shadowy figure was moving down the path and that this had inspired the warning.

It was Wesley Parks, wearing a black raincoat poncho and a black knit cap, looking over his shoulder and scuttling forward in a mincing, idiot pantomime (as though he were a student in some impromptu acting class and had been asked to illustrate "suspicious behavior").

A sound came from behind Jack, and he turned and peered into the tangle of branches, tree trunks, bushes. He saw nothing.

Looking back, he saw Parks approach the man by the tree.

"You got it?" Parks said, his voice urgent and easily audible in the crisp air.

"Let's see the color of your money first, counselor."

Wesley grumbled, dug around under the black poncho, produced a wad of bills.

"Shit. I thought you people weren't interested in money," Parks grumbled, as the man took the proffered cash and began counting it. "I thought you just wanted to raise everyone's goddam consciousness."

The guy looked up, shrugged. "If you didn't pay for it, it wouldn't mean anything. Don't blame me; it's your value system."

"Just give it to me," Wesley said. His voice trembled.

Jack heard the noise behind him again, turned, expecting to see nothing, resigned to the tricks his nerves were playing with the shadows and night sounds.

The dog was three feet from Jack, crouched and growling, the low rumble in its throat an imperfectly tuned but powerful motor. Jack was a child again, his mind filled with the voices of his companions. *Don't let him see you're afraid. Show him who's boss. Pet him.*

This was not a dog to pet. *Feed him your hand,* was the proper parsing of that suggestion.

This dog was all hackles and yellow teeth and blood-red eyes with silver—shivering, migraine-mote silver—floating in the pupils. The beast was vibrating, stretched taut with rage. Its fur was wet in parts, black and matted in others. And parts of its body boiled with trembling silver patches, a bright, metallic mange.

Talk to him. Say soothing things, the voices in Jack's head counseled.

"Dr. Bob," Jack whispered, amazed at this info his subconscious supplied. Yes. He saw the truth of it. This was the dog—but larger, stranger—that had fled Martin's shotgun, this was the one that had survived. "Easy does it,

IRRATIONAL FEARS

Bob." The dog's hindquarters shifted, twitching. Jack remembered that never, never had the counseling voices offered a single effective suggestion.

The dog leapt into the air and Jack screamed and rolled away.

Jack had not been its intended prey. It raced down the hill, barking. Jack twisted and stared after it, heart burning up adrenaline, throat still aching from the crush of imagined jaws.

Jack watched as the dog sailed through the air, hurtling toward the two men who stood near the base of the tree. Wesley turned and threw an arm up in front of himself.

The hand that Wesley used to protect himself was holding a brown paper sack, which broke, spewing its contents into the air, a bee-cloud of pills that hung suspended in the air and then tumbled onto the packed ground of the path. "Aaaaaaaah!" Wesley screamed.

The Clear's drug rep was already running down the path, back the way Wesley had come, arms pinwheeling wildly, an ungainly long-striding flight that was nonetheless effective and quickly took him around the bend and out of sight.

Dr. Bob had the bag in his mouth, twisting, turning it into wet shreds.

Wesley was howling, kicking, pummeling the dog's back with his fists.

Jack scavenged a rock from the dirt and stood up.

"Hey!" he shouted, hearing his voice, thin and fainthearted (as though a rabbit were attempting to disperse brawling wolves). He flayed his way through the underbrush, digging his heels into the sloping ground to keep from sliding and tumbling headfirst.

Neither Wesley nor Dr. Bob paid Jack any heed. Alcoholism counselor and dog were rolling in the dirt, wrestling, bellowing and growling. Had Jack been so inclined—and not dead frightened by the prospect of inserting himself between Wesley and an insane monster dog—he could have conjured an apt allegory for this struggle in which Wesley symbolized new alcoholism treatment modalities (medication and cognitive behavioral modification therapies) and Dr. Bob symbolized AA's pragmatic, keep-it-simple approach.

But Jack lacked the leisure and serenity for such an allegory—and, indeed, the allegory wasn't a perfect fit. Both man and dog were gobbling the scattered pills with unholy ardor.

Dr. Bob's jaws dug into the earth, gulping wet leaves and dirt along with the colored pills.

Wesley was equally indiscriminate, hands clawing the ground and feeding whatever was discovered to his howling, ravenous mouth.

WILLIAM BROWNING SPENCER

They would pause in their desperate pill gorging to bite and shake each other with a strange, ritualized ferocity, then, distracted by need, scramble for more pills.

Jack stumbled out onto the path, trembling. He raised the rock, feeling the futility of the gesture.

Blue sparks popped and hissed from the dog's black coat as it sank its teeth into Wesley's forearm. Wesley pushed himself to his knees, then, incredibly, stood, the dog rising onto its hind legs. Now both man and dog were surrounded by a blue nimbus, and the air crackled and smelled of heated steel. Wesley's capelike poncho billowed; for a moment, it seemed to Jack as though Dracula and the werewolf danced. Then Wesley roared, leaned forward, and bit the dog's ear.

The combatants flipped in the air, gymnasts in a magic show. They began to dwindle in size as they spun in a sphere of quivering blue. They were shrinking, dolls raging against each other. Jack stumbled backward, baffled.

The sphere suddenly took on weight, with a cosmic sigh, as though the universe of natural law had had enough and now, exhaling sharply, was finished with supernatural tomfoolery.

The blue sphere, basketball-sized and bearing its cargo of tiny, tumbling figures, hit the ground and bounced down the weedy bank toward the trickle of muddy stream.

It hit the stream and winked out with one flash of blue-green light (a tiny, condensed point that lived in the back of Jack's eye for the next fifteen minutes). The bright blip was accompanied by a hollow bang, the sound a cherry bomb makes when demolishing a coffee can.

Jack climbed down to the streambed. Gates, reluctantly, peered down. There was a faint odor of wet ashes, and a small buzzing noise that grew less distinct as Jack sought its source, quickly vanishing.

"They's gone," Gates finally said. "You sure they didn't just run off in the woods?"

Jack shook his head. "That bang you heard was the last of them."

"You might not want to be telling everybody that Wesley Parks and a dog done bit and squeezed themselfs into a little blue ball that exploded."

"You saw them getting smaller," Jack said. "You had to see that even if you didn't see them wink out of existence."

"I'm not saying what I saw or didn't," Gates grumbled. "I'm just advising you not to share it with the rest of the world."

Jack climbed back up. Gates offered a hand and hauled him the last two feet. Jack was exhausted, sick with a surfeit of strangeness. He leaned over and picked up one of the remaining pills where it lay near the base of the maple. He was not surprised to discover that it was not a pill at all, that it was a yellow gummy bear.

Jack was accosted by sudden, dizzy dread. He threw the rubbery little candy into the trees. Just for a moment, he'd thought of popping it into his mouth, his tongue seized with longing for the satiny embrace of its sweet, golden limbs.

No.

"Let's get out of here," he said.

The sign read:

> **IF YOU WANT TO**
> **TALK ABOUT DRUGS,**
> **GO ON OPRAH**

Martin Pendleton saw Jack looking at the sign and said, "This group is an older crowd, very fundamental. The attitude here is: Alcoholics Anonymous is for alcoholics."

It was the day after Wesley Parks's disappearance. Jack had decided to risk it, to tell Pendleton everything that had happened the previous night.

"Why you want to do that?" Gates had complained. "We gonna find ourselfs in one of them mental silos where they hose you down when you holler."

"I think we owe it to Martin," Jack said. But he knew that the real debt was to Kerry. He remembered her look of reproach, how she had felt betrayed by his silence regarding Hinkle's departure in The Clear's van. That silence had, by Kerry's reckoning, jeopardized the group. Now Jack was trying to do the right thing, trying to let New Way's director know as much about the situation as possible, to know, at least, that drugs had led Wesley away and that The Clear were not all gone.

Besides, Pendleton had been in Dorian Greenway's madhouse. His mind had already been stretched some by circumstance.

Jack had gone to Ed Tilman's room before going to Martin.

"Come on," he'd told Tilman. "I've got something to tell Martin, and you might as well hear it at the same time. It's plenty weird; I expect one telling is all I'm up to."

So he'd told them.

We caught our alcoholism counselor scoring gummy bears from a derelict cult member. Yeah, out there in the woods near the friendly red maple. The mad dog Dr. Bob came along and he and Wesley got in a fight, and the both of them squeezed up into a blue ball that went bang like the Fourth of July and that was the last of them, dog and man transmuted into one firecracker fart and good-damn- bye to the both of them.

Like that.

Martin Pendleton didn't express any incredulity, any skepticism; he just looked grim. Tilman, much interested in the dog's silver shimmer that suggested Tilman's own physical affliction, was silent and thoughtful.

Martin finally spoke. "I'm gonna keep on the road, the recovery road of happy destiny. I'm not gonna veer off into a ditch at the first sign of adversity. I got an obligation to you folks. I'm gonna steer you to victory over alcoholism as long as I got breath in my lungs and blood in my heart. But I been too long without guidance, thinking I could navigate without a compass. I need help, and tomorrow I'm gonna seek it. We'll be going to a new meeting tomorrow."

So here they were. It was a small wooden house on the corner of Banks and McAuley, in a neighborhood of such houses. The lawn was covered with dead oak leaves. The house was in need of a paint job, and someone had actually embarked on such an enterprise, so that half of the front of the house glowed with a light blue makeover while the other half continued to molt gray flakes. A passerby might have assumed that an elderly couple lived within, battling against time's implacable advance.

The room Jack entered was gloomy, the bare ceiling bulbs of such low wattage that he found he could stare directly at them without squinting.

The denizens of the room (about a dozen people) sat on folding chairs facing another chair where the meeting's leader sat, hunched behind a squat lectern.

WILLIAM BROWNING SPENCER

It was an elderly crowd, mostly old men with a scattering of old women. Jack found an empty chair next to a woman who was working on a piece of needlepoint. In the dim light she was laboriously pushing green thread through a calligraphic stencil that read: *Analysis, Paralysis*.

Martin sat down next to Jack.

"They don't hold with rehab folks," Martin whispered, "so just sit quiet. For newcomers, the rule is: *Take the cotton out of your ears and put it in your mouth*."

Jack nodded. He hadn't been planning to speak anyway.

The meeting began as they normally do. The beginning of Chapter Five was read; the leader, a thin, bald man, rattled through some announcements, and said, "My name's Al, and I'm a *real* alcoholic."

Jack had heard people say this before, and he had wondered then—as he wondered now—why on earth people who were not "real" alcoholics (frauds, impostors, wannabes) would infiltrate AA meetings. Would someone wish to claim an addiction to alcohol that he did not, in fact, possess? For what reason? In order to be admitted to closed meetings of AA? Such behavior would be analogous to a healthy man claiming some disease in order to undergo painful surgery (mental illness on a grand scale). Surely no one was drawn to AA meetings because they were inherently entertaining?

An old man with a long, odd beard of the spare and nibbled sort that eccentrics cultivate, was holding forth on the topic chosen by the leader.

"If you ain't grateful for the Lord's blessings, you ain't got a chance," he said. He spoke in the rolling tones of a television evangelist. "If your attitude ain't gratitude, every day and every tick of the clock, then your soul is slipping down, sliding into perdition as sure as a mouse slides down a serpent's throat. If a thank-you don't ever pass your lips, if you ain't nothing but a whining pullet, you're goners, and all I can say is better you than me. I'm grateful. Some people even call me Grateful Grady, and I'm flattered they do cause it means they hear me saying thank you to the rooftops."

The man began to work himself up, holding forth on the low morals and ultimately hell-bound character of ingrates. "Sons of bitches think they did it all on their own!" he roared.

Grateful Grady ended with, "You ask me, I think the lot of them should be horsewhipped!"

This speech inspired others to pursue the topic of ingrates (as opposed to what Jack saw as the original suggested topic: Gratitude). Everyone allowed as how they hated and despised ingrates. Some anecdotes about the dire things that happened to ingrates when they finally stretched God's patience to the breaking point were offered up. Ingrates drank, of course, and after they drank they would lose their limbs, their minds, their friends and possessions, their lives.

Gates spoke then, standing up. He was clearly worked up, trembling. "I come here in a van," he said. "I'm living off rehab food out on a damn fahm. We sufferin out there, and we droppin off like fellers in a TV mystery, one then another, old truck driver rednecker, sweet little girl, slippery dude counselor…I'm sayin I don't need you sorry-assed deacons telling me gratitude, dissing poor, sick muthers just cause they ain't lying up a storm bout how rosy and lucky their asses are. Truth is, I ain't happy to be here. I ain't grateful to be sittin in this tiny room full of corn-fed farts listenin to a load of bullshit."

Gates sat down, his speech lying on the silence the way a used condom might lie on the floor of a nunnery.

Jack sensed a certain animosity in the room, a poised wave about to roll down.

A deep voice boomed from a darkened corner. "I'm Hubert, and I'm an alcoholic."

"Hi Hubert," the room said. Jack was struck by how much this chorus suggested children welcoming their teacher.

Hubert was a small shadow in the corner. He wore a flannel shirt, gray trousers. His face was in shadow, but Jack could make out a white cloud of hair. The man's small, veined hands were in the light, resting on thin blue-jeaned thighs.

"That's the truth being spoken. We need it here, and I thank you. The truth is that old Grateful Grady used to be called P&M Grady back sixteen years ago when he came here. That P&M was short for Pissin and Moanin Grady, and I can't honestly say that the new Grady is much of an improvement. The old Grady wasn't fun to listen to, but at least he wasn't so gawdawful pleased with himself." Hubert paused, coughed, struck a match which illuminated his face (a narrow, hawk-beaked countenance with a cigar planted firmly between thick lips). Hubert inhaled, making the tip glow under the match. "But you got to forgive us all," he said. "Accept us for the assholes we are and let any slights, imagined or real, go. I been sober sixty-eight years, sober longer than AA's been standing, and that's my advice to a newcomer. Sure Grady's a blowhard. Sure I'm a pompous fool. Why should it be different? Who the hell did you expect to find sitting in these rooms, holding forth? You think a normal, insightful, well-balanced human with a gram of humility would spend it here? Course not. You got to have some compassion for us. I know that's a lot to ask of a new person, but that's the secret, that compassion. If you can find it in your heart to love us, or at least think, 'That old fart's doing his damn-poor best,' then you have given us what we need to help you. It's simple: You can't judge us harshly and then just dance off with the angels. The angels will be willing, sure, but that hardness in your heart won't be letting you take wings. It's in your best interests to give us some slack."

Hubert coughed again, and then coughed some more, his shoulders shaking, smoke huffing from his lungs as though he were a dusty sofa being whacked with a broom. He put a frail hand up and waved it, indicating that he was done.

The old man's talk had inspired Eunice, who raised her hand and said that she was grateful Jesus had led her to this meeting. "I see that we are all brothers and sisters, and that I have been wrong to think AA can't help me just because it has a heathen element. I have let pride blind me, forgetting that my mission is to love you in spite of your sinful natures."

Jack felt that there was something condescending about this speech, but heads were nodding.

The next person to speak, an elderly woman named Natalie, plugged her alcoholism novel, *Champagne Hearts*, and announced that she was going to be appearing on television speaking about her abuse issues and that she hoped, in her small way, to change the manner in which the world viewed alcoholism and AA (improving the present dismal image). She said that her novel was about people with fashion sense and intellectual style coming to terms with AA's reputation for off-the-rack clothing and lowbrow tastes.

Jack could sense that the others in the room had heard this before. They seemed somewhat listless, neither offended nor inspired. It was a given that, in any AA meeting containing more than ten people, at least one person was writing an AA novel or twelve-step recovery text.

After the meeting, Martin spoke to Aaron. "I got some business with Hubert," Martin said. "Me and Jack and Tilman here will get someone to drive us back later. You go on and take the others back." Martin handed over the van's keys.

Martin walked over to Hubert. Eunice was already there, giving the man a hug. Eunice was gushing. Her voice had a kittenish squeak that Jack had never heard before and which he found unsettling. "You opened my eyes," she told the old man.

Up close, Hubert bore a remarkable resemblance to a sly, hundred-year-old Mick Jagger.

He grinned up at Eunice and said, "You come back anytime, young lady. This meeting has always been short on good-looking women. I was forgetting

I had a pulse. Sometimes there ain't a female in this joint, and old George will be going on about his prostate, and I'll be trying to remember why being alive is preferable to being dead. Well, there you are!" He thumped a silver cane soundly on the wooden floor. "The damn answer, sweet as honey in milk, obvious as the sun at midday. You are a fine-looking woman, Eunice, and I appreciate your sharing the bounty of your beauty with us old dinosaurs."

Eunice giggled.

Martin interrupted. "Hubert. I need to talk to you about some difficulties we've been having out at New Way. I'm hoping you can help."

Hubert turned, grinned at Martin. "This young lady staying out there with you?"

Martin nodded.

"Okay. You know my thoughts on rehabs. I don't care for them. Too much administrative deadweight, too much damn therapy cheerleading, but that's a personal opinion, and I've never let it stand in the way of our friendship, and anything I can do to help this young lady find her feet on recovery's road…well, I am at your service, and my first suggestion is that we adjourn to my house."

Hubert drove. Eunice came too, sitting up front in the passenger's seat. She had already adopted a proprietary air toward Hubert, touching and squeezing his shoulder to punctuate her remarks, and she was now telling him about the injustices visited upon her by her children. She had found a fresh and sympathetic ear in the old man.

"Children can be vipers," Hubert said. "Some of them hold a grudge forever—and don't even admit it's a grudge although that's just what it is. You keep them from pooping their pants, and they hold it against you. *Fascist*, they're thinking. *Wait till I get older. I'll get you.*

"I had a couple of children, tried once to have me locked up, but I'm rich, so I run them off with lawyers. Don't hear from them anymore. I could lend you some lawyers, should you feel the need."

Jack and Martin and Tilman sat in the back. Plenty of room; this was one of those long, station wagon trucks—what had Hubert called it? *The Burb* ("Let's all get in the Burb here")—and the old man drove it as though he were on a suicide mission, rolling through enemy lines, paying no heed to the stop signs and red lights that attempted to destroy his momentum.

The house was a mansion on a hill, white stone, white columns. There was even a butler, dressed elaborately in black.

"Don't call attention to his condition," Hubert said. "McPhee's very sensitive and he is trying. He has failed to comprehend AA's First Step, but he will."

McPhee the butler was drunk and wisely refrained from speaking. His eyes were very red and his hair stuck up oddly in back and he reeked of whiskey. His inebriation manifested itself in extreme caution. He shuffled, not lifting his feet from the carpet, and kept his elbows high, for balance, as though walking a plank. He brought each person a saucer, then a tea cup, then finally the teapot which—again wisely—he left for others to pour. He tripped once, but righted himself and smiled (possibly the most wretched smile Jack had ever seen, a smile that said, *Pay no attention to this smile, its wearer is worthless, beneath contempt*).

After McPhee deposited the teapot on the low rosewood table and left for the last time—"That will be all, McPhee," Hubert called after him— Hubert leaned forward and spoke in a whisper, "Man's a chronicle of tragedies, dead wife, dead daughter. I'm not going to go into it. Right now he's a little slow on the runway, little skittish about abandoning alcohol, but once he gets the hang of sobriety, he'll soar. You mark my words, he'll do fine."

No one disagreed.

"You probably think I should let him go, fire him. You don't know his history, but you are probably thinking it never does an alcoholic any good to be coddled. That's what's called *enabling*, you'll say. *Practice detachment*, you'll say. Well, I've seen plenty of fine, sober folks refuse to lift a finger in the name of detachment, and it ain't a pretty sight. Truth is, there ain't nothing more fastidious than some drunks when they sober up. They don't want anything to do with the filth and mess of a real slobbering, puking booze hound.

"You clean up some drunks, and they get like old Grateful Grady, full of fine sentiments and hot air and not a lick of recall for their miserable pasts. You don't ever see guys like Grateful Grady hauling some poor hallucinating sinner to the VA hospital or talking to somebody in trouble at three in the morning. The Grateful Gradys of this world prefer to hold forth around the coffee pot, like that fat guy on the television who's always explaining the world based on some books he's read and some unpleasant experiences he had in college."

Hubert paused, took a deep breath, grinned. "Well, I guess I was about to go off there. Sorry. I feel strongly about this, but I didn't invite you over here to rail at you."

"I like a man with opinions," Eunice said. She smiled warmly.

IRRATIONAL FEARS

No one else said anything. They drank their tea. Finally, Hubert slapped his knees and said, "Okay, what can I do for you, Marty?"

"It's a long story," Martin said. "And I should warn you, parts of it will stretch your powers of belief. There is a weird element here."

Hubert nodded, leaned forward. "Let her rip," he said.

Martin was thorough in his telling, and it took some time.

Jack gulped the last cold dregs of his tea and wondered why his recovery had to be so complicated, so harried by loss and conflict. Here he was, involved in some bizarre intrigue (insane, murderous cults and paranormal events). All he wanted was quiet, the hope of salvaging some sort of a life.... Self-pity sucked him under, where he encountered Sara.

She was leaning over a restaurant table. She was in a contemplative mood, tapping her perfect teeth with a celery stick. "When you were a kid, did you practice looking sad in mirrors? Looking, you know, tragic?"

"Sure," Jack said.

"Me too. Why do we do stupid things like that? Tragic isn't hip. Little eight-year-old kids giving that grim, existential stare, what's that all about?"

"I've already thought about that," Jack said. "Actually, I've spent considerable time pondering the evolutionary utility of the tragic, brooding look in young people."

Sara leaned closer, broadened her smile, tapped Jack on the nose with the celery stick. "And your conclusion, Dr. Lowry?"

"It's a *save-me* look we're cultivating. *Find me*, we are saying. *I'm inside this troubled look, come and get me.* In teenagers, it also embodies the hope of getting laid."

"I think evolution is getting too clever for its own good," Sara said. "I think we should all try to be more straightforward."

Oh, Sara.

Sara began to fade, still smiling as the room intruded, imposing its reality.

Martin was winding down. "...So I was hoping you knew more about this cult, this Clear. Looks like we haven't seen the last of them, and there's a score to settle anyway. There's a girl we'd like to find, if she's still alive."

Hubert stood up, sighed. "I know about The Clear. I know about Dorian Greenway, and I know Ezra Coldwell. That dwarf in the hospital bed, that mummy that Tilman saw..." Hubert nodded at Ed Tilman. "You were looking at the lord of the manor when you were studying that dried-up invalid. You were looking at Ezra Coldwell. It was Dorian who went down to Staunton and took Ezra out of the mental hospital there and brought him back here."

Hubert sat back down. He looked tired, almost sullen. "There is some weirdness in what you've told me. But I recognize the fabric. I've watched it being woven for a long, long time. Here I've been talking about those no-count AA members that dodge their obligations, and you've come and slapped me with a warrant for all my sins. It's true, I was hoping to dodge this debt. Now here it is, like a cat you've tried to drown, mewling at the back door."

He shook his head, a fit of anger, snatched a cigar from the table and lit it, igniting the match with his thumbnail. "I don't know where to begin, although I suppose it's all the same tangle and any strand will lift the whole knotted-up mess. I might as well start back when Ezra Coldwell killed his wife. That was in 1976, a dirty cold January, and he was drunk, drinking again after a brief dry spell, maybe a month, maybe two."

t was snowing that night," Hubert said. "We were over at the AA club, the only one in town at the time…it's gone now, used to be called Merchants cause that was the street it was on…whoa, I'm never gonna make it to the end of the highway if I go down every dirt road I see. Anyway, we were playing poker, me and Jim Wallace and a newspaperman named Heller when the phone rang. It was Anita, Ezra's wife, and she was upset. Ezra was drinking again, getting mean and threatening the way he would, and she wanted a ride over to her sister's and could someone from the club take her? We didn't refer her to Al-Anon, tell her she wasn't an alcoholic and her problems with an alcoholic required a different program. Heller, who took the call, didn't say anything about detachment. He just said we'd be right over."

"I was scared," Hubert said. "I didn't say anything to the others, but I didn't want to go where Ezra Coldwell was drinking. I'd been out to his house a couple of times in the past under similar circumstances, and the last time, when I'd dropped by to take him to a meeting and found him dead drunk, I'd seen a thing I was trying to forget."

Hubert had to back up again, the story just kept pushing him back in time like a bully shoving some poor kid down a hall.

Hubert backed all the way to 1930 when he was twenty-nine years old. In 1930 he had stopped drinking after a drunk that damn nearly got him drowned out on a lake in a storm. He just swore off and somehow it worked, and he didn't go to AA until 1948, about a year after the AA club appeared in Harken. He went then because a friend had just stopped drinking and was filled with AA zeal. "Thought I was doing him a favor, being supportive. I'd stopped drinking without AA and didn't feel the need for it. But I took to it, just plain liked it and still do." The meetings back then generally had four or five people, and there would always be a few who were in and out. A wet drunk in a meeting was nothing unusual.

Ezra Coldwell walked into a meeting in 1968. He was a rich man's son, the same as Hubert, and so they knew each other from the country clubs and those closed circles the rich go round and round in. He was a stunted, arrogant little man in his late forties, had a law degree but didn't practice, managed various properties that his parents (off somewhere in Europe) owned. He always wore a suit and was something of a dandy. "He was maybe five feet tall then, but he got shorter as the years went by. It was some disease of the spine, maybe, although I never thought of it that way. I just saw him as a man who naturally grew smaller, his body shrinking right along with his soul."

Ezra Coldwell said he had to get sober or Anita would leave him. She was the one person he loved, the only thing on the planet that had his heart's attention. He was ready to do whatever it took.

He asked Hubert to be his AA sponsor. "He didn't like me any more than I liked him, but I had the most time away from a drink, and Ezra always had to have the biggest, the best, the most."

Ezra Coldwell stayed sober through sixty-eight and sixty-nine and drank in January of 1970. "People who aren't alcoholics ask why, looking for some circumstance that sent him back," Hubert said. "But we know it doesn't work that way. Thing is, Ezra went to meetings every night that first year, and there was a big celebration when he hit that one-year-without-a-drink day, with Anita in a bright red dress, looking radiant and proud, looking like her man had just won the Pulitzer Prize, hugging him while the applause rained down (we must have had near forty people in the room that night; most of them not alcoholics at all, just cobbled-up well-wishers, relatives, people that owed him money, maybe). Then he stopped going to meetings that second year. When I'd run across him, I'd ask about it, but he'd say, the way they always do, that he was fine, that AA had braced him up, but he didn't need it anymore. An old story: He figured he'd learned his lesson."

Ezra Coldwell started drinking again in 1970, and he would get a few months sober (eight and a half months being the record; that was in seventy-four) and then go back. "Anita left him once," Hubert said. "In seventy-three. But he got so miserable and defeated she feared he would kill himself or drink himself to death. She went back. She loved him and didn't know what to do. That's another old story."

Hubert saw that his cigar had gone out, and he lit it, his head briefly enveloped in smoke. He began again: "Everyone was telling Anita to leave Ezra, but she was voting with her heart."

Alcoholism is a progressive disease (a fancy way of saying it gets worse). In Ezra's case, worse meant physical deterioration, blackouts, wilder rages when drunk, and mental illness.

The mental illness sounded, at first, like a metaphor. "I got an evil spirit inside me," Ezra said. "I can't keep it down, sometimes, when I drink."

Hubert had been there; he understood. *First the man takes a drink, then the drink takes a drink, then the drink takes the man.* What alcoholic didn't know about being possessed?

But, as time went by, Hubert understood that Ezra's demon was, for Ezra, utterly real.

"So it was snowing!" Hubert roared, as though, by brute force, he could leap ahead, wrest control of this unruly history. But then he shook his head, realizing that he wasn't there yet, sighing.

"I guess I gotta go back some still. Before it was snowing, it was a blazing, dog-weary August, and I was stopping at Ezra's because I'd told him, just the day before, that I would. He'd only been out of detox, that time, a week, and I was trying to keep an eye on him, take him to some meetings, listen if he had a mind to talk. I pulled into the driveway and saw Anita sitting in the rocking chair on the porch and smiled and said hello and saw then that she was crying, rocking and crying. She looked up and said, 'No sense in taking him tonight. He won't get much out of a meeting tonight.' Anita was twenty years younger than Ezra, but worry and defeat looked to be closing the distance. She looked beat.

"'I'll just say hello then,' I said.

"I found him in the basement. I just followed the racket. He was down there, hammering nails into a two-by-four. He was in his underwear, dead drunk, hair falling in his eyes, going at that board like it meant something—only it didn't. He would fish a nail out of the jar, hold it upright over the board, and try to slam it with the hammer, miss as often as not. The nail would ping out, spinning on the floor. Occasionally he'd get lucky and hit one right on, driving it down. 'Bingo!' he'd holler, a shout of satisfaction. He wasn't making anything, just whopping nails into the board. I didn't think he knew I was there, but then he spoke to me, 'Don't let Anita down here,' he said, not looking at me. 'He's crazy tonight, Hubert. You get her away, you hear?' Bang! He slammed the hammer down again.

WILLIAM BROWNING SPENCER

"'Who's crazy?' I asked, but he didn't hear that, whacking that board in a sudden fury, making it jump."

Hubert was going to speak again, shout, but something caught his attention, a green blur in the air. It was Anita's parakeet, Nigel, flying from one ceiling beam to another.

As Hubert watched, the bird wheeled in the air and descended, landing on Ezra's shoulder.

Ezra hadn't been expecting it, and he shouted, surprised, panicked. He turned, the hammer in his hand knocking over the jar of nails.

The bird took to the air again, a fist-sized fury—and a silver cloud of steel wasps pursued it.

"I didn't know what I was seeing," Hubert said. He saw something, but his mind was way behind what was happening, as though he were a translator thrown off by some unfamiliar, alien language.

The parakeet was harried by a swarm of nails. In less time than it took to tell, this ball of splintered steel engulfed the bird, shot through the air, and slammed against the pegboard behind the workbench, knocking a hanging saw to the floor, nails flying everywhere.

What was left, pinned to the pegboard, looked like a crushed flower made from green and yellow feathers, leaking a blood-red glue. That was Nigel, one wing still ticking reflexively, bristling with bright nails.

"Get out!" Ezra shouted.

Hubert remembered turning to stare at Ezra's sweating, frightened countenance. Behind Ezra, a glittering cloud of nails was rising.

Hubert scrambled up the basement stairs, raced through the kitchen and living room, banged out onto the porch and shouted for Anita to run to the car as he closed the front door behind him.

She ran, knowing better than Hubert, no doubt, the occasional need for sudden, decisive flight.

They were in the station wagon, already moving, already rounding the corner, when she said, "You're hurt."

Preoccupied with escape, he hadn't noticed the throb in the side of his palm. The nail had gone in an inch.

There was a toolbox in the back of the station wagon, and he'd had to root through it and find the pliers.

"Thought I was going to heave, working that sucker out," Hubert said. "Course, it was fear more than pain. I was scared sick."

* * *

IRRATIONAL FEARS

"So it was snowing," Hubert said. That August day had passed and been damped down by reason and distance. But, sitting in the backseat of Heller's jeep while he and Heller and Jim Wallace raced to Anita's aid, Hubert had to fight an urge to shout for them to stop, to turn around.

"Anita let us in when I rang the doorbell. She had that tired look, but, coming in out of the blowing snow, the room felt, for just a second, like sanctuary." The house was quiet, warm, full of cooking smells, spices, onion and oregano.

"He's in the kitchen," Anita said, and she led the way.

"If Anita hadn't felt the urge to take us back there," Hubert said, "things still might have turned out different. But, I don't know. I've thought about it. The way my mind replays it, it always seems inevitable. If it hadn't happened, something like it would have.

"Ezra was sitting at the kitchen table, wearing a white shirt, his sleeves rolled up. He was quiet, looked at us all and nodded. 'Gentlemen,' he said. 'To what do I owe the pleasure of your company?'"

Hubert could see that the man was drunk, red-faced, his composure an effort of will. His words were only slightly slurred; Hubert remembered that struggle for control, like feeling your way through a dark room. There was a cutting board on the table, diced onions like frosted ice chips on the wooden surface. A knife, its silver blade blurred by the brightness of the overhead fluorescent lights, lay next to the cutting board.

A shadow flickered in the corner of Hubert's eye, and he turned to watch something pale writhing on the wall. He saw, then, that the walls were splattered red. He saw the overturned sauce pan on the floor near Ezra's feet. His mind connected the dots (visual to olfactory to visual). The walls were painted with spaghetti sauce and cooked noodles. The noodles were peeling free, dropping to the floor in a grisly simulation of life.

"You've come to fetch my wife, haven't you?" Ezra said.

"Yes," Hubert said.

"A man drinks a little in his own house, just looking for some peace of mind, a little goddam relief, and his wife walks out. Is that right? I ask you, Hubert, is that *goddam standing by your man?*"

There was a noise, and Hubert looked at the table. The knife was beginning to spin.

"Ask her is she ever coming back?" Ezra said. His hands were shaking now, and he clasped them, his eyes bulging, watching his hands wrestle. He seemed unaware of the knife, now spinning more rapidly, the handle going *clack, clack, clack* on the tabletop.

"Ask me yourself," Anita said.

Hubert couldn't take his eyes from the knife. It rose into the air (a miniature helicopter blade), leaving the table-knocking noise behind (replaced by the huff of air being sliced).

Ezra was now looking straight at Anita. Neither of them paid any attention to the knife. They were caught in each other's eyes, like old warriors impaled on twin swords, so full of old antagonisms that they were unaware of the killing steel.

"We are just taking her to her sister's until you get right," Hubert said, hearing his voice rattle with desperation, sounding like a hurried lie.

"I'm not coming back," Anita said. "That's right, Ezra. I'm going for good."

"Bitch!" Ezra shouted. He jumped up, knocking his chair back, trembling like a small dog in a rage. "You think—" He stopped, struck dumb. His eyes widened. He'd seen the knife spinning in the air (or, more precisely, his brain had finally logged it). His voice changed, a hoarse, dead-sober whisper. "Don't move, honey." The blade was moving toward Anita.

"Give me your jacket," Ezra whispered.

"I was wearing one of those big, down-stuffed quilted jobs," Hubert said. "I shucked it off and tossed it to him. I think I understood what he intended as soon as he asked."

Ezra flung the jacket over the hovering blur. "Run!" he screamed.

They all just stood there, silly with shock, watching Ezra clutch at the bottom of the jacket. It strained away from him, ripping, a gray fuzz of feather dust suddenly blooming in the air.

Hubert ran past Ezra, yanked open the fridge door, screamed, "Here!" and Ezra understood what was required, fell backwards dragging the jacket with its upward-straining, rending fury.

He pushed the animated, down-spewing jacket into the fridge and Hubert launched his shoulder against the door.

And, in one last frenzied burst, the knife spun free of its shroud, leaving its slashed cocoon behind to collapse amid jars of mayonnaise and pickles and aluminum-wrapped leftovers.

Anita had turned, was fleeing through the doorway. The knife careened far to her left, powered wildly by its violent escape, scratched and screeched (a frustrated banshee) as it banged against the brick facade behind the stove, then flipped and darted past Anita and stuck, quivering, in the wooden face of the cupboard.

IRRATIONAL FEARS

Hubert saw that Ezra was bleeding, one of his hands cut in his battle with the ravenous knife.

Hubert helped him to his feet. "It's okay," Hubert said.

"Anita!" Ezra screamed, standing up, pushing Hubert away.

"She's all right," Hubert said.

Ezra stumbled past Hubert and through the doorway.

Hubert heard him scream.

"I was wrong," Hubert told them, his voice choked with the dust of old, remembered emotion.

Anita lay face down on the floor. Her husband turned her over, and Hubert, coming into the room, thought she wore a dark scarf.

The knife had, indeed, darted past her as she turned and fled the room. It hadn't even paused as it flashed in front of her flight, had cut her throat in one elegant, mortal second, and she had lost consciousness and tumbled into death as blithely as a child, racing through a long day, falls into sleep in a tangle of limbs.

The ambulance came and they took Anita away. They took her husband too.

Ezra attended Anita's funeral in the company of two orderlies from Winchester Hospital (where he'd been sent for another detoxing) and a young, solemn boy of perhaps ten or eleven. Hubert and his companions testified that an accident had occurred, and the lawyers that Ezra always retained leapt into action, devising a story that was, essentially, true without taxing the court's credulity. In the end, no charges were filed.

Ezra's grief was genuine. He was numb, dead and ancient, a dwarfed husk. It was time, certainly, for him to drink himself to death. The only person he had ever loved was dead, and he was, no matter what any court might rule, the guilty, living one. But he did not drink, at first. Instead, he got out of detox and continued to go to AA meetings. After five or six weeks, he began drinking again, sporadically, and he was always in a rage, drunk or sober, and he was governed by a single, burning obsession: To convince the world that an evil entity had robbed him of his beloved Anita.

"I believe," Hubert said, "that Ezra Coldwell killed Anita. I don't believe in ghosts. Somehow it was Ezra, his rage and drunkenness and craziness, that animated that knife. But he could never look at that, never face up to it, so he told himself a ghost story. We alcoholics are always on the lookout

WILLIAM BROWNING SPENCER

for someone to blame. Ezra blamed an invisible monster. 'An evil spirit killed Anita,' he would say. It was a pathetic self-deception. Then the boy came to stay with Ezra, and that boy…Ezra was already in Hell, I guess, flames flapping round his soul. That boy was gasoline."

"At the funeral—" Martin said.

Hubert nodded. "That was the first time I laid eyes on Dorian Greenway."

ubert stood up, shaking his head. He looked at his watch. "Tell you what," he said. "I'm damn sick of my own voice, and we've still got time to make a late-night AA meeting that will be very instructive. It's called the More Will Be Revealed Group—and it's the best example of Dorian Greenway's influence on AA in this town. Satan…no, better I don't say anything now, and you judge for yourself."

The meeting was held in Harken's high school auditorium. There were probably a hundred people in attendance. Incense burned, candles flickered, a generic sort of New Age music floated in the air (vague, synthetic, faintly asthmatic sounds, "The Universal Star Dance of Asynchronous Time/Space/ Love"—that would be the title of this piece, something like that).

The meeting was already in progress, and a woman in a purple robe was saying, "After they inserted the probe, their leader, whose name is not translatable but, in our time continuum, means One-Who-Can-Multitask-Effortlessly, said, telepathically, 'Earth One, you are the lost goddess of the seventh moon of Mercor, and your memories are waiting for you there. But before you come to us, you must solve your alcoholism, which is a problem, like a math equation. The solution will require four tasks and three mentors.'"

The next man introduced himself as a sex and love addict. He described, in explicit detail, an explosive sexual encounter with a cousin ("very distant and well over the age of consent in many countries"). His wife had discovered him, and he was now seeking a sofa to sleep on until he could rent an apartment or reconcile.

"I am shot through with remorse," he said.

Jack doubted the man's sincerity. Remorse shouldn't come with so much enthusiastic detail. Instantly, Jack reprimanded himself. Let he who is without sin lob the first stone at some poor pervert.

No one in the meeting seemed offended by the man's detailed narration of his sexual encounter (another example of AA's commendable tolerance/indifference).

A skinny woman with blond hair and large, mascara-enhanced eyes told about her dream animal (an otter) and how it had been captured by the white man's death-science and tortured. Her alcoholism was the otter's bad dreams. An angry man spoke of his outrage at having been cloned as a child and cast off, sent to an orphanage. "I was robbed of my birthright!" he shouted. This created some crosstalk (from a man whose psychiatrist had been cloned, and another man who had realized, two years ago, that he was, himself, an "experimental" clone, the nature of the experiment being to determine just how much alcohol abuse a man could endure. At night, when he was sleeping, scientists would conduct a variety of tests to see how he was faring. Not well, in his own opinion).

It was a meeting which, even by AA standards, contained an unnerving diversity. There were the astral travelers, the Elvis worshippers, the white witches, the satanists (Jack sensed a coolness between these two factions despite AA's militant live-and-let-live policy), the conspiracy advocates (Bill Wilson and Doctor Bob had been CIA operatives; Scott Peck was a zombie manipulated by Jesse Helms), and a large astrology contingent. Jack heard the names of strange deities and entities, including Azathoth and Nyarlathotep. He recognized these names from the Happy Roads AA Club.

"So what did you think?" Hubert asked. The meeting was over, and Hubert was driving them back to New Way.

"I don't hold with all the psychological issues stuff," Pendleton said. "I'm not saying I don't believe in it, I'm just saying it doesn't belong in AA. Take that fellow who was going on about what a wonderful human being he would have been if he had had better parents. I don't know. Even with better parents, he might have been somebody you would wish to avoid. There's no way to tell. It's all hypothetical."

IRRATIONAL FEARS

Eunice, still exalted by revelation, said that, although the crowd appeared to be hopelessly lost to heathen thinking, she would love them; she would be on them with love like a bull terrier on a rat, like a tornado on a lake. She would not let up until they were dizzy and sick to their stomachs with the power of her caring.

Ed Tilman said, "There was some truth in that meeting. Lot of chaff, but some truth. Bill Wilson did do some covert work, but none of it was for the CIA."

Jack said he'd heard the names of strange deities—and that he had heard these names before, at the Happy Roads Club.

Hubert nodded. "They got a big dose of that horror writer Lovecraft there. Dorian Greenway had a Lovecraft period when he was going to Happy Roads, so they got the most of that. But he don't stick with any one kind of craziness. One month it's aliens, the next month it's a government plot, the next month it's alternate worlds, the next month it's some kind of old Indian curse. During his Lovecraft period, he wrote a book, something about a pentagram, and that was all Lovecraft, outer-space stuff, but the point is, the thing I've come to believe over the years, is he doesn't believe any of it. He's just trolling the waters for crazy fish, and he doesn't care what he uses for bait, as long as it hooks them. The main thing is, he hates AA. He gets that from his uncle—who wasn't the first alcoholic to hate AA. I call it hating the messenger. People come to AA, sick and full of self-pity; they've been blaming things all their lives, and the next thing you know they are blaming AA. You'd think, to hear them talk, that they caught their alcoholism at a damn AA meeting."

Hubert shook his head. "Some people think we old-timers have grown surly, going off and hiding out in meetings with like-minded, sour old duffers, talking about how the message has been sullied with therapy and cosmic bullcrap. But the truth is, we're just trying to survive. Dorian Greenway has—intentionally, maliciously—set out to tear AA apart, creating dissension with his Clear cult and infecting AA meetings with all manner of alcoholism theories."

Martin Pendleton said, "I could sure do with a soda," prompted by the sight of the Glad Whiz convenience store coming up on their left.

"I wouldn't mind stopping myself," Eunice said.

Hubert turned in, and they all got out.

Jack had no desire for a soda. He considered getting an ice cream cone. But studying the various cones and chocolate frosted bars made him feel low, somehow, as though the rest of his life would be a series of halfhearted decisions (celery or a carrot, an apple or an orange, bran flakes or puffed rice). What he really wanted was a beer. He pressed his face up against a glass door and stared at the siren shapes within. Then he deliberately turned away, leaving his hand prints behind, each finger an exclamation of yearning.

Eunice, escorted by Hubert, was looking at a rack of postcards. Her new enlightenment had brought forgiveness, and she wanted to send her children a postcard, assuring them that she was well and held no grudges and was praying to Jesus that they would be happy and not mired in sin and complaint. She considered getting a postcard of the Glad Whiz convenience store.

"What do you think?" she asked Hubert, showing him the card.

"Well, it will get the job done," he said.

Eunice settled on a postcard of a gypsum mine (located considerably to the west of Harken, in a different state actually). This postcard was very informative, explaining that gypsum (hydrated calcium sulfate) was a common mineral used in the making of plaster of paris, fertilizer, et cetera. The card explained the mining procedure, with historical dates and a chemical formula.

Eunice read the card to Hubert as they drifted toward the Glad Whiz counter where a robbery was in progress.

Eunice stopped reading when she looked up and saw what was occurring.

The same skinny clerk was behind the register and, again, he was drunk. He was smoking a cigarette, the smoke snaking up the side of his cheek, making his left eye squint shut. His arms were raised in the air. He was undulating some, a kind of slo-mo hip roll, like someone full of heroin doing the hula.

"Don't do nothing rash," he was saying.

"Open da rejish," the robber said, sounding chemically challenged himself, wobbling back on his heels. He wore a black hooded jacket, the gun poking the pocket forward in tumescent threat.

Everyone was silent. Jack could see Eunice and Hubert in front of him, Ed and Martin to his right by the sodas.

Jack felt his heart beating faster, thought that images of his past might crowd through his mind. Instead, he remembered a Glad Whiz television commercial in which four singing nuns (polar bears in nun habits, to be precise) sang about the merits of really, really cold beer.

If he were gunned down in a Glad Whiz, these ecumenical mammals might attend the funeral, might sing.

Jack was not happy with this thought. It would be undignified. It made the prospect of dying less attractive.

The Glad Whiz clerk was talking. "I'm telling you, it's not worth it." The clerk suddenly leaned forward, shouted, giggled. "They'll catch you, man!"

IRRATIONAL FEARS

He crushed his cigarette in an ashtray, jabbing angrily, snatched the beer bottle from the counter and took a long pull. "I saw on TV that they are sending all prisoners, every fucking felon, to Texas, yeah, because Texas got a shitload of prisons, everything is a prison, they got like prison *franchises*, and you don't want to be in the slammer in the Lone Star State, no sir. You—"

"Just give me the fucking money, limp dick!" the robber shouted, and he yanked the gun out.

It wasn't a gun though, just a finger pointed forward, thumb cocked rigidly.

"Easy!" the clerk shouted. "Okay. I'm getting the cash."

The clerk began to wrestle with the cash register, shook it, cursed—and leapt/scrambled over the counter, grabbing the robber's simulated-gun arm.

"Muther!" the robber shouted.

They rolled on the floor, grunting. Jack felt that something was missing from this tussle. Of course. *Music*, he thought. A frenzy of overwrought instruments was required. The wrestling-for-the-gun scene was such a staple in movies and television that it was hard to accept this unadorned show. No music. No gun for that matter, although the robber gamely held his index finger stiffly pointed forward, thumb up.

The clerk had the upper hand, though, drunk and self-righteous. He was on top of the robber now, slamming his gun hand against the floor, screaming, "Drop it!"

The robber sighed, went slack. His fingers unfurled, releasing the imaginary gun to the ether.

"Okay then," the clerk finally said, lurching to his feet. "I guess that's that."

The robber sat up. He was gasping for breath. The hood of his jacket had fallen back. A black tie was tied around his right arm. His pants were torn, his shoes scuffed.

"That guy's a member of The Clear!" Jack shouted.

Martin moved quickly, Tilman right behind.

"You're coming with us," Martin said, dragging him roughly to his feet.

On the way back to New Way, the failed robber sat between Tilman and Martin. When asked, he said that his name was Monk. He said that he also had a Clear name, given him by the Gatemaster-in-Waiting, Dorian Greenway. "I can't tell it to you though, so don't ask. It's a secret name, and if I was to tell you, it would call down the wrath of the Otherness that sits at the door of the Flickering Abyss."

He fell asleep then and snored loudly.

WILLIAM BROWNING SPENCER

Hubert coughed. "That fellow's got some potent drugs floating inside him. We won't learn anything helpful from him in his present state, might as well let him sleep it off."

Hubert spent the rest of the drive to New Way relating the last of what he knew about Dorian Greenway and his uncle Ezra Coldwell.

He didn't know much, only that the boy came to live with Ezra right after Anita's death. Some folks said Ezra had hired an investigator to track Eulalia Greenway (Ezra's sister) and induce her to send the boy. Others said that Eulalia (a resident of Fergus, Montana) had written Ezra herself, saying she was no match for the boy, that since her husband had been killed (by a wolverine according to later, embellished accounts), Dorian had been wild.

No one really knew just how Dorian came to live with Ezra. They suited each other, though. You might think that a bitter old man like Ezra would be a bad influence on a young boy, but, in truth, it often seemed that Dorian was the corrupting force, Ezra simply a muddled, beaten fool, broken forever by the loss of his wife.

It was young Dorian who would stagger out onto the porch and scream at AA members when they came to the house. "You stupid fucks!" he would scream. "Damn you all! Get out of here. We don't need your goddam slogans and your steps and your stinking blue book!"

On such occasions, the boy was deemed drunk or (another theory) so psychically linked to his uncle that he manifested the symptoms of inebriation.

Other times, a sullen Dorian would accompany a sick and shaky Ezra to AA meetings where the old man would mumble that he had not killed his wife, that an evil spirit had been responsible. Everyone would listen politely; they'd heard it before. Dorian, silent and seething, would scowl at them all.

When Dorian began attending Harken High, he impressed the other students with his personal style (at this time he was wearing all black, a black jumpsuit, what appeared to be a black bathing cap, black sunglasses, a black cape). The school was not academically rigorous, and, without much effort, Dorian graduated near the top of his class. He could make friends, and did, but he would sever these ties with some act of cruelty that suggested the relationship's goal had always been betrayal. He was a voracious reader of science fiction and horror, speaking in an arcane tongue decipherable only to other geeky, fast-talking SF freaks (at Harken, this group never comprised more than half a dozen students). He never talked to girls, shunned them, in fact, and there was some speculation that he was gay (based almost entirely on the cape).

It was probably Dorian who talked Ezra into buying the gothic mansion when the horror film folk were done with it.

IRRATIONAL FEARS

It was Dorian who saw the old man's mind receding into a dim, inaccessible realm and convinced Ezra to hand over the financial reins while he could. It was Dorian who summoned the lawyers to draw up the necessary documents for Ezra to sign.

In a small town, such prudent legal planning is always seen as sinister, but, in truth, Ezra had no one else to assign his fortune to. His only other relative, Eulalia, had died four years after Dorian came to Ezra. She had been found frozen in a snowdrift (in what was, most folks believed, an alcohol-related death; she'd been drinking all night at the local tavern).

Ezra's mind did, inevitably, crumble, and Dorian blamed it on AA. Grieving, he entered an AA meeting and hurled a balloon filled with pig's blood at a guy named Mort Sedders. Mort ducked, and the balloon burst against an EASY DOES IT plaque. A woman attending her first meeting fainted.

Mort had been Ezra's sponsor at the time of Ezra's last, mind-blowing debauch. Ezra had gone through many sponsors (firing some, being fired by others), and Mort just happened to be the one there when Ezra went blank, his condition diagnosed as Korsakoff's syndrome. The alcohol had tunneled holes in Ezra's gray matter, had finally routed all signs of sentience. The doctors convinced Dorian that there was nothing reversible about this condition, and Ezra was shipped off to Western State.

Dorian blamed AA for his uncle's transformation into a mute and withered husk. He specifically blamed Mort. Six days after the pig's blood incident, Mort didn't show up at Happy Roads, and when folks went to his apartment, he wasn't there. He never was anywhere else again that anyone knew of, and the sheriff had a talk with Dorian. Dorian said he didn't know anything. "Maybe his sponsor knows where he's gone," Dorian said.

Mort's sponsor, a salty curmudgeon who attended an old-timers' meeting once a month (and always said the same thing: "Clean house, pray, help another alcoholic, and keep that rascal in your pants"), was, it turned out, also missing. Dorian's remark seemed fraught with significance in retrospect, but there wasn't a shred of evidence to link him to any crime.

Dorian Greenway left Harken and did not return for almost ten years, finally showing up at Happy Roads with his entourage of white-shirted disciples and his crazy, infectious theories. It's likely that Ezra Coldwell returned with Dorian, retrieved by Dorian from the state mental hospital in Staunton, Virginia.

Rumor had it that Dorian Greenway had acquired a medical degree, had tripled his fortune developing computer-game software, had spent the years in prison, and had been hospitalized for mental illness.

There was, Hubert said, probably some truth in all these rumors.

WILLIAM BROWNING SPENCER

he next morning, Martin gathered everyone in the day room. Hubert was there too—he'd stayed over—and Jack guessed that the millionaire was fighting his natural urge to take charge, deferring to Martin (New Way was, after all, Martin's turf).

"I don't need to be deprogrammed," the Clear member, Monk, said. He was, in the light of day, a lanky kid with a goofy, self-deprecating air, ducking his head, rubbing the back of his neck. "I don't need to be electroshocked or prozacked or nothing. I come to my senses. Anyway, they all just packed up and left. World's supposed to be coming to an end, big what they call Unraveling, and off they go, fuck it, can't be bothered."

"Do you know where Dorian Greenway is?" Martin asked, pulling a folding chair up and sitting directly in front of Monk.

"No, sir, I don't. Our leader slid off without us, not even a farewell speech. Maybe he took a few of his generals with him; I can't say. We got burned out and that was it, done. You can stop calling us The Clear; you can call us The Street, that's where we are living. There's a bunch of us hanging downtown, promoting loose change, sleeping in doorways. We're pretty fucked-up, but that's not our fault. We weren't responsible for our actions, because we were all in a trance state, dressing up like Jehovah's Witnesses, that sort of thing."

"Do you recognize this woman?" Martin asked. He leaned forward, showing the polaroid. It was Kerry's intake ID. Gretchen, New Way's secretary, had taken the photo.

"Don't be expecting something flattering," Gretchen had said. "I'm not a photographer, and this camera takes a kind of greenish, fuzzy snap. I can't help that, and this was never part of my job description."

Kerry's photo looked, nonetheless, radiant, her glow unsullied by the cheap equipment (which did, however, render a portrait of Jack that could have been entitled: *Dead, decomposing indigent, city morgue*).

"Yeah, I recognize her," Monk said. "I heard she was around, that she had returned as was written, but I never did see her." Monk frowned. "Oh, I saw her in the dreams, sure, we all saw her in the dreams. But there was supposed to be other stuff, too. Promises, promises..." Monk's lower lip stuck out. "They kept telling us stuff, and nothing ever come of it. Like, the women. We were supposed to have this end-of-the-world orgy that was gonna get things charged up, ready for the Gate to open. Well, ask me did it happen?" Monk waited, blinking at Martin who glared back, no hint of asking in his demeanor.

Monk spread his hands, palms up, displaying emptiness. "Nope. Didn't happen."

Al leaned forward, his teenage libido instantly alert. "You were gonna have a big orgy for the end of the world?"

Monk grinned, sensing a peer. "Sure. Beer, party favors, a live band, naked women, the works."

Hubert gasped. "This is Anita Coldwell," he said.

Jack turned, as did everyone else. Hubert was holding the photo—he had reached down and plucked it from Martin's hand. His voice was low, thick with incredulity and an earnestness that was like a shout.

"This is Anita Coldwell."

Martin squinted at Hubert. "No, that's one of our patients, the one that Dorian Greenway kidnapped. Her name is Kerry Beckett."

Hubert raised his eyes from the photo. His expression, dazed, faintly annoyed, was one Jack recognized: that of a man surprised by a flurry of memories (a covey of quail breaking cover, right under your feet, making your heart stammer in shock).

"The hair is different here, curlier, wilder," Hubert said. "But...this is the spitting image of Anita, when she was young, high school."

"That would explain Dorian's interest in her. I heard him say, 'It's you,' like he recognized her. I remember that," Martin said.

"I never did see her except in the dreams," Monk said, still complaining. He remembered something, pulled the frayed paperback from his back pocket. He flipped pages, found one he'd turned down; squinted his eyes at the type and followed a sentence with his finger. "Says, 'She will return to stand by the new Gatekeeper, and all her handmaidens will *offer succor* to the faithful and'… That's it right there, that 'offer succor' that's the orgy part, and what? I guess it's canceled, that's what, and I quit a job at Video Vendor for what?" Monk shrugged his shoulders, disgusted, and tossed the book on the end table.

Jack picked it up. *Alcoholism and the Pnakotic Pentagon*, by Dorian Greenway. It was, obviously, a self-publishing venture: Old English lettering on a blue background, a pentagram with pen-and-ink sketches of winged snakes and gargoyles menacing the perimeter and, within, a woman, blindfolded, her arms raised toward a star that radiated squiggly lines. Like many self-published books, this cover promised an unbalanced intensity, the self-absorption of the insane, the incoherence of the unedited.

"What dreams?" Martin asked, leaning forward. He clutched Monk's shoulder. "You saw this woman in your dreams?"

Monk nodded. "Sure. Everybody did. It was what you call a communal dream." Monk was looking nervous. "Should I have a lawyer or something and you say that stuff about anything I'm saying could be held against me in a court of law?"

"We aren't police," Martin said. "We are looking for a girl. We need your help. Tell us about the dreams."

Monk nodded. "Okay. I was gonna leave out about the drugs, but I guess it's cool, huh?"

Martin nodded. "It's cool."

"Well, we'd take this drug, little blue syringes that would be handed out by this bull dyke nurse, and we'd lie flat on mats, and we'd drift off and dream about this girl in your picture there. Different dreams, but always her—only her hair was different. Sometimes we'd be dancing with her, or maybe at the beach, just having fun, you know, but then the dream would always narrow down somehow and we'd be walking down a hall and into this kitchen. There were other people in the kitchen, but they were always a blur, couldn't make out their faces or anything.

"People would be talking, shouting and shit, but their voices would be too big to hear, you know how that can be in a dream, and then we'd see this big knife on the table, and the knife would fill up the room. It would always start to move, to spin, and it would become this white disk, and the kitchen would fade away, just the white disk spinning and then it would be her face and someone would shout, "Run!" just the one word, like a gunshot, and—well, we'd wake up, like that, all of us thrashing around, sick, puking. They had these metal buckets by each mat, because the fuckers knew we were gonna heave. I tell you, the sound of a couple of hundred people emptying their guts is one you don't forget."

Monk was quiet, thinking, then said, "I sort of miss that sound. I know, that sounds crazy, maybe disgusting, but… Well, there we were, all together, you know. I never had a family, hung with Dad some between foster cares, but I was mostly on my own. And the dreams were good, until the last part, when you'd see her face and she'd start to bleed, blood coming out of her nose, her mouth. We knew it was gonna end bad, but it was a whole package, and the part that rocked was worth the rest and besides, it wasn't always gonna be that way."

Monk said there were other dreams too, bad dreams some of them. It had to be that way, according to Dorian. You couldn't go around the bad dreams, you had to go through them to get to the Gateway.

Monk said he thought people died during some of those dreams. The dreams were like real places (a luxury hotel, a foreign city, an office building, a strange, many-roomed hospital), and some people didn't come back, or they came back different, maybe missing something like an arm or maybe just a couple of fingers—no blood (as though the maiming accident were in a distant past and long healed, long forgotten).

Monk couldn't be sure about that, because sometimes he thought that a woman's missing fingers had always been missing, a man's leg always curiously truncated. But, other times, it struck him as strange, and he couldn't get past the strangeness.

Monk was not an articulate young man, and when Martin asked for more detail regarding The Clear's doctrine, Monk couldn't supply it. Since Dorian Greenway routinely changed his crack-brained theories, Monk could be forgiven his confusion. He did say something that reminded Jack of what he had read in The Clear's proselytizing flyer (a document read mere weeks ago and not, as it seemed, in a long dead past). Monk said, "We addicts and alcoholics, we are a tribe, Dorian says, a tribe with some fancy name, and we been cursed with a condition of *unlove*." Monk nodded, offering himself encouragement to continue. "Unlove. Means we got a hole that can't be filled, and it can't be filled with drugs and alcohol and money and sex no matter how hard we try. Want to know why it can't be filled?"

Martin did not seem on the edge of his chair, but he nodded grimly.

"Cause the hole ain't really in this world, it's in another world. It's got to be patched there, we got to go in there and patch it." Monk was nodding rapidly now, looking scared, as though aware that his listeners were way back in the dust of disbelief, looking around, hoping to catch some more credible ride.

"Did this condition ever manifest itself in the people around you?" The voice made Jack turn. Tilman had left his seat on the sofa and was standing in the middle of the room. He was agitated, the flesh of his face almost as white as his mustache.

"I don't—" Monk began.

"You ever see anything like this?" Ed Tilman yanked the black glove from his right hand, unbuttoned the cuff of his shirt sleeve, rolled the shirt up his forearm and extended his hand, palm down, arm stretched parallel to the floor. Shimmering silver holes rolled lazily up and down his arm, like jellyfish made of mercury. His fingers glittered when he moved them, the shape of his hand shifting. The air surrounding his arm seemed imbued with a new, liquid translucence.

Eunice said, "Oh dear." The others stared in silence.

Finally, grimly, Monk said, "I seen it before."

"And what," Tilman said, "was the final fate of those so afflicted?"

"I couldn't say. Not in just every case."

"They melted away, didn't they? Just sort of filled up with holes until there was more hole than human, right?"

"I never saw it," Monk said, swallowing hard. He tried to keep his eyes from Tilman's silver arm, but he couldn't. "I guess that's what I heard."

"Is there a cure?" Tilman asked. "Did you ever hear of anyone being cured?"

Everyone waited for the boy's reply. He gave it some thought, frowning. "Well, we were told that we were doing it to ourselves, that it was an *inside* job, that's how Dorian put it." Monk sighed. "But I don't know as that helped anyone. They just kept thinking they were sick, and…" Monk was rubbing the palms of his hands on his knees, unhappy with the bad news it was his to impart. He didn't say anything else.

Ed Tilman shook his head, rolled his sleeve back down, carefully worked the glove back onto his hand, said, "Well," and turned and left the room.

Soon after Ed left the room, the meeting broke up. Martin wanted to make some phone calls and so canceled group. He told Monk that he could stay if he was willing to go to AA meetings. Monk readily agreed, and Al said he'd show him around. They went off together, Al saying, as they walked out of the room, "I ain't hardly an alcoholic, I'm just here on the advice of my lawyer."

IRRATIONAL FEARS

Hubert said he had to get back, check up on his manservant, McPhee, who was suicidal lately and needed close watching. Hubert and Eunice hugged warmly and at length before his departing, which caused Gates to frown and, turning to Jack, say, "That's called thirteenth steppin. You got the twelve steps and then you got what Mr. Bill W. called the thirteenth step which is the hanky-panky step. Some folks don't care for it, say it will send you to drinking in a wink, but I say it's natural, birds getting on with those bees." Gates shook his head. "Course, thirteenth steppin could kill an old geezer like that Hubert feller. That's his look-out, though, and if you gotta pitch off the deep end sometime, that might be the best way to go."

At lunch, New Way's secretary, Gretchen Payne, sat across from Jack and said, out of nowhere, "I'm in love with Martin, and I've a mind to tell him. What do you think?"

There are days when a theme is in your face, written on every event, and this, apparently, was such a day. Jack told Gretchen that he was not an authority on love, not someone who should be giving advice on the subject. "Probably honesty is the best policy," he said.

"What if I tell him and he is disgusted?" she asked.

"You could say that you were kidding and laugh wildly," Jack said.

Gretchen frowned. "You're right. You're not too great with advice. Where'd you ever get advice like that?"

Jack shrugged, saying nothing, although he could have said that this advice was based on his own experience. In the second grade, he had declared his love for a small, blond girl and her response had been to stick her tongue out, and he had told her that it was a joke and laughed wildly and unconvincingly, and she had said, inscrutably, her brown eyes bright as a ferret's, "Laugh if you must, from dawn till dust," (perhaps something learned from her mother) and she had run away, Jack's heart bouncing after her like a can kicked into a quarry.

Remembering, Jack had felt suddenly exhausted. He excused himself, went back to his room and lay down, rallying briefly for mail call and then returning to his bed where he studied another postcard from his mother. The photo was of some European village, the houses scrubbed white, a blue sky with a sensible serving of clouds, a man in a suit, riding a bicycle, shoulders back, stiff with dignity as though aware of the camera preparing to glue him to historical time. Her mother's scrawled words were few: "Dear Jack—Drat! Had hoped to meet you in D.C. for Thanksgiving—your choice of restaurants—but schedule's in shambles, expect I won't see the New World until Jan. Hope you are well and thriving. Love, Ellen."

WILLIAM BROWNING SPENCER

Thanksgiving? Was that coming up? November, right? Was time flying or dragging?

Dante had, in the middle of his life, found himself lost in a dark wood, not knowing how he got there. Jack wondered if Dante had been a drinking man.

They went, that night, to an AA meeting in Leesburg. Martin said he needed a break from Harken. The meeting was small and dull. Jack could not remember one word, although this was not necessarily a bad thing in an AA meeting.

On the drive back, Jack sat next to Ed Tilman. On the seat in front, Al and Monk laughed raucously. The youths seemed to have bonded instantly and were communicating in primal teen-speak. Al was bouncing up and down, performing a rap song while slapping the back of the seat in front of him. There was, Jack thought, only one delivery for rap, a pissed-off huff, coming down with both feet on the end of each line, didactic and scolding. "It gotta burn like a bitch, you puke in a ditch, rather fight than switch, scratch it when it itch…"

Tilman said, "I've lost faith, Jack."

Jack smiled weakly. He didn't know if he was up to a discussion of faith.

But Tilman continued. "Maybe that's why I took to drinking—and yes, I did do my share of drinking, might as well admit it. I lost faith. We thought we could steer the world, a nudge here, a pat there. Take a madman out, bolster a few malcontents until they bloom into a cause. It was what you call the illusion of control. And that's alcoholism, pure and simple, thinking you can handle it, thinking you just need to switch what you drink, only drink on weekends, only drink in social situations, always remember to eat…all that bullshit.

"Well, I'm weary of it all, and if being sick and tired of being sick and tired is the beginning of acceptance, then I'm on that road. But it seems like a damn long road. Oh, I know, one damn day at a time, easy does it, have a nice day. The thing about this"—he held up his gloved hand—"there's a hunger for oblivion here, termites in the soul. I been having some restless dreams, and I can't remember them when I wake, all I'm left with is the restlessness, that wanting to do something rash. If I had faith that there was a purpose, I'd hang onto that, but I got no faith. It is easy to let go when the thing you've been hanging onto has turned to air. I'm thinking all that keeps me from racing into madness is a scum of fear, and I can feel that being washed away, licked clean by cold waves. There won't be anything to hold onto soon."

IRRATIONAL FEARS

"I know what you mean," Jack said, realizing that he was uttering what amounted to an AA mantra. But it was true. He did know.

Neither of them found anything else to say. In front of them, Monk and Al laughed loudly, filled with the stupid hilarity of immortal youth.

Back in his room, Jack got undressed and fell into bed. He tried to read some, a self-help text entitled, *The Jello Papers*, written by a man named Herman Goldbeam and published by a small press (HG Literary Books, Inc.). Goldbeam tirelessly pursued the metaphor of jello in discussing life concepts. His entire philosophy had, he wrote, come to him during the final days of a rigorous diet, a bad time for him personally (his wife was leaving him and his novel had been receiving particularly vituperative rejections from publishers). At that time, he realized that life was, in its essence, like plain gelatin. The flavoring, strawberry, cherry, peach, was imposed by what Goldbeam referred to as *existential savor*. Happiness, Goldbeam explained, was a cheat. "If you want happiness, go to the movies," he grumbled. Goldbeam said that happy people were "like stinking chocolate-covered doughnuts filled with banana cream pudding."

Jack could almost see Herman, a fat man in his underwear, sitting on the bed, glaring morosely at the refrigerator.

According to Goldbeam, the trick was to embrace your own flavor of sadness, to savor its bitterness. "Substance is sadness," he wrote.

Goldbeam's sentences, strangely impenetrable, must have been fashioned with some art because they did, indeed, fill Jack with sadness. He felt incredibly weary, incapable of moving, as though his bones had turned to jello. He put the book down, turned the light off, lay his head back on the pillow, and closed his eyes. But he couldn't sleep and, finally, admitting defeat, clicked the light back on.

Kerry's desire chip winked on the nightstand where he had tossed it with his loose change.

He touched the silver medallion with the tip of his index finger and instantly felt that curious tingling sensation imparted by the coin. Was this guilt, resonating within?

He picked the chip up, closing his fingers around it. It hummed in the center of his fist. He lay back down, soothed somehow, and closed his eyes.

The vibration eased its way up his arm, slowly turning to music as it filled his body.

It was a country song, not one he recognized, although it had a stark and lonesome quality that suggested a bygone era. "Bartender, bartender, don't tell me that it's closing time," the singer wailed. "She just walked in my memory, and I got to drink her off my mind." A pedal steel mourned for every lovesick fool who ever lurched through a haze of cigarette smoke to search, muddled and blurry-eyed, for the jukebox song that told the truth about heartbreak.

The truth—the gritty, buried-in-the-basement truth—was stupid, melodramatic, insipid. The singer's voice was defeated ("I cain't see nothing but her face. I cain't hear nothing but her voice. Don't tell me that you're closing; I got this memory to chase.").

Some fool, smashed and soaked with self-pity, would play that song over and over, thinking of his own Louise, Mary, Ellie, Jane, Erin, whomever. The hunger got so big it became something else, an object of torture and worship (like Humbert's Lolita, Gatsby's Daisy).

"All I ever wanted was to be loved," Dorian said. He was sitting there in the booth. "What a joke. Uncle never had any love to spare. And those phonies never helped him. They just liked lording it over him. Fuck them!"

A *dream*, Jack thought, as Dorian shrunk, became a child again, his eyes red from crying, his face round, puffy, naked. "Fuck that *unconditional love*! That's a laugh. It's not for nothing. They want to see us crawl."

Tears were running down the boy's face. He picked up the beer mug, drank. He wiped his mouth. "Fight the fear, have a beer," he said, in obvious imitation of someone else. "You love me, don't you?"

"Yes," a voice said, Kerry's voice, her warm and lilting affirmation the answer to all those haunted songs.

Jack woke, sweating, frightened. The desire chip, clutched tightly in his hand, was cold. The clock's red numbers told him it was a long way till morning, and he knew he wouldn't sleep again.

**Part 3
Slip**

he man next to Jack at the bar was saying, "You seen that movie? Hey, you seen it?"

"Huh?" Jack said. He could not say just where he was; he had fogged out and just come back. He was drunk again and had been since the last week in November.

"That movie called *Leaving Las Vegas*," the man said. "You seen it?"

Jack indicated that he hadn't by shaking his head, a bad idea since it caused the man's image to blur into several.

"You should see that movie. It's about a drinking feller, like you and me, who goes to Vegas and hooks up with this really fine-looking whore. He's drinking himself to death, that's like his plan cause he lost his job, but she don't care cause she loves him. She'd do anything for him. I been thinking, maybe I should go to Vegas, someplace where they appreciate a drinking man, don't treat him like dirt. In Vegas, you can be shitfaced, walking sideways, and you can go up to some fine-looking woman and say, 'I'm drunk as a coot, and I'd sure like to dance the naked fandango with you,' and that's it." The man stopped, smiled. He was a small, wizened man with a head full of big, yellow monkey teeth.

Jack squinted, trying to narrow the man down to just one image.

IRRATIONAL FEARS

"That's it," the man said again. "I mean, she's yours. She'll do anything cause she'll understand that you are troubled and can't help the drinking. She won't be always on you to stop, won't be telling you that you are nothing but farts and promises, won't be throwing up her brother-in-law all the time, saying how he went to AA and is now as straight as a goddam ruler."

Jack nodded. He'd been to AA. But he wasn't straight as a ruler. One day, maybe, but not this one.

"I got to go," he said.

"Hey, one more," the man said. "I'm buying." He shouted at the bartender. "Henry. Give us two more Millers."

"Really got to go," Jack said, and he slid off the barstool and headed for the door.

"Think you are too good to drink with me, don't you buddy? Fuck you!" the man shouted.

Jack turned and shouted back, "You're right. I never did like you." Jack was pretty certain he had just met the man, but you never could tell. There were a lot of guys in bars who resembled each other. For instance, bar guys often knew a lot about sports. Bar guys often smoked and told lies about money and women. And bar guys thought that their opinions were inherently interesting (what they thought about Madonna or the Orioles or the stock market or youth today). Bar guys were often ancient and full of complaint.

Hell was probably full of bar guys, moving slow, shouting at the wide-screen TV, arguing about whether it was hotter this year than last, killing whatever charm Hell might have with the tedium of their routines (unwrapping a Slim Jim, lighting a cigarette, sprinkling salt into a beer).

Jack came out of the bar into cold weather. It was night, cold rain falling sporadically. Fortunately, he didn't have to drive in it. His motel was just across the street.

Before going to the motel, he stopped at the convenience store located at the end of the strip mall.

He bought two six-packs.

The oriental clerk smiled, seemed to recognize him, said something and laughed. Jack thought he would have to move soon. This intimacy was insufferable.

Back at the motel, he put the six-packs in the cooler filled with ice. This wasn't a room to write home about—for one thing, it was home. He'd been planning on finding an apartment to rent after leaving New Way, but the way it turned out, there hadn't been any transition time.

WILLIAM BROWNING SPENCER

He lay on the bed, tapped a cigarette from the pack—he was smoking again too—and opened a beer. He turned the television on, muted the sound, and started going through the channels with the remote. He had a lot of channels.

I'm rich with channels, he thought. He flicked along brightly. Here was a made-for-TV movie about the Old West, the acting so bad that it made Jack wince (even without the sound). Here was a man writing on a blackboard, explaining some pyramid scheme (and drawing a pyramid). Here was *It's a Wonderful Life.* Here was some sitcom (spirited old people mugging for the camera). Here was an evangelist, surrounded by the kind of people that made Jack feel sorry for God. Here was a documentary about bees or a man who had gone to live with bees. Here was a talk show, the sofa filled with what had to be basketball players. Here was an ad for cold medicine that soothed the brain by turning it green. Here was...

When he woke, the television was still on, another talk show, kids dressed in black, a rock band or maybe vampires. The clock on the nightstand read 3:20. He got up, went to the bathroom to empty his bladder. Then he went to the cooler and got another beer. He lifted a slat in the blinds and peeked out. It was dead black, rain falling like a sermon, the strip mall across the street dark except for a shivering yellow stain, the parking lot's single intact beacon.

So it was night. A good time to mull things over while drinking a few beers, to calmly assess the situation, to plan one's next move. Here at the Blue Pines Motel—a popular retreat for meditative drunkards.

Oh god of bullshit, Jack thought, *smile on your humble servant.*

Jack had long ago ceased to believe that alcohol would grant him clarity. That was a younger man's dream.

He turned the television off, inadvertently hitting the volume button first and catching a fragment of a line ("We think the audience is ready for something new, something that stretches their..." one of the black-clad girls was saying). *Pop.* Gone.

Jack wished he had a copy of the book, *Alcoholics Anonymous.* He would have opened it at random, discovering guidance in the same way that devout Christians found solace in the Bible.

Jack promised himself he would go to a meeting, get a new copy of the Big Book. He needed a newer edition anyway. The one that he had owned— freely given him by a small, ancient woman at one of his first meetings— was a second edition and lacked some of the insights offered in later editions.

IRRATIONAL FEARS

Jack had discovered that his book was outdated several weeks after he heard a member urge another to read page 449. "You need to get out of all that self-pity and find some acceptance," the man had advised. "Read page 449." Jack had not raced home and read page 449, but, in subsequent meetings, he had heard others refer to this page, and finally he had given it a look.

The book *Alcoholics Anonymous* consisted of one hundred and sixty-four pages of historical material (including a discussion of the program of Alcoholics Anonymous) and another four hundred or so pages containing first-person accounts of drinking and recovery written by members. Jack flipped to page 449 and found himself in the middle of a story entitled "Joe's Woes" in which Joe, hospitalized for drinking, was complaining to his doctor that his wife had only left him with a dollar—and that *dollar*, the doctor informed Joe (weary of Joe's whining), was her *last* dollar. Learning this, Joe felt "pretty cheap."

Jack liked this story, sympathized with Joe (who had had a hard time of it, and had, once sober, lost a teenage son to a trolley accident). But Jack couldn't understand why people were always urging others to go directly to this page when acceptance was an issue. Finally, in a Big Book study meeting, the actual passage was read, and Jack discovered that the third and subsequent editions of the Big Book contained an entirely different page 449—and a different story! This story was entitled "Doctor, Alcoholic, Addict" (a physician's account of his drinking and drugging problems) and contained the popular "acceptance" paragraph on page 449 in which acceptance was held to be the answer to all problems.

Jack found himself strangely troubled by this updated edition. While this new story was instructive, and the new page 449 was obviously important to many AA members, the question remained: *Where the hell was Joe's story?*

Jack imagined Joe opening up a revised copy and saying just that: "Where the hell is my story?" No doubt, Joe would read the new story, read the famous 449 paragraph in which he is assured that absolutely nothing happens by accident in God's world. Would Joe agree, nod his head…in short, *accept* this? Or would he scream, "Where the *blazing hell* is my story!"

Jack drank his beer and thought about Joe, thought about how this was the way of the world. The smooth and easy answers always pushed the awkward, struggling questions into the shadows. The world wanted comfort. The "light" in enlightenment had better be flattering or it wouldn't find a market niche.

Having no Big Book at hand, Jack reached for the book which had been in his back pocket the night he had parted company with AA and his friends at New Way.

WILLIAM BROWNING SPENCER

He opened *Alcoholism and the Pnakotic Pentagon* by Dorian Greenway, turned to the place he had marked and began reading.

It was rough going. A lot of it made no sense. Perhaps it would all be more intelligible to a reader of Lovecraft. Jack had read nothing by Lovecraft. But the words and odd names that were spilled on the pages like loose change, words written, perhaps, in a amphetamine-induced rush, did not seem likely to ever yield to logic.

In a sense, this book felt like certain products of the sixties, dense texts written by gurus and visionaries and read by kids who, fueled by LSD and other mind-altering substances, could tunnel their way into the heart of the message.

Trying to read this stuff and puzzle it out sentence by sentence was another matter.

Jack read:

> **Nyarlarthotep is in thrall to the Outer Gods. The Gatekeeper has sickened and now orbits a single fixed point. This is the key to alcoholism, this spiral, always downward, and the cycle can only be broken by entering the pentagram, navigating by the rules set down in the *Sathlattae*.**
>
> **The full power of the Outer Gods cannot be harnessed until the cycle is broken. She-at-the-Center must be usurped, replaced by a new goddess so that the new Gatekeeper can claim his kingdom.**

Jack flipped forward, read:

> **And Shub-Niggurath, in a burning cloud, told me that I was the chosen and should gather the faithful unto me and proceed so that the Unraveling could bring peace to those afflicted by the curse of the K'n-Yan.**

Jack flipped pages again, and came to one of those stark, autobiographical bits that occasionally surfaced amid all the arcane rhetoric:

> **The Alcoholics killed my uncle. They killed him with kindness and lies.**
>
> **I swore I would not go to them when the curse ravaged my own soul. Instead, I entered the labyrinth.**

Jack put the book back on the nightstand, got up, and went to the cooler.

IRRATIONAL FEARS

He plunged his hands into the ice, fumbling for another beer. He paused, hands in the freezing sludge, and thought, *Am I okay?* He waited for the answer. *Yeah. Fine so far.*

These little spot checks were important. When you returned to drinking, it could get out of hand quickly. You might find yourself hallucinating in a strange bathroom while something, a dog, a bear, a crazy person, whimpered behind the door. That was just an example (drawn from last summer's files). The point was: You'd be some place you hadn't intended to be, and you would not be at your physical, mental, emotional and spiritual best.

Jack retrieved a beer and dried his hands on a dish towel. He went over to the room's only chair, an overstuffed armchair upholstered in green vinyl.

He'd been drinking for about two weeks. Had he been eating? Well, not today. He would eat tomorrow, maybe get a big breakfast.

Jack sat in the chair and lit another cigarette. He knew that the concept of breakfast was enticing when bolstered by several late-night beers. But it would be different tomorrow. Tomorrow he would be sick, shaking, confused. *Who is the President of the United States?* would be a trick question.

He might drift around the room, might throw up some, might contemplate killing himself, joining a Christian commune, calling an ambulance. He might sob helplessly for a while or sit very still attempting to decide if, in fact, the left side of his brain were melting or if his tongue were turning to cheese. He might drink several more beers, shaking violently, then, curiously renewed, feel on top of things, imagine that he had already conquered his alcoholism through some mystical insight. He might call his old high-school girlfriend—a dozen calls first to discover her number—and, when she answered, he might scream, "You bitch!" and slam down the receiver. He might do many things, but he suspected that the one thing he would almost certainly not do was eat breakfast.

There were some potato chips somewhere in the room. Maybe he should eat them while he was thinking about it. He found the bag lying next to the chair. That was easy.

The chips were flavored: steak and onions. Not bad. He stuffed a few handfuls into his mouth.

He spied his reflection in the gold-framed mirror over the sofa. "I know I'm pathetic," he told his reflection. "Don't you have anything better to do than to watch me eat potato chips?"

Jack stopped, scared, suddenly aware of what he was doing. He was talking to his reflection. Didn't he ever learn anything?

Talking to reflections was why he was here, drinking his way toward the nuthouse or death in a motel in—well, the newspaper called itself the

Clifton Clarion but then there was that knockout question: *Where in the gypsy-jesus wilderness was Clifton?*

To be honest, it wasn't just one thing that had sent him here. It was a set of circumstances, tumbling like dominoes.

Maybe he needed to think about that. If he was going to get out of here intact, maybe he needed to have a very precise idea of how he had come to be here in the first place. AA members would approve of that, of assessing the situation, of taking a hard look at his own part rather than easing into some victim role.

Jack saw that Martin and Hubert were convinced that Kerry was still out there somewhere, and they intended to find her. Jack wondered if their aggressive optimism was the result of having been in AA for years (where people did rally in extraordinary ways, derelicts sobering up to become company executives, parents reunited with errant children, hopeless recidivists celebrating years of clear-eyed recovery in the company of spouses and offspring).

Jack had no history of miracles. For him, good times had a way of going bad, celebrations carried the seeds of sorrow, and the most unbearable stories were the ones that began, *That morning, they were very happy. They had packed a picnic lunch; the day was balmy, the sky cloudless and blue.*

The best Jack could do, in the optimism department, was keep silent.

He did this while being chauffeured to AA meetings at night and, during the day, traveling around with Martin, Hubert, and Tilman in an attempt to discover something that might lead them to Dorian Greenway. The drifting, derelict kids who had once comprised The Clear and now sat hunched in doorways or attended AA meetings where they sat, vacant-eyed and silent (like birds returned to a bulldozed nesting site) were no help. Some of them did not seem to recognize the name Dorian Greenway, and none of them knew where he was.

Jack was uncomfortable in the presence of these ex-cult members, noting a girl with two missing fingers, a boy on crutches. Had they left parts of themselves in some alternate dream world? Or had young Monk's imagination been goosed into overdrive by illicit drugs?

In any event, these lost children knew nothing of their leader's whereabouts. Neither did anyone else.

Hubert had hired investigators. They ransacked Dorian's past—and his uncle's as well—hoping to find some clue to his present location. When it was learned that Dorian had lived for several years in Chapel Hill, investigators down there were engaged. Perhaps Dorian was back in Chapel

Hill. A laconic PI in a brown suit, when asked by Hubert to explain why Dorian might be expected to turn up in Chapel Hill said, shrugging, "We go where we been."

Those words had come at the end of the first week of the abortive search for Dorian and Kerry. The investigator had been leaving New Way, preparing to get in his car (a battered, boat-sized Cadillac that suggested past success and present decline). Hubert had shouted the question, and the man had shrugged, answered and ducked in his car, driving away in an oily cloud of smoke.

We go where we been. The words sank to the bottom of Jack's heart, lay in the muck there, a black ooze of experience that recognized such sentiments. We go where we been. Truth. We scrounge up a couple of patterns when we are young, and we ride those poor, blind horses till they drop. Around and around.

Life is short. Nonsense. Life is way too long not to notice its circular nature.

It is embarrassing to do the same dumb thing over and over. Surely there are plenty of ways in which a man can misfire, can sabotage his life. Why not more variety?

But most men and women seemed stuck with a half dozen dysfunctional tricks, using them over and over again. The man who kept marrying women, kept being amazed that they turned into bitches. He'd tell you about it, pausing to leer at the blonde laughing near the coffee pot. The woman who always got mixed up with men who stole her money never learned not to flirt with ex-felons.

Being a human being was embarrassing. It was like being a chipmunk perched on the head of an elephant. You had to make the best of it. If that elephant decided to lumber off to the lake and hurl itself in, you could salvage your dignity by saying, "I'm thirsty; think I'll mosey down to the lake." But whatever you said, you were going to get wet.

We go where we been.

They went, again, to the Happy Roads AA Club. Jack hadn't wanted to go. The strangeness of those meetings, their strong psychic echo of Dorian's Lovecraft days, made Jack uneasy.

Sitting in the overheated, smoke-laden room, Jack closed his eyes and watched, again, as Wesley Parks ran down the snowy steps and climbed into the black van. This vision initiated a mental film fest, all the stock footage of that night, and ended with Dorian Greenway licking Kerry's hand.

It had started here. Jack hated this place.

WILLIAM BROWNING SPENCER

An old man wearing a flat straw hat and a red striped shirt as though dressed for some musical revue talked about the death of his dog with such poignancy that Jack found himself drawn in, in spite of himself, sucker-punched by empathy for someone whose appearance should have guaranteed distance.

The next person to speak, a pear-shaped woman with frizzy hair, told everyone that she was pleased with herself, having, that very day, told her mother to go to Hell.

Everyone nodded. "All right!" someone shouted. Had the woman told the group that she had *refrained* from telling her mother to go to Hell, heads would have nodded with equal fervor, and an "All right!" would have erupted from another corner.

Jack still didn't know what to make of this phenomenon. In sobriety, any change in behavior could be the object of self-congratulation if viewed in the proper light. The woman who had told her mother to go to Hell was applauding her newfound assertiveness. The woman who had refrained from telling her mother to go to Hell could congratulate herself on her restraint.

Human nature was such a knot of arrogance and humility, self-deception and simple decency. In the course of any AA meeting, Jack could find himself being deeply moved, bored, disgusted, amused, skeptical, angry, inspired.

He loved this place. And hated it.

And, for the moment at least, he needed fresh air.

He walked down the stairs, past the framed photos of Lois, Dr. Bob, the house in Akron. He peeked into the social club on the first floor, saw the usual ancients engaged in earnest games of bridge, and kept going.

Outside it was cold, a metallic chill that pressed against his face, numbing the flesh almost instantly. Had there been the slightest wind, it would have sent him back inside, but the stars were out, the air still, and he was determined to smoke a cigarette. Besides, the room within would seem more welcoming if he let this hostile night bite at his flesh for a few minutes.

He thought the unoriginal thought: that life was only appreciated in contrasts. He'd heard someone say at a meeting that, for an alcoholic, the absence of pleasure was pain.

Ouch, Jack had thought.

Emerson had said that the unexamined life was not worth living, but it seemed to Jack that there was an endless, busy-monkey analysis that could, with time, render the examination meaningless. When Jack's self-pity reached out and embraced his fellow humans, he felt sorry for the whole jabbering lot. He saw them crowded on an imperiled planet that was rocketing through the terrifying vacuum of space. They all were talking in rapid-fire, tiny voices, because they had the gift of speech and the curse of self-awareness that drove them to fill up the mystery with words, hoping no one would notice what a paltry defense those words were against the void.

Ouch.

Jack heard it then, a slippery sound that poked at his heart, tentatively, the way a child's finger might test the frosting of a chocolate cake.

The sound of a pedal steel guitar.

Jack blinked at Bob's Beer Palace, the beer-mosaic sign, the parking lot with its half dozen cars.

He found himself walking across the street, his heart beating faster with the certainty that it was—yes—*that* song, the song from his dream. He reached in his pocket and found the desire chip. It vibrated. He clenched it in his fist, his talisman.

When he pushed open the door, he was greeted by the smell of stale beer and cigarettes and ammonia. And he heard, blooming inside his skull, that weary, working-man's voice, pleading, "Bartender, bartender, don't tell me that it's closing time."

He walked into the bar, wending past empty tables in the dim light that excused the dirty floor, the chipped tables, the stains on the walls. Instinctively, he moved away from the few people clustered at the center of the long bar. He moved to the end, pulled himself up on the stool, eased his elbows onto the counter.

"I got to drink her off my mind," the jukebox crooned.

He inhaled the atmosphere, dank, thick as Faulkner's densest prose. It was not a welcoming atmosphere to the uninitiated. To Jack, it was splendid. He realized that the two odors that packed the most punch for him were odors that would not win prizes with any olfactory connoisseur. The second of these beloved odors was the reek of bars such as this. The first odor—the effluvia that was freighted with a thousand fond memories—was the smell of old libraries and small, used bookstores, the smell of mildew thoughtfully masticating the words of geniuses and hacks.

Both of these odors were not, of course, attractive per se. His response was Pavlovian, the excitement engendered by delights to come.

Probably there were many things that were loved, not for what they were, but for what they heralded.

An old girlfriend, who loathed anything alcoholic, had asked (with an air of great disbelief) if he really liked the taste of beer, and he had said, "Absolutely!" But how did you separate the taste from the effect?

WILLIAM BROWNING SPENCER

Jack sat at the bar, quiet. He pressed Kerry's desire chip between his palms. It fluttered softly, like a moth. His heart had ceased beating rapidly and he felt calm. He studied himself in the long mirror that ran behind a carnival of bottles. He was wearing a black sweatshirt, so that his face floated in the dim light, pale, an innocuous, forgettable countenance, the sort of face which might change depending upon what you knew about its wearer (like a newspaper photo of some smiling young man revealed to be, say, a serial killer; now something not-right lodges clearly in those too-blue eyes; those lips, too red, are charged with a rapacious, deadly hunger).

Jack was staring at his reflection when the door behind his reflected self opened and Kerry walked in. Jack turned quickly on the stool. The barroom door was closed, and he did not see her. He blinked at the people at the center of the bar, didn't see her there either. Perhaps she had turned around and walked out, or moved briskly into the hall where the telephone and rest rooms were located.

"Jack."

He turned again, responding to the voice.

He gripped the bar counter to keep from falling, as the room seemed to shift. His reflection was gone from the mirror and a woman in a dark blue dress (with tiny white dots) was sitting where his reflection should have been. Her hands, sheathed in white gloves, lay on the counter's surface, a small black purse at her elbow. It was easy to see how he had mistaken her for Kerry. She was older, and her hair was short, clipped straight across her forehead, but her eyes, her mouth, the strangely exotic curve of her cheekbones, her compact youthful body, all conjured a teenager named Kerry Beckett (so powerfully that some part of Jack's mind expected Kerry to snap into focus, shedding the last vestige of the stranger).

"I'm Anita," the woman said, her rueful expression the work of years. "Do I look like your young paramour? Dorian seems to think so too. I suppose I should be flattered." Her voice was warm, assured.

"Are you—"

She held a gloved hand up. "You'll need to ply me with alcohol if you intend to ply me with questions. A gin and tonic would be nice."

Jack might have, eventually, said something, but she continued. "It's simple, really. You order a gin and tonic, and the bartender will bring me one too. Mirrors, you know, repeat things." She waved her hand vaguely, as though directing his attention to the surrounding world and its ways.

Jack was aware that the bartender was standing off to the left. Jack moved his eyes.

IRRATIONAL FEARS

The man wore a light blue shirt, a black vest and a string tie. His hair was short, blond, his teeth even.

"A gin and tonic," Jack said.

"Cheers," she said when it came, and they lifted their drinks in unison, properly mirrored.

Slip, Jack thought. That's what it was called in AA, this taking a drink after months of abstinence—as though you were walking on ice and had suddenly lost your balance.

His body welcomed him home. Far from feeling guilt or a sense of violation, or the vertigo of falling, he felt warm, solid, centered again.

Anita leaned forward, her eyes already bright. "I can't stay long. Poor Ezra will be wanting to kill me again…oh, that's not fair. He will be wanting to save me, actually. But that's not what happened; I died. We go around and around, but it comes down to that, the sad, dirty fact." She sighed. "It's a great bore, though, being killed over and over again. You don't suppose you could buy me another one of these, do you?"

Jack bought her—and, incidentally, himself—another gin and tonic.

Anita was serious now. "I need your help, Jack."

Jack waited. She continued, "I need you to stop it. Ezra thinks his nephew loves him, but I know better. Dorian is evil. Dorian cares nothing for Ezra. As far as Dorian is concerned, Ezra is just a battery, just a source of power. Dorian would torture a thousand Ezras if he could find a use for their screams. I know Dorian Greenway, I know him the way someone who has been sick for years knows her disease."

She finished the drink, rattled the ice, smiled. "I never drank when I was alive. Ezra drank enough for both of us, and I never understood the attraction. Now I do. In fact, I would like another one, if you don't mind."

Jack didn't mind. He bought her quite a few drinks that night.

He couldn't remember all she said. She talked about her childhood, about an aunt named Harriet whom she had loved. She talked about her parents, hard-working folks who had distrusted a rich man's son like Ezra and had never been able to understand her sticking by him.

Anita Coldwell sang a song she had learned as a schoolgirl (her singing voice was light and girlish), and she recited an Emily Dickinson poem.

Jack thought that she might be rambling some, and that this might be the result of the alcohol, but the gin in his own system may have impaired his ability to follow her.

WILLIAM BROWNING SPENCER

Jack did remember asking her if she were a ghost.

She had chuckled at that. "Worse than that. I'm the ghost of a ghost. And your little girlfriend has come crying and raging into this…this tomb…and she has invigorated us all, made us all just a little more lively. I see you have something of hers."

Jack looked down, saw Kerry's desire chip on the bar in front of him. Jack touched it with a finger. It no longer vibrated, felt cold to the touch.

"I'll pass it along to her."

Anita opened her purse, picked the mirrored medallion up from where it lay next to her drink, and dropped it in her purse, snapping it closed.

Fuzzy-headed, Jack blinked at the counter in front of him. Kerry's desire chip was gone. *Good trick.*

"You have to help us," she said.

"How?" The door opened behind her and someone entered, moving immediately to the left and out of the mirror's frame.

Anita was trying to stand up. "*Need* will collapse the universe. I *need need neeeeeed* you, they whine. This one wants that one wants this one wants that one wants this one wants that one." Her words were slurred. Jack realized that she was drunk. She'd rubbed the back of her hand across her lips, smearing her lipstick, lipstick on the back of her glove. The lids of her eyes were drooping, her features numbed and sullen.

When she stood, Jack stood too, as though trying to maintain their game of mirrored images.

"Where is Kerry?" he shouted, hoping that a straightforward question would elicit a straightforward answer.

The sound of glass shattering accompanied Anita's scream and Jack watched, stunned, as she was propelled across the bar counter, slammed against her side of the mirror, as though it were a windowpane, her face pressed sideways, flat, a dime-sized splotch of blood at the corner of her mouth, her cheek and nose distorted and pale, her eye tightly shut. Her hands were pressed, palms flat and cotton-white, against the glass.

Dorian Greenway, eyes glittering maniacally from a face painted white, clutched Anita's shoulders and pressed her against the glass. He grinned at Jack over the woman's shoulder.

"Hey Alcoholic," he said. "You are some kind of lady's man, aren't you? You don't let a fuck-ing-wo-man-go-by." He thumped Anita against the glass (bottles jangling) in sync with each syllable.

Jack watched as Dorian reached past Anita, out of the mirror's frame, retrieved a long-necked beer, and slammed it against the counter. It broke, beer foam flecking the mirror. He held the shattered neck and shouted, "Discipline! We need discipline if we are ever going to rise above our circumstances. I don't know why—"

Jack leapt the counter and hurled himself, shoulder first, at the mirror. He heard Dorian laugh, a gleeful bark. The mirror held, bouncing Jack, his bones humming. Bottles toppled around him, like glass buildings in Godzilla's wake. Jack clutched a gallon jug filled with amber firewater, and, turning his head away, swung it in a low, wide arc. He heard shouts—distraught, shocked. A scattered surf of glass danced like wind chimes in the air. Glass rain pummeled his neck and shoulders as he spun and crouched.

He turned, prepared to do battle with his enemy, who would no longer be able to hide behind the safety of the glass.

A bare wall greeted Jack, some last shards of mirrored glass still sticking in it. A larger piece of the mirror, a triangle perhaps eight inches long, swung lazily, suspended by a wire, and Jack saw the palm of a white-gloved hand slide down the upside-down vee, each finger drawing a fuzzy line through a pink mist of blood.

Someone tackled Jack from behind, and he staggered forward and fell. Amazing, there were still some bottles standing, and these now joined him on the floor. He turned, saw that the bartender, his features distorted with rage, muscles and veins writhing with aerobic vigor, was raising a meaty fist.

Jack could not be sure what happened next. Conjecture was required. They threw him out of Bob's Beer Palace, obviously. He had no idea why they hadn't called the cops; maybe Bob had an aversion to all authority figures. Or maybe…maybe Bob's was something else, a place that wouldn't bear investigation.

Jack had not gone to jail. He would have remembered that. He remembered being in another bar. He remembered waking up on someone's sofa. An old man was watching cartoons on television. It was morning. The old man was eating fried chicken out of a cardboard bucket.

Jack remembered calling a cab. He could not say if that was the cab that had brought him to Clifton and his present motel. He felt that there were intervening motels, intervening bars, intervening conversations.

Simply put: He had slipped at the edge of the great ocean of alcohol, and the tide had taken him out and he had washed up here, at the Blue Pines Motel.

WILLIAM BROWNING SPENCER

he next morning, Jack did not eat breakfast. Instead he drank several beers and watched a talk show about men who cheat on their wives. The point of the show was unclear, but a number of philandering husbands had agreed to come on the show and confess to any sort of perfidy as long as the television camera was pointed their way. The audience, largely stout housewives (some clutching infants as props), reviled the guests, who responded in kind, one man shouting, "If I was married to you, I'd cheat on you in a New York minute!"

No one on the show was sexually attractive, although Jack realized that saying such a thing out loud in the company of women would have revealed his true brute-lout colors. A compassionate woman might shake her head sadly, say, "You have been duped by the media."

Jack had been to parties where every male libido in the room was lying low. Testosterone would be hissing like a live wire down in a rainstorm, while the men would be shaking their heads sadly at a world so tawdry and immature that a woman's breasts might be used to sell a car or a music video.

Some men had moved entirely into the women's camp, in the hope of enlightenment. These men sought escape from the company of their own crude sex (and, peripherally, a chance to get laid if that were mutually agreeable to all involved and not simply an invasive, male-dominance display).

The audience was howling at a man who was trying to explain that male promiscuity was written into the genetic structure. "Nature don't care about marriage," he said. "Nature's like a used-car salesman, she just wants to close the deal. Here's that sperm, here's that egg. There you go." The man, a thin man with glasses like safety goggles, slapped his hands in hearty explication.

Jack did not, at first, hear the knock at the door. The audience was unhappy and loud, roaring for blood. And drinking beer seemed to deaden Jack's sense of hearing, so that, with each beer, he'd cranked the volume up some (this same phenomenon had often frightened him during his drinking/driving days when, after a night of tooling around the highways in an inebriated condition while listening to the radio, he would climb into his car in the morning, turn the ignition switch, and have his heart battered by the ear-shattering body slam of bad rock as loud as ragged woofers could roar it).

The knock at the door was eventually heard and identified for what it was. Jack realized that he was in his underwear. He found a pair of khaki slacks under the bed and pulled them on.

No one knew he was here, did they? He hadn't, foolishly, given his name out to some chance bar acquaintance, had he?

Jack peered through the peephole but couldn't see anything. He opened the door.

"Mr. Lowry?" the man inquired. He was a tall man in a black suit. His long face was red, hound-jowled, a purple darkness under his red-rimmed eyes.

Jack recognized him but couldn't think from where. The man reeked of whiskey so it was probable Jack had met the man in a bar in the recent, murky past.

The man, apparently sensing Jack's confusion, said, "McPhee, sir. I am in the employ of Mr. Hubert Henslow. I was hoping I could enlist your aid."

Jack recognized the man now. Hubert's tragic, drunken butler, the man Hubert resolutely refused to give up on.

"Please, come in," Jack said, opening the door wider.

"I am sorry to impose," McPhee said, entering the room with an air of deep sadness. "I took the liberty of locating you through my employer's investigators. I was not, strictly speaking, authorized to do so, but, well…" He sat down on the edge of Jack's bed, withdrew a flask from his pocket, unscrewed the top, offered the flask to Jack who declined, leaned his head back and drank deeply. Then, methodically, he rescrewed the cap and put the flask back in his pocket.

WILLIAM BROWNING SPENCER

"How were they able to find me?" Jack asked.

"They didn't say, sir. Perhaps they didn't wish to reveal trade secrets."

Jack nodded. He went to the cooler, fished out a beer, noted that only two remained and yet, in the interests of hospitality, offered McPhee one. McPhee declined.

Jack sat in the armchair, popping the beer. "What can I do for you?" he said, pleased with the sound of the sentence which suggested a speaker capable of powerful, decisive action.

"I know you are conducting your own search for this Dorian Greenway and the poor kidnapped child," McPhee said.

Instantly, Jack was deflated, his grandiosity grounded. It was a lie he had told himself, that he was taking a few days to rally after his disastrous return to drinking and that, then, he would rise heroically to the task of finding and rescuing Kerry. In truth, he had been pursuing nothing but the impulse to drink, to flee, hoping that while he floundered in an alcoholic haze, sober, responsible souls would set the world to rights.

Jack could not tell this grave, sorrowing man the truth. What had Hubert said, something about this man's great tragedy, the death of a wife, a child? Jack lifted the beer to his lips and drank, incapable of revealing his own empty, helpless, and morally deficient state.

"I'm afraid Mr. Henslow is missing—along with Martin Pendleton. Mr. Henslow has not called me in the last forty-eight hours, and this cannot be an oversight. My employer is too meticulous a man to forget or ignore this arrangement. I must conclude that he is being prevented from making such a call. He may be dead." McPhee closed his eyes, surprised and embarrassed by emotion. He stretched his neck, reflexively adjusted the knot in his tie. His voice was under control when he spoke again. "So I believe that my employer and your Martin Pendleton have discovered Dorian Greenway and, presumably, your young lady. It is, therefore, one location we both seek. I thought we could help each other in that search."

Jack spoke before caution could stop his tongue. "I think I already know where Dorian Greenway is," he said. He hesitated, then said, "I've just been afraid, afraid to go back."

Often, it is a single sentence that is blocking the truth, the dead mouse in the drain which, when plucked out by its tail, empties the sink.

Jack didn't feel healed by this one cathartic sentence, but he felt a potential for healing, something like hope firing up within.

Hope or an ulcer.

IRRATIONAL FEARS

ack woke and could not move. He saw the straps running over the cotton blanket, an embrace that locked his arms to his sides. Something skittered across his cheek; he gasped.

"Easy. You're all right," a voice said. Jack turned his head, saw a man sitting up in the next bed, a book on his lap.

"It just takes a while to sort things out after the electroshock," the man said. "It will all come back to you...well, most of it anyway."

"I know you," Jack said.

The man nodded. "See. That's a good start. I'm McPhee, Mr. Henslow's manservant."

"Ah," Jack said. He sensed a whole sea of memories beneath him, as though he were a swimmer buoyed on the waves of some mile-deep ocean. If he ducked under, he would see it all, but the thought of doing so made him sweat, a rancid-butter film of fear.

"Where are we?" Jack asked.

McPhee sighed. "A hospital. The wages of sin. An ambulance brought us here, I'm told. We went on an extended binge, it appears. I suspect that I have finally exhausted Mr. Henslow's patience and am no longer in his employ."

Jack turned away, studied the pale green ceiling. His brain felt like overcooked rice. Jack calmed himself by visualizing white towels spinning

WILLIAM BROWNING SPENCER

in a laundromat's dryer. He was just a child, sitting hypnotized, while his mother was all industry, folding sheets, the smell of heated linen and bleach enclosing them both.

He slept.

Later, when they released him from the straitjacket, when he was standing in the meds line, as patient as a potted plant, he thought, *The unexamined life is just fine*.

His green paper slippers slicked down the corridor with a reassuring rhythm.

He made an ashtray out of clay. A skinny kid next to him said, "That's a pretty good ashtray. You could sell ashtrays like that."

Jack was pleased by the compliment but said nothing. He didn't want to get too close to people who were crazy, didn't want to encourage conversation.

The skinny kid was definitely crazy, saying that he had jumped into a swimming pool full of monsters, been wrapped round with huge tentacles, chewed up by a silver beak, and spit out, landing in this hospital. "How about you?" he asked.

"Alcoholism," Jack said. He was frightened by the young man's madness because (in a way that he didn't even want to look at sideways in a dream) Jack believed the kid.

There were no AA meetings in this hospital, and that was a relief. AA stirred too many thoughts. *Happy the man whose self is unexamined*. This was just a quiet nut ward with an occasional echoing scream traveling the corridors.

In the evening sometimes, Jack and McPhee would sit in the nearly empty dayroom.

The television did not work and neither Jack nor McPhee was much inclined to conversation. They would sit and watch the few other patients (a shuffling old man with a very precise route around a sofa, over a low coffee table, behind the television; a thin, brittle girl with what looked like self-inflicted short hair who rocked in a corner, hissing; and a short, middle-aged man who talked out loud—or, more precisely, spoke into the cardboard core of a toilet-paper roll as though dictating).

Jack felt safe and at peace.

On a slow night, when the dayroom was empty, Jack thought that McPhee looked particularly unhappy, and Jack said, "I'm sorry."

"Beg your pardon?" McPhee said.

Jack felt immediately foolish. "I…well, you don't want to talk about it, I'm sure. I remember Hubert saying something about the difficulties you've experienced, the tragedies."

McPhee looked blank. "No, can't say that it has been anything out of the ordinary. Regular, steady folks, a brother in Cleveland. Never been married, always been a loner, I suppose. But I've been happy in my work, a man who likes having a task and the strength to carry it out."

Jack said no more although he seemed to remember Hubert saying something about McPhee suffering the loss of a wife and daughter.

Jack woke in a sweat, heart racing. He must have been chased through a bad dream, couldn't remember it though.

He got up and padded down the hall to the bathroom. After he relieved his bladder, he went to the sink and splashed water in his face. His face and hands tingled, as they often did these days. As one got older, one adjusted to new sorts of discomfort, strange physical signals, inexplicable infirmities which were far too tentative for any doctor to address.

Jack suspected that really old people had lost touch with what tiptop physical health was all about. An octogenarian might say, "I feel fine," and mean it. If a teenager were magically lifted from his young body and dropped down in the ancient, feeling-fine oldster, the first use the teenager would find for an old man's vocal chords would be to scream, "Aaaaaaaaargh!"

Jack looked up and saw his face in the mirror above the sink. Someone had scrawled red words on the glass—lipstick in the men's room?—and Jack leaned forward. Not English, something…not foreign characters either. Jack stepped back and looked at the whole message:

> DEATH
> IF I DIE WHILE I'M ASLEEP
> NOT EXPECTING IT
> I WON'T BE SURPRISED or
> JUST A LUMP UNDER THE
> SOMEBODY ELSE'S PROBLEM

Jack remembered the backward "E"s. As a kid, they had played this game, Jack and his father. Mirror messages, his father called it. Jack would take the message his father had laboriously printed and race to the dresser and hold the ruled paper in front of the mirror and in the mirror would be some instruction, the next step of the treasure hunt, something like, *UNDER THE JUNIPER BUSH BY THE MAPLE TREE*.

Jack puzzled it out, right to left. It was Kerry's poem, "Death," some of the long lines chopped off by the mirror's edge. Trembling, he moved toward the glass and touched one of the red letters. He scratched with his fingernail but failed to etch a line in the lipstick. How could he, when she had most certainly scrawled it from the other side?

Jack pushed his face against the mirrored glass as though, by pressing hard enough, he might see beyond the limits of the frame.

He was sick, frightened, lost. "Kerry," he whispered. "Where are you? Where am I?"

He rested under the sink, knees pulled up to his chest. He began to feel better. His buttocks ached from the hard tiled floor, but that was the price of a dissociative life style.

Finally, he stood up. The poem was gone. In its place was a new, concise message:

Denial. The first property of alcoholism—perhaps of life itself—this ability to avoid reality, to declare that a wake of destruction (failed relationships, lost jobs, sickness, hallucinations) was nothing more than a personal slump, bad luck, a karmic misstep.

It was a skill, this avoidance, and the best practitioners had honed their craft to such an art that it was reflexive. The actor forgot he was in a play.

How do you get out of denial?

Just saying "Hey I'm in denial" wouldn't do it. Jack tried it, though, leaning over the sink and repeating the words "I am in denial" very slowly and precisely.

Nothing. The faucet dripped; his hands clutched the rim of the sink. Nothing magical occurred. How many times had he sat in a chair, at two in the morning, dead drunk, and said, "I am an alcoholic," and believed the words and thought, "And now I am ready to stop," and walked to the fridge and snagged another beer and opened it, and slugged half of it down in a single swallow, pleased with his new resolve?

Self-knowledge was worthless. That's what they said in AA meetings, said it in a way that suggested they were quoting from text ("self-knowledge avails us nothing").

So.

Jack walked back out into the hall. *Here I am in the nut ward*, he thought. *Mt. Denial Memorial Hospital. Great.*

He walked into the dayroom, empty at this late hour, and flopped down on the couch. He dozed some, woke with something poking him in the ribs. It was a videotape, sticking out from under the cushion.

Jack turned the plastic rectangle in his hands, revealed the title, *Sara*. No.

He stood up. There was a VCR, but the television was broken, too bad, no way to view a video entitled *Sara*.

It will work, Jack thought. *Tonight, the television will work.*

He wanted to hurl the tape against the wall, flee. If this were a dream, if he were comatose somewhere, living in the fitful firing of the last surviving brain cells, he still had choices. He didn't have to play this tape.

He walked to the television and punched the power button. Of course, it flared into life, gray motes dancing, no picture. He turned the VCR on and inserted the videotape which was swallowed, the word *PLAY* lighting on the LCD.

"Hello Jack," Sara said. "I miss you."

Jack sank to his knees, watching. He was chained to this spot now, breathless, full of hot anguish and desire and desperation and any and all emotions that human creatures coveted or scorned.

"Oh Jack, you are in a fine pickle. I won't take the blame for it, you know." She was sitting in a high-backed chair, in a room of feminine sensibilities, a big window, silk curtains drawn, a large vase of roses blooming with a red beyond the monitor's capabilities, color smeared outside the lines. A phone, modern and sleek, sat next to the vase.

"Oh God, Sara," Jack whispered. He reached out, touched the cold glass of the TV screen.

WILLIAM BROWNING SPENCER

"I'm not really here," Sara said. "Not even a video. You are, I guess you could say, talking to yourself, just as poor, crumpled Ezra is talking to himself, just as Dorian is talking to himself. It's very sad, all these long, long monologues. That's the sadness of alcoholism, how the self leaks out and swallows itself."

The telephone began to ring and Sara ignored it. "I don't have time to tell you all about it. Somehow, Ezra started it all. He could make things happen with his mind. His alcoholism cared nothing for this mental power, rode roughshod over it and destroyed him. But his mind was—and is—still busy, still trying, with the megalomania inherent in the disease, to change that one terrible moment when he killed her, killed Anita. He could not change that. There are miracles that God reserves for Himself. Ezra can only replay the moment of Anita's death, driving himself insane with self-inflicted pain. Meanwhile his nephew, drawing energy from his uncle's obsession-driven powers, makes up stories, stories of demons and creatures from outer space—and he infects others with these brain fevers. Your detox mate, Hinkle, caught the Demon Belief, and that's a hard one to shake—it is, after all, Ezra's own—and Hinkle killed himself with the creature he conjured. I guess it didn't look much like suicide from where you were standing."

The phone rang, and Sara shook her head, lifted the receiver. "This too is inevitable, I'm afraid. I've got to take this call."

Jack heard his own voice, small, metallic, self-righteous, coming out of the receiver. Jack knew every sobbing word of the speech, for he had rehearsed it before the call, although, in drinking down the courage to make the call, it had finally been altered some.

Still, he knew what he had said. He had said that he could not go on seeing her unless, that very night, she ended her loveless marriage, told Winslow Janson she was leaving.

Now Sara held the phone to her ear and stared out at Jack. "But Jack—" she said. She waited, nodding. "Yes, but—" She paused again, waited, licked her lips absently. Finally she spoke again. "All right," she said. "I'll tell him. Yes. Tonight. Promise. I'll talk to you tomorrow." And she hung up the phone, blinked at the screen. "That was you," she said.

Jack nodded, numbly. Yes, that was the truth of it. Sara had been reluctant to leave Winslow—the power of inertia, the power of fear, who knows?—and so Jack had felt it his duty to demand and plead. Jack had prevailed. Sara had told her husband. And Winslow Janson had responded promptly, no hesitation on his part. He had killed Sara that same night.

The truth will set you free.

Free to despair.

IRRATIONAL FEARS

Sara was still talking. She spoke as if anticipating his thoughts. "You don't have time for guilt, Jack. There are people who need you. First, you have to leave this place. McPhee has been here before, and he can show you the way. But he is asleep in his heart, and he doesn't want to wake up. You can wake him. It will hurt him. In other circumstance, I'd say let him sleep, but too much depends on his helping you leave. So this is what you are going to have to tell him...."

When Sara had said all she had to say, she said, "I love you."

She was gone then, fading to black. Jack turned everything off and left the room.

"McPhee." Jack whispered into the sleeping man's ear. "McPhee."

McPhee opened his eyes but didn't move. His eyes were the color of a winter sky on Scotland's rocky coast.

"We have got to leave here. This isn't a hospital. It's some dungeon conceived in the minds of Ezra and Dorian."

"Go away," said McPhee.

Jack shook him. "We are prisoners here. We might as well be dead."

McPhee was shaking his head now, sitting up. "We are not dead," he said. "We have food; we have shelter. We are staying away from the drink. In a world of strife and hardship, there's plenty who would say we have it good."

Jack was shaking his head. "We don't have it good. If you don't want to leave, that's fine. Just show me the way out. You have been here before, and you know how to leave."

"You are talking crazy," McPhee said. "And that's your right. This is a madhouse, after all, so talk away. I can't help you." He fluffed his pillow, lay back down.

"All right," Jack said. "I'm sorry."

"Huh?"

"Her name was Katherine O'Leary. You married her in 1978."

"Go away." His voice had changed, cautious, tense.

"Your daughter's name was Kaitlan, but you both called her Keeper as in 'You think this fish is a keeper or is it too small?' Finally, when she was three, she insisted you call her Katie and you bowed to her wishes."

"You have me confused with someone else," McPhee said, but he was sitting up again. He wore blue pajamas.

"No, I don't have you confused with anyone else." Jack sighed. "You were the factory foreman. You were right to fire the man; he was a foul-tempered brawler and a drunk. You didn't drink back then. His name was Adams. You fired him. Anyone would have done the same, but he didn't see it that way, thought it was something personal and decided to retaliate."

"For the love of Christ," McPhee said. "Leave it." There were tears rolling down McPhee's cheeks, but his eyes remained the color of cold February skies.

Jack nodded. "I'm sorry. I just need enough of the truth to set myself free. If you can remember who you are for long enough to help me leave, that's all I ask."

McPhee nodded, pushed himself up. "There's no choosing, once you open the door. I'll have to come with you, I guess. Back to Hell."

"I'm sorry," Jack said.

"Katherine and Katie are dead, murdered by a crazy sonofabitch who knew how to build a bomb. That's the whole story, right there. He meant to blow me up too, and I damn his soul to Hell for his failure to allow for the late shift I always pulled on Tuesdays—*always!*" There was fire in McPhee's eyes when he said this, a devout disgust that would never abate.

Jack waited.

"I don't ever forget they are gone," he said. "Sometimes, in drink or a place like this, there is something that comes over me; I think maybe I can just run along the tracks until I die, not thinking overly much. But there's always something that comes along. This time it's you."

Apologies grow hollow with repetition, so Jack said nothing.

"Come on," McPhee said. "We have to go through Freud's office to get out."

"Freud?"

"Azzam Freud. He's our resident psychiatrist, no relation to Sigmund. He's sensitive about the name, though."

McPhee knocked on the door, and the voice from within, heavily accented, said, "Please. Open her."

"He's Iranian, I think," McPhee whispered as they entered the room.

Jack saw a handsome, dark-skinned man seated behind a large rosewood desk. His hair, black and combed straight back from his forehead, gleamed as though he had just come from the shower. He wore a white lab coat. On the wall behind him was a calendar with a photo of a naked woman lying on a couch. Her pose was more peremptory than suggestive.

"No twos," he said, shaking his head. "I see one and then one. Who has the appointment first?"

IRRATIONAL FEARS

"We don't have appointments," McPhee said. "We just wish to leave." McPhee motioned toward a door behind the doctor. "Really leave."

"Hah. If wishes were the pretty women, we could fornicate with them," the doctor said.

Jack said, "We are in a hurry."

"Ah," the doctor said, standing up. "How can you be patients and not have the patience?" He laughed to demonstrate that this was, indeed, a joke, his laughter articulated carefully (Ha hah ha ho).

"Follow me," McPhee said, racing past the doctor and grabbing the doorknob.

The door did not open and the doctor, his lab coat flying, was on McPhee, hands clutching at his neck.

"No," the doctor said. "You have not achieved the transference or even the insight. You are no good yet. You cannot go so—"

McPhee turned and shoved the doctor, who stumbled and fell. McPhee threw his shoulder against the door. It did not give. Jack ran to help. "On three," McPhee said.

"Help!" the doctor shouted. He flung open the door to his office and shouted into the hall. "Crazy people here! Help instantaneously!"

"Three!" They hit the door together. Behind them, Jack heard voices, shouts. He turned his head and saw three white-uniformed orderlies hustling toward him.

He tumbled into darkness, grabbed at a rusted railing, missed, and somersaulted into the icy night.

"Aw shit," he said (or perhaps only thought).

He landed with a *whump* which he thought he heard before blacking out. (He went to see the Pope, at the Vatican, had to wait hours, sitting next to a woman who kept saying, "I can't believe it; I'm in the fucking Vatican!" Finally, the Pope came out. The Pope looked a lot like the alien in that movie called *Alien*. The resemblance was uncanny, actually, and threw Jack off balance. "What do you want?" the Pope asked. Jack said, "I would like you to consider the possibility of declaring 'Aw shit!' some sort of official, authorized prayer. It's short, heartfelt, and is often uttered just prior to death. It's popular…" Jack realized, with some dismay, that the Pope's second set of teeth were trembling in a disconcerting manner.)

Jack woke. He had fallen onto a dirty mattress, lying flat behind the dumpster (perhaps the Pope had, despite appearances, been receptive to the prayer concept). Above Jack, a fire escape clung to a brick wall.

Jack saw McPhee. The man was lying facedown (dressed in his black suit, no pajamas in this world).

WILLIAM BROWNING SPENCER

Jack ran to the man, knelt down. "McPhee." Slowly, Jack turned the tall man over. There was blood on his forehead.

They had tumbled from their alternate-world asylum to land next to the dumpster belonging to the Happy Roads AA Club. Jack called an ambulance from the club's pay phone and, enlisting the aid of AA members, brought McPhee inside.

Jack wondered if McPhee had had time for his own prayer on the way down. If so, it had probably been answered: He was dead.

Jack called New Way from the hospital. Aaron answered.

"Jack!" Aaron said, delighted. "I can't tell you how glad I am to hear from you. We have been in positive *turmoil* out here. You would not believe it. Martin is gone, went off with old Daddy Warbucks or whatever his name is. *Hubert!* How could I forget? Eunice is going around wringing her hands like Lady Macbeth, sighing 'Hubert, Hubert, Hubert.' And Gretchen is no better. 'Martin, Martin, Martin!' She and Martin just declared their undying love for each other, and now he is gone. Well, I suggested that there might be a connection, and I thought that girl was going to scratch my eyes out. *Turmoil.* And those teenagers ran off—bound for trouble, I'm sure. Well. Where are you, honey?"

aron came and got Jack. "You don't look so good," Aaron said. "I bet you have been neglecting your vitamin supplements."

Jack confessed that he had been drinking since leaving New Way.

"Well," Aaron said, "I'm sorry to hear that." He ran his hand through his flaming hair. "Fortunately, today is a brand-new day."

Aaron flew down the road, taking the country turns without braking, perhaps in homage to the absent Martin (another fearless driver). Jack pined for Hurley detox's Earl Simms who drove as though the whole world were a school zone.

Jack got back just in time for group, which was being led by Gretchen.

"I am leading this meeting because I am staff," Gretchen said. "And I know Martin would want us to continue until he returns. My primary expertise is in word processing and accounting, so you are just going to have to bear with me. I know you would rather have Martin here." She paused. Her eyes, round and wide, blinked behind her glasses. "Well, so would I," she said. "So would I!" She took her glasses off and sobbed into her hands. Eunice got up and walked over to the sofa and sat down next to Gretchen and hugged her. Eunice's eyes were red, and she started sobbing too. Their shoulders shook as, locked in a sisterhood of sorrow for their missing men, they wept.

"This ain't doing nothing for me," Gates said to Jack. Gates seemed to have gotten darker, smaller and angrier since Jack had last seen him. "This ain't helpin my alkyholism one bit."

It wasn't a big group: Aaron, Jack, Gates, Ed Tilman, and the two women sobbing on the sofa. Their numbers had been pared down. *We are the…survivors*, Jack thought, although the first word that had come to mind—and been discarded for its negative connotations—had been *dregs*.

Gretchen regained control of herself and led group.

When Jack confessed that he had been drinking, she hit him with a rolled-up *People* magazine.

"That's no way to lead group," Tilman snapped. "Get ahold of yourself, woman."

"Oh, I didn't hurt him," Gretchen said. "Did I hurt you, Jack?"

"That's not the point," Tilman said. "It's not professional. It's therapeutically unproductive." Jack noted that Tilman still had the black glove on his right hand and that he rubbed his forearm a lot, as though scratching an itch through the fabric.

Gretchen's voice quivered. "I'm just trying to carry on. I just…"

"Don't anyone be cryin," Gates grumbled.

Jack interrupted. "I don't think it is another group therapy session we need in any event," he said. "I think we need to settle on some course of action that gets Martin and Hubert and Kerry back."

Everyone agreed. Since it was almost time for dinner, they decided to hold their council of war on full stomachs. Group was adjourned.

Jack drifted into the rec room and Tilman, seated on a sofa in front of the TV, turned and shouted, "Jack. Come over here. Look at this."

Tilman had been watching a local news broadcast. He had wanted to find out what the weather was up to. Interest in the weather, like the conviction that you have left the house without turning off the stove, was something that increased with age. "I'm getting old," Tilman had told Jack. "I need to get the weather three, maybe four times a day."

So Tilman had turned the television on and discovered a local news announcer, a sharp-featured, pretty woman in a suit who was smiling fiercely (and probably thinking, *What am I doing on this cold, windy fucking mud flat?*). She was speaking into the camera. Behind her, bright yellow and red tents were going up amid much industry, big trucks and canvas tarps flapping.

IRRATIONAL FEARS

A pond, its black water rippled by gusts of wind, shivered with colored lights.

"It's going to be a big day in Harken, Virginia, tomorrow," the announcer was saying. "An estimated thirty thousand folks will be attending the four-day Whole Addiction Expo. Last year, this event, the recovery event of the year, was held in San Francisco, a logical choice. But what brings the Whole Addiction Expo, and its dozens of celebrity writers, actors, singers, and recovery experts, to Harken? The answer is local millionaire and philanthropist, Dorian Greenway, who is with us today. The Expo will be held on his property. Only weeks ago, Mr. Greenway was the victim of arsonists and many thought that the event would have to be rescheduled but…"

Jack blinked in disbelief.

"Yeah," Tilman said, nodding his head. "I just plopped down here, turned the TV on, and look. What's this load of crap?"

Jack's nemesis, Dorian Greenway, wearing a blue windbreaker, was nodding his head, smiling. "Oh, I wasn't about to cancel," he was staying. "We lost the house, but all the other buildings are intact—and I'm told there will be no problem heating the tents. The Expo is personally very important to me. I've had my own problems with addiction, and my uncle…well, Harken is a small town, and everyone in Harken knows his story, and all I can say is his tragedy has become my cause. I want to see alcoholism and drug addiction defeated in my lifetime."

The interviewer smiled at this wrap-line and said, "So just what is the Whole Addiction Expo? Let's go back to the studio for a look at an event that could easily be called the Woodstock of the nineties."

Jack thought about Dorian Greenway, philanthropist and millionaire, welcoming the world's recovery community.

What the hell? Jack thought.

The news show ran interview clips of some famous folks scheduled to attend the Expo. A celebrity actor named Alan Cort, who had been chemically clean for three months and was completing a book entitled *My Struggle with Darkness, My Commitment to Light*, said he just wanted to help people. Brad Budge, author of ten self-help best-sellers, touted his latest, *Twelve Steps in Twelve Days*. He was a large man with a beard, very serious. "I want the whole world in recovery," he said, frowning at the camera.

There were people hawking vitamins, crystals, dream therapy. A man with a round face and long blond hair, dressed in Native American garb, beat a drum and chanted. He was identified as Owl Laughingfire, author of *Drums to Recovery*.

WILLIAM BROWNING SPENCER

A stern, dark-haired woman glared at the camera and gestured with her cigarette. "Addiction is a feminist issue," she said. She nodded her head violently. "Exactly. Somebody's got drugs, somebody needs drugs. That's about power, right? Where are women in any power struggle? The bottom. Male dominance equals drugs, that's the equation." She glared at the camera, nodded her head, sucked on her cigarette.

A popular spiritual guru named John Mahler (author of *The Astral Kiss*, *The Astral Kiss Diaries*, *My Search for the Astral Kiss*, *The Astral Kiss Workbook*, *Beyond the Astral Kiss*, et cetera) said, "Addiction is a product of imperfect perception. As though I were to look at you and see the suit you were wearing and not see you. Addiction is a manifestation of spiritual confusion, mistaking fabric for essence."

Tilman aimed the remote at the television and turned it off.

"If I were evolution, I'd be ashamed," Tilman said, and he got up and left the room.

At dinner, everyone was subdued. Dessert was banana pudding, and Jack found himself thinking fondly of Wesley Parks and wishing the counselor had not been dragged off to an alternate world by a mad dog. Missing someone you never liked is one of the top seven signs of an impending breakdown. Jack realized he would have to watch himself, keep a very close eye on his mental health.

After dinner, everyone sat around the dining room table. Jack brought them up to date, beginning with that moment when he had left the AA meeting at Happy Roads and drifted across the street.

"Bob's Beer Palace," Jack said. "That's where Dorian Greenway is. At least, that's where he was. He might not actually be inside the building. I mean, it may just be a sort of doorway to where he actually is, where he goes. He may be in some sort of alternate dimension created—*made possible* might be more accurate—by his uncle. I spoke to Ezra's murdered wife, Anita Coldwell—well, a simulacrum of her, I guess—and I've since thought about what she said, that Dorian was using his uncle as a kind of battery. I think Ezra is the source of psychic energies that Dorian can harness to his own ends."

It was rough going explaining this, and Jack couldn't read the expressions of his comrades. "I don't know if Dorian and his uncle are still at Bob's Beer Palace, but I know they were there. I know because that's where I was headed with McPhee. I have no memory of what happened once we got there. I know I woke up in a straitjacket in a mental ward that doesn't exist in this world. Obviously, McPhee and I encountered Dorian, and he sent us there."

IRRATIONAL FEARS

Ed Tilman spoke. "Okay. Fine. Assuming Greenway is still holed up in that bar, what are we going to do about it? You don't know how it went last time, but you know the result. There you were in a straitjacket. If we all go breaking down his door, what's to keep the lot of us from waking up in straitjackets? And maybe, this time, there won't be anyone to lead us back, to say, 'Wake up.' What are we going to do different? You don't even know what you did last time except that you obviously didn't slip up on the man's blind side. He saw you coming."

Jack nodded. "McPhee and I were both pretty drunk. I expect we may have acted rashly. We'll use caution this time. Happy Roads AA can be our base of operations. We'll have to trust that more will be revealed once we have the lay of the land."

Ed was shaking his head. "You are saying you don't have a plan."

"Not yet. I think we need to drive to Happy Roads, take it from there."

"Okay," Tilman said, "but let me make a phone call first. I don't have any authority, but I've still got some friends."

Aaron parked the van in the lot, and they all walked across the street to Happy Roads. Overhead, a helicopter diced the cold night air.

Tilman looked up. "Those boys move fast," he said. He turned to Jack. "If two crickets are humping behind the dumpster, those guys up there know about it."

There were about ten people downstairs at Happy Roads. Four of those people were playing bridge, silent, serious players with no interest in small talk. The others—except for a man reading a newspaper in a far corner—were clumped around the television.

The whole surviving rehab had come (Aaron, Gretchen, Ed, Eunice, Gates and Jack).

Jack steered them to a table and took out a deck of cards.

"I have to make another phone call," Tilman said. "Give me a quarter."

Jack fished a quarter from his pocket and handed it to Tilman, who tossed it jauntily in the air, caught it, and was already moving toward the pay phone.

"He's a spry old muther," Gates said. "And up to something."

By the time Tilman returned, Gates and Gretchen had already gotten into an argument about the poker game underway.

"Eights and black threes are always wild," Gretchen was saying.

WILLIAM BROWNING SPENCER

"That ain't poker," Gates grumbled. "That's old-maids-in-a-closet and that's for chillun and simple people. We are playing honest poker, ain't nothin wild but your gamblin heart."

Tilman was smiling when he sat down. "I just checked on the operation. Here's the lowdown. There are four people at the bar—probably regulars, probably not involved. Then there is the bartender and his girlfriend. Upstairs there are two men; both have weapons, automatic rifles. All the rooms appear to be empty except for one with a bed. There's someone in that bed. It's a three-bounce shot, so that's the best they can do."

"Ezra Coldwell," Jack said.

Tilman grinned. "People can bad-mouth the government all they want, I'd say my old coworkers did us proud."

"Guess you didn't work for the postal service," Jack said.

Tilman frowned. "That's a joke, right?"

"Well, yes," Jack said.

"There are places you don't want to tell a joke like that. Not every post office is what it seems, and some of those postal workers with machine guns weren't firing blindly."

Tilman regarded the others at the table. He stood up. "You folks go on playing your game," Tilman said, smiling at Eunice (who, if Jack wasn't mistaken, was furtively studying Gretchen's cards as they were reflected in the glass of a framed serenity prayer). "Jack and I will be back shortly."

Tilman clapped an arm around Jack's shoulder and led him outside. The helicopter was gone; the sky full of stars. Bob's Beer Palace looked welcoming, the words *Miller Lite* scrawled in a blue neon script just to the right of a small, square window full of golden promise.

"I went ahead and made an executive decision," Tilman said. "Didn't have time to consult you." Tilman sat on the steps, fumbled for a cigarette, found one and lit it. He stared at Bob's Beer Palace. "You don't have a lot of helicopter traffic in Harken, so they were bound to get suspicious. I told my boys to get the hell out, come back quiet."

Tilman shot Jack a look that seemed fraught with meaning. "This is a hostage situation; they got Martin, Hubert, Kerry. There's only one word for the sort of response you want in a situation like this." Tilman was squinting at Jack. "Decisive," Tilman said.

"Decisive?"

"Exactly."

Tilman offered a cigarette to Jack. Jack shook his head. "I'm trying to quit," he said.

IRRATIONAL FEARS

The front door of Bob's Beer Palace opened, and a dark figure leaned out, waved, and ducked back inside. Ed Tilman stood up. "Come on," he said. "Looks like we got the ball."

Jack followed.

"Commander," one of the men in black said, smiling. He balanced an assault rifle in the crook of his right arm.

Tilman nodded, looked around. "So, John? How are we doing?"

"Everything secure, sir. We have a guard on the one in the bed."

"And the others?"

"All down."

Ed nodded, turned, and headed for the stairs leading to the second floor.

Jack followed. "Down?" Jack said. "He means dead, right? I thought you said the people in the bar had nothing to do with any of this?"

Ed started up the stairs, one veined hand on the banister. "I said they *probably* weren't involved. We had to move fast here," Tilman said. "It's too bad about those people. Seeing as how we are both alcoholics, undergoing treatment, it might make sense to view those recently departed in the context of alcohol abuse. If they had stayed away from the enticements of Bob's Beer Palace, they'd be alive now."

"Those were innocent people," Jack said.

"Let's not wallow in guilt," Tilman said, reaching the top step. "Alcoholism is a disease, we both know that, and I'm not about to take responsibility for every alcohol-related death that comes down the pike. This the room?" Another soldier nodded and moved away from the door.

Kerry.

She lay on top of the bed, her arms at her sides. She was wearing a blue dress with small white dots. Jack recognized the dress; it was the same dress Anita Coldwell had worn when she had sat across from Jack, drinking gin and tonics in the bar's mirror.

Kerry's eyes were closed, and she looked different. Her hair, Jack realized, was cut short, was... Jack reached down and removed the wig to reveal a shaven head. Kerry opened her eyes as he did so, smiled lazily. "Hey, Jack," she said. She turned her eyes, "Ed."

They helped her up. She wobbled a little.

"You are going to be okay," Jack said.

Kerry smiled wanly.

Downstairs, one of the soldiers wrapped a jacket around her shoulders.

"Let's get out of here," Jack said.

WILLIAM BROWNING SPENCER

 had a dream about you," Kerry said. They were back at New Way, sitting in the dining room. It was one in the afternoon, the day after Kerry's rescue. They had just finished eating lunch.

Jack smiled encouragingly.

Kerry smiled back. "Yeah. I dreamed that you had been drinking again and that you wound up in a mental hospital. I could see you, through a window or something, but you couldn't hear me when I shouted. You just shuffled along, looking so sad and sort of, well, stupid, like I wanted to kick you. I decided to write my poem on the window, hoping you would see it, maybe—I don't know, you do things in dreams that aren't entirely logical, you know—and, sure enough, you saw my poem, and you shouted, *Where am I?*, and I knew, I knew where you were, although that was kind of crazy, like something I'd heard in a meeting, you know."

"You took your lipstick and wrote on the window," Jack said. "You wrote, *You are in denial.*"

Kerry blinked at Jack, her mouth half open. Jack wanted to touch her lower lip with his index finger, but he was fairly certain that giving in to this impulse would shock and appall the girl.

"How did you know that?" Kerry said.

"Because I did drink again, and I did wind up in such a place. Because..."
Jack didn't know how much to tell. Kerry remembered very little about the
last weeks, and what she did remember was floating up in fragments she
identified as dreams. Jack thought it was probably best to let this
remembering continue its slow, piecemeal materialization. She was dressed
in jeans and a sweatshirt now—and had abandoned the wig.

"I kind of like this look," she said. "What do you think?"

"You look good," he said. It was true. She had the high cheekbones,
regal bearing, and youthful insouciance to carry off this shorn state. Seeing
her, hairdressers would despair.

Ed Tilman came into the dining room and said, "There's something
you need to see on television."

Ed had rounded everyone up, and he sat them down in front of the
television. He knelt down and popped a tape into the VCR. "I want to get
this on tape," he said.

A man with a mustache was saying, "...epidemic of religious persecution.
In fact, these bombings are not, as was first surmised, motivated by religious
zealots. Churches were only incidentally the targets. These bombs were, in
fact, detonated in church basements for the purpose of disrupting and
destroying meetings of Alcoholics Anonymous. The New York bombing
and the videotape that came in its wake have confirmed this."

Jack watched as the newsroom switched to the press conference that
occurred after the bombing of the Alcoholics Anonymous General
Service Office.

"One fatality," a grim-faced public servant was saying. "Yes. One of the
officers on the governing board of Alcoholics Anonymous, Dr. Bradley
Blackburn."

The room was packed. A reporter shouted a question. The man at the
podium leaned forward. He hadn't heard. The question was repeated: "Was
Dr. Blackburn a recovering alcoholic?"

The room was silent, the whir of activity suddenly stilled. Jack could
feel the tension in that faraway room.

"No, Dr. Blackburn was not an alcoholic," the man said. The audience,
many of whom obviously *were* recovering alcoholics, breathed a collective
sigh of relief. Someone even laughed, a reflexive release of tension.

"But alcoholics were certainly targeted," the spokesperson said, ensuring
an atmosphere of grave attentiveness. He said that Blackburn had probably
triggered the bomb, which had been hidden in a desk. Had Blackburn not

been working late, the bomb would probably have been set off the next morning, at which time it would have accounted for quite a few people—most of them alcoholics.

The news show returned to its local moderator, who ran the video sent to a New York television station hours after the GSO bombing. Ed leaned over and whispered in Jack's ear, "I've seen this a couple of times now. I think it's our boy."

The video was grainy, the man's voice—perhaps intentionally altered—mechanical and crackling with static. The man was wearing camouflage fatigues and was seated in front of a blue wall upon which a white AA symbol had been painted. He stared at the audience through slits in a black silk hood. He apologized for the mask. He could not, he said, divulge his identity. To do so would be a violation of an AA tradition. He was an AA member and it was his sacred duty to remain anonymous at the level of press, radio, and film.

"It's not commonly known," the man said, "but in the late sixties there was a plot to assassinate Bill Wilson, the cofounder of Alcoholics Anonymous. Dedicated AA members felt that the man who had started AA was now leading it astray. He had written the Twelve and Twelve, a text many felt was heretical. He was advocating megavitamins, taking LSD. He was leading AA into pop psychology, trivializing its triumph, subverting its truth.

"Well, word of this conspiracy got to Dr. Bob Smith, AA's other founder, a solid, simple man who loved AA with a dog's sweet loyalty. I'm not sure how he got wind of it, but I wouldn't be surprised if he was simply approached. There was every reason to believe that Dr. Bob might be in sympathy with the would-be assassins.

"Dr. Bob said, 'Don't do this thing. If you do it, you'll have to do it over my dead body.'

"The whole plan fell apart. Everyone loved Dr. Bob. So it didn't happen. If it had, well maybe we wouldn't have to be taking the measures we are taking now."

Jack listened, horrified. The man, who described himself only as a trusted servant, said that he and other concerned members were willing to give their lives to regain the sanctity of AA. In an emotional display—his body was shaking—he shouted, "No more inner children, no more emotional dumping, no more special interest, no more New Age bullshit. Back to the Steps! Or die!"

He calmed himself, turning away from the mike, hunching down. He grabbed something from the table, but Jack couldn't make it out. His

IRRATIONAL FEARS

shoulders rose, a sigh perhaps, and then he turned back to the camera. His voice was altered, deeper. "The backsliders cannot be coddled. Some will say, 'What about *Live and Let Live*, that sentiment enshrined on the wall of every AA meeting place?' I say, when order is restored, when the patient is healthy again, *Live and Let Live* will be relevant again. Now we are at war. Hard measures are required. There is nothing arbitrary about our vengeance. If you are an AA member, and you can honestly say that the AA meetings you attend have not subverted or distorted the teachings laid down in The Big Book, then you have nothing to fear. If not, may God have mercy on your soul."

This man was claiming that his group was responsible for the bombings presently occurring in at least four states: Virginia, New York, Maryland, and Pennsylvania. Another group, calling themselves Enlightened Recovery, had already responded, taping a message which they sent to the same New York television station.

This video message could not be shown, since its speaker was wearing a Mickey Mouse mask, and the networks feared the massive litigation Disney could muster. But the text of the speech was read: "We will not turn our backs on progress. We will not cower in corners while fanatical AA fundamentalists attempt to bomb us back into the Dark Ages. We will embrace all legitimate, caring recovery alternatives, including nonrepressive AA. And we will retaliate against those who would intimidate us." ER was already claiming responsibility for several New York City bombings and the destruction of a fundamental all-men's group in Reston, Virginia.

"Here's what I want you to take a look at," Tilman said when the broadcast was over. He rewound the videotape he had just recorded. He punched *PLAY*, saw that he had rewound too far, and cued the tape forward until he was well into the terrorist's diatribe. Tilman punched play again. "...New Age bullshit. Back to the Steps! Or die!" the terrorist said.

"Watch here," Tilman said.

The hooded man turned away from the camera, grabbing something from the table. Tilman pushed the pause button, holding the frame. "That's one of those inhalers, like for asthma," he said. "It's black. I've only seen one other black inhaler."

"Dorian Greenway," Jack said, remembering that night, Dorian on the stairs.

"Yeah, he's turning away to take a hit. See him shiver? It's quite a jolt."

"The voice doesn't sound like Dorian," Jack said.

WILLIAM BROWNING SPENCER

"It doesn't. But we know our boy is a high-tech kind of guy. Laying down a different voice, someone else's or a synthesized one, isn't going to tax a guy like Dorian."

Ed Tilman rewound the video and played it again. "That's Dorian Greenway. I know it."

"Jesus," Jack said.

"More like the Antichrist, I'd say." Tilman flopped down in a chair. "If that's Dorian Greenway—and it is—there's one thing you can count on."

Jack waited, but Tilman apparently wanted him to ask, so Jack asked. "What?"

"There's not a word of truth in what he's saying. He's not interested in preserving the purity of Alcoholics Anonymous. Hell, this is the same Dorian Greenway who is promoting that carnival of craziness called Whole Addiction Expo."

"What is he up to then?"

Tilman shrugged. "Maybe he really is the Antichrist. If so, then sowing dissension is what he's about, driving us all toward the chaos of Hell. You read his book, that alcoholism pentagram nonsense, what do you think?"

"Revenge," Jack said, realizing, as he spoke the word, that it rang with truth. "He wants to destroy Alcoholics Anonymous itself. He holds it responsible for his uncle's ruin. He intends to bring it down. He said as much, he said..." Jack fumbled for the quote. "He said...'AA, that empire of falsehood, will unravel. In the Great Unraveling, the Old Ones will return and only the just will survive the righteous anger of the Dark Gods.'"

Tilman nodded. "I expect Greenway numbers himself among the just. And, like most of his kind, he doesn't count too many by his side."

Tilman sighed, stood up. "I guess I better make some phone calls. I don't like to ask my friends for favors, and it seems that's all I've been doing recently, but if Armageddon is upon us, I guess I don't have to worry about accruing obligations. When I get back, maybe we should think about driving over to the opening of The Whole Fucking Addiction Expo. Maybe I can find a good stress management book."

Part 4
The Unraveling

he Expo was mobbed. Terrorist threats had not, apparently, stopped anyone from attending—and may, indeed, have prompted some to come that would otherwise have stayed at home.

"It's that stubborn streak," Ed Tilman said. "Just try warning an alcoholic off."

Young people wearing fluorescent orange vests were guiding cars to parking places in a roped-off field.

There was a fifteen-dollar entrance fee, which Aaron tried to get waived. "We are a county rehab," Aaron said.

"I got to have fifteen dollars a head, unless your head is under twelve years old," the kid in the booth said. "That's just the way it is."

"I got it," Ed Tilman said. "This party is on me."

They got out of the car and walked up a hill. Jack studied the crowd. Quite a mix, he thought. There were aging hippies, gray-haired, the men looking dazed but game, the women (many with children in tow) looking weary in the manner of women who have seen too many feckless men. There were upscale couples with upscale kids, sturdy with privilege, and older folks looking tentative (*where were the crafts?*), and teenagers, much-pierced and tattooed, in costumed clumps, and fat men in overalls wheezing their way up the hill with red-faced purpose. There were dogs too, racing through the chilly twilight, barking with indiscriminate joy under the banks of blazing yellow lights. Dogs, Jack thought, were suckers for any sort of crowded outdoor event.

Live music was being broadcast from overhead speakers. A rock band was covering an old Stones song, taking some liberties with the lyrics. A shrill, preadolescent voice whined: *I can't get no self-actualization, though I try, and I try, and I try.*

A clump of teenagers, jostling and joking, saw Kerry, and a girl wearing a rhinestone dog collar shouted, "Sinead! That's Sinead!"

"That ain't Sinead," her companion said.

"Is too!"

"Is not! Sinead grew her hair back."

"Well, she must have cut it off again. I'm telling you, that's her."

"Is not."

They kept at it until Kerry turned and shouted at them. "The Pope's a murdering dog!"

"See," the first girl said, looking smug. "It is Sinead!"

Jack turned and frowned at Kerry. "Cut it out," he said. Kerry smirked.

There were booths with people selling cotton candy, glazed apples, hot dogs. Another booth sold balloons and dolls and T-shirts.

Jack stopped at a booth that sold something called a Pocket Sponsor. It was a little calculator-sized device with a small LCD screen. It was, Jack thought, fairly sophisticated. Set it in the OLDTIMER mode and the tiny screen spelled out straightforward messages like, "Keep the plug in the jug" and "One day at a time." If you clicked on the GURU mode you got more elaborate stuff like, "The unfolding of any event is neither right nor wrong; it simply is. The event is always God-manifest; it is in the context of self that the world is altered, judged, found wanting."

This same booth sold a board game called Chemically Challenged. A player could choose his addiction (alcohol, narcotics, glue, PCP, marijuana, cocaine) and then draw cards from the pile of his choice. A marijuana card might read, "Dude, your girlfriend has been gone for two weeks! She is not coming back, man! Speed King's Carry-Out Pizza called. You are fired. Lose two turns." A PCP card: "You shot your dog. He was your best friend, asshole! Pay dealer ten self-respect credits." Alcohol: "No insurance. Go to social detox. Cigarettes stolen. Go to AA meeting in van. Admit powerlessness; collect First Step card. All other players must hug you."

WILLIAM BROWNING SPENCER

Ed Tilman came up to Jack. "My people are here," he said. "The guy eating cotton candy. And that guy with the plaid jacket, standing in line for the Bad Trip ride." Tilman held up a cell phone. "They get a line on anything, they'll let me know. In the meantime, we might as well look around ourselves. Everybody stick together."

They all entered a big yellow tent. Gates was, as usual, complaining. "This ain't got nothin to do with nothin," he said. Gretchen patted his arm, absently. She was trying to be supportive, but her eyes kept sifting the crowd, as though Martin Pendleton might be standing in line to get his picture taken with the cardboard cutout of Bill Wilson or buying a gag beer bottle (you squeezed it and a snake popped out) at the Drinking Novelties booth.

Jack marveled at the entrepreneurship on display in the various booths. He stopped in front of a sign in bold red caps announcing Sam and Martha's Cut Rate Detox. A cheerful man in a sweatsuit introduced himself. "Sam," he said. "You in AA?"

Jack supposed that the Expo was a place where that sort of question could be asked without giving offense. Jack said that he was, yes.

The man handed him a business card and said, "Well, might be you'll come across a wet drunk that needs drying out. You'll take him to every hospital in Northern Virginia, Maryland, and D.C., and they won't, any of them, take him. 'He don't have insurance,' they'll say, or 'He's been here before, and we aren't taking him again.' That's when you might say to yourself, 'Hey, that fellow gave me his business card at that Whole Addiction Expo.' You might take that card out and give me and Martha a call. We are an inexpensive detox alternative. We got alcoholism tapes, relaxation tapes, vitamins, Gatorade, television (with cable), and AA speaker tapes. Martha and me are both recovering alcoholics. I can relate to hangovers, withdrawals, paranoia, panic, DTs, hallucinations. I'm a good listener. I don't take it personal if you don't laugh at my jokes. When you are feeling better, I drive you to AA meetings. I'm even working on a mild electroshock device that will work wonders on a nervous person. That's still experimental, you won't find it in the brochure, but I could have something by next March."

Jack was impressed.

At another booth, Eunice bought a wallet with the serenity prayer stenciled on it. "I'm getting this for Hubert," she said, fiercely cheerful, daring anyone to say that Hubert had disappeared, that he could be dead—dead and in another dimension, a dozen times dead.

Everyone smiled, like it was a good idea, and Gretchen said, "I bet Martin would like one of those wallets," and fumbled in her purse for the cash.

IRRATIONAL FEARS

Jack felt the usual swirl of conflicting emotion. He marveled at this aggressive optimism and trembled at the shadow of the giant jackboot descending to crush it.

At the back of the tent, standing at a lectern in a roped-off area, a large woman in a frilly dress was speaking. Her topic, according to the upright sign at the entrance to this enclosed area, was, *WRITING THE RECOVERY ROMANCE*. She was identified as Hermoine Radcliff, the author of over thirty recovery romances.

She had attracted a good-sized audience, mostly women, seated in a dense thicket of folding chairs.

"Plucky," she said. "You want a plucky heroine. She is a survivor, a tough cookie, and she doesn't let life get her down."

Someone in the crowd raised a hand. "In the novel I'm writing, the heroine marries a recovering alcoholic at the end. Is that all right?"

Hermoine Radcliff looked thoughtful. "That's being done these days. I'm told that Jessica LaVerne does it, and her novels are quite popular. I..." The woman smiled ruefully. "Well, I'm old fashioned, I guess. When it comes to marriage...well, I like to think that my girls can do a little better than that."

Jack moved on as another woman rose from the sea of folding chairs and began to explain, in some detail, the genesis of her unpublished novel, *Breath Mints for Breakfast*.

The night wore on, taking on the fragmented quality that Jack associated with his college days and trips taken on acid of uncertain lineage. He felt anxious and disoriented.

They entered one of the white buildings, drifted through rooms of addiction-inspired art. Jack moved quickly past a room where young people were reciting angry poetry. He paused and peered into a room identified by a hand-printed sign: *SOBRIETY LAUGHFEST*. There were seven people in this room, and the six sitting down clutched note cards, were, Jack suspected, novice comedians awaiting their turn at the mike. An elderly man in a black cowboy hat was speaking. "Low bottom. That's when the room you rent has roaches that do hits of Black Flag to get going in the morning. Low bottom. That's bragging about the fancy cardboard box you used to live in. Low bottom. That's..." No one was laughing.

Ed Tilman came up and said, "I just got word that something big is being powered up, underground. Subterranean turbines are kicking in. My man's worried. He wants to know what all the sound and fury is for."

Jack stared at Tilman.

Tilman nodded. "Yeah. I think he's right to be worried. I think we never really shut this place down properly. Greenway's mansion burned down, and maybe the machinery sustained some damage. But most of it was underground, I bet, and if it wasn't triggered to blow, it's still there. It is up and running now, humming away under a lot of happy addicts. I don't feel good about this."

Jack didn't either. He remembered the roaring hurricane machines, the turbulent air misted with blood, the churning swimming pool, huge tentacles flaying the blood-black water, naked cult members plunging to oblivion.

There was not a comforting image in the lot.

"We are supposed to meet my man over by the Bad Trip ride," Tilman said. "I say we leave the others here. They will just be a liability if things get ugly."

"Gretchen," Tilman said, turning to New Way's secretary, "you and Aaron are in charge here. Try to keep everybody together. Jack and I will be back as soon as we can. We will meet you over there." He pointed to a blue tent where signs announced a dance (with live music by a band called *Freddy and the Unfortunates*). Later there would be a drawing for prizes and some lucky young woman would be elected Whole Addiction Expo Sobriety Queen.

"Where are you going?" Kerry asked.

"Ed wants to check out an underground power source. He's worried that Dorian is planning something unpleasant for everyone."

Kerry frowned, looked troubled. "Jack," she said. "I just remembered something."

Jack waited, raised his eyebrows, the silent signal to proceed. Kerry clutched his arm.

"I just remembered. I'm in love with Dorian."

"Kerry, he kidnapped you. You are the victim of—"

"Just like that," Kerry said. "I don't feel dizzy or dreamy or excited or sick or…or anything. I just remembered that *I love Dorian*. It's sort of like in a dream when you remember you should be in school, but you are not, in fact, or maybe you are in school, naked, in the hallway, but you haven't been going to classes all fall and it's almost Christmas and…well, you know. It's just a *surprise*, remembering."

"We have to get going," Tilman said.

"Kerry," Jack said, gripping her by her shoulders and staring into her eyes. "Dorian Greenway is your enemy. He has tampered with your brain. Any feelings of affection you have for him are the product of chemical and psychological tampering."

IRRATIONAL FEARS

Jack expected instant outrage, perhaps a physical attack. People were loyal to their emotions and did not welcome logic in these matters.

Kerry said, "Well, sure. I'm not a fool. I know I've been tampered with. You should give people more credit. Love is always somebody up to something sneaky, *somebody* fucking with you."

Jack was about to say something more, but Tilman had turned and was walking, briskly, away. "I've got to go," Jack said.

Kerry waved. "Be careful," she shouted.

They found the man waiting for them at the entrance to the Bad Trip ride. He was standing quietly, ignoring the two guys who were fighting, wrestling in the cold. They were drunk. This was, Jack reminded himself, Harken, Virginia, a town where people who were not actively in recovery were generally drunk.

A well-dressed woman in an expensive gray parka was leaning down, explaining to her equally well-groomed towheaded children—twins?—that the combatants were under the influence of alcohol. "Their judgment is impaired by alcohol," she said. "They are probably alcoholics. They should not be despised for their behavior. Alcoholism is a disease and not, as people used to think, a moral failing. Jonathan, Michael, can you say *al-co-hol-ism?*"

Neither child attempted to. They fixed their grave blue eyes on the brawlers.

Suddenly, the two young men stood up, staggered away from each other. "Fuck you!" the one shouted, turning and running down the hill. "Double fuck you!" the other screamed, racing after the first one.

"There's those damn prodigal sons," Ed said.

Jack nodded, nonplused. The fighting teens had, indeed, been Monk and Al, both of them looking much the worse for wear.

"They are going to have to look out for themselves," Ed muttered, turning toward the waiting agent. "We have more pressing matters."

The man in the plaid jacket was big. He held a small computer, the size of a paperback book. He consulted the screen and said, "It's definitely underground. Southwest of here, maybe two hundred, two hundred and fifty yards."

Ed nodded. "Yep. That would be under the house." Ed frowned. "Soldier, we don't want whatever is down there to get up to full power. How do we get to it?"

The man nodded. "It looks like this ride goes down there. I've been around once, and it looks to me like you could get off the train near the vomiting gargoyle and you'd be close. There's a walkway along the tunnel. I saw a door."

"What's this 'vomiting gargoyle?'" Ed asked.

"Just that," the man said. "You'll see what I mean."

"Okay. Jack and I are going to take a look around. In the meantime, I'd like you to rustle up some explosives, something compact but with plenty of punch, and bring it back here. I want it within the hour. Will that present a problem?"

"No sir," the man said.

"Good," Tilman said. He turned to Jack. "Let's go for a ride."

Tilman snapped the bar in front of them. When the cars began to move, he punched the button on his watch. "I haven't been on one of these fun-house rides since I was a teenager. Wanda Meeks threw up on my shoes. I didn't mind. She was pretty as a pinup, and the act was sort of intimate, like a bond between us. I guess almost anything can seem an erotic overture when you're young and randy."

The cars suddenly lurched forward and down a sharp incline, into darkness. People squealed (there was, as always on such rides, a large contingent of young couples). Wind, generated by fans to heighten the effect of speed, fluttered Jack's hair, nipped at his hands.

Strobe lights flashed. Jack was in the midst of a party, people bouncing to techno pop. A woman in a tiny black dress moved through the crowd, directly toward Jack, her lips bright red, her hair white-yellow and flashing like neon in the staccato light. She opened her mouth and said (the words amplified by speakers hidden in the tunnel walls), "Try this!" She held out her hand, a pink square of paper. The music picked up the words: *Try this try this try this try this*.

The dancing people disappeared into darkness. Jack was at another party, giant faces looming toward him. A man with silver hair was leaning forward, his face the size of a truck, the pores of his flesh like potholes in a bad road. Sentence fragments came from his mouth, cold bits of boring stuff ("deconstruction...paradigm...we see...context...a bias of relevant...my dissertation...feminist studies..."). Very realistic, Jack thought—and containing an insight into the nature of bad hallucinogenic trips. LSD produced the reality break, but the dislocation took an unpleasant turn when the catalyst was—yes, this seemed irrefutable—professional academics, graduate students, professors (people already immersed in a hellish, mind-numbing alternate world). The combination of bad drugs and a suffocating closed system produced temporary psychosis.

IRRATIONAL FEARS

Here we go, Jack thought, as they plummeted into darkness again. He found his heart was beating faster, realized that he was getting a little too caught up in the moment. *This is just a ride*, he told himself.

He was in an empty room. It was breathing, the walls expanding and contracting. He was doing that, his breathing. *Uh-oh.* It stopped. *I'm dead.*

No, he wasn't. But he couldn't breathe because he was underwater. Fish came in through the windows, fish floated across his lap. And snakes, sea snakes.

I don't like this ride.

Darkness. A blinding light. Lots of balloons. Nope. Not balloons at all. Floating heads. Well, balloon heads. The balloons exploded like glittering Fourth-of-July fireworks.

The ride seemed to go on and on. They would fly down dark inclines in darkness. Hearty folks were still shrieking and laughing, but there were some who were sobbing.

They traveled deeper into the earth, through various tunnels. There was the tunnel of tentacles, the tunnel of screams, the tunnel of flashing lights, the tunnel of zombie nuns (or perhaps penguins), the ghastly tunnel of friends (in which huge white faces leaned forward and their amplified voices boomed, *IT'S GOING TO BE OKAY OKAY OKAY* or, in voices stretched tight with terror, *JUST DON'T PANIC PANIC PANIC*).

Finally, the car slowed. Jack had the sense that they were deep within the earth. He could hear the slow drip of water, feel the earth-rock indifference press against his shoulders, the back of his neck.

There were carvings on the walls, gargoyles, lizard heads, bats. Stone hands, reaching, imploring, sprouted from a chiseled relief of tangled serpents.

They turned a corner, and Jack saw the giant stone head of a squat and toadlike gargoyle, grinning. Floodlights illuminated it as it leered from high on the wall.

The ride's passengers were quiet, subdued as they passed under it.

It opened its cavernous jaws as they passed, and the air was filled with a mighty retching. The sound sent a queasy, sympathetic shiver through Jack's flesh. Eels churned in his stomach.

Green, glowing vomit poured down onto the passengers, who were shrieking now. Jack put his hand up to protect his face from this otherworldly bile, and caught one of the green, luminous crepe paper streamers with his hand. A mass of glowing ribbons covered his feet.

Everyone was laughing now, the raucous laughter of relief.

WILLIAM BROWNING SPENCER

"This is where we get off," Tilman said, clutching Jack's shoulder. "The old vomiting gargoyle landmark." Tilman looked at his watch. "Fourteen minutes, twelve seconds," he said.

I'm not doing this again, am I? Jack thought as he followed Tilman along the narrow, stone-cobbled walkway. He could hear the laughter of his fellow passengers dwindling, already distant and faintly inhuman, transformed by the subterranean air, the corridors of stone.

Tilman had turned and was ascending a steep stone stairway. Tiny blue lamps mounted on the wall created small orbs of light in the dark.

Jack would leave one beacon and, pressing the palm of his right hand against the cold, sweating stone wall, begin a halting, laborious climb to the next dwarf moon.

"Let's hope it's not locked," Tilman said, the words floating down to Jack.

Apparently it wasn't. The door unleashed the sound of vast, malevolent machines, the furies of physical law tortured on racks of unreason, inertia defied.

Jack, remembering, resonating with terror, followed grimly.

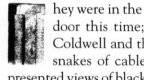hey were in the control room again. There had been no guard at the door this time; they had met no one on the journey here. Ezra Coldwell and the hospital bed he had inhabited were gone. Thick snakes of cable littered the floor. The banks of video monitors presented views of black-and-white corridors and rooms, empty of humanity. Four screens on the top flickered with life, and Jack saw that these were scenes from the world overhead, where the Whole Addiction Expo presented a panorama of activity. On one of the screens, a dance was in progress.

Kerry was in there somewhere. So were five or six hundred others, a writhing mass of humanity animated by inaudible music.

Jack noticed that another screen, in the middle of the bottom row, was jumping oddly. It was a shot of an empty corridor, twisting as Jack watched, turning to reveal a row of black, sinister machines, another long corridor. A door was growing larger, curiously familiar, this door… It was opening— there were two people in this room, you could see their backs, one seated in a chair studying a wall of video screeeeee—*Jesus!*

Jack dove for the floor, rolled. *Ka-pow, ka-pow, ka-pow!* Glass shattered. Jack heard Tilman shout, "Christ! It's us, Martin!"

Silence. Jack peered up from behind the overturned chair.

WILLIAM BROWNING SPENCER

Martin Pendleton stood in the doorway holding the rifle.

He stared openmouthed at Ed Tilman, turned and blinked his bewilderment at Jack.

"What the hell are you guys doing here?"

"We are trying to rescue your sorry ass," Tilman said. "You might want to stop trying to kill us while we do it."

Jack sat in a chair and shook.

"Gave you a scare, I guess," Martin said. "Sorry."

"If that weapon hadn't had a video camera mounted on it—or if you'd turned the damned thing off—I'd be dead," Jack said, pointing to the shattered monitor. "That's where my head was."

"Well, I said I was sorry," Martin said. "I didn't expect to find you here."

Martin added, in his defense, that he'd been disoriented recently. He and Hubert had been in some sort of strange mental ward, although it was never clear just how they had gotten there in the first place.

"Hubert and I were looking for Dorian Greenway; next thing I know, we are in a hospital. It's a bogus hospital, doesn't feel right. Nobody seems to know anything; the staff doesn't know your name or your diagnosis, the resident shrink can't speak English. That was all authentic, nothing out of the ordinary there, but I still had this feeling that the place wasn't really a hospital. I spent most of my time playing checkers with a crazy shrink; he'd fly into a rage when he lost."

"I was in that place, too," Jack said.

"Small world," Martin said.

"Funny we didn't see each other."

"Probably weren't supposed to," Martin said.

Ed Tilman had come up. "Where's Hubert?"

Martin shook his head. "I don't know. The hospital lights started going on and off. I thought there were generator problems, electrical storms, who knows? Next thing you know, I'm not in my hospital room. Hubert's gone. So is everyone else. Or maybe it's just me who's gone. I'm here. Machines are roaring like Hell. I walk out into the hall, and this rifle is just lying there, propped up against a chair. I remember this place, remember those sonsofbitches kicking me in the head. So I grab the rifle. I'm walking down the corridor, and I hear voices…"

"Shoot first, ask questions later," Tilman said.

Martin glared at Tilman. "I suppose you are perfect."

IRRATIONAL FEARS

"Wait a minute," Jack said. He was looking at the video screens again. Ordinarily, he wouldn't have spotted her; the images were too small. But of the five women (all wearing white swimsuits) who were standing on the stage, she was the only bald one.

"Is there some way to enlarge this?" Jack asked Tilman. "That's Kerry."

Tilman moved to the console. "There should be a remote for the camera," he said.

The screen went completely blank, blipped back on and slowly panned across the crowd. Tilman cursed softly, fiddled with the controls. The camera came to rest on the stage again, and the field of vision narrowed as the five contestants grew until they filled the screen.

Tilman turned a dial, and the young women blurred into fuzzy cybershapes, then snapped back into triumphant focus. Blue ribbons were draped diagonally across their bodies, reminding Jack of the sideways slash within a circle, the symbol of nullity that meant NO (*No smoking, No food or drinks*, et cetera) and which could have meant, in this context, *No thinking what you are thinking regarding these nubile bodies*. But it didn't mean that at all, quite the contrary. So sharp was the picture that Jack was able to read the letters on the ribbons: *MISS SOBRIETY QUEEN 1998 FINALIST*.

How the hell had Kerry gotten mixed up in this? And how, for that matter, had she done it so quickly? Granted, she was an alcoholic, an addict, and a teenager and therefore vested with an almost supernatural capacity for mischief, still...

The emcee stepped in front of the girls. He was holding the mike in one hand. Although the image was soundless, Jack could see that the man was singing, his mouth an O, his right hand stretched out in a corny, theatrical gesture. He wore white face makeup, red lipstick, a top hat, a tuxedo, a large red bow tie.

Jack recognized Dorian Greenway. Which explained Kerry's involvement certainly (*I remembered I love Dorian*).

"We've got to get back—" Jack said. He stopped, distracted by a motion in the full-length mirror on the wall. The yellow lights that outlined the mirror were unlit, several of them broken.

The mirror was not reflecting the room. It was a window on a long corridor, a hospital corridor with green walls, a brown-tiled floor, much polished from use. The ceiling lights cast yellow pools on the floor.

WILLIAM BROWNING SPENCER

Far down the corridor, doors so distant they were the size of a matchbox banged open and a figure came running out of the white glare, running toward Jack, sprinting down the middle of the hallway, bare feet slapping the waxed floor so solidly that Jack's inner ear supplied the sound of flesh smacking the tiles (in defiance of the mirror's uncanny silence).

Jack stumbled toward the mirror as Anita Coldwell, wearing a gray hospital gown, a cloud of white gauze wrapped around her neck, reached the mirror, pressed her entire body against it, and shouted.

Jack could hear nothing.

She slapped the palm of her right hand against the glass, shaking her head, furious.

Jack leaned close, pressed his face against the glass. Nothing. Behind him, the room was filled with the sound of doomsday machines, but the mirror was inviolate, a vacuum sealed against her screams.

Jack backed up. "I can't hear you!" he shouted.

She shook her head, impatient, and slapped her palm against the glass again. Jack was struck by how much the woman resembled Kerry. Anita looked younger, wilder in her rage, and the wildness seemed to summon the teenager's image.

Jack shook his head. "What?" He had realized, suddenly, that it was not impotent rage that drove her; there was meaning to the slap of her hand against the glass. She was pointing with her other hand; her eyes, alive with purpose, were focused beyond Jack.

Jack turned, saw Tilman standing there. "What does she want with me?" Tilman asked.

"I don't know—"

But Tilman was moving closer. "Damn, I think I do know," he said. He pulled the glove from his hand and walked toward the mirror. His hand seemed made of glass.

Anita Coldwell was nodding her head violently (*Yes, yes, yes*).

Ed Tilman stood staring in the glass, staring at this beautiful, determined woman. Flecks of blood were melting through the gauze scarf, blooming like tiny wildflowers through snow.

Anita slapped the palm of her hand against the glass and held it there. There was no possibility of mistaking her expression, or what she wanted of him.

Ed Tilman raised his glittering, crystal hand. "For the record," he said, "I'm not happy about this."

IRRATIONAL FEARS

He pressed his ghost hand against hers, leaning across, right hand to right.

The glass rippled from their palms. Anita seemed immersed in silvery water. "Jack!" she shouted, the word entering the room like a rock thrown through a plate glass window.

"Anita are you all right?" Jack shouted.

"Of course I'm not all right," Anita shouted back. "I've been dead for years. I suppose I'm the good part of Ezra, trying to make amends. It may be too late. Listen!"

Jack glanced at Tilman's face, saw that the man's features were a grimace of pain, the flesh white. His whole body seemed to stretch away from the glass, trembling.

"Ezra is dying," Anita said. "When he's dead, that's it, game's over, we'll never see his like again, with luck. He's been replaying my death for decades—this, incidentally, is the emergency room part—and somewhere in that obsessive passion play, Dorian has found a way to play his own tricks with reality. It's as though Ezra is a turbine that Dorian harnesses. Now Ezra is dying and Dorian needs his own ever-repeating horror scene, something to facilitate the changing of the guard. Maybe he is even right. Dorian is crazy, but he is also a genius. With his own version of me, maybe he'll be able to fire up this creaky engine. I don't know. How the hell should I know!"

Anita shook her head. Jack saw figures behind her, running down the hall. Anita must have sensed them too; she turned, shouted something that Jack couldn't make out, and then turned back. "You've got to stop him. He will kill a lot of people if you don't. And more will die as a consequence of what he does tonight. He calls it the Unraveling." The white gauze encircling her neck was soaked red now. "Give Ezra a message from me."

Jack listened, distracted by the approaching figures, afraid of interrupting. Anita said what she had to say. "You understand?"

Jack nodded.

"Take me to Ezra," she said.

"How do I take—?"

"Break the mirror. Then take a piece of it with you. Any piece."

"I—"

"Do it now! You don't want to see this—" Jack had assumed the figures coming down the hall were orderlies, and so they were, but they were Ezra's perception of orderlies, dead-eyed, monstrous golems, heartless, rotting things who had refused to restore Anita to life, had, in Ezra's damaged perception, killed her again. These were the creatures that now reached Anita, sought her with their clawed and crippled hands.

Anita's scream was clipped short as she turned, yanking her palm from the mirror. Ed Tilman staggered back, moaning, and Martin shouted, "Stand back!" and Jack moved clear too and the rifle coughed and the mirror burst into a thousand ragged, silver shards.

he fire that had destroyed the mansion had been thorough. When Jack came up into the basement, the night sky loomed over him. They climbed the concrete stairs and began moving rapidly back up the hill toward the carnival lights, the tents.

Tilman stopped, punched a number on the phone, spoke into the mouthpiece, "Tilman here. I talked to a soldier about a package. Yes. I want you to evacuate the Bad Trip ride. I want you to send the payload down on one of the cars. That's right. Rig it to activate remotely. After the bomb is onboard and it's on its way, give it fourteen minutes and twelve seconds of travel time. Then stop the car—cut the power if you have to. It will be in place then. Let me know when it is, then keep your finger on the button and wait for my command. Good. Well, I hope so too." The phone made a small beep as Tilman turned it off.

Tilman smiled at Jack and Martin. "We are going to pull the carpet out from under Dorian Greenway's monster machines. With any luck, the explosion won't blow the rest of us to Hell. If it does…" Tilman shrugged, winced with pain.

"Are you all right?" Jack asked.

Tilman had tugged the black glove back on, but he was holding that arm as though it were broken. "You are asking that question a lot. You get any positive responses? I feel like a man who has been turned inside out and dropped in a nest of fire ants. My mind isn't too good either, like right now everything is sort of leaking colors; the sky's like a finger painting by an untalented chimpanzee. Other than that, I feel fine."

They squeezed their way into the crowded tent. The contestants were still up on stage. The judges sat at a long table off to the left. This critical panel consisted of two gray-haired ladies, a young man whose good looks suggested that he might be a celebrity (Jack didn't recognize him; *television*, Jack assumed), best-selling author John Mahler in a monk's hooded robe, and—my God!—Ezra Coldwell, propped in a wheelchair, his head lolling to the side. The small silver box had been removed from his temple, leaving a rectangular, purple bruise. The man looked like he might already be dead— and imperfectly stuffed by some incompetent hobbyist.

Dorian Greenway sat at the head of this table, smiling beatifically, his white-gloved hands folded in front of him.

Jack followed Martin and Tilman as they skillfully pushed through the crowd, moving toward the left side of the stage. Huge screens were mounted on scaffolding behind the contestants, so that their young and radiant faces, captured by video cameras, could be translated into full-color fifty-foot icons for the crowd to gawk at.

One of the judges was leaning into a mike, asking a question. "Contestant number two, Rosalind, what would you say if you were at a party and someone offered you a beer?"

Rosalind smiled. "I'd say, 'No thank you, I'm a member of Alcoholics Anonymous, not to mention NA and OA, and I don't drink.' I would then relate my story (how it was, what happened, and how it is now). I would try to share this experience in a positive, engaging manner, taking no more than fifteen or twenty minutes. I would note that I was not speaking for AA, but only presenting my personal path to recovery."

"Thank you," the judge said. "How about you, contestant number three...ah...Kerry? How would you handle this situation."

"Does it matter what kind of beer it is?" Kerry asked. "I mean, if it's one of those lite fuckers, I'm not even tempted."

"Let's assume it's your favorite beer," the judge said.

Kerry folded her arms, frowned deeply as though trying to remember who Millard Filmore's vice president was, then smiled. "I'd scream and run out of the room."

The room applauded.

Oh, Kerry, Jack thought, *you don't want to win this competition.* As with every recent event he could think of, he had a bad feeling about this.

The contestants were excused while the judges entered into final deliberation. Kerry and the others were ushered backstage, and punk rockers *Freddy and the Unfortunates* shouted out a song whose only lyrics, as far as Jack could tell, were, *Don't be breaking my An-no-nim-mity.*

While the rock band played, Tilman, Martin, and Jack managed to wend their way to the edge of the stage. The large, wide-bellied, black-shirted motorcycle guys who frequent any live event in their crowd-control capacity were guarding the wooden stairs. Tilman ducked under the skirt of the raised platform. "Come on," he said.

Martin and Jack followed. Jack saw that Martin was still cradling the rifle. Jack tried to stay out of the line of fire.

It was dark under the stage, and cold, the night air leaking in from somewhere in back. Thick cables snaked off in every direction. The rock band shook the boards.

Jack scrambled forward. *I'm really tired*, he thought. Then he remembered that he had once read a self-help book that urged its readers never to say they were tired. Jack couldn't remember why the author was adamant about this; perhaps the author found it personally irritating, or had had a spouse or girlfriend who dodged sex by professing fatigue. Who knows?

Still, I'm really tired, Jack thought.

They crawled out from under the platform. The wall of canvas behind them bellied inward as a cold wind pressed against it.

Crouching beside Martin and Tilman, Jack slowly raised his head until his eyes were above the platform's edge. A skinny, bearded guy was fiddling with an instrument panel. The rock band had ceased to play, and the five contestants were poised behind the red curtain, their bodies eloquent with youthful anticipation as they awaited some signal. In their white bathing suits, they were, Jack thought, a fit subject for a modern Degas.

A burst of applause, and they ran back onto the stage.

Great! Jack thought. As usual, his timing was less than impeccable. He had hoped to spirit Kerry away before this occurred.

He scuttled to the right, found a break in the curtain, and peered out.

Dorian Greenway walked to the lectern, nodded to the girls who had taken seats in folding chairs on the right side of the stage, and said, "I know

WILLIAM BROWNING SPENCER

you are all eager to learn who this year's Whole Addiction Expo Sobriety Queen is. The answer is right here." Dorian held up the envelope. "But before we tell you, I've asked a man many of you know to say a few words. It seems fitting that he should present tonight's award. He's a man who knows more about sobriety than most. He's a man who has been sober for sixty-eight years! That's longer than AA has been around, folks!"

Dorian paused dramatically while the crowd—always obliging when cued properly—murmured to themselves, amazed and delighted.

"I will tell you the truth. Hubert Henslow and I have had our differences. I was younger then. I was a little difficult, a little skeptical of the wisdom of my elders. Some of you younger members can probably relate." Dorian paused for laughter, which was sparse. "Hubert and I still don't agree on everything, but I knew it would be wrong not to let him have his say. You won't find too many people who can put sixty-eight years of sobriety on their recovery résumé. Please welcome the presenter of this year's Whole Addiction Expo Sobriety Queen award, Mr. Hubert Henslow."

Dorian left the envelope on the lectern and moved quickly back to the judges' table as the audience applauded enthusiastically and Hubert, who had been seated in the front row, climbed the stairs and walked across the stage. Years of telling his story at AA speaker meetings had made Hubert comfortable in front of audiences. Jack, studying the man's profile from the side, found something too self-pleased in the toothy smile.

Jack instantly reprimanded himself. *Give the guy a break.*

The timing of the speech, however, was bad. Like many old people, Hubert had no feel for the present's mood (inhabiting a rough-and-ready time when opinions were delivered with force and hurt feelings were considered a natural consequence of human interaction). Hubert did seem unaware of two pertinent facts: 1. A fundamentalist AA terrorist group was bombing more liberal-minded meetings, thus generating some ill-feeling, and 2. The audience gathered in front of him had come to the Whole Addiction Expo because they were, for the most part, of an eclectic spiritual temperament.

"I'm Hubert, and I'm an alcoholic!" he shouted. "If you can't hear me in the back, just holler. I was in a hospital recently—can't remember why, but I feel fine now—and the first thing I did when I got out was go to an AA meeting. Fact is, first thing I *remember* is sitting in a meeting. I love meetings—old-fashioned AA. The new stuff…" He waved his arm in the air, a dramatic gesture of dismissal. "Bells and whistles, folks! A lot of damned bells and whistles! The fancier a thing gets, the more apt it is to break. And what do we say in AA? We say, *If it ain't broke, don't fix it!* Say it with me, *IF*

IT AIN'T BROKE, DON'T FIX IT!" Hubert scowled, leaned forward. "All this New Age bullshit has been around forever. Ask them holy men and self-appointed self-helpers, and they will be glad to tell you that. You got your ancient wisdom that was around when Jesus was in diapers. That's fine. There's nothing like wisdom with a pedigree. But here's the thing. Ain't none of that wisdom knocked the bottle out of an alcoholic's hand and set him on his feet. None of it. All them long years. No. Some old stockbroker, drunk and down on his luck, had to do that, get another drunk and puzzle it out, get a bunch of drunks and sit around in the kitchen drinking coffee and talking a lot of shit that you just know you wouldn't have wanted to hear. But somebody had to do it. So it gets done, and they put it in a book called *Alcoholics Anonymous*, the Big Book, and before you know it, you got all these sonsofbitches saying *Yessir, that's the way to do it, old AA.* It's a grand old program, and they know how to make it grander. They can supercharge it. They got a book or a videotape or a weekend course that will get you enlightened or on the road to getting enlightened or just more comfortable with being an asshole, I don't know." Hubert paused dramatically. "They say, 'AA's fine, but we got other issues, too.' Well, I expect only the dead don't have issues, and I can't speak with any authority on that. What I can…"

There were many topics that Hubert did feel qualified to address, and he addressed a number of them.

Jack could sense that the crowd was getting restless, even hostile. Didn't the old man hear them hiss when he referred to John Bradshaw and Scott Peck as a couple of grandiose assholes?

But Hubert just kept on, oblivious, cheerful. He told a joke about a drunken priest and another about a drunken rabbi. He referred to women as "gals," gays as "queers." He was not endearing himself to this crowd— primarily young—who seemed incapable of placing him in his proper historical context.

The crowd was turning ugly. "Old fart!" someone shouted. "Step Nazi!" someone else shouted. "Bleeding deacon!"

Something else was occurring, something that the crowd, distracted, may not have noticed. The ground was shaking.

At first Jack had thought the tremor was communicating itself to him through the platform he leaned against. Then he noticed that his knees, sunk into the dirt, were buzzing too.

He glanced at Tilman, saw that the man was aware of this phenomenon and not pleased. Tilman was speaking into the cell phone. "How are we doing?"

WILLIAM BROWNING SPENCER

Tilman listened, said, "All right." Tilman looked up, saw Jack studying him, and said, "It's on its way. It's been traveling for ten minutes, so we've got another four before it's in place." Tilman spoke into the phone again: "We got some tremors here. What's the power source doing?" There was a long pause here while Tilman sucked on an invisible lemon. "Jeez. Has it peaked yet? Look, I'm just going to hang here, keep the line open. I may want you to blow it as soon as it's in place."

Several fights had broken out in the audience. There were some who agreed with Hubert and were defending his right to speak his mind. The fat guys in black were attempting to restore order, moving with surprising agility, shoving, bellowing with back-off authority.

Hubert was winding down. He snatched the envelope from the lectern. "I know, I know, you'd rather look at a pretty girl than listen to an old man. That shows you got your priorities straight." He tore the envelope open, squinted at what was written therein—predictably hamming it up some— and said, turning to look at the seated girls, "Every one of you is a winner, having achieved the status of finalist in the Whole Addiction Expo Sobriety Queen competition. Acknowledging your accomplishment, the sponsors of this contest have seen fit to dispense with the categories of second, third and fourth, delineations that seem to shave this honor too close. We are here only to award one prize, the title of Miss Sobriety Queen 1998. That award goes to…" Hubert paused dramatically, looked down again as though making sure he had it right, looked up and shouted, "Miss Sobriety Queen 1998, Kerry Beckett!"

The rock band launched into a raucous rendition of "You Are My Sunshine" and Kerry, beaming, ran across the stage and hugged Hubert, who hugged her back (his left hand, in Jack's opinion, resting a little too familiarly on her waist).

One of the gray-haired ladies got up and rocked across the stage, unsteady on high heels, a painful grin inspired by the weight of so many eyes. She was carrying a blue ribbon and a crown.

Hubert took the ribbon and draped it over Kerry's shoulders, then lifted the crown and placed it on her shaved head. "You Are My Sunshine" rose in volume, a dismal rendition that revealed what many had suspected, that the artlessness that characterized the music of *Freddy and the Unfortunates* was genuine and not some clever, self-mocking pose.

The floor seemed to be undulating now. Jack looked up and saw that the bright vaulted ceiling of canvas was tearing, long ribbons of blue whipping in a hurricane wind.

IRRATIONAL FEARS

The black night shone through, and sinuous columns of gray fog, smoke perhaps, drifted down, as though the sky were burning, smoke sinking rather than rising, lethargic tentacles, heavier than air.

Jack heard the sound of hideous machines. He turned and saw Tilman, crouched low and shouting into the cell phone. Jack could not hear what the old man shouted, but he knew the words had to be the only sensible ones: "Blow it! Blow it!"

Hubert was holding up his arms, shouting, attempting to calm the throng, his expression and gesture as old as the first caveman's (exhorting his comrades not to panic as the volcano erupted)—and just as effective, oil on flames. The crowd was screaming as the smoke settled on them, took shape, became white, mottled serpents with their heads whipping about, jaws flashing.

Hubert waved his arms. Jack heard a sharp explosion, saw Hubert stagger back, blink up at the glaring lights. The old man clutched his shoulder, slumped forward onto his knees, keeled over sideways. Kerry screamed. A second bullet blew splinters into the air next to Kerry's left foot, and she turned, running.

Two explosions—so close together that they amplified each other— barked in Jack's ear, and he turned, saw Martin crouched and firing, the rifle aimed high and toward the back of the crowd.

Jack saw someone pitch forward from a platform near the tent's ceiling. Rifle and man, separated, fell at the same speed, lost in shadows and smoke.

"Gotcha, you sonofabitch," Martin muttered, standing.

Jack climbed up on the stage, blinked at Hubert's prone figure. The gold sobriety crown lay next to him, rocking slightly on the floorboards. Kerry was gone. Jack's frenzied eye searched the crowd.

Later, when his memory would reconstruct the scene, it seemed obvious that the ghost serpents were invisible to the people below, but that may have been the mind taking editorial liberties with the past, revising with new knowledge. The snakes were swarming, all sizes, from foot-long, ether-wriggling creatures to monstrous, barrel-bodied leviathans whose full length was lost in coils and shadow. *Serpent* was a word the mind settled on, an imperfect fit. These creatures seemed to be made of rope-like veins, their eyes small and animate with malice, their teeth a mouthful of needles licked by a dozen barbed tongues.

Jack watched as one of the serpents bit a black-garbed biker on the elbow. He screamed, turned, and grabbed the man behind him by the throat.

WILLIAM BROWNING SPENCER

In retrospect, it was clear. The crowd was being goaded, whipped to a fury of blind hatred.

"Hate," a young, bearded boy said later, looking at the interviewing cameras as though he were seeing the world with a new, uneasy awareness. "Like hate flooding into a vein, you know—a dirty rush. I never got that expression 'seeing red,' but now I do. I wanted to kill somebody."

The crowd was fighting itself, screaming, biting, kicking, a beast devouring itself, harried by devils.

Ed Tilman shouted into Jack's ear. "They're setting it off. God willing we—"

The explosion made the tent buckle. Supporting beams leaned forward, ripped from their moorings. The great canvas, shrieking like some winged monster nailed to the earth, too brutal and vast to be so easily crucified, roared and rose. Folding chairs skittered across the stage like crippled insects, and Jack was thrown backward, knocked from his feet by a wall of wind. He lay on his back, still dragged by the wind as though he were a doll dragged by a dog, splinters sliding into his shoulders and back, the pain unremarked in a body filled with a terror so large it might have been wonder, joy, enlightenment.

He saw, above him, the canvas rise, a blue jellyfish jerking toward the stars, wheeling away.

The wind tore the serpents to pieces, flinging them like rags. Jack saw a small serpent's body ripped from its head. The head clung briefly to a wooden pole and then flipped away, rising into the sky.

The crowd was running, breaking in all directions, fleeing their release from madness.

The judges were gone, their table overturned. Dorian Greenway was gone. Eunice was up on stage, kneeling next to Hubert. "You are going to be all right, honey!" she was shouting. Amazingly, Hubert was saying something in response.

Jack ran across the stage, saw the overturned wheelchair and righted it and the man within.

Ezra Coldwell's eyes were white, blind, barely visible between swollen eyelids. "Where's Dorian?" Jack screamed. "Where's Kerry?"

Ezra Coldwell might as well have been dead—a dull, mummified husk.

"Help if you can, you poor sonofabitch," Jack said. Jack reached in his pocket, pulled out the crumpled tissue with its shard of mirror. He took the silver shard and placed it in the old man's hand, gently closing the fingers around it. The hand slumped open, the mirror falling to the ground. Jack

IRRATIONAL FEARS

picked it up and replaced it in the man's hand. Jack moved the hand to the man's lap. This time the fingers remained closed.

"Anita says…" *Can you hear me, old man?* "Anita says you've spent so long manipulating the world that you have forgotten. She says, 'If you can move mountains, you can *move yourself*. It doesn't matter if your mind is imprisoned, if all the connections are cut, if you are crouched in a dark corner of your own ruined body. If that body were a dead dog, you know you could make it walk. Animate yourself.'"

Jack might have been talking to dust, to a hole in the darkness of space. He had no time for this. He had to find Kerry. He stood up.

Blood was leaking from Ezra Coldwell's clenched fist.

"Over there!"

Jack turned, saw Ed Tilman pointing. Jack followed the line of Ed's finger. He saw the two small figures, hand in hand, enter the long white two-story building.

Jack and Tilman leapt from the stage and raced in pursuit of Dorian and Kerry.

ack pushed the swinging doors open warily. The room, one single long, football field of a room, was filled with seated people. In the far distance, some people were seated alone on a stage. A large banner across the back wall read, *AA MARATHON CLOSED MEETING.*

An usher came up to Jack and Tilman. "You just made it," he said. "This way."

Jack and Tilman were led to two empty folding chairs on the end of a back row. Jack sat, looking around, hoping to catch a glimpse of Kerry and Dorian. They were in here somewhere.

A woman toward the front of the meeting was standing up, speaking. "So I said to my mom, 'No way am I coming up there for Christmas and engaging in dysfunctional behavior now that I am clean and sober. I don't see why I have to come there to get the money so I can pay my rent anyway; we got the postal system, you know.'" She folded her arms and looked around the room, pleased with this response. The room was silent except for someone coughing as though he'd swallowed a kazoo.

The woman continued. "That night, when I went to sleep, I had a dream. I dreamed that I was dancing topless at a PTA meeting. This guy came up to me that I knew from high school and he said, 'Wanda, I would sure like to have sex with you, what do you think?' He was kind of cute, but

IRRATIONAL FEARS

I told him that I had discovered a new way of life and wasn't interested in cheap thrills. Well, I saw that he had turned into a bear, that bear with the little hat, the one that puts out fires, Moses, Henry, Toby, you know the one. Anyway, he said…"

My God there are a lot of people in this room, Jack thought. Could Dorian and Kerry have slipped back out the door? No, there was the one aisle and he would have seen them.

The woman went on and on. Jack fidgeted.

When the woman finally sat down, a short, dark-haired man immediately jumped up. "I'm Bob, and I'm an alcoholic. Mr. Chairperson, I timed Wanda. She went on for sixteen minutes. We have approximately two thousand people and, as I understand it, the plan here is for every one of us to share. Well, if everyone goes on as long as Wanda, that's going to take, by my reckoning, over twenty-two days. We have got to speed things up, maybe have a time limit of two, three minutes each."

This statement stirred the whole room, a noisy ripple of controversy.

A big man stood up, "Mr. Chairman, I don't go for people timing me when I talk. If you gotta talk for sixteen minutes to stay sober, I say do it."

An even bigger man stood. "I agree, but I say, let's leave out telling dreams. I mean, telling your dreams or the plot of a television show you have seen, that should be ruled out. That kind of thing has no end to it, and it's not real experience."

"It is if you go and drink over it!" someone shouted.

People were interrupting each other now. There were about twenty people standing, trying to get the chairperson's attention.

Ed Tilman clutched Jack's shoulder. "There." Jack turned as directed and saw Dorian and Kerry sliding out a door on the left at the end of the room.

"Let's go."

The last words Jack heard before the door shut out the marathon meeting were "…if a dream has drinking in it, I say…" The door closed and Jack found himself in a narrow stairwell that smelled like stale cigarettes and coffee made from dishwater.

He climbed the stairs quickly, catching the door that Tilman had flung open before it banged shut.

They were in a narrow, dimly lit hallway. The wallpaper was some ancient, faded print (butterflies or female genitalia). Tilman was trying the first door. Jack ran on, flung open a second door.

WILLIAM BROWNING SPENCER

Dorian Greenway stood there, smiling, elegant in his emcee outfit, although some of the white face paint was gone, revealing pink flesh. The red of his lips was smeared. "Yes? I think we already gave at the office. Or are you here to save my soul? Whatever." He raised his hand, slowly—Jack thought, later, that he had had plenty of time to jump back if only he could have abandoned his role of avenger. There was an aerosol can in Greenway's hand, and it released a green mist that became the world, a world of green wonder, green confusion, green arguments and green rebuttals.

"I am the boss here," the man said, smoothing his black hair. "I am Dr. Azzam Freud. I am the professional one, and you are the patient." Jack could see his own feet, enclosed in tennis shoes. He was lying on a sofa. The dark-complected Dr. Freud sat in an armchair, his attitude casual, the ankle of his right foot resting on his left knee. His pants were sharply pressed, and he held a blue-black revolver in his right hand. The room was comfortably overfurnished, a sort of Victorian study with framed diplomas, glass-enclosed bookcases, potted plants, a brass lamp.

Jack felt a sense of urgency, but he could not seem to move. "I have to leave," he said.

"Hah!" the man said. "You always want to leave. Hello good-bye as your Beatle Boys say. Well, time is the thing that it takes to get well. No way of getting there otherwise." He smiled, perfect white teeth. He stood up. Behind him was an ornately framed mirror. Jack could see himself in the mirror, blinking stupidly past the shrink's shoulder. He lay on the sofa like an invalid, something comfortably defeated in the limpness of his body, the fey angle of his neck. He was suffused with self-loathing.

"I'm dreaming," Jack said. "You are a dream. I know because I've had it before. I think."

The man nodded. "Good, good. Dreams are very important, very expensive, very full of the insights." He pointed the gun at Jack. "Did you know that when a man dies in his sleep it is because he has died in his dream?"

Jack didn't say anything, but he knew that he was frightened, realized that he did believe dreams could kill.

"Why you want to go on living anyway, Mister?" the psychiatrist said. "You are full of the complaints and the unhappiness. 'Fix me!' you holler, but who are you kidding? You like the wallowing and the sighing and the slumping in the chair. Ha! There are plenty of peoples in the world, and just so much of the medicares and the insurance. The medicares and the insurance are peoples too, and it is not right to take their monies for nothing, for moping and crying the spilled milk! Ha!" He stood up, keeping the gun pointed at Jack, and backed away (anticipating, perhaps, some cat-quick leap, some desperate, last defense). Stopped by the wall, his back against the mirror, the psychiatrist stretched out his arm, closed his left eye, took aim.

"If you have the final insight, make it now," the man said.

Jack could think of nothing.

The man nodded slowly, as though Jack's silence confirmed a diagnosis. "Then—"

Azzam Freud's head slammed back against the mirror, jerked by a glittering forearm that had pierced the mirror to encircle his neck. He gagged, fired the gun into the air, the report bigger than the room. The shrink struggled to break free. He dropped the gun and clutched his assailant's arm with both hands. The arm jerked him back again. The shrink's skull whacked against the glass, sending ragged white lines shivering to the edges of the mirror. The man lurched forward, was yanked back again, harder, glass suddenly exploding outward, the man sliding to the floor, blood streaking the wall as he collapsed, the room filling with glass, a snow storm, a whiteout of fat, flying needles.

Jack tried to stand, throwing his arm in front of his face, fell backwards.

Ed Tilman was helping Jack to his feet. Tilman's sleeve was rolled up, his arm red with blood.

"Thought I lost you there," he said. The room was empty, nothing but shattered glass covering the floor.

Leaning against each other, they staggered back into the hall.

Dorian Greenway (and Kerry) were gone. A search of the other upstairs rooms showed them all to be empty. The fugitives had obviously sidestepped their pursuers, slipped into that alternate refuge, the labyrinth that Dorian Greenway had made his home.

Jack and Ed sat on the steps outside the marathon AA meeting and welcomed the cold air into their lungs.

"I heard you holler," Tilman said. "Found nothing but an empty room with a mirror on the wall. I don't care much for mirrors these days, but I thought I'd try the trick of looking with the palm of my hand. There you were."

"Thanks," Jack said.

They sat there on the steps. The cold was leaking into Jack's bones, and, with it, that despair, that moping and wallowing (as Azzam Freud so

WILLIAM BROWNING SPENCER

aptly put it), that crying the spilled milk. Dorian had eluded them, had stolen Kerry back and would certainly rise again to create new havoc.

Jack heard the wail of sirens, watched two fire engines and an ambulance, all festive with flashing lights, bounce across a field. *Well,* Jack thought, *what's a Whole Addiction Expo without a few emergency vehicles?* He could see a thick column of smoke billowing from the basement of the ruined mansion. Thanks to Ed Tilman, the machines that would have—Jack was convinced of this—goaded thousands into killing each other...those death machines were silenced.

If the Whole Addiction Expo had ended in a frenzy of killing, that carnage (in combination with the church bombings and the attack on AA's General Service Office) could have, quite possibly, expanded into a civil war, recovering faction against recovering faction, America burning.

Jack closed his eyes and envisioned such a horror. He trembled at the thought. The images possessed such power, such an authority of dread.

He opened his eyes, turned and looked at Tilman. They both felt it, that thundering, earthquake roll, a subterranean dissent.

"What the hell?" Tilman said, standing up.

Jack stood too.

"He's turned them back on," Jack said.

Tilman shook his head. "No, not back on. Those babies are finished." Tilman nodded at the column of smoke. "The sonofabitch had something in reserve."

Tilman began to move quickly down the hill. Jack followed, the ground humming through the soles of his feet.

"Wait!" Jack said.

Tilman turned, and Jack pointed.

A tiny figure was limping toward the pond, its progress clumsy but rapid, falling toward its destination with convulsive, obscene purpose.

"Come on," Jack said, breaking into a run.

When they reached Ezra Coldwell, he was standing in front of a thicket of pines and smaller evergreen shrubs, a clump of vegetation perhaps twenty feet in diameter. A cold wind sent leaves scudding across the nearby pond and riffled his thinning white hair with invisible fingers.

He stood perfectly still in baggy brown pants and a red flannel shirt (also too large). The wind slapped at his pants; there was a dark stain in the region of his crotch. He wore black socks, no shoes. The question of whether or not he was comfortable seemed, to Jack, a moot one, since he looked as dead as any of the brown leaves floating on the pond, as dead as the belly-up flies on a farmhouse windowsill.

There was one sign of life; blood dripped from his clenched fist.

Neither Jack nor Tilman called his name.

They stood beside him, towering over him, and Jack had the thought that they might, the three of them, stand there the rest of the night, stand there, indeed, until something terrible jarred them into motion again.

Jack wondered if the rest of the world had this fear of a blank patch, a silence or mental smoothness that would stretch out and swallow them. Did the rest of the world fear, for instance, that a lull in a dinner party's conversation might freeze into an icy stillness, and that, once frozen, inertia might prevail and no one would be able to summon the scream that would set them in motion again?

Probably not, although it was the sort of thing which wasn't helped by thinking about it. Jack felt panic shift in his chest.

Ezra Coldwell lurched forward. He plunged into the thicket, making no attempt to duck the branches and thorny leaves that tore at his face and blind eyes.

Animate yourself. That had been Anita's message to Ezra Coldwell, and it did seem as though some invisible, brutal hand were shoving the old man forward.

Ezra Coldwell tumbled to his knees, clawed the dirt, and stumbled backwards. The metal door fell open with a heavy *thunk.*

"Are you claustrophobic?" Jack asked.

"No, why do you ask?" Ed Tilman said.

They were in a small elevator, the floor perhaps eight by eight feet, the light above them blinking fitfully as they descended. Ezra Coldwell, giving no indication that he was aware of their presence, had pushed a button and turned back into stone. The rumble of machinery was growing louder, filled with its resonance of fear. The tiny chamber reeked of sour earth and coppery fire. They had been descending for perhaps fifteen minutes.

"Just making conversation," Jack said—and trying to distract himself from a disorienting phenomenon (i.e., the way the dirty sheet-metal walls kept shifting into something else). Jack thought he saw an old-fashioned refrigerator (small, round-shouldered), a kitchen stove, kitchen cupboards, yellow walls splattered with red spaghetti sauce and noodles.

Jack closed his eyes, and when he opened them, the walls belonged, again, to an elevator. He breathed deeply, studied his shoes. *You are just fine,* he told himself.

WILLIAM BROWNING SPENCER

Something gleamed on the floor, a knife with a wooden handle and a big, shining blade. As Jack watched, it began to spin.

Jack closed his eyes again. The elevator car howled as it slowed and came to a groaning, rocking stop. Jack opened his eyes. The knife was gone.

The din of the machines was like an explosion that did not end. Jack and Tilman followed the stumbling, broken dwarf as he moved rapidly down a narrow hall. Walls of cinder block surrounded them. Ed Tilman, ever resourceful, had produced a gun which he held in his good hand. His other arm had ceased to bleed, but it swung limply at his side as though it were a prosthesis made of clear plastic.

Ezra Coldwell paused before a metal door, reached up, turned the knob, and entered, Jack and Tilman right behind him.

The door closed behind them and, incredibly, the machines were reduced to a distant rumble.

They had entered a movie theater, rows of empty red chairs curving in wide arcs, row after row. On the screen in front of them, in garish, primary colors, half a dozen figures in large, yellow, moon-walk space suits were leaping slowly in zero gravity, waving red pom-poms. Jack recognized the scene, the movie: *Revenge of the Cheerleader Space Zombies*.

The scene shifted. The music rose in dissonant waves. The hero, last of the surviving teenagers, was carrying his girlfriend up the mansion's curving stairs. The camera angle was low; you could see the girl's white cotton underpants, but she was dead, dismally dead, and this twinge of eroticism was, consequently, poignant rather than provocative. Who said that B-movie horror flicks did not have their moments of high art?

Jack recognized the carpet's ornate design. That staircase was the one that Dorian Greenway had walked down to enter Kerry's life.

The lights went on in the theater, washing out the screen, its shadowy horror and tense music score instantly relegated to the indifferent interest of two dimensions. Then the screen went blank, the music slumped to silence.

A figure walked onto the stage, slowly, encumbered by the bulky yellow space suit.

The figure stood in the middle of the stage, stared out at the audience. The sparkle of footlights gleamed in the glow of the space helmet.

A voice, amplified through a microphone, came echoing out over the empty seats.

"Uncle, are you there?" Silence. "Well, I know you are out there. I watched you come in on the monitor, you and your friends. It's good to see you getting around, Uncle. You have always resisted exercise, and I have always felt it would do you a world of good. A little fresh air racing through the lungs can do wonders for depression."

Dorian Greenway put his hands behind his back and took several slow strides up the stage. "Well, we have had nothing but setbacks. I'm sorry, Uncle. I thought I might avenge you. I thought I might set us both free, you from your eternally dying Anita, and me from…well, from you, my damned Uncle Ezra."

His voice changed, grew higher, petulant. "It's wonderful to have gifts, talents, but it has its downside, you know. I've tried to help you, tried to enhance your powers, and I've sensed that you have never really appreciated my efforts. Well…I'm sorry. What can I say?"

Dorian eased his bulky body down into a sitting position on the edge of the stage. "I tried witchcraft, I tried spacecraft, I tried Lovecraft. *No one* can say I didn't try. There's one last chance. I intend to enter the event, to alter its causality, to shift the weight of its implication. You will be free to…well, to die, I'm afraid. I'm guessing that all that keeps you alive is the repetition of the event. When it comes to an end, so, alas, will you. Don't worry about me. I know, in the past, that I have relied on your wild talents to fuel my own. But now I will control the new order."

Clumsily, Dorian stood back up and walked slowly to the side of the stage. He paused, one hand on a red lever jutting from the wall. "Here we go," he said. He pulled the lever down, a motor hummed, and the white movie screen rose toward the ceiling.

Jack found himself staring at a white room that contained a white table, white chairs. Dorian flicked switches and overhead lights flared, lights so bright that the room burned in Jack's brain, a fever of white boxes, rectangles and squares. Jack recognized that minimalist set design that generally heralded an experimental play, the sort that approached art by eluding the audience. Kerry, dressed again in Anita's blue dress and wearing a wig, sat in a white chair at the table, facing the empty rows of chairs. Her eyes were blue and empty, her features as free of expression as a glass of springwater.

"Here we go," Dorian said, his amplified voice bright and echoing. "Welcome to the nineteen-thousand, four-hundred-and-seventh consecutive performance of Ezra's Nightmare sponsored by Coldwell Guilt and Psychokinetic Enterprises. Glad you all could come."

WILLIAM BROWNING SPENCER

Dorian stepped to the side, waited. Nothing happened. "Uncle," Dorian shouted, "why resist? Let's get rolling here." Still nothing. Dorian, in his yellow space suit, poised like a child's toy, arms outstretched, nodded his fishbowl head. "Okay. I guess you need the cue. Here goes." Dorian shouted: "I'M NOT COMING BACK. THAT'S RIGHT, EZRA. I'M GOING FOR GOOD."

The whole room shivered, hologram figures blinking into life.

When Ezra Coldwell stood up and began marching toward the stage where the drama of his wife's living death (and his damnation) was playing, Jack and Tilman followed him. Later, Jack realized, there was nothing else he could have done. If this were a play, it was one with total audience involvement. From the minute the kitchen came into focus, it seemed to be the world, its detail and truth so absolute that all other places and things were shadows. Jack could even smell the onion and oregano in the air. Although his heart was held by the knife that slowly spun on the kitchen table (*gathering, gathering speed*), he saw everything else as though it had been his life's work to catalogue the specifics of this room, these people, this moment.

A much younger Hubert Henslow was standing in the room next to his two AA friends, the three of them seeming to own a single expression (uncomfortable, embarrassed, resolved to do the right thing). Anita Coldwell stood in the doorway, one hand touching the door frame, her blue eyes sad and unwavering as they studied her husband, who sat at the table, red-faced, hair in his eyes, sullenly drunk, muttering, "A man drinks a little in his own home…"

The sound of the knife (*clack, clack, clack*) filled Jack's head.

"Ask me yourself," Anita was saying.

Dorian Greenway walked into this kitchen, as foreign to it as the moon's surface had once been to men. He had removed the space helmet, and his head seemed small and cartoonish as he smiled over the swollen suit. He walked behind Kerry, placed his gloved hands on her shoulders, grinned.

"Time for something different," he said. He leaned forward and spoke in Kerry's ear. "Miss Sobriety Queen 1998. What a triumph for one so young. How glorious, how tragic. Wouldn't you like to hold this moment forever, keep it like a jewel in a box, a memory in every facet?"

Kerry opened her mouth and said something.

"What did you say?" Dorian asked. "I don't think they can hear you. You'll have to speak up."

IRRATIONAL FEARS

"I love you," Kerry said, speaking as though in a dream, addressing, perhaps, a dream lover.

Dorian nodded. "That's very important," he said. "Love is the glue, love is the fuel. Don't you think? Ezra could tell you…"

The knife was rising in the air, spinning. Dorian turned, reached out, and deftly snatched it.

"Here is where everything changes," he said. "A new circle is drawn, and I am its center."

He brought the knife to Kerry's throat. The rest of the room proceeded as though he was not there. Anita was saying, "That's right, Ezra."

Ed Tilman, having reached the edge of the stage and climbed it, knelt and fired the gun, twice.

Dorian blinked at the report. He smiled. "Sorry," he said. "I'm afraid you missed by a mile, missed by a light-year."

Jack ran across the stage, anguish and loss howling in him. The pity he felt for Ezra Coldwell was palpable, mixed with his fear for Kerry's life. The name on his lips, unconsciously there (a wound in the heat of battle that would go unremarked until later), was Sara.

A wall of pain bounced him back, sent him rolling on the wooden floor.

"Nope," Dorian said. "You are not allowed in here. That goes for you too, Uncle."

Ezra Coldwell had laboriously climbed the stage and stumbled toward the center of his universe, the glowing kitchen. He pressed his face against some invisible barrier that distorted it. Jack saw the old man's skull flickering through flesh.

The mummified dwarf spoke, his mouth moving, but the words came from the air itself and did not match the shape of his mouth (as in a foreign film, imperfectly dubbed).

"Nephew, you cannot keep me out. This is my room, *my room!*"

"Go away!" Dorian said, his voice oddly petulant, the voice of a child sulking behind a door.

"No. If there is one thing you cannot bar me from, it is this room. God knows; so does the Devil."

Ezra Coldwell leaned into the force that licked him with silver foam. Translucent bubbles broke away, spiraled upward, carrying bits of his flesh, beads of blood.

And he was within, falling on the floor, swimming across linoleum tiles, clutching the table and hauling himself upright.

WILLIAM BROWNING SPENCER

"Well," Dorian said. "I hope you are happy. You have secured a ringside seat. It changes nothing. Say good-bye, Kerry."

"Good-bye," Kerry said, her voice a whisper that could pierce through decades. The knife blade moved.

Ezra Coldwell did not leap forward. He was launched into the air, a puppet hurled by an angry master (*animate yourself*). Dorian Greenway howled, fell back, and Ezra's fist came down, again and again, striking at his nephew's face and neck, and the room expanded, flooded outward as though poured, the kitchen becoming the whole theater—oh such a spacious kitchen!—and Jack felt the tiles under his hands and struggled to right himself. Vertigo seized him; he was too sick to move, filled with a nausea that might steal his reason forever.

Ezra Coldwell stood up. He dropped the shard of mirror on the floor, looked around, lost. Jack saw the bloody mess of Dorian Greenway's face, a red inkwell of blood where an eye had been, a tattered ear.

Kerry had fallen back and lay on the floor next to Dorian. Neither of them moved. Jack could not see her face, her throat, could not see what damage Dorian had managed to inflict.

The knife on the floor began to spin again, slowly, then faster, then... The ancient little man grabbed it—Jack saw it twist, saw the blade bite his forearm, urging more blood from the bleeding body—and Ezra Coldwell turned, nodded to Anita, and said, "Forgive me," and turned again, caught the hair of his younger, drunken doppelganger. This younger Ezra seemed dazed, drugged with horror, perhaps, raising his hands ineffectually, too slow to stop the swift-moving blade. His fingers fluttered as though magically summoning the gush of blood. His chair pitched back and the room shivered again, the floor moving beneath Jack.

Jack convulsed, felt something churn in his stomach, gagged, opened his mouth. He was coughing, choking, his chest like molten lead, his heart some poor, terrified sparrow trapped and shaken in a tin box.

Never again, he thought. But what *never* was this, what morning after, what retribution for what debacle? He might promise to do the right thing, to march forthrightly into a new morning, a better person, a triumph of new resolve.

Too late. He seemed to be fading, going under.

Death? All right. Fine.

Jack came to with Ed Tilman standing over him. "I'm going to go see if I can turn these machines off," Tilman said.

IRRATIONAL FEARS

"Kerry," Jack said, sick again, reading the worst in Tilman's grim features.

"She's all right," Tilman said. "We want to get her topside and in a hospital, but she wasn't cut. She's out with the drugs. Our boy hit her with something heavy."

Tilman stood up, turned away. "Hang in there, this shouldn't take long."

Jack didn't care to study the sprawled bodies of Dorian and his uncle. He gave them a wide berth and knelt down beside Kerry. Her wig had fallen off; she lay on her back with her eyes closed. Tilman had pushed a folded curtain under her head, black velvet that made her flesh seem more pale and vulnerable, her shaved skull fragile, mysterious.

She opened her eyes when he spoke her name.

"Jack," she said.

"You are going to be all right."

She reached up and touched his cheek. "Jack?"

"It's okay. We are going to get you out of here."

"Jack?"

"Yes."

She smiled. It altered her, this smile, as pouring milk in a glass alters the glass. "I love you," she said.

It lifted Jack's heart, although he knew it was not true.

WILLIAM BROWNING SPENCER

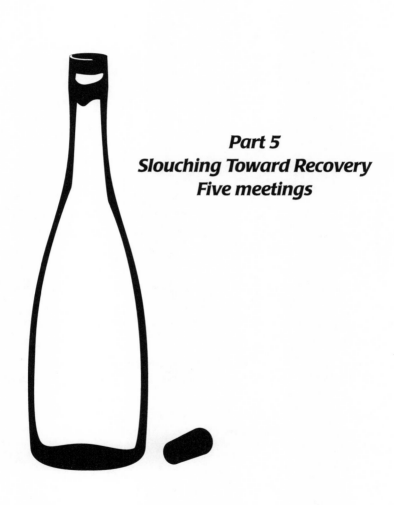

Part 5
Slouching Toward Recovery
Five meetings

 t the AA meeting, Al and Monk got in an argument about who had precipitated their downhill slide. "I said, 'Let's go to the arcade,' and you said, 'I'm sick of that geek stuff, let's take a bus downtown and go to a titty bar.'"

"Yeah," Monk said, "but we was already wrecked on your brother's pot when I said that. You're the one who…"

"Enough," Martin said. "Nobody gives a damn. Wait for me in the van; I want to talk to Jack."

Jack grinned. "Thanks for coming out to see me get my three-month chip."

"Sure. Leesburg's not such a drive. I like to come out here now and again anyway. The residents like it too. A steady diet of Harken meetings can be kind of rich."

"How's Hubert doing?"

"Fine. Eunice has moved in with him; they are living in sin although she says she's worked it out with Jesus. She's nursing Hubert back to health—which, if you ask me, isn't much of a feat. The doctor couldn't even keep Hubert in the hospital overnight back when it happened.

Shooting a guy like Hubert in the shoulder is like trying to kill an elephant with a BB gun."

"Looks like Wesley's in trouble," Jack said.

Martin shook his head. "Seeing as how I meant to kill him, I'd say he's doing all right. There's a lot who sympathize with him."

They talked about Wesley Parks, the risks of any "addiction defense," and AA's take on personal responsibility.

Martin said that Gates was back in D.C., living in a halfway house, going to meetings.

"How's he doing?" Jack asked.

"He says AA ain't what it used to be. He says it's all hugging and sweetness, but he says he's whupped, don't want to drink, even if AA is nothing but sissies and perverts these days. Sounds like he's doing good."

Jack asked about Tilman, but Martin had no news there. Jack was still at New Way when Tilman announced, in group, that he had decided he wasn't ready for retirement. Everybody thought that statement was an expression of discontent, some vague resolve to look for a job when he left, but the next day a black limousine arrived and Tilman left in the company of three men in suits.

"And Gretchen," Jack said. "How's Gretchen?"

Martin looked worried. "I don't know about mixing romance with work, you know? That's risky. I mean, she's a fine woman, but women tend to weary of me. I don't have many sides, you know, just my work."

"I wouldn't worry about it," Jack said. "I think she's smitten with you. Anyway, one day at a time, right?"

Martin grinned. "This AA suits you. You have already learned slogan sagacity. Well, I've got to go before those alcoholics in the van get to thinking they're living in a democracy."

Martin shook Jack's hand, turned to go, turned back. "Speaking of smitten, you hear from young Kerry?"

"Yes, I see her at meetings. I even run across her on campus sometimes; she's taking a couple of courses." Jack had begun teaching at the community college. The job had just fallen into his lap; a colleague of a colleague needed to fill a slot after the abrupt departure of one of the English teachers. Grammar and Composition wasn't American Lit, and Jack didn't think he'd be doing this a year from now, but...well, one day at a time.

"She was head over heels for you," Martin said. "I didn't notice it those first weeks, but toward the end...right before you left, she was following you around like a puppy."

WILLIAM BROWNING SPENCER

"Infatuation," Jack said, feeling uneasy now.

"She's a beauty, that one," Martin said, eyes going glassy.

Now it looked like Martin would just stand there, dazzled stupid by a vision. Jack slipped past him. "It was good seeing you," he hollered as he headed toward the parking lot.

short guy wearing a black T-shirt and suspenders was giving his test for alcoholism. *Everyone*, Jack thought, *has a test*.

"Here's the test," the guy said. "If the thought of never taking a drink again for the rest of your life sends a chill wind blowing through your soul, then you're an alcoholic."

Fair enough, Jack thought.

The next person to talk was named Camille, but she was not of the delicate, sickly Camille school. She looked like she could eat that Camille for breakfast and maybe had.

"You leave my girls alone," she said, addressing the predatory men in the group. "They are vulnerable children trying to get sober, and they don't need you men sliding up on them with promises of program talk when that's not what's on your minds at all. No he'ing and she'ing during the first year, I say. Just get some magazines and relieve yourself looking at the pictures. What does it take, five, ten minutes? My girls…"

Camille had been sober thirteen years and she sponsored many new women. She was married, and Jack had met her husband at a party. He was a man devoid of personality, so colorless that he was impossible to focus on. If he stood next to a cat or a plant or a television (some commercial with the sound off), any of those things would exert a stronger pull, a greater gravity of fascination, than this man.

Camille had, Jack assumed, sucked the soul from him years ago.

AA meetings could be shrill. People who slipped would return to AA filled with remorse and a desire for self-flagellation. An ugly kind of cause-and-effect reasoning could rear its head. You drank because you did not do a rigorous enough Fourth and Fifth Step, you didn't make every amend, you did not meditate, you did not believe in God (or you did not believe enough). Careful, careful, careful. Circumscribed by caution and blame, some men and women lived in a world of fear. *I'm not good enough*, they would say. *I was born vile*.

Gates could have told them. That wasn't no AA. That was superstition, and Mr. Bill Wilson and Mr. Doctor Bob had no use for it.

"We need ground rules," Camille said.

So the trains can run on time, Jack thought, but he wasn't really worried about Camille or her soulmates. AA was a benign anarchy, and like tended to gravitate to like. Grim deacons gathered grim flocks. Heretics harangued each other at late-night coffee shops (where the staff invariably hated them, these coffee-drinking, quarter-tipping, loud, long-staying meeting people).

Jack had only been in AA four months, but he already knew the true object of fear, glimpsed in others when they stood just so in the light of his attention. The fearful thing was his own wayward heart and the darkness it kept for company.

After the meeting, Kerry came up.

"Hey Jack," she said. "It doesn't look good for Wesley, does it?"

Their alcoholism counselor had been on the news again, as the jury deliberated over his fate.

It was Wesley Parks who had shot Hubert. Martin had then shot Parks; and Jack had actually seen his alcoholism counselor drop through the air on that fateful night, although he had not, at that time, identified the would-be assassin.

Parks had a tale to tell, of being indoctrinated into a strange cult, of hallucinating (at one time he thought he had merged, psychically, with a dog named Dr. Bob), of being coerced into taking drugs until his soul was no longer his own, his reasoning processes impaired by chemical need.

The media was much taken with this tale. Here was an alcoholism counselor who had shot a recovering alcoholic (an AA member with an incredible sixty-eight years of sobriety). There were some who sympathized, some who reviled Parks, and some (most, no doubt) who appreciated the distraction of someone else's troubles.

It was the addiction defense that got Wesley in trouble. "I didn't know what I was doing because my reasoning was impaired by alcohol" (or drugs if that was the case) was a dicey defense. If addiction were a disease, than the addict was not responsible.

The victims of crime were not inclined to say, "My assailant was suffering from alcoholism" and leave it at that. And AA made it clear that one had to accept the consequences of one's actions.

But here was an alcoholism counselor, run amok after encountering a cult, a slave to a drug habit acquired in the practice of who knows what sort of despicable, movie-of-the-week perversity.

His lawyers thought his case was a good prospect for the addiction-is-a-disease defense.

No one asked Parks the crucial question—no one, that is, on the defense team.

The question was put to him by the prosecution.

"Gummy bears," Wesley said. "I had a bad gummy bear habit."

His defense never rallied from that moment.

"It's too bad," Kerry said.

Jack agreed.

"So we should go to a movie sometime," Kerry said.

She was growing her hair back, having finally tired of shaving her head. It was in a sort of transition stage. She looked beautiful, as she would in all transitions, the immutable soul stuff of K. Beckett not something disguised by clumsy fashion or cosmetics.

"Sure."

"Hey, I turned eighteen last week. I'm legal."

"Happy birthday."

"You don't take that Camille woman seriously, do you? No he'ing and she'ing during the first year. You think anyone pays any attention to that?"

"No, but it gives the people who don't get laid something to feel self-righteous about."

"Exactly," Kerry said, leaning into Jack. "So are you shooting for self-righteousness or what?"

"You know what," Jack said.

Kerry sighed. "Yeah. I know. I'm the victim of a love potion. An evil cult leader messed with my mind, fired up my love receptors. I opened my eyes, you were there, so naturally, I'm in love with you. That's the way you read it. Sounds utterly loony, but you believe it."

"It's true," Jack said.

Kerry stamped her foot. She turned, headed for the hallway, stopped at the door. "So when does it wear off? When do I get to really loathe you for the asshole you are?"

She banged on out the door, not waiting for an answer. Which was just as well; Jack didn't know.

inter had melted away. There were flowers by the roadside. The grass was aching green, and Jack could hear T.S. Eliot saying, "Well, maybe *May* is the cruelest month."

Poets were such weasels with the truth, so easily corrupted by the sound of a word, fickle in their affections when counting syllables.

Jack was thinking of poets because Kerry had given him another poem. She had been waiting for him in the hall after his class, had handed him the poem and dashed away.

LOVE was the title of this poem, another brave title, like DEATH. But didn't everyone have a right to the all-caps questions? Wasn't everyone at sea?

LOVE Kerry wrote:

> "You're just mixed up,"
> the blind man said.
> "You took a drug
> and lost your head.
> Now you think
> your heart's a boat

WILLIAM BROWNING SPENCER

and in my sea
you want to float."

And she said,
"Jack,
maybe you're right,
but don't you know
it's not polite
to tell someone she's
out of touch.
A kiss,
is that asking so much?"

The meeting that night was rotten. Sometimes an AA meeting could be dreadful. And why not? Any event in which humans featured had the potential for going bad.

The slogan under discussion had been *Live and Let Live*, and someone had talked about the flurry of AA bombings that had occurred in the winter and which—it was discovered—were all the work of a cult leader named Dorian Greenway (there had been no retaliating group called Enlightened Recovery; that spurious opposition had been an attempt to fan the fires).

"I don't know why different kinds of people can't stick to their own kind," the man said. "You live and let live over there, and I'll live and let live over here. That's the way to do it. You got your gay groups and your young people groups and your couples groups and your drug addict groups and your Celestine Prophecy groups and…"

Others objected, pointing out that it was diversity that gave AA its strength. A truck driver could enlighten a lawyer. One human heart looked much like another.

A fat man in a tank top and those spandex bicycle shorts that—Jack felt strongly about this—should never have been allowed out of France talked at length about various personality types in AA that he didn't like. He didn't like people who told jokes. He didn't like people who had petty problems. He didn't like people who were dishonest (and admitted that his own ruthless honesty had cost him some friends). He didn't like rich people, old ladies who owned cats, and people who quoted Hazelton literature that was not GSO approved.

The next man to talk kept saying "Listen!" probably aware that people weren't. He felt that everybody had it wrong, and he wanted to steer them back onto the narrow path. He kept saying "The Big Book tells me…" Jack had been in AA long enough to recognize this locution as a sign that the speaker believed he was channeling either Dr. Bob or Bill W.

So not every meeting is perfect. Jack did not feel like drinking, but he felt a sense of loss that the warm evening magnified. T.S. Eliot again: Memory and desire were mixing in the lambent air.

The moon was full and philosophy lurked on its dark side. It was not good, they said, for an alcoholic to entertain deep thoughts. Like inviting a vampire into your home, the rule was: Don't.

Jack went home to his efficiency apartment and lay on his bed. He reached for the phone, tapped Kerry's number (which he knew by heart although he'd never called her). Kerry's roommate, Angela, answered and Jack hung up.

I am just restless, he told himself.

But was it true, as many would insist, that any impulse, any twitch of yearning, was the new secular devil: Self-indulgence? Was addiction the itch at the heart of everything? Was greed the apple Eve ate?

Jack closed his eyes and dreamed he was in a bar. It was a bar of old men and bitterness. The jukebox played Hank Williams. A man with broken teeth said, "Listen! I'm telling you for your own good. Listen!" The man was too drunk to say more than that, toothless, a stubble of beard.

Jack turned and saw her at a booth and walked to her and sat down.

"Sara?" he said.

But she did not recognize him, or pretended she didn't. "Do you come here often?" she asked.

He did not know what to say, realized that tears were filling his eyes. He was—what an asshole!—weeping.

WILLIAM BROWNING SPENCER

ack rarely spoke at meetings. He didn't feel he had anything wise or impassioned to relate. Jack had a dread of becoming one of those people who chronicled their lives in detail at every AA meeting, as though the daily shifts in their internal emotional weather could possibly be of interest to anyone else.

But that evening Jack said, "I don't seem to have any sense of direction. Can confusion be considered an emotion?"

After the meeting, a man came up to Jack and suggested they might go for coffee.

His name was Ken. He had been sober for nine years, worked in the vague world of computers, was married, had two kids, a house.

"Confusion's good," he said, studying Jack over the rim of his coffee mug. "When the world explodes, it takes a while for the debris to settle."

"I've been sober almost ten months," Jack said.

The man nodded. "Exactly. Stuff's still floating in the air."

"They say you are not supposed to make any big decisions in the first year," Jack said.

The man nodded. "They say a lot. You might have noticed."

Jack liked this guy.

IRRATIONAL FEARS

hen Jack celebrated one year without a drink, the chairman of his home group asked Jack to tell his story. Jack didn't want to, but his sponsor, Ken, said, "It's a positive experience. You should do it."

Jack was nervous, but once he began to talk, he lost himself in the story. He wanted to explain how accepting his alcoholism had given his life a *theme*, an organizing principle. This thought was somewhat complicated and might, he realized, elicit shouts of *Keep Coming Back!* (an exhortation which, while loving, often meant, "You need all the help you can get, you poor wretch").

After Jack spoke, Ken came up to him. "Good job," Ken said.

"Maybe I shouldn't have mentioned the alternate world stuff," Jack said.

"Oh, they always like that part. You did a terrific job. Congratulations."

Jack excused himself to find a restroom. He was washing his hands in the sink when he looked up. In the mirror, he saw one of the stall doors opening.

WILLIAM BROWNING SPENCER

Jack turned as Ed Tilman came out. Ed was smiling.

"Didn't want to startle you," he said. "I'm not supposed to be in the country, so I'm doing the furtive thing. I didn't want to miss your one-year anniversary, though. Congratulations."

Jack was surprised when Ed Tilman leaned forward and hugged him. Tilman was not a demonstrative man.

"I heard your story. Edge-of-the-seat stuff. You're wondering about this hand, are you?"

"Oh, well—" Jack was embarrassed, flustered. He'd been caught staring.

Ed removed the glove, revealing solid flesh. He was missing the ring and little fingers.

"It's a small price to pay," he said. "I thought I was going to have to go through life half ghost. Worse, I thought I was going to have to go through life like a man walking on a log, apt to topple off at any time. I'm lucky. How do you say it? I got an attitude of gratitude."

Jack wanted Ed to meet his sponsor, but Ed shook his head. "I got someone else I have to talk to. People think he's dead, but he's fine. He learned his lesson too, tries to get to meetings regularly." Ed ducked back into a stall, closing the door just as the restroom door opened and a tall man entered. The man wore a black leather jacket. He studied himself in the mirror, ran a comb through his pompadour.

His sideburns were graying, but, if he was who Jack thought he was, he'd lost weight.

He turned and looked at Jack. "Your momma ever tell you it's not polite to stare at strangers?"

Jack said, "Sorry," smiled foolishly, and got out of there.

Jeez, Jack thought. *Jeez*.

Outside, Kerry was waiting for him. She had a card she had made and she wanted him to open it.

"Come on, come on!" she urged.

She turned her car's heater on, reached up and flipped the overhead light. Her hair was long these days, swirling around her cheekbones. The chill air had brightened her eyes.

"Open it, Jack."

IRRATIONAL FEARS

Jack tore the envelope and pulled the handmade card out. It said, in big printed caps, *HAPPY AA ANNIVERSARY, JACK. DON'T QUIT BEFORE THE MIRACLE. PLACE FINGER HERE.*

Jack looked up at Kerry, smiling. "Go on," she said.

A red paper heart was glued in the middle of the card, an arrow aimed at it from the instruction, *PLACE FINGER HERE.* Jack put his finger down, felt the gritty, pebbled surface.

"Okay," Kerry said. "So open the card."

Inside, a stick-figure girl was grinning (each square tooth carefully delineated) with her arms spread apart, welcoming. The card read, *YOU HAVE JUST BEEN ZAPPED BY MAGIC CRYSTAL LOVE DUST. YOU WILL BE THE HELPLESS LOVE SLAVE OF THE FIRST PERSON YOU CAST YOUR EYES UPON.*

Jack smiled at Kerry.

"So," she said. "Did it work?"

Jack smiled ruefully.

Kerry looked suddenly glum, the effort of willed lightness and hope eroding. "It didn't work."

"Kerry, I—"

"You don't love me."

"Kerry, I have *always* loved you. That was never the point. That was—"

Had he frightened her? She looked terrified. Jack turned, imagining some monster pressing against the passenger window. Nothing. He turned back, and Kerry was leaning toward him, her lips pursed, eyes closed.

This is never going to work.

He saw a closed door, behind it the wreckage of his future, the heartbreak, the despair to come.

He saw all the yearning trouble, the obstinacy and desire, the predictable foolishness, the facile censure of his peers (*he's twice her age, an old story*), the exhilaration and fear…all this behind that door.

He opened it and kissed her.

WILLIAM BROWNING SPENCER